HOT SLEEP
The Worthing Chronicle

HOT SLEEP

The Worthing Chronicle

By Orson Scott Card

Baronet Publishing Company, New York

HOT SLEEP

First Baronet edition April 1979

Published by arrangement with The Condé Nast Publications, Inc.

ISBN: 0-89437-054-5

Library of Congress Catalog Card Number: 79-50589

Baronet Publishing Company
509 Madison Avenue
New York, N.Y. 10022

HOT SLEEP
The Worthing Chronicle

JAS Worthing was being kept alive by State Paper FN3xxR-5a, and he knew it. He didn't need an assistant professor of education to tell him that. But once Hartman Tork had begun a lecture, he was unstoppable.

"There's no way, Jas Worthing, that you could have made a perfect score on that test. The information is classified, it was only bumped onto the computers by a mistake in the program—"

"Your mistake," Jas pointed out.

"Maybe not a mistake at all," Tork said, his face turning red with anger. "Maybe we've found out something about you that we desperately wanted to know. You couldn't possibly have copied off anyone else's paper—"

"Are you accusing me of cheating? Because the juvenile code requires a proper hearing and substantiating evidence—"

Tork whirled around on his swivel stool and stood up. He walked around the glowing teacherboard until he stood only a meter or less away from Jas. Again, as a hundred times before, Jas felt the vertigo of childhood, realizing that everything is up, that only when he tumbled into the future would he be as large as those who manipulated him today—or tried to, anyway.

"I've had enough," Tork said, softly, trying to be menacing;

and though Jas knew that the menace was a facade worn to intimidate the small and weak, he also knew that behind the facade the threat was very, very real. "I've had enough of your cocky smartass self-assurance. Now you're going to take that test over again."

And in spite of himself Jas was trembling, though he kept the quaver out of his voice. "Unless you can prove malfeasance—"

"I know the juvenile code, Jas. And I don't have to prove malfeasance if I can prove something else."

His look of triumph was disconcerting. Jas gripped the sides of the nearest console. "I didn't cheat, Mr. Tork, and unless you have a witness—"

"The law, boy, is a lot more open when it comes to the question of the Swipe." Tork pounded his finger on the teacherboard for emphasis.

"Are you calling me a Swipe, Mr. Tork?" Jas asked. This time the quaver came into his voice. "That's slander, Mr. Tork, unless you can prove—"

"I'm working on that, boy. Now get out."

Jas got out. But at the door he heard Tork call after him, "You got those answers out of my head and I'm going to prove it! You passed that test by picking my brains!"

Jas turned around and said, "Assistant professor Tork, no one in his right mind, given a choice, would pick *your* brains." Tork didn't answer, just smiled savagely. But Jas felt a little better for having said it.

He was shaking and weak all the way home.

His mother met him at the door of their flat. "What happened?" she asked, trying to keep the fear out of her voice, as if it couldn't be read on her face.

"Tork yelled a lot."

"What about the proof? Did you have the proof?"

"Your blood test came out okay, mom." Jas sat down on the bed that doubled as a sofa in the living room. "Sorry you had to get jabbed."

His mother sat next to him and took his hand. Her palms were clammy. "I was so afraid. They were so sure."

"I guess they can't cope with somebody outsmarting their stupid tests." Jas lay back on the bed and breathed deeply. "I need to rest, mom," he said. His mother nodded and got up and went to the kitchen-dining-bathroom to ring up dinner.

Jas lay on the bed, his heart still pounding. He had been stupid, not to realize that they'd know. But it had been so easy—the test in front of him, and then just by looking at Tork the answers so clear, sitting right behind Tork's eyes. It was as if for a moment Jas had forgotten that telepathy was a capital crime. In fact, of course, he hadn't really realized, not for sure, that what was happening was telepathy. It had grown so gradually, his gift—beginning when he turned twelve—fleeting glimpses at random of what people thought, what they felt. And then in the room last week, just as a child might discover a new muscle that let him wiggle his ears or twitch his scalp, Jas had realized he could control it. Not just random glimpses, but a deep, hard, long look into their minds.

The Swipe? Swipes were monsters, Swipes were planet-wreckers, Swipes weren't kids in schoolrooms taking calculus tests.

He stared at the picture of his father on the ceiling. The tiling had been there since their last authorized remodeling, when Jas was seven, and he had instantly seen the picture. That squiggle was the nose; the dark space his eye; the lips the gentle curves just below. It was a benign face, kind if monstrous, trustworthy if incredible. How had he decided that it was his father? Jas knew. After all, he had seen no other picture.

He wanted the face to smile, but it always just smirked, as if just about to laugh, or as if it had just tired of laughter. Or as if it knew that a meal was coming. Jas shuddered.

And as he did his mind gave his body a reason for the fear. How was I to know, he asked himself. How was I to know that the last three questions were cross-programmed from another classroom, a classified, advanced, damn-it-but-it-all-made-so-much-sense classroom, and Jason rolled over and dug his hand

9

into his mattress, partly because it felt good, and partly because his mother had told him, "When you muck up the mattress it has to be replaced early, and if it has to be replaced early, the government gets angry."

Advanced astrodynamics. Well, it just felt like more math, how was I to know I was playing little games with stars and planets? And I understood it, once I got the answer. Jas rumpled the bed again. Once he got the answer: that was the problem. He couldn't show them any figuring. He couldn't show them how he arrived at the correct answer. "I figure in my head," he said, and they showed him the paper where he had done some other figuring, and Jas had smiled and said, "Sometimes, anyway."

If only Tork had been a moron and had remembered astrodynamics wrong.

If only God were still alive and not just a face on the ceiling.

"I'm a Swipe," Jas said under his breath, trying out the words.

Suddenly a hand was fiercely clamped over his mouth. Startled, he opened his eyes to see his mother glaring down at him.

"Fool!" his mother hissed. "An intelligence that can't be measured and you talk as if the walls weren't listening!"

"I was joking," Jas stammered. "I didn't think—"

"In this world, boy, don't ever not think. Why do you suppose your father died?" She wheeled and left the room.

Jas looked after her. "Father didn't have a chance!" he shouted.

"Shut up and eat your dinner," his mother snapped, surly again. Again? Still.

The answers had just been sitting there, like a disc ready to be played, a book ready to be read, waiting for him behind Tork's eyes. Jas looked up and saw his mother watching him. He looked at her tightly-set lips, glanced at her wrinkled forehead, and saw (just behind the eyes) that she would suffer any torture if it would bring Homer Worthing back to her for one bright day, for one penetrating touch, for one last kind, delicate, ravishing night.

"I wish I looked more like him, mother," Jas said, wanting the wrinkles on the forehead to go away.

She just narrowed her eyes at him. "Don't," she whispered, and then pushed a plate of the stiff gel that was called *soup* in the catalog across the table toward him. Jas sat for a moment, then leaned across the table, took his mother by the shoulders, and pulled her close. His mouth by her ear, he spoke so softly that he could barely hear his own voice, and said, "It's true."

She tried to pull away, shaking her head.

"Mother," Jas insisted, pulling her closer still, "I'm a Swipe. I got the answers from the teacher's mind."

She shuddered. "Impossible," she said softly.

"I know."

She got up from the table and took him by the hand. Together they left the flat and walked down corridors and ramps to the tube. At that hour it wasn't crowded. She dragged him along until they got to a women's lavatory. She started to pull him in.

"I can't go in there," Jas whispered.

"You're sure as hell going to," she hissed back, her face ugly with fear.

He went in. It was empty. His mother leaned against the door, facing him.

"Maybe," she said, "this place isn't bugged. But if it is, we won't be known."

"Voiceprints."

"Whisper, then," she whispered. "I said it's impossible. I've had two blood tests. Once before your father's trial, and this time for you. I do not have the Swipe on any of my lousy DNA. My X chromosomes are clean. Do you understand that?"

"I know what I did."

"You couldn't have gotten the trait from your father," she said, holding tightly to the boy's arm, "because it's carried on the X and he only gave you a Y."

"I've taken genetics."

"Then why did you say what you did?"

"Separate mutation," Jas said, and she clenched her grip on his arm. It hurt, but he was afraid to try to pull away. He had never seen her this angry and afraid at the same time.

"Do you think they didn't check that? It's the first thing they check. Your cells don't show any mutation."

"Then it's magic," Jas said, and she relaxed just enough that he felt safe in trying to pull his arm free. She let him.

"Magic," she said, and then she covered her face with her hands, digging her fingers into her eye sockets so fiercely that Jas worried, fleetingly, that she might be trying to blind herself, even though the cost of a transplant would wipe out her earnings and her pension for years. He gingerly reached for her arms, to pull her hands down, but when he touched her she erupted, shouted at him, forgetting the danger that one of Mother's Little Boys might be listening. "Listen to me! It's impossible! You're just hallucinating because of your father. They warned me it might happen, that children of Swipes sometimes react this way, pretending to be Swipes because of guilt feelings about the way their parent died. But whether it's real or not, it can get you killed if you go around claiming to be a—"

"I don't feel guilty about my father's death!" Jas said angrily. "I wasn't even born when he died. I wasn't even *conceived*. If you didn't want a crazy child, why did you go to the sperm bank—"

"I wanted him to have a son—"

"Well, he's got one! But don't try to transfer *your* psychoses onto me!"

She fell silent, her jaw slack. And as Jas leaned against the washbasin he again had a flash; but this time not a thought, this time a picture:

A man smiling—not a handsome man, but a man used to power, a man sure of himself, a man with huge, powerful, sweet hands that reached out and touched—

"No!" his mother shouted at him, and she pushed his hand away, and he realized that he had touched her just as she was

12

remembering his father's touch, that he had been acting out her memory.

"Don't touch me!" she said. "Not like that."

"I'm sorry. I just—I couldn't help it—mother, why do you remember him laughing, when he—"

His mother shook her head violently. "You didn't see," she hissed, more to herself than to him. "You didn't know, you didn't see." She was not looking at him. Is she even sane, Jas wondered for a moment. And then realized that the answer to his question was no, had always been no.

Suddenly his mother relaxed and smiled. "Of course," she said. "You're just insightful. It's a family trait. Your grandfather was just like that. As if he could see into your soul." She laughed. "Little Jason Worthing, just like your father's father."

"And my father."

"No!" she said fiercely. "He was a Swipe. But your grandfather. He just looked at me the first time Homer brought me home, just looked at my eyes and then he smiled and he said to me, 'Nita, you're a good woman, you're right for my son.' And from then on it was like he'd known me all my life. He knew he could trust me. And he could, he could."

Somebody pushed on the door, trying to get in.

"We've got to leave, mother," Jas said.

"Not until you promise me," she said.

"What."

"That you'll never say that again. To anyone. About being a—"

"I promise. Do you think I want to get killed?" Jas lunged for the doorknob. His mother backed away, and the door slid open as Jason twisted the knob.

A woman with a little girl who was dancing up and down shot them a dirty look as they came out. Then she did a double take when she realized that Jas was a boy.

"Perverts!" the woman spat as they hurried through the cars to the exit.

13

The next day at school they tried to trap him. Tork wasn't in the test room. Jas went in for his regular weekend quiz, and an empty-headed woman with thoroughly observable decolletage greeted him in a whispery voice and told him his test was ready. Jas guessed what they were going to do. To make sure, he looked into her head. Behind her eyes? A love life. No answers to tests.

And sure enough, the test was not on the topology of speed-of-light motion, the study topic for the week. It was, once again, astrodynamics. All new questions, of course. But the same topic.

Jas had to work on this one. Of course, his mind being what it was, he remembered perfectly everything he had taken from Tork's mind the week before. Now he had to apply the principles, think them through. But his logic kept up with the questions on the test.

He did miss one question. But ninety-nine was close enough to a hundred to be statistically insignificant.

When the computer printed out his score, Jas stood up and announced to the woman, "All right, lady. When you see Tork again, tell him for me I'm going to press charges. This test was illegal."

The woman was genuinely surprised. "What could be illegal? I just pressed the button and—"

"I know, I know. Just tell Tork for me. Can you remember that long?"

She sniffed her disdain. "You boy geniuses all seem to think you're the only ones with minds."

When Jas left the school he had every intention of going straight to the CRL for a lawyer to press his case—it was airtight, there'd be no way to hide their tampering with the computer program to put the wrong test on it. And without a writ they had no right to double-check his score.

But then he realized that he didn't want to attract too much attention with this. Because if rumor got around that he was suspected to be a Swipe, the doors would start to close to him.

His unmeasurable intelligence would be worth as much as a moron rating.

No, let them sweat, but don't make too many waves.

Somehow the tests had all come out negative. But Jas knew he had the Swipe. And they might have other tests that would discover it.

"Insightful," his mother had said, "just like your father's father."

Father. And me. And grandfather?

But grandfather was dead.

Jas went to a directory and found the listing: "Genealogical programs, G55Nxy3. He put his credit card (nearly worthless for purchasing, but good enough for this) into the computer outlet and punched in the program.

"Genealogy: Name research, 4n; inheritance tie-ins, 4i; name similarities . . ." Finally Jas found what he wanted, punched in his own name and birthdate, and waited for the reading.

"Male relatives of common descent by male lines only:" and then came a list of names that threatened to go on all day. Jas interrupted the readout and punched in a new instruction. Now the screen flashed, "Five nearest male relatives by common descent by male lines only."

First on the list was Talbot Worthing. He lived on a planet only forty-two light-years away.

Next on the list was Radamand Worthing. GE-44h rating—government employee on the district management level.

Again he put his credit card into the slot, and this time asked only for an address. His fifth cousin Radamand was supervisor of District Napa-3. A good position not more than an hour by tube from Jas's home district.

Nice to know that a relative had done well with himself.

It was 1600, and Jas figured he'd have time to get there before the man left work—and get back before his mother had Mother's Little Boys out looking for him. So he got on the tube, wondering all the time if this wasn't a wild goose chase. And then in the part of his mind that always took over when he was

15

worried, he free associated, and tried to calculate what in the world the phrase *wild goose chase* meant.

Radamand Worthing had his name on the *outer* door of the office complex, and no name at all on his private door. Jas was aware enough of status symbols to be impressed.

The secretary was also impressed—by Radamand, not by Jas.

"Do you have an appointment, little boy?"

"I don't need one," Jas said, putting on his most irritating voice.

"Everyone needs one," she said, getting just as irritated as he wanted her to get.

"Tell him his blue-eyed cousin Jason is here to see him," Jas said, sneering—a facial expression he had long since learned infuriated adults.

"I have instructions not to bother him."

"Tell him or you'll have new instructions to be out of here with your desk left empty behind you."

"Listen, little boy, if you've disturbed me unnecessarily—"

The noise of the disturbance opened Radamand Worthing's door. "What's going on out here?" the portly, middle-aged man with bright blue eyes demanded. Bright blue eyes, Jas noted. His grandfather's holo had blue eyes. His mother's memory of his father had those same bright blue eyes. "Uncle Radamand," Jas said affectionately. At the same moment he focused on the spot just behind Radamand's eyes.

What he read there was Radamand's immediate fear—and the fact that Radamand was also seeing Jas's fear. Their bright blue eyes locked.

"You're impossible," the older man said. "You can't *be*."

"Apparently you're hallucinating," Jas said.

"He just broke in here and *demanded*—" the secretary said, righteously indignant.

"Shut up." Radamand was sweating.

So was Jas. Because he could hear in the man's mind the decision that Jas had to die.

"Is that the way to greet a long-lost relative?" Jas asked.

16

"Get out of my—" Radamand stopped, but Jas knew he had been about to say—

"Mind?" Jas asked.

"Office." Radamand bit the word, and then Jas heard/saw/felt Radamand's panic, his rage—

"Why are you afraid, Uncle Radamand?" Jas asked in his sweetest voice.

In the older man's mind he found the answer: Because you have it too, and if they catch you, they might catch on, they might realize it's hereditary on the *male* line, and they'll trace the genealogies and find me—

And as Jas heard Radamand's thoughts, he realized that Radamand had heard what leaped into Jas's thoughts: that assistant professor Hartman Tork already suspected he was a Swipe, was laying traps for him.

"I'm afraid for *you*," Radamand said sweetly, through gritted teeth. "I'm afraid you might fall into a trap somewhere."

"I'm smarter than they are," Jas said.

But not smarter than me, Radamand thought loudly, fearfully, angrily.

Jas saw the laser in Radamand's mind before Radamand could find it in his pocket. Jas dropped to the floor, rolled. The laser seared the floor behind him. A moment while the weapon recharged, and in that moment Jas was out the door, running down the corridor.

An alarm sounded somewhere in the complex.

The door ahead of him slammed shut. A guard stood in front of it. Jas stopped and frantically searched the man's thoughts for another way out, another exit. Where were the doors? He found them just behind the guard's eyes, even as the guard noticed Jas's fugitive appearance. The gun raised—Jas was already gone.

Through this? No, this door. Out and down the stairs. And through this last door and into corridors branching off into the endless underground city of Capitol, which stretched in an unplanned and unplannable labyrinth from pole to pole to—

17

Home? Not home, Jas thought, because the plan already forming in Radamand's mind was to arrest Jas on some charge or other—breaking and entering? Resisting inquiry? For someone at Radamand's level, and with his obvious influence and prestige, it shouldn't be hard to get Jas put away forever behind bars.

Or in a little plastic box in the cemetery.

Jas's mind kept wandering as he loped down corridors, losing himself in the turns and the rises, putting as much as possible of three dimensions between him and his cousin. He smiled to think of how Radamand had probably acquired his influence and prestige: for he could easily spot a superior's guilty secrets and then drop subtle hints—not enough for blackmail and the subsequent murder, just enough to let the superior know that Radamand shared his secret. And *understood*. Would never tell; could be trusted; was a friend who knew all and loved anyway.

And so promotion. And so power. And so all of the wealth and position that Radamand was afraid he would lose because now someone shared *his* guilty secret.

Jas came to the tube and got on going away from his home.

Then he got off at the second stop and changed to the first tube leaving for anywhere.

Then got off and caught another.

And another.

And then left the tubestop and went to a computer terminal and pushed in his card. Dangerous? Perhaps—but access to the master files of the computer was closely guarded by Mother's Little Boys, and Jas doubted that Radamand's considerable influence was quite *that* considerable. No, it would be the constables that Radamand had on his trail, not the computer police, not the listeners in the walls.

So probably the computers were safe.

Jas punched for a readout on criminal law. He specified. And specified again. "Exemptions from all class 2-8b felonies and all misdemeanors."

18

Then Jas specified for exemptions accessible to juveniles. There were only two: the Service and the Colonies.

Never the Colonies. Not the one shot of somec, and then waking up fifty light-years away on an empty planet, doomed to live out the normal hundred or so years of life and then die, with neither fame nor power nor hope of the somec doses of immortality. Colonies were for the despairing, not for the merely desperate. Jas still had hope.

Had to be the Service. There at the end of the somec sleep through space the captains awoke, fought a battle or did a short term of duty and then went back under the somec to return to Capitol, where they were heroes—at least the successful ones—and wealthy, whether spectacularly successful or not; and, most important, the captains were on somec, waking only one year out of every thirty or forty or fifty, watching the centuries slip by and laughing at time—

The Service then. And it would be ironic, too; for his father had been a ship captain, before the Swipe crisis that killed him. It would be somehow appropriate to follow in his father's footsteps.

And then Jas remembered his mother's warning that sons of Swipes tried to expiate guilt. Maybe, he thought. Maybe after all I'm just trying to relive my father's—

A hand gripped his shoulder.

"Jason Worthing, age thirteen, number RR3njw-4, status juvenile, state your business in this district."

Jason leaned limply against the wall, and the man made sure he wouldn't leave the wall abruptly. The man's voice sounded official, but he wasn't in uniform. A constable not in uniform? Behind the man's eyes Jas learned that he was one of Mother's Little Boys. Then he must have guessed wrong, and Radamand did have that much influence.

"Well, little boy, your mother's worried about you. Seems you didn't come home after school."

"I just went—I went exploring," Jas said, using his young

19

voice, his unintelligent voice. "I was trying to find my way home."

"Your mother asked us to run a missing persons check. You shouldn't stick your credit card into computer outlets if you want to run away," the man said.

"I don't want to run away," Jas said, longing to run away.

"Good thing," the man answered with a smile, "because you can't."

They rode in the closed compartment of the tube back to the station only a few corridors away from Jas's flat. The man didn't let go of his iron grip until Jas's mother opened the door.

"Jas, you're all right." She hugged him, acting for all the world like a parent who had been worried that her little boy might be hurt. But Jas knew what the real fear had been. Though he was already a little tired of looking into people's thoughts, it was almost reflex already, and he saw his mother's flashing memory of a visit from Hartman Tork.

"Thank you, officer," she said, tears of joy in her eyes.

"Any time, ma'am." The man left. Jas's mother closed the door. She looked at Jas in fear.

"Hartman Tork came," Jas said. She nodded, biting her lip in an exaggerated show of fear. Again, Jas was convinced for a moment that she was mad.

"Looking for you," she said. "He has proof. He said you had passed the second test, that it was proof positive—"

"Proof when I *passed* it?" Jas asked, surprised.

"He said it contained information that had only been fed into the computers this week, completely and totally restricted, there was no way you could have studied the information, so obviously you got the answers by—"

"But I *didn't* look into anyone's mind, mother. I just used logic, I just figured it out—"

"Apparently," she said bitterly, "your logic has just caught up with the latest advances in astrodynamic theory."

Jas leaned against the wall. "I thought the test went the other way. I thought that if I *failed* it they'd think it was proof that I'd cheated, or something else. I thought I had to get a good score."

"Smart smart smart, but so stupid, stupid, how can you be so wrong." She fiddled nervously with the fabric of her dress. "I've figured it out, Jas. What they did was illegal. Your intellect —surely we can get a court to believe that you simply discovered it independently—it's not impossible—"

"It's not impossible because it happened that way. But I can't go to court."

"You have to. We'll just call the constables, get a holding order—"

"Mother, listen." Jas touched his mother's cheek and she fell silent, watching him. Behind her eyes she was still tense, ready to jump in any direction, ready to scream. "Mother, listen. We can't call the constables because they're already looking for me. If they find me I'm dead."

"Why?"

"I—did something. And now they're after me."

"What did you do!"

"I can't tell you."

"Tell me." She gripped his shoulders, as if squeezing them would force the answer out of Jas's mouth.

"Let go," Jas said.

Her hands began to shake violently, and she let go.

"I can't tell you what I did because if you know then your life's in danger. Your life's probably in danger anyway. We have to get out of here, now."

"They can't get in here without a warrant," she said tentatively.

"They'll have a warrant, mother. That's probably the only reason they aren't here now—they're getting the warrant. Now let's *move*."

His mother's fear made her meek in the face of authority, and she let him pull her out the door. She made a momentary, half-hearted resistance, saying, "I have to get some things, my bag,

21

I have to—" but he kept pulling her and in a few moments they were down the ramps and on the tube. Her hands now danced and fluttered constantly. She hummed. Her eyes kept moving constantly, and she kept looking over her shoulder. Great, Jas thought. Great. This is all she needed.

He went down the list of wonderful events of the last few days, and tried to think of something he might have done differently. But every path he could think of led him here: Hartman Tork after him with the threat of death as a Swipe; dear long-lost cousin Radamand after him to put him away before he was exposed as a Swipe; and mother.

Mother knew. Mother was pretending she didn't, but she knew. And knowing, she could be made to tell. What was Jas to her? A son, of course, but more: her only link to the man who had dominated her life. More in death than in life, it seemed. Hadn't she named him Jason Harper Worthing? Harper, because it was in the Harper system that Homer Worthing had been trapped, had been killed.

And now was about to die again, and she couldn't handle it. She smiled at him and squeezed his hand. "And where shall we go today?" she asked him, cheerfully, as she had done years ago, seven-year-old Jason leading her from the park to the zoo to the dome to the cave, all the sights; and she proud, happy, following where he led, devoted to him.

But he was no longer seven years old. He was thirteen. He was frightened. He was leading his mother on an excursion that had no destination, whose only goal was escape. Where to, on a planet where there was no outside except the thin sky, no away except on starships—

Colonies.

The sign blinked. Colonies were one of the few projects the government considered important enough that they could be allowed a lighted sign.

Colonies put people on starships and sent them far beyond the reach of Mother's Little Boys. Colonies asked few questions, and answered none. To go with the Colonies was the next thing to dying.

But it was only the next thing. And when dying was the alternative. . . . Jas stood for a moment, looking at the sign. *He* had the option of joining the Service. His mother didn't.

So Jas led his meekly following mother through the impressive archway leading into the plush Colonies reception room. Lighted panels on the walls depicted huge fields of a golden plant, extending to the horizon, with blue sky and a yellow sun. "Earth Colony," the panel said, in a muted, feminine whisper. "Return home again." Another panel was in motion—hundreds of tiny human beings scrambling over red rocks and black cliffs, raising a mesh of fine metal strands. The mesh began to glow. "Catch stars on Manookin," the virile masculine panel-voice said, "and bring them home as frozen light."

Bring them home—Jas laughed silently, bitterly. No one came home from a colony. A hundred years just to get established with any degree of security. Another two hundred or so before anything worth exporting could be developed in exportable quantities. And without the somec sleep, who would still be alive? None of the original colonists. None of their great-great-grandchildren, either.

"A new home," sang a chorus of children's voices, "where children have room to run and play under the sun. Carter. The children's dream planet."

And they were at the desk. "Both of you?" the woman asked.

"Just her," Jas answered. "A place where you can walk around in the open."

The woman pretended to think hard. "Capricorn? It's a yellow sun planet, just like Capitol."

Jas wasn't taken in. Obviously Capricorn was what they were pushing today. "What do they export?"

"Oh, exciting things."

"Excite me," Jas said.

"Aluminum," she said. "And platinum. And chrome."

Jas smiled wanly. "You don't do much walking in the open when you're down a mine shaft, ma'am. A planet that exports food."

"Duncan, then. Sol-type planet, they didn't even have to terraform it. She'll love it."

"Papers?"

And the papers appeared on the desk. Jas insisted that the receptionist write in Duncan as the legal contract destination, and in the preferred work space Jas wrote, "Clerical." The chances of anyone getting a clerical assignment on a colony world were very slim, but there was no harm in asking. And then the papers were in front of his mother, and she meekly picked up the pen and signed, writing the name very, very carefully, as if for the first time, though she was a legal scribe, both longhand and punching.

"You have a few minutes for good-byes," the receptionist thoughtfully said. "And then these nice men will take you with them." These nice men were two blond, blue-eyed gorillas with cheerful smiles on the front of their microcephali. Jas felt a strange lightness in his stomach, a gentle twisting that he recognized as guilt, though he had never felt much guilt before.

He turned to face his mother. She was looking at the two guards.

"You selfish bastard," she whispered gently, "I'm not crazy enough not to know what you just did."

"I had to," Jas said, not believing himself.

"I would have done it gladly if you had asked."

Jas took her hand. It was lifeless as it lay in his. "I'm sorry," he said. "I love you."

And in his mother's mind he saw his father, heard him say, "I'm sorry. I love you."

His mother's face contorted. "Selfish," she said loudly. Then she screamed: "Selfish bloody flaming Swipe bastard, you're your father's son, you're no son of mine!"

Jas had made a gesture as if to stop her when she said the word Swipe, and she noticed it. "That's right, Jas, boy, look out for number one, the old lady's going crazy, but all you care about is who can overhear us, well I can shout it out, you know—" and her voice rose to a high-pitched scream—"I can yell to the whole world that you're a stinking—"

"Sedation?" asked the receptionist. Jas didn't answer, but one of the gorillas came over with a needle anyway. Jas's mother tried to back away, but there was no retreat. The needle dug into her back, and in less than a minute she was smiling sweetly. "Hi," she said to the gorilla. "I'm Nita Worthing. Are you coming to Duncan, too?"

The gorilla smiled and patted her shoulder.

Nita turned to her son and smiled again. "Thank you, son. Good-bye. Wish me a happy voyage."

"Have a happy voyage, mother."

"It'll be happy because at the end of it, I'll have memories of you."

The gorillas led her away. She was telling them a joke as they went through the doors to the inner complex.

The receptionist leaned forward over the counter. "Your mother signed on as a volunteer, didn't she? No legal problems, right?"

Jas nodded, shook his head. "Volunteer. She's not wanted for anything."

"Don't worry about her," the receptionist said kindly. "They often react that way. The minute the papers are signed they're frantic to change their minds. Silly, isn't it? You'd think they'd just signed their own death warrant or something. Why, they're absolutely lucky to get away from this tin can of a world."

Jas smiled. "You're right. No doubt you've already signed onto a colony ship."

The woman's smile disappeared. "Get out of here, smart-mouth," she said. As Jas left he heard her muttering, "Some people, you try to get friendly and they get so. . . ."

Jas took another tube and ended up in one of the huge parks that were placed in every borough by some politicians who had visited Earth and had thought it would be wonderful to spend

25

tax money duplicating it on Capitol. Live trees growing out of real lawns. The residents were unimpressed, by and large—most of them had never seen a tree, and chlorophyll smelled dirty, somehow. Green growing things were just large forms of mold, and mold meant you had to have your humidifier adjusted.

But Jas had been drawn to the parks since childhood, and as he stepped onto the lawn he remembered coming to this very park with his mother, several times. She had sat on the grass, spooning beef out of a dish, as Jas had climbed that rock, and jumped onto the lawn, laughing and laughing.

Well, I don't feel like laughing now, Jas reminded himself. And then wondered what it would be like on a colony world—green, like this? Only without the ceiling. Without the walls. Without the crowded corridors leading off in six directions.

The park was nearly empty, as always, and Jas hoped that though cameras monitored the comings and goings here as everywhere else, such an unfrequented place might not be too well monitored. He crept into the middle of a large clump of bushes and curled up around the base of the tree that grew out of the middle. It was shady, and so darker than everywhere else in the open corridors. In the darkness of the shade he tried to think. Had to decide what to do.

He daren't be caught by the constables because of Radamand. And only the constables could offer him any protection from Hartman Tork and the mobs that would form if word got out that a Swipe had been found. Mother's Little Boys? Jas shuddered. You just don't go to Mother's Little Boys. For finding missing persons, yes. For protection? Who would protect you from the Little Boys?

If he used the computers he could be found, and yet the computers were the only way he could get into the Service. And the other escape route—the Colonies, he wouldn't do that. Jas had dreams of an impressive and important future for himself. People on Colony ships didn't have impressive and important futures.

26

He thought of his mother, and the future she had, and again felt the twist of guilt; maybe she wouldn't have been caught, maybe they wouldn't have tortured her and got the answer, maybe—

There were no maybes. And when they had proved that Jas was a Swipe and killed him, they would have executed her, too, because the trait is passed from mother to son. That's all they know, Jas thought. Mother to son indeed. I'm like my father. He thought the words again and again. I'm like my father.

He woke about six hours after he had crept into the bushes. And when he woke he knew what to do. How long had it taken Mother's Little Boys to find him when he had used the computer terminal the last time? Not long—three minutes, perhaps. But that would be long enough, if he hurried.

For a moment he wondered what he was so worried about. For all he knew, Mother's Little Boys weren't even looking for him—just the constables and the school.

But it was too easy to file a missing persons query, and the constables and the school would have little trouble proving right-to-know. Mother's Little Boys would be looking for him, all right.

He walked to the nearest public terminal. Five specifications got him an application form for entry into the Service. Then he punched memory and coded it to his private number, snapped on a cover code, and then retrieved his card and hurried away from the terminal. Mother's Little Boys wouldn't find him there—it had taken only one minute.

Jas took the tube (did they monitor the credit cards at the tube stations? Probably—but not even the Little Boys could board a moving tube), and switched at the first station. Then he got off again, went to another terminal, punched in the memory code and the cover code, and started filling out the application.

After a minute, the same thing—a dash through the tubes, a new terminal, and a few more items on the application. And since the application wasn't long, that finished it; Jas punched the send button, and left.

Another tube, another terminal, and he requested an answer. Fifteen seconds, and the screen said, "Reject."

He queried.

"Personal."

He queried again. Specify.

"Personal. Father killed in Swipe Wars."

He quickly punched in, desperately punched in a rebuttal, a request for voice contact. It was an agonizingly long wait. Then a face came on the screen, and immediately Jas said, "Can you hold? For just a minute?"

"I'm busy," the woman said, irritated.

"Please," Jas said, acutely aware that he had been at the terminal for nearly three minutes.

"All right, hurry," she said.

Jas ran from the terminal, bumping into a man, and behind the man's eyes Jas discovered in a moment that the man was one of Mother's Little Boys, coming to fetch him from the terminal. No doubt now—they *were* after him.

This time Jas didn't bother with the tube. He ran to the nearest terminal, only a few ramps away, and punched in. The woman's face reappeared.

"What was that all about?" she asked.

"I'm sorry." Jas didn't have time to explain. "I need to know" breath "why my application" breath "was rejected."

"Your father was killed in the Swipe Wars," she said, as if that explained everything.

"But *I* don't have the Swipe. Telepathy isn't passed from father to son!" he insisted, wondering if she could possibly guess that it was a lie, that she was talking to a member of the one family in which the Swipe was, in fact, inherited on the male line.

"Of course the Swipe isn't hereditary," she said. "We aren't the least bit worried about that. In fact," she said, as Jas inwardly urged her to hurry, "in fact, you're a remarkably bright young man, widely educated, ridiculously high test scores on your record, and ordinarily we'd accept you in a moment."

"Thanks. Then accept me."

"The Swipe isn't hereditary. But revenge is. Sorry."

"I don't want revenge!" Jas shouted.

"If you're going to shout, please turn your volume control down. I'm not deaf."

"I won't try to get revenge—"

"Of course you'd say that, but our statistics make it almost a probability that—"

"Dammit, my father burned three planets and killed eight billion people, do you think I'm going to try to avenge his death?"

She shrugged. "We have the psychological profiles, and I'm afraid the policy can't be reversed without a lengthy process of appeal. Go ahead and try. It'll take only two weeks, and maybe you can change somebody's mind, though I doubt it. I wish you luck, young—"

An iron hand gripped Jas's shoulder. Involuntarily he cried out. The woman smiled. "Do you have him, officer? Very well then. Out."

The screen went blank.

The iron hand turned Jas around to face the man. Jas looked behind his eyes.

Amusement. That warm feeling of success. "You've been leading us a merry chase, boy," the man said.

Jas smiled weakly. "Tag I'm it?"

It worked. The man smiled back. "You're from Rockwit?"

"I'm from Capitol. But I know the game. I studied it."

"Then I'll feel a little worse turning you in. How did you guess I was from Rockwit?"

I saw it in your mind, of course, Jas thought. But he said, "Your accent."

"That bad, huh?"

"I study accents. It's a hobby."

29

"Accents and archaic games," the man said. "Come along now, boy. I don't know why, but somebody important wants you real bad."

Radamand, then. No one could call Hartman Tork important. But Jas went along peacefully enough. No sense struggling and increasing the man's vigilance. Just wait for an opportunity.

The opportunity was the commuter traffic in the tubes. The rush hour was starting, and as with commuters in all times and places, the signs saying *enter* and *exit* were regarded as mere decoration. Those getting off the tube rushed out, making rivulets around those struggling forward to get on. Of course there were dozens of people who stopped, greeted each other, blocked traffic—others, caught in the rush, desperately trying to reach a destination different from that of the crowd that swept them along. Three times a day the shifts changed, as the night boroughs, morning boroughs, and afternoon boroughs in each district lived their separate and rarely interconnecting days.

In the shoving and elbowing at the door, Jas lurched into the secret policeman who was holding him, then tripped and fell, ripping his shoulder painfully away from the man's hand. Someone tripped over him; someone else stepped on his leg; the crowd pulled Mother's Little Boy away from Jason. In a moment friendly hands helped Jas to his feet, and he began moving away in the crowd.

"He's cut!" shouted the security policeman. "Get him!"

He's cut? Jas realized as he threaded through the crowd that the security policeman wasn't alone. There had been more of Mother's Little Boys close enough to call to. Who?

For a moment Jas tried identifying people as they passed, before they came near him, but he couldn't—it was too dizzying, darting from mind to mind. And moving that quickly, impressions became vague, too fleeting to catch.

A hand grabbed at his hip. Jas lurched away. Again the hand was stronger than he expected, and pulling away took so much force that Jas fell to the ground. Someone stepped on his hand, hard, and Jas cried out in pain, but pulled his hand out from under the heavy boot. Blood leaped from torn-open veins, but Jas ignored it, scrambling to his feet. Hands reached for him. He swerved away, ducked, and then spotted a break in the crowd, ran through, and shoved his way into the mass of people piling up around the station doors.

Now the crowd that had helped him escape helped Mother's Little Boys to catch him. Where the people had been moving fast, his small size let him dodge through much faster than the police could. But with the crowd moving slowly, shoulder to shoulder, his small size was a disadvantage. He couldn't shove people out of the way, and Mother's Little Boys could. In a moment rough hands gripped him everywhere, and he was lifted off the ground and tossed into the air. When he came down there were six men around him.

He panted for breath. So did they. They looked angry. Wary, too, waiting for Jas to try something, to move. Jas didn't move. Blood dripped from his hand.

"What do you guys think I am?" he finally said. "Six of you to take a thirteen-year-old kid?"

The one who had first caught him smiled. "For a minute there, we were wishing for an even dozen."

"Well, you've got me," Jas said, still panting from the chase. "What now?"

But they just watched him, and the exhilaration of flight and pursuit gave way to the despairing knowledge that he was, indeed, caught, and there was no way he could stop them from doing whatever they wanted. Would it be the school, and facing charges as a Swipe? Or Radamand, and death to protect a rising politician?

Jas waited several minutes before it occurred to him that he didn't *have* to wait for answers to questions. He looked behind their eyes, and. . . .

Just then a short stout man dressed in thirty-year-old styles that looked brand new came up to their group.

"I'm amazed that you haven't hog-tied him," the man said.

Jas tried to find the meaning of the archaism, but *hog-tied* wasn't catalogued in his memory.

"Let him go," the man said. "And fix his hand, he's bleeding."

"If we let him go," one of Mother's Little Boys said, "we might never catch him again."

The stout man pushed his way into the circle and looked at Jas with soft, kind eyes. He was so short that Jas looked down at him a little. Someone wrapped the injured hand. "Dale Carnegie cringes at their methods," the man said. This time the allusion rang a bell, and Jas smiled, reciting back: "You can catch more flies with a drop of honey than with a gallon of gall."

"Actually," the stout man interrupted, "Carnegie was only quoting someone else. Odd that you should know Carnegie and not Aesop." The man turned back to Mother's Little Boys. "He's in my custody now."

The policemen looked at each other uneasily. The man pulled out a little card and showed it to them. They nodded obsequiously and moved away.

The man turned back to Jas. "You have a name," he said.

"Jas Worthing."

"Jason Harper Worthing, a most remarkable young man. Jason Harper Worthing, don't get any clever ideas about escaping from me. Because where Mother's Little Boys trust to brute strength, I rely on technology." The cockle flashed momentarily in his hand, safety off.

"Who are you?" Jas asked.

"A question I've been trying to answer ever since adolescence. Shall we walk?" They walked. "I finally decided I was neither God nor Napolean. I was so disappointed I didn't try to narrow it down any further."

The stout man escorted Jas to the officials-only door in the station and they went down the lift to the private cars. They got into one that looked rather old and shabby. And ridiculously out of date.

"I'm an archaist," the man said. "Like you, I collect old things. The difference is that you, being poor, can only collect ideas. I, being rich, can collect things. Things are worth much more money than ideas."

The man chuckled gently, and as the car took off, skimming the tube on its delicate magnetic balance, he laid a kind hand on Jas's knee. A good, strong hand, though small, and the gesture of affection was all it took to push Jas over the edge. The tension before had been too great—the relief now too sudden. Jas began to tremble and his breath came in short gasps like sobs.

"Please try to avoid hysteria," the man said, and then continued his pleasant conversation. "I also collect new things. But new things are hard to judge. One never knows if they'll last. One never knows if they'll appreciate or depreciate. Quite a risky investment, new things. Here we are."

The car stopped. It hadn't traveled far. The man led Jas to a door and they stepped into a lift and rose for a long time. When the ceiling was right above their heads they stepped onto a bare wooden floor.

Wood. Jas realized that it didn't feel like wood. He said so.

"Ah, your curiosity is beginning to function again. Good. It doesn't feel like wood because you've never touched wood in your life, you've touched plastic. This, Jason Worthing, is *wood*. From *trees*. I needn't tell you that you can't buy any of it on *your* credit allowance."

And then they were through a door and Jas gasped.

At first, for a moment, he had thought it was a park. But it was too large, and there was no ceiling. Instead the walls just ended, and a dazzling bright blue arch crested over him, just like the pictures of sky. The trees seemed to go on forever. The grass underfoot was real. Something living moved in the branches of a tree.

"I collect old things and new things," the man said. "But mostly I collect living things. Like you."

Jas turned to look at him and suddenly realized that the eyes were no longer soft and kind—had they really been before?

And the man seemed to be staring past Jas's clothing and his skin and into his soul. Jas realized he had trusted this man without reason, and he looked behind his eyes.

The man's name was Abner Doon. (Silly name—never heard of him.)

His job was assistant minister of colonization. (Colonies again. Mother.)

He honestly believed he ruled the world. (Crazy? Or am I?)

And he knew Jas was a Swipe.

"I'm dead," Jas said, suddenly feeling despair. Why had he thought he was no longer in danger with this man?

"Very nearly," Doon said. "It depends on some decisions you make in the next few hours. You know my name, of course."

Jas shook his head to say no.

"You know my name, you know my title, you know my real function, and you know that I know what you are."

Jas took a step back. Abner Doon only smiled. "Surely you don't fear any kind of physical attack?"

"You're insane," Jas said.

"That's been said before," Abner answered mildly, "by men and women with better credentials than yours."

"I often wondered who really ruled Capitol and the Empire, but I really never supposed it was the assistant minister of colonization," Jas said, wondering how quickly he could get the door open again. He decided that he couldn't possibly do it faster than Doon could get the cockle into action.

"Well, it all depends on what you mean by *rule*. Mother rules us, officially. But everyone knows that the Cabinet rules Mother, and they're right. She's just a figurehead. But who rules the Cabinet?" Doon took off his jacket and tossed it to the ground. "And even more important, who owns the people who carry out the Cabinet's orders?"

Abner Doon took off his shoes.

"Walking in grass with shoes on is a waste of an opportunity," he told Jas. "Take your shoes off. Join me in a swim. Hmmm?"

34

Jas took his shoes off, and they walked deeper into the park. A large white bird flew nearby, then skimmed the surface of a lake, stopped, dipped its head, and flew off with something silver dangling from its mouth.

"A fish!" Jas shouted, and he hurried past Doon to the edge of the water.

"Clever deduction. What else did you learn from the bird?"

Jas turned around. The assistant minister of colonization was taking off his clothing.

"Is this a test?"

"Oh, no, not at all," Abner Doon answered. "I just thought you might have guessed from the species of bird what planet this park is modeled after." Jas watched him undress to the skin, and was mildly surprised to discover that the man wasn't stout at all—just wore layers of protective clothing.

"The water's relatively warm," Doon said. "Swim with me."

"I don't know how to swim."

"Of course not. I'm going to teach you."

Jas undressed and followed the man uncertainly into the water. They stopped when it was up to Jas's neck.

"Water is actually a very safe medium of locomotion," Doon said. Jas only noticed that it was cold. Numbing. If this was what Doon called relatively warm, Jas wondered what in the world he called cold.

"Now here, my hand is against your back. Lean back against my hand. Now let your legs just come loose from the ground, just relax, I can hold you up."

Suddenly Jas felt very light, and as he relaxed he felt his body bobbing lightly on the surface, only the gentle pressure of Doon's hand under him to remind him of gravity.

Then the world turned upside-down, Abner Doon had a back-breaking hold on him, and Jas's face suddenly plunged underwater. He gulped, swallowed water. His eyes, when he opened them, stung in the water. He hadn't taken a breath, needed one desperately. He struggled to come up, but couldn't break the hold. He struggled, he twisted, and tried to strike with his hands

35

and feet, but he couldn't get free, and not breathing became agony.

Then he felt himself pulled to the surface. He gasped for air. Coughed.

"Don't cough, it splashes water everywhere."

"Let go!" Jas cried out, still gasping. "Let me go—"

"Never," said the man. "I'll never let you go, Jason Harper Worthing. I have collected you. I never break up my collections."

Jas looked behind his eyes, struggling to find a motive, but found only an emotion of—love? Kindness? The man was threatening his life, and yet all Jas could find in his mind was kindness.

"This," Doon said, "was an object lesson. May I assure you that you are in over your head? A figure of speech that you may not have known."

"I knew it," Jas said. "Me Gook system."

"Much older than that," Doon said, "but of course that's where it's still current. Very good. You get the point, I'm sure, even if you haven't read Aesop. Even when we step out of my lake, you'll still be deep in water, and believe me, in that water you don't know how to swim. I have only to flick a wrist—" suddenly Jas found himself dipping into the water again, and Doon's sentence was muffled and yet strangely clarified by the water "—and you will certainly drown."

This time Abner Doon let him up almost immediately, and Jas coughed and spluttered only because he knew it annoyed the man. "What are you arresting me for?"

"I'm not arresting you. Whatever gave you that idea? I said I have collected you. Like the Cabinet. Like Hartman Tork. Like Radamand Worthing. The only difference is that I'm *telling* you. You should be flattered—very few people know."

"I would have known anyway, Mr. Doon," Jas said, and that was his surrender, admitting that he had the Swipe, that Doon therefore had control over him. "What are you going to do with me?"

"Why, teach you how to swim, of course," Doon answered.

36

"May I suggest you start by swimming on your back? Much easier, and you don't have to fuss with learning how to breathe. Just kick lightly with your legs—that's right, shallower kicks and more rapidly, very good. Arch your back. The other way. Yes, yes, very good. I'm going to let go."

Jas felt the hand go out from under him, and for a moment he felt himself sinking. But he kicked harder, and arched his back more, and floated.

"Now, one at a time, raise your arms in front of your head and draw them back down to your side, through the water. That's right, Jas. Very good. Not a champion, but you'll float." And then there was a splash, and Jas felt the water shift violently as Abner Doon swam past him, not on his back, but on his stomach in the water, breathing under his arm. Jas turned his head to watch, and was rewarded with an eyeful of water and a dunking as he lost flotation. Sputtering, he tried to find bottom with his feet, and couldn't—his swimming had carried him out where the water was deeper than his head. But his instincts were right—he splashed his way to the surface, and kicked violently, bringing himself back up into a backfloat.

A bright, golden sun passed slowly overhead. Jas saw to his surprise that it moved detectably. All the books said you couldn't see the motion of the sun. And besides—he could look right at the sun. And suddenly his vision shifted, and he realized that the sky was just what it seemed to be—a dome of blue—and the sun followed a track across it—a dazzling disc, not a sphere millions of kilometers away.

When the swim ended, the sun was nearly set, though it had barely been an hour. The man and the boy lay on the grass, drying. The sky grew dark, and reddened in the "west." The sun set.

"I've never seen a sunset before," Jas said. "Is this anything close to what a real one looks like?"

"At least on the world this park imitates. My home world, in fact," Doon answered. "It certainly isn't this way on the surface of *this* planet. The sky of Capitol is absolutely greasy with the filth of our planet. Jut looking at it makes me want a bath. Sunset topside is downright purple. Pink is noon. Blue sky is impossible."

"Garden," Jas said.

"That's right," Doon answered softly. "The most perfect place in the universe. So far, anyway. I was a fool to leave Garden. But I had visions of being great. One does not pursue greatness in a beautiful setting. Only peace is possible where things are invariably beautiful. Greatness only comes in ugly settings. And that made Capitol seem the best place to go."

"Is it ugly here?"

Doon laughed. "Oh, my. My, oh, my. To think a human being should even have to ask that question. But you aren't exactly a normal human being, are you?"

"Count the arms and legs," Jas said. "Even the right number of heads."

"The only difference is that you can leave your head and walk around for a while in mine. The Swipe," Doon said, "is such a strange thing. Such a great power that for a time most ship captains in the Empire fleet and among our illustrious Enemy were Swipes. Instantaneous communication. No need for spies. Too bad that Swipes couldn't teach the gift to others, you know? But that little X chromosome modification just can't be transferred. Only passed from mother to children, and the gift only crops up in boys, whose pathetic little Y doesn't have the dominant to block out the telepathy link. How we do dance with the helixes, yes?"

Jas pulled a tuft of grass and sprinkled it on his naked chest and abdomen. It prickled. He brushed it off.

"But I don't have that chromosome. Neither did my mother."

"Irrefutable. You are correct. You are clinically not a Swipe. Bravo. Too bad the mob takes blood tests *after* they tear reputed Swipes to little pieces."

"Can't the law protect me?'"

"If the law knew about you, my small, brilliant, naive friend,

38

the law would certainly be stretched to include you. No, Jas. Your only safety lies in being part of my collection. If you should leave it—well, I simply couldn't stop them, could I?"

A breeze passed over them in the starlit darkness. Jas shuddered.

"Cold? Or merely afraid?"

"Cold," Jas said.

"Actually, the temperature is quite comfortable. Don't be afraid, Jason."

"I can't help it," Jas said, his teeth chattering a little.

"All your life you've been completely under other people's control. Your mother, the school, the constables. Now, suddenly, it isn't *they* who rule you anymore, it's one man, it's I, and that makes you afraid."

"I don't know what you're going to do with me."

"Why don't you look in my mind and see?"

Jas wondered why he didn't. But he didn't. "No."

"Do it. Test me. See what you find out."

Jas shook his head. "I don't want to."

"Why not? I'm asking you to. Or do you only like to peer in people's minds when they don't know you're looking?"

Jas shivered now with the cold he felt. "I don't want to look."

Abner Doon sighed. "I suppose my mind isn't all that lovely a place to visit, anyway. Never mind."

He got up and dressed. Jas still lay on the ground, except that he curled up on his side. His back was cold as the air touched it. Why don't I look in his mind? I'm afraid, Jas decided. I'm afraid I'll find my own death there.

"Tired?" Doon asked.

"Yes."

"Does your hand hurt?"

Jas nodded.

"Do you feel weak?"

Jas smiled. "No. I feel like ripping a tree into toothpicks."

Doon, dressed again in the steel and asbestos protective clothing, the stuffy, out-of-date suit, knelt beside Jas in the grass. "Jas, you've done a lot of studying over the years. Your teachers seem to feel that you never forget what you've read. Ever heard of the Estorian twick?"

Jas's mind reflexively found the reference. "Yeah. Deadly little animal. Wiped out the first colony on Estoria."

"What else do you know about it?"

"Marsupial mammal. Teeth like razors. Small, but it hangs on with its claws while it bores with its teeth. Once it gets on a person he has maybe thirty seconds to get it off. If it lands near something vital, you've got only five seconds or so. Could cause nightmares."

"Very good, Jas. How do you kill it?"

Jas laughed. "A laser. A cockle. I remember reading a story where somebody tried beating it with a rock and it just jumped on and started eating his hand."

Jas watched uncomprehendingly as Doon gathered all of Jason's clothing from the ground and held it in a bundle under his arms. "You don't happen to have a laser or a cockle, do you?" Doon asked.

"Yeah," Jas said. "I hid 'em both in my mouth. I was only waiting for an opportunity to get you."

"In other words, no."

"I don't even have a toothpick," Jas said. "What are you doing with my clothes?"

"Getting them out of the way," Doon said. "Good luck."

"Good luck for what?"

"Good luck in the upcoming battle. In a few seconds an Estorian twick will be turned loose at the other end of my little garden here. He'll be headed your way."

And then Doon took off at a run.

Jas jumped to his feet, started after Doon, but only got a few feet when he realized that Doon was too far, already at the door, already closing it behind him. Jas turned back and looked into the darkness around the lake. The moon was rising, but there wasn't enough light. And if there was, Jas wasn't sure if he could tell what a twick was. Had he ever seen a picture? Yes—and as he remembered what it looked like, he saw a living one crouched on a tree branch about thirty feet away.

Weapon? Unlikely. Doon wasn't the kind to leave spare lasers lying around.

The twick darted forward on the branch. So quickly that Jas could hardly see the movement—it was simply a few meters nearer. The twick didn't take its eyes off Jas.

The words of the book flashed back. "Toys with its victims. Tries to seem harmless. Many fatalities among children who try to pet it." Useless information. What Jas needed to know was how to kill one without a laser.

I should have looked in Doon's mind, Jas told himself. At least I would have known the method he planned to use to kill me. Some kind of pervert, Jas decided. Likes to watch bloody death. Have fun, Doon. This one's on me.

Jas's injured hand throbbed.

The twick wasn't on the branch. One minute it was on the branch and the next minute it wasn't.

Jas looked down at the ground. Two meters away the twick crouched in the grass. It was absolutely motionless. Jas couldn't remember seeing any movement. Was the animal smiling? Jas wondered if an animal was capable of gloating over a victim. Its fur glistened. Apparently Abner Doon groomed his assassins well.

And suddenly Jas felt an excruciating pain in his right calf. He reached down to pry the animal off. For a moment the twick clung, still boring into Jas's leg. Then it wriggled out and in less than a second was burrowing into Jas's upper arm. The leg gushed blood.

With the twick tearing at his right arm, Jas could only strike at the animal with his left hand. It did no good.

I'm going to die, Jas shouted in his mind.

But his survival instinct was still strong, despite the terrible

41

pain and the worse fear. Like a reflex he realized that the twick would simply jump from target to target on Jas's body. It was only a matter of time until it hit a vital artery, or until it found the boneless cavity of his abdomen and devoured his bowels. But Jas could delay. Jas could force it to move.

He threw himself to the ground, trying (hopelessly) to crush the animal under the weight of his body. Of course the twick was uninjured. But the maneuver had won Jas a moment's respite —the animal wriggled out and away, and it crouched two feet from where Jas lay on the ground.

Jas leaped to his feet and started to run. Of course the twick struck, but Jas's back was turned, and the animal only dug into the muscles under the shoulder blade.

Jas threw himself violently to the ground, backward. This time the twick made a sharp sound (pain?) and scurried a little further away. Jas tried to run again. He knew he couldn't outrun the twick, especially now with his back ripped open and his calf torn up so that every step was agony. But at least he was doing *something*.

The twick landed on his buttocks and tore at him. Jas broke stride, fell to one knee. Then he noticed that the lake was only twenty feet away, parallel to his line of flight. He had instinctively been avoiding the water. But maybe—

He got up again and staggered toward the water. The twick kept boring into him, tearing at the great muscles that controlled Jas's left thigh. The animal struck bone just as Jas hit the water.

I can't swim, Jas thought.

Oh well, the coldly intellectual part of his mind answered. Maybe the twick can't either.

It was impossible for Jas to relax enough to float. He just crouched under the water, holding his breath forever, trying to ignore the agony pulsing upward from his buttocks, from his leg, from his arm, from his back. He could feel the twick burrowing along the edge of his pelvic bone. His analytic mind noted the fact that this was taking the animal away from the vulnerable anal area. Muscles can heal. Muscles can heal. The repetition kept him underwater despite the agony, despite his lungs bursting for air. He concentrated on the rhythm of the words muscles can heal muscles can heal muscles can heal.

And then the twick stopped burrowing. A moment later it dropped off Jason's body.

Jas lunged for the surface. He gasped air. He gasped again. A few inches away from his face floated the twick. It was moving feebly, also gasping. Jas grabbed it and forced it underwater again. It wriggled, but it didn't get free, and after forever it stopped moving at all. Jas threw it (with his left arm) out into the deeper part of the lake, breathed again, then felt irresistibly weak and sank back into the water. The water closed over his eyes.

He woke in a gel bath. Only his head and his knees broke the surface of the green slime. He was vaguely aware of throbbing in his leg and arm and buttocks, a tightness in his back. But the gel kept the pain away, kept pressure off the wounds. Jas closed his eyes and went back to sleep.

When he woke the next time he was in a conventional bed, and his wounds hurt more. He groaned with pain.

"Ouch," agreed a pleasant voice. "Well, that's it. Conscious and almost no chance of coma now."

"Very good." Jas recognized the second voice. Doon.

Someone got up and walked away. Someone else didn't. Jas was aware of breathing near him. He opened his eyes. The light was dazzling. He closed them again.

"Abner Doon," Jas said.

"Feeling better?" the man asked cheerfully.

"Than what?" Jas asked. Abner laughed. It was as if he hadn't tried to have Jason killed in the garden. As if they had last met at a cocktail party. As if they both shared a very good joke. "Why?" Jas feebly asked, because he was too tired and enervated to say what was really on his mind.

"You're a survivor, all right," Abner Doon said, patting Jason's hand. "So many people never use their heads. Even people with fine minds. You'll do. You'll do very well."

Jas didn't ask what he'd do very well *for*. He knew that in the opinion of an Estorian twick, he'd do very nicely for supper. Jas disregarded the vague fear and anger he felt in his stomach and turned his head away.

"I'll come visit you later," Doon said, still cheerful.

"Don't bother," Jas mumbled. Then he slept again. He dreamed of tearing Doon with his teeth, burrowing into his throat and ripping out his voice and then opening the jugular vein. The hot blood leaped from the throat. Then, suddenly, the blood was coming from the picture of his father on the ceiling in his mother's flat, and Jas felt the blood warm on his face. He woke up, grief-stricken and guilt-ridden.

Doon was washing his face with a warm cloth. "Quite a dream," the man said. "You were sweating quite a bit."

Jas pulled his head away from the cloth. His wounds didn't feel as painful as they had before. Tight, though, and Jas still felt weak and sleepy.

"Don't pull away, Jas," Doon said. "I'm only trying to wash your face."

Jas turned his back, holding on to the opposite side of the bed.

"Don't be absurd," Doon said. "You're acting like an adolescent."

Jas turned back over, and the quick motion made him grimace with a sharp pain from his hip. He looked at Doon, who again seemed to be kindness personified.

"Sorry that I didn't die on schedule," Jas said.

"Schedule? I have you scheduled for several centuries from now."

"You tried to kill me, you bastard!"

"Oh, that," Doon said, dismissing it with a wave of his hand. "That's not worth arguing over. Come along."

Doon beckoned to an orderly, who brought over a wheelchair. The orderly helped Doon lower Jas into the chair. Then Doon himself pushed Jas out of the room.

They went down corridors whose doors didn't open, until the corridor itself opened into a large room. Prominent at one end of the room was a desk. Behind it the wall was an elaborate computer terminal.

Doon wheeled Jas over to the computer terminal.

"Here's where I found you, Jas."

But Jas studiously did not look at the terminal. Instead he gazed at his injured upper arm. Of course the bandages had long since been removed, while he was under the healers' sleep, and the connective tissue now looked purple and disgusting. Doon didn't seem to mind that Jas wasn't paying attention, though, and soon the boy gave up and looked where he was supposed to.

"I have two basic files here—they hold everything I need to know. One is the nonsense file. The other is the contradiction file. I found you in nonsense, of course."

A code. Jas noticed, too, that Doon had a double cover code on the program, besides the basic search and specify. The screen flashed: "All left-handed blue-eyed women with an IQ of 97 who eat more than two pounds of meat a week and who have more than three lovers." The list took three flashes to read out fully on the screen. "You'll be amused to know, Jas, that the list you just saw includes not just one, but *two* mistresses or former mistresses of Cabinet members. Incredible, isn't it, that they could both meet that description. Amazing things in this computer."

"And you found me under the program for all blue-eyed thirteen-year-old orphans with telepathic gifts," Jas said.

"No. You were part of a much more random search. Everyone knows the computer knows everything—the trouble is that you have to have the keys to find what you want. I have the keys. And here's the program that found you."

The screen flashed: "All children IQ greater than measurable, PQ above 3.8, health excellent, with unfavorable reports from at least two teachers."

Jas's curiosity was stirred. "Why the unfavorable reports?"

"It's possible to be brilliant and utterly uncreative," Doon said. "But brilliant *and* creative people always antagonize the merely bright, who lack, shall we say, originality. Your odds of running into such unoriginal persons in the school system of Capitol are about 8,000 to one—a reasonably good guide, then, to creativity. Better than any test I've seen."

"And you had unfavorable reports from two of my teachers?"

"Actually, Jas, you stuck out on this list because you've never had a teacher who *didn't* file an unfavorable report on you, despite the fact that your PQ shows you adjusted at the 3.9 level, which is neurotic but certainly not antisocial. Why the reports? I could only conclude that you were exceptionally creative. So I had the computer file you and gather all data. Merely routine, of course, but I was aware of you. That was five years ago. Between then and now I've been asleep on somec. Normally I take twenty years—" which, Jas realized, meant that Doon was getting more somec sleep than was legally permitted outside the service "—but because of you I came out only three weeks ago."

"I didn't mean to wake you. I'll be quieter next time."

"I had the computer set to wake me when a certain kind of contradiction came up. The contradiction that triggered it was, of course, your score on the astrodynamics test."

"I wish I'd flunked it.'"

"No you don't. I don't mean the first astrodynamics test. That was routine. It merely identified you as a Swipe, and the computer would have been content to let you die. Luckily for me and the Empire—and you, of course—you're a survivor. You lived long enough to take the second test."

Jas remembered how he had labored over the answers to that one. "I didn't pass that one by checking in on anybody's mind, Doon."

"I know. After all, whose mind would you check in on, as

46

you so colorfully put it? There isn't a single mind—or computer, for that matter—in the Empire or out of it that could have given you all the answers. You missed one test question, of course. But there were three questions on that test for which we didn't *have* an answer."

Doon paused. Jas slowly realized the implications of that.

"You mean I moved beyond—"

"I mean," Doon said, "that you are a reasonably bright young fellow with prospects for a satisfactory career in astrodynamics. My engineers assure me that they can now construct a ship that moves not the piddling triple-light-speed that our scouts now muster, but rather a dazzling eleven lights. Nothing, my young friend, goes eleven lights. And you twisted up the physicists' understanding of mass somehow, though they despaired of trying to explain the difference to me. I'm not mathematical. I hardly need tell you what this does for the Empire."

"I suppose it will speed up the mail."

"You have a very flippant attitude today," Doon said.

"I always antagonize the merely bright," Jas retorted.

"You might recall that I can have you killed if I like."

"You might recall that I have already faced about the worst you can do to me. Kill me if you like. I hardly give a damn."

Doon punched something else on the computer, and in the space over a large table in the middle of the room, a star map formed. The stars were fairly dense. Another code, and most of them disappeared. Now all that were left were pale blue stars and bright red stars. "Us," said Doon, "and Them."

"They surround us," Jas said, surprised.

"Colonies all around, yes indeed. We're hemmed in. And much as we hate to admit it publicly, this war is all about colonies. Whoever has room to expand will eventually win. Whoever is hemmed in will eventually lose."

"Too bad for Mother, then, I suppose," Jas said, though such an unpatriotic attitude jarred even him—one didn't forget one's entire upbringing in a single fit of pique over a mere attempted murder.

47

"Too bad until now, anyway. With the new eleven-light drive, my young friend, we shall soon be colonized far beyond them—and before they can steal the drive and duplicate it, we'll be firmly entrenched. It will remove the whole question of encirclement forever, I am quite confident."

"So play the national anthem and give me a medal, Mr. Doon. Don't have me eaten alive by little animals. It doesn't feel like a suitable reward."

"Does that still bother you? Surely you understand that it was a test."

"What were you testing for, how good I taste? Or how long I can hold my breath underwater?"

"Actually, I was testing to see if your clever and creative mind would keep you alive in a situation of high pressure. You're a survivor."

"And what if I had failed the test?"

"You'd be dead. I was willing to risk my whole waking on that one test."

"A whole waking. While I merely risked the rest of my life."

"You are annoyingly egocentric, Jas. What difference would it make to the world if you dropped dead right now? An infinitesimally smaller daily food demand for Capitol. In this universe you don't amount to horse manure—you recall what horses are? No matter how bright you are, my boy, you are worthless and trivial to the universe until and unless you get into a position where you can make a difference."

Doon walked behind Jas and abruptly began pushing the chair toward the door.

"I spent the first thirty years of my life, Jason, just getting where I am. For thirty years I manipulated and connived and sacrificed—I passed up five chances to go on somec before I was finally satisfied that I had the organization that I needed. I let myself reach thirty physical years of age, in order to get the position I have."

"Assistant minister of colonization."

"I had that at twenty-two. The rest of the time was spent

48

getting control of the computers, winning Mother's Little Boys to my group, getting men and women who ultimately reported to me in every level of the bureaucracy. And I had to keep it all secret so that someone didn't pull the plug while I was under somec."

Jas involuntarily started to laugh at the juxtaposition of the archaic phrase "pull the plug," but caught himself, and merely smiled. "The ultimately efficient megalomaniac," he said.

"Of course. Megalomaniacs are simply people who know damn well they can run the universe better than God or the present governors."

"You've been doing a super job," Jas said. "Everybody's happy."

"What the hell do I care if anybody's happy?" Doon asked. "Least of all you. Heredity has dealt you a full deck, my boy. So you're going to play cards until you win or go broke. You're in my collection, and if you do as you're told, you'll eventually reach a position where you *can* make a difference to humanity. But if you decide to do things on your own, you'll step outside my protection. Do that, and if Radamand Worthing doesn't get you, Hartman Tork will."

Doon pushed the chair quickly down the corridor. And as Doon's last statement hung in the air, Jas felt a tremendous vertigo. The chair was not moving forward, it was falling *down* the corridor, and he was powerless to stop it. He wasn't afraid of hitting the end—it was the falling itself, the powerlessness itself that made him throw his hands out in front of him and shout, "Stop me! Let me stop!"

And Doon stopped pushing the chair. A sudden silence fell in the corridor. The rhythm of Doon's running steps made the stillness shout deafeningly. Jas covered his face with his hands.

"What's wrong, Jas?" Doon whispered. "Why are you afraid?"

Jas just shook his head.

"Brilliant or not, Jason, you are still a child, I suppose. If you would only talk like a child, people would remember to treat you like one."

"I don't want to be treated like a child."

"Well, you sure as hell don't want to be treated like an adult. Remember that you applied for the Service?"

"They turned me down."

"They've already reconsidered. You'll begin pilot school as soon as your skin is healed."

"Pilot school?" Jas was surprised. "That was just my escape, to save my life—I never really wanted to be a pilot."

"Too intellectual for the Space Service, is that it? Well, consider it a lifesaver anyway, boy. Pilots live longer than anybody. If they don't get killed, of course—but you're a survivor, right? On all their twenty- and thirty-year flights, they're only awake for a few months at the most. The rest of the time, somec. Pilots are on a somec level that will keep you young and alive for five hundred years."

"And after that?" Jas asked, trying to be sarcastic.

"Why, further instructions, of course," Doon answered with a bland smile. "There are only a few people in the Empire who are on the somec level that pilots take for granted. The whole Cabinet will die before you. Only I will stay alive. And the head of the Little Boys. And a few of my most needed assistants."

Jas stared. "The somec usage is determined strictly by law!"

"And once upon a time there was a little girl with long blond hair that got involved with three talking bears. *I* control the people who control the somec, and that means I have control over life and death everywhere in the Empire. Rather a secure position to be in."

"I don't want to be a pilot."

"Then you want to be a corpse. That's the choice."

"I thought you said you didn't think you were God!" Jas shouted.

"I don't."

"Then get out of my life!"

"Why? Just because I want to make you great, whether you like it or not?"

"If I'm going to be great, I'm going to do it on my own. And

50

I don't know if I even care about 'greatness'. Not everybody's a would-be worldmaker, Doon."

"You have no vision, Jas."

"I see better than anybody I know."

"Better, but not very far. Your father's dead."

"You think I didn't know that?'"

"He died because he and some other Swipe ship captains weren't content to serve. They went into business for themselves, and so they lost the protection of the Empire. They thought they didn't need it. So they took a dozen ships and made war with the universe. They were heroes for a while, of course. Everybody loves a rebel—from a distance, and as long as the rebel loses gracefully. But when they were about to lose, they burned over some planets as a last-ditch effort. Then suddenly the Swipe heroes became Swipe bastards, and Swipes were hunted down and killed all over the Empire. And do you know why your father burned those planets?"

"No." Jas was grinding his teeth and couldn't stop.

"Because they wouldn't let him land. He requested permission to land and refuel, and they turned him down. He had to teach them a lesson."

"That's not true. They fired on him."

"You know that there's no weapon that can be fired in an atmosphere that can possibly do damage to a ship, Jas."

"My father burned them in self-defense."

"He was angry, and he had to teach them a lesson."

"No!"

"Like father, like son," Doon said.

Jason half-rose from the wheelchair, until the pain stopped him. "That's not true, you bastard! I'd never burn a planet, I never would—"

"You would, Jason. Right now you would, if they got you angry enough. Because you have no vision. You have nothing important to accomplish, no magnificent goal that keeps you from destroying yourself to achieve petty, transitory objectives. You don't even have a *right* to be free until you have vision and pur-

51

pose. And so I'll rule you, Jason, and keep you safe until you're able to rule yourself."

They moved again down the corridor. Jas tried to look into Doon's mind, to see, if he could, what Doon eventually planned to do with him—having been betrayed once in the garden, he didn't plan to be betrayed again. But he couldn't twist around to see Doon's eyes, and whether that really stopped him from seeing into the man's mind or whether he simply couldn't control the gift well enough to see a person's thoughts without looking at him, Jas found nothing, could tell nothing.

They got back to the hospital room, which was still empty. Without a word Jas gingerly lifted himself out of the chair, and though he wanted to refuse Doon's help, he had to lean on the man as he made his way to the bed.

"Thirteen years old," Doon whispered. "Well, heaven knows you're ready for pilot school, anyway. They'll undoubtedly bend the rules and make you a pilot before you turn twenty-one— why they chose that age anyway is beyond me to fathom. You should go on two or three voyages, and then sometime, say a century or a hundred and twenty years from now, when you return to Capitol from a voyage, come to the Ministry of Colonization and ask for an appointment with me. They'll know that they should wake me then. I'll look forward to seeing you again, my boy."

"Going back to sleep now, Mr. Doon?" Jas asked.

"In a few days. I've spent far too much time with you as it is, and I'm behind schedule on all my other work. You'd better be worth it."

"I hope I'm not."

"You like being excellent too well, Jas. You won't be able to stop yourself."

"I will not be part of your bloody vision!"

"How do you know that your resistance to me isn't exactly what I want from you?" Doon asked, amused.

In despair Jas threw himself back on the pillow, staring at the

52

ceiling. There was no picture there. Through gritted teeth he said, "There isn't a damn thing I can do."

"You can trust me," Doon suggested. Jas laughed bitterly. Doon sighed. "Why don't you just look, and see who I am?"

"Look inside *you?*" Jas asked.

"Or are you afraid that if you knew me, you couldn't hate me anymore?"

And so Jas leaned up on his left elbow and looked behind Abner Doon's mind. It wasn't just a glance this time, as it had always been before. This time he looked deep, looked far, found the hidden places, found the lies and the lies behind them and finally came down to the truth. He held it in his mind—the basis on which Abner Doon thought, decided, acted—and was amazed. And then he stopped being amazed, and only withdrew from Doon's mind. Painfully, reluctantly removed himself, and then, because he had left, he wept. Doon went away. Finally Jas slept.

When he woke, he remembered vague words that Doon had said, but whether Doon had actually said them or Jas had only dreamed them, he didn't know. He remembered them, though, and over the next few weeks, as bureaucrats processed him into the Service, tested him, trained him, as he consented to everything done to him, he stopped despising himself for the memory of Doon's words, and began, instead, to call them back, to listen to them again in his dreams, and in his daydreaming.

One day they came to him and told him he was ready for his first Service assignment. It was on the other side of Capitol, a long journey, and at the end of it he was assigned a tiny cubicle in a far corner of the officers' section of the command center. It was lowest in the hierarchy of privilege and perks, but it was a private room all the same, and in officers' quarters, too. And there was a full-length mirror on the wall.

"Ha," Jas said when he saw himself in it.

He was surprised to see that he was still only thirteen years old, still only a little over 165 centimeters in height, his main growth still ahead of him. Somehow during the last week he had stopped thinking of himself as a child. He was surprised at how young the face was. How slight the body.

He grinned, and the boy in the mirror smiled slightly back at him.

Then Jas turned and unpacked his few belongings, then began memorizing the list of command center rules and regulations that had been given him upon arrival. He was going to be the best damned new officer they'd ever had. Because the sooner everyone was happy with him, the sooner he'd become a pilot. And the sooner he became a pilot, the sooner he'd be on somec, and then he could sleep through most of the years until he could wake up at the end of a century and come back to see Doon.

He knew it was ironic that he should look forward to seeing the man who had tried to kill him, but Jas understood that a little better, now. For he had seen Abner Doon as no other living person had seen him. From the inside. And inside Abner Doon, behind the memories and pain, Jas had found what no other man could show him.

Peace. Utter discontent, but peace with his vision of the possibility, peace with his commitment to fulfilling that vision.

And Jas remembered the words he had heard Doon say. "I love you, son."

He set the list aside, closed his eyes, and recalled, or tried to recall, the face on the ceiling in his mother's flat. He couldn't. It was gone from his memory. When he tried to remember his father's face, all he could see was Doon, smiling.

THE amusements in the Empire depended more on social class than on location. Though some games and sports were restricted to certain planets, they were few and fading—those that had universal appeal, like the mismating simulacrum game of Exeter, ceased to be provincial, while those that didn't catch on off-planet, like cockball on Campbell, eventually died away.

The truly popular games, however, spread throughout the Empire rapidly—only the limitation of space travel kept their acceptance from being immediate. Spectator sports were immensely popular, and the outcome of football, basketball, and undercut games were rushed by courier ships to every planet in the Empire. It was here that the first division between classes occurred: somec users began to time their wakings to fit the expected arrivals of courier ships, in order to watch the game and learn the outcome. Those not on somec, of course, could rarely see the same off-planet team perform twice in their lifetime, and so only live, on-planet games were readily available. Thus the somec users watched games on vast screens in huge banquet halls, where only the elite could come, and where prices were prohibitive, while non-somec users crowded into vast arenas, watching live athletes of the second rank slug it out on the local playing field.

Participant sports also faced the same division. Team sports gradually became the prerogative of lower class enthusiasts, who could get together at frequent intervals, and who didn't have to worry about timing their wakings. Somec users, however, found it difficult to time their wakings just to get a team together. A seven-year sleeper would not be too terribly tempted to waken two years earlier in order to play on the same team with a superb rugby player who happened to be a fiver. Instead, individual players would "pair up" in "duels," and these would be taped and replayed for other somec users later. A great deal of gambling focused on these duels: Sleepers, upon waking, would consult lists of upcoming duels, study past tapes of the players, and place bets. On their next waking, they would learn the outcome of the duel and watch the tape, learning why and how they guessed right or wrong. The most common games were fencing, rapiers, tennis, wrestling, boxing, and knife-throwing, the last being an illegal game, with tapes secretly taken and preserved, since many deaths and injuries ended particular contests prematurely.

Aside from sports, amusement centered around computers. "Arcades" catered to the lower classes, offering many complex computer contests called "pinballs." Similarly, the wealthy also played with computers, but instead of simple one-person games, played vast multiplayer games such as "Soap Opera," "Monopoly," and "Empire," in which individual players, upon waking, could purchase an already existing persona from a player ready to go under, and play against other players already in the game. It became a point of pride to manipulate one's persona to the strongest possible position, and many players became so involved that they adopted the persona name as their own, purchasing the right to play in the same game at exorbitant prices at every waking for centuries. The same game, with different players manipulating the personae, could continue for centuries, and the Monopoly players of Sonora even today take great pride in the fact that throughout the Somec Revolution and the Dark Ages, their game missed only one year, and that because of a power failure.

But the most all-pervading amusements were the theatrical media: loops and plays. Plays, of course, were for the lowest classes, those who couldn't afford to see reality in the loops, which commanded high prices. But for once the division wasn't along somec lines. A majority of non-somec users were able to pay to see loops, and this one amusement brought them in contact with the lives of the somec society.

Loops were made of practically everything. Notably beautiful women were paid astronomical fees for allowing their private lives to be looped—audiences would sit for hours watching the unedited holo broadcast, enduring (or enjoying?) the endless trivia, all for the sake of the dramatic moment, the argument, the intercourse. Naturally, budding actresses and actors would pay dearly for the privilege of taking part in that "totally true" looped life, and these women were the top money-makers in the Empire, rising to somec levels unreachable except to the highest government officials.

Next to the actresses in the lifeloops were the starship captains, pilots with such legendary names as Carter Poor, Jazz Worthing, and Ngao-ngao Bumubi. These pilots paid a small percentage of their earnings to the Service, and then allowed broadcasts of their victorious battles to be made throughout the Empire. They, too, received phenomenal wealth, and since they were already at the highest possible somec level, all their income could be—and usually was—invested in business. Some pilots ended up owning entire planets; others magnanimously sponsored universities; still others kept the uses of their money entirely secret.

And others brought their own downfall by getting embroiled in government. Perhaps the most famous case was the phenomenally successful pilot and loopstar Jazz Worthing, whose man-

*ager, Willard "Hop" Noyock, apparently involved him in the fa-
mous Shimon Rapth Coup.*

Excerpt from *The Complete
Public Pleasure Book,* Onger
and Haight, 6645, p. 12.

HOP Noyock woke up feeling hot and flabby. Hot because the reviver always left him sweating. Flabby because somehow, over the last three hundred years, he had gotten a little out of shape.

He rolled onto his side, and his stomach followed a moment later, hitting the metal of the bed with a disgusting slap. He belched.

"How," he asked the nurse who stood by with a sponge and a towel, "can I possibly belch after five years of sleep?"

The nurse shrugged and began to wipe him down. The sponge was ice cold and the water trickled freezingly along his back. Hop was vaguely ashamed that the nurse had to lift his stomach out of the way to wipe down the sweating crease. (I have got to exercise. I have got to diet.) But he knew that he wouldn't have time for exercise, that food would taste too good to worry about dieting, that in only five weeks he'd be eligible to return to the Sleeproom and go under for another five years or until his client came back (aye, there's the rub).

Hop got up and walked stiffly to the hooks where his new clothes hung waiting for him. As he took his first steps he felt

59

a sharp pain, a stiff uncomfortableness in a region of his body that should not be causing him any pain. Could he possibly have developed hemorrhoids while under somec?

"Excuse me," he said to the nurse, who immediately turned away. Nurses had to be very deferential to the sleepers—but obsequiousness was a small price to pay for the privilege of somec, even at the nurses' rather trivial rate of two years up for one year under.

Hop Noyock reached behind himself and found the source of his discomfort. It was a small piece of paper, soaked in the sweat of his revival. On it was written, in Hop's own handwriting, a short message:

"Someone trying to kill Jazz. Must warn."

What in hell did that mean? He looked at the paper for some possible hidden clue. There was none. It was just the ordinary paper they kept by the sleepbeds to satisfy the paranoia of those who were convinced they would think of something absolutely vital between the time when their brains were taped and the time when the somec flowed into their veins, emptying all memories from their minds. Memory slips, they called the papers, and Hop had never used one before.

Now he *had* used one (or *is* it my handwriting?) and not only that, he had gone to the bother of putting it in a rather effective, if undignified, hiding place.

Apparently, when he had written it, he had thought it was vital.

But if (*if*) there was a plot to kill Jazz Worthing (alias Meal Ticket) how in hell had he found out about it between the taping and the somec? It was strictly illegal for anyone but the nurses to come into the tape-and-tap; that was in the contract —it was imperial law, for heaven's sake, forget the contract.

And who would try to kill Jazz Worthing, the Empire's most successful starship pilot, not to mention the star of the five best-selling loops in trade history (I made the boy a star, he'd be nothing without his agent); killing him would not only hurt the

Empire's war effort and tear down morale, it would also leave the fans disconsolate—

And thinking of the war effort, what about it? Hop went to the history sheets that hung from the wall. He was proud of the fact that he had a five-year summary, a reminder of his high somec rating.

The news was basically good. The Empire was still intact, more or less, win a little, lose a little but the war is far from home.

Then, practical as always, Hop checked the gossip sheets and spent an amusing five minutes as he dressed, reading over what happened while he was under. Of course, most of the people he had never met—their somec schedules never coincided and so he knew of their escapades only from the sheets—

The flight schedules showed that Jazz was coming in only three days. Hop glanced up at the calendar on the wall (they never bother with clocks in the Sleeproom) and realized that he had been wakened almost three months early.

Damn.

Oh well, it could have been three years, that had happened before, and it was a small enough price to pay for his twenty percent of all of Jazz Worthing's revenues. Without Jazz, Hop Noyock wouldn't be on somec at all.

Somebody trying to kill Jazz? Asinine.

(If I find them, I'll tear them apart, the bastards.)

Hop met Jazz the minute the smoke had been pumped out of the landing hall. The two-kilometer-long ship always took Hop's breath away (either that or the long climb up the ramp), just as the ridiculous narrow tube that held all the payload made him laugh. It looked like it was tacked onto the huge stardrive as an afterthought. The tail wagging the dog. A hammer to drive a needle through nothing.

Over the ship stretched the huge girders that supported the roof, now looking like fine lace in the distance. Only here, in the shipcradles, were there large doors in the metal roof that sheathed the entire planet of Capitol.

Hop watched as, far below the audience, gates were opened and the crowds flooded in. Jazz's arrival was big news on Capitol. Hop felt the old resentment as he watched the crowd fill all the available space around the base of the cradle. He had made a fortune by charging admission to Jazz's arrivals—but some of his competitors, sponsoring less popular pilots, had managed to convince the government that it was illegal to charge admission for entry to public government facilities—and they had even made Hop give back the money he had already made on it. Damn poor losers, that's all they were.

And then the door of the ship fell open and out stepped Jazz Worthing. Two hundred meters below, the fans started screaming so loudly that the sound could be heard even above the roar of the machinery that was testing the stardrive. Hop Noyock threw out his arms and made the theatrical gesture that had been seen by billions at the end of every Jazz Worthing loop. He strode to the tired-looking pilot and embraced him.

"Jazz Worthing, Capitol is grateful that you're home safe and victorious again."

"Nice to be back," Jazz said, smiling slightly, his bright blue eyes flashing in the dazzling lights. He was several centuries old, and looked younger than twenty. One last pat on the back, and then Hop reached down and flipped off the loop recorder. Jazz relaxed as soon as the taping was finished. He tensed again, though, when Hop whispered in his ear, "Somebody may be trying to kill you. Don't leave the crowds."

"Hop, I don't even want to *see* the damned crowds."

"No one'd dare try anything in the crowds. We'll talk in a minute."

Hop led Jazz to the railing and showed him off to the cheering fans. Their roar of approval was quite stirring. Hop felt quite stirred.

"Hop, what the hell is going on?" Jazz asked.

"*I* don't know," Hop said. "Bow for the bastards, Jason, give them their money's worth."

Jazz looked at Hop in surprise. "You don't mean the government's letting you charge admission again?"

"No, no, figure of speech, little figure of speech, you know."

"I just want to go home and go to bed, Hop. Don't give me any trouble about it or I'll fire you."

Hop shrugged. "If you get killed, I'll be out of a job anyway."

Jazz sighed and listened as Hop told him about the note.

"I especially like your hiding place," Jazz commented as they walked down the winding ramp.

"It's my body's only built-in pocket."

"How are we doing?"

"Financially? Latest audit was five years ago, and it said about seventeen billion."

"I left about forty years ago. What would it have been worth then?"

"Eleven billion. Inflation's getting worse."

"That note. Are you sure you weren't just playing a joke?"

"On myself? Ha ha, what a riot."

Jazz set his lips tightly. "Why would anyone want to kill *me?*"

"One of the other captains?" Hop suggested, lightly.

"We're all friends. We all like each other."

"Are you sure?"

"I'm sure."

Hop shrugged. "One of their managers then. Out to wipe out the competition."

"Do you believe that?"

"Hell no. It sounds more like treason. Must be *something* involved with the government, or how could the information have reached me in the Sleeproom? Somebody thinks your death would help or hurt some faction in the government. I wish you'd stay out of politics."

The ramp seemed to go on forever. The roar of the stardrive test grew softer; the roar of the crowd grew louder. "Are you

63

sure," Jazz asked, "that you didn't already know the information, and put it together after you were taped?"

"I've been racking my brains. Nothing. I didn't know anything about any threat on anybody's life. I don't know anybody with a motive. I was *told,* after the taping."

"Damn."

"How are the loops from this trip?"

"Oh, some good stuff. My fleet got caught in an ambush near Kapittuck and we fought our way out without losses. Very dramatic. Some good close-ups, too, you'll be in gravy for the next five or ten wakings."

"So will you," Hop said.

"Sure," Jazz answered. "And I have so much time on Capitol to enjoy it.'"

(Don't complain, you bastard. When I started working for you three centuries ago we were both in our teens, subjectively speaking, and now count my gray hairs. I wake up every five years, while you coast through life waking only three or four times a century, staying young forever—)

"You look great, Hop," Jazz said.

"You, too, Jazz old man," Hop said, using the obscenity freely.

They reached the bottom of the ramp, where police were struggling to hold the crowd back from charging up to meet them. "Here are the lions," Jazz said, and then they waded into the crowd of outreaching hands and hungering eyes.

They went to a party that night—after all, wakings were short and all the pleasure had to be crammed into only a few short days and weeks. Besides, eleven actresses doing lifeloops were there, and all of them had paid a tidy sum to get Hop to promise that Jazz Worthing would not only attend, but also spend at least three minutes talking to them. Jazz took care of the duty calls right away, and then proceeded to win a small fortune (a drop in the bucket) at pinochle, losing his preoccupied look for a few hours. The hostess, Arran Handully, a former actress who had now "retired"—which meant she only made guest appearances in other women's lifeloops—was forever fluttering around Jazz and Hop, bringing them drinks, making charming conversation: obviously Jazz was her prize for the evening. Hop fleetingly wondered if she had arranged her waking just to coincide with his coming. That would be flattery indeed.

After the party had been going for about four hours or so, Arran Handully called for silence, which after a few minutes was grudgingly granted to her.

"One of the reasons for this party is that Fritz Kapock has designed a new costume that is so compelling, so magnificent, that I had to show it to you the best way I know—on me."

Since there was nothing remarkable about the dress she was wearing—floor-length white with long sleeves that ended in gloves and a high neck—everyone knew she was going to dance, which would be fine, she had a Capitolwide reputation for interesting effects, and one of the best-selling lifeloops in history had been her "Rehearsal Day" tape in which she had practiced every conceivable dance pose and motion, nude.

The Kapock design was interesting enough—as she danced her ordinary-looking dress began to glow brightly, dazzlingly, and slowly the guests realized that it was dissolving somehow in the process. The bright aura lingered for several minutes after she was completely naked, and when she ended her dance sparks still seemed to dance around her. The guests applauded wildly —some with lust, some with real appreciation, and a few with gratitude: with this on their loops, more than one budding young actress would have a good start to her career.

After her bow, she brought out Kapock, the designer, who also bowed stiffly.

"Poor guy," Hop commented to Jazz, "he hates the bitch, but who can turn down a commission these days? Inflation eats it up faster than you can spend it. And the price of lower somec ratings is always going up."

Arran picked up a drink from a passing tray and walked out among her guests. The other women soon realized that she had no intention of dressing again, and so they sighed and undressed, too, wishing they hadn't bothered to spend so much money on costumes for the party.

Arran went to Jason Worthing and handed him the drink. Immediately a group of lifelooping women and interested onlookers gathered to see what would happen, hoping perhaps to interject some witticism that might turn the incident to their favor —some clever remark that might get them invited to another, grander party on their next waking, or the one after.

"Did you like Fritz's little costume?"

"Very clever," Jazz said, smiling and accepting the drink. "How is it done?"

Fritz Kapock, who had followed Arran, smiled and said, "I'll never tell."

"He told *me*," Arran said, tossing her head prettily, "that it's oxidation."

Fritz laughed. "Of course. That much is obvious."

"Oh, and now Fritz is telling everyone how stupid I am," Arran pouted.

What a great act, Hop thought. Billions of loopwatchers, seeing this scene, would nudge each other and say, "See, there's Arran Handully, pretending to be dumb. She'll get 'em in a minute."

Fritz Kapock awkwardly denied her accusation. "Of course I'm not."

"It's still a dazzling effect," Jazz said, and Hop was pleased that Jazz was making an effort to be pleasant company, even without being on contract.

"That calls for a drink," Arran said, taking a glass out of the hand of a servant near her.

Kapock held up his glass and said, "To Arran Handully, who managed to upstage my small effort by wearing a costume far more beautiful—her lovely self."

"What a poet," Arran whispered, and then she brought a gasp from everyone by stepping toward Jazz Worthing and putting her own glass to his lips. A declaration of intent, and everyone

66

waited for the completion of the ritual, Jazz sipping and then placing his own glass up to Arran's lips.

He didn't do it, though. Instead, he stepped back, rejecting the offer, and raised his glass into the air. "And let me add my own toast to her courage—who else would dare to try to murder me at her own party?"

It took a moment for the words to sink in. And then the guests murmured as Arran protested, using her body coquettishly in a reflexive attempt to disarm and win over all watchers. "What a thing to say, Captain Worthing. There are politer ways to say no to a girl."

"You mean you deny it? Then take a drink from your own glass, my dear."

"After I've been refused? I could almost wish it *were* poisoned."

"Really? And so could I," Jazz said. "Shall we see if your wish is fulfilled?" He stepped toward her abruptly, taking the glass from her hand, seizing her by the hair with his other hand, and putting the glass to her lips. No one intervened. Let the action flow, as they all said. However things turned out, this would sell a billion loops.

"Take a drink, sweet Arran Handully, from the glass you offered me," Jazz said, smiling.

"What an actor you are," she said softly, and Hop was sure now that he saw terror in her eyes. For the first time it occurred to him that somehow Jason might well have uncovered the very murder plot he had been warned against. But how? They hadn't left each other since he disembarked from the ship.

Jazz began to tip the glass up to pour over her smiling mouth. Suddenly she writhed away, knocking the glass on the floor. It broke; the liquid splashed.

"Don't touch it," Jazz commanded. "It's now time for at least one of our kind and watchful observers to show himself and take a fragment of glass for analysis."

Suddenly several women moaned in disappointment, punching at the buttons on their loop recorders. A grim-faced man came up, holding a suppressor, and the moans stopped. Mother's Little Boys could do whatever they liked—including cutting out a choice scene from a lifeloop. The man knelt down by the fragments of glass and in a very businesslike way mopped up a sample of the liquid and took four pieces of glass, dumped them into a small bag he pulled from his pocket, and then, nodding to the company, left.

Arran was sitting down, shaking.

Fritz Kapock looked at Jason Worthing in hatred. "That was incredibly crude, doing a thing like that," he said.

"I know," Jazz agreed, smiling. "A more courteous man would have drunk, and died gracefully." Jazz excused himself from the group in a way that informed everyone that he preferred not to be accompanied. Hop, of course, accompanied him anyway.

"How did you know?" Hop asked.

"I didn't. But it seems like it was a pretty good guess, doesn't it?"

Guess? Hop knew perfectly well that Jazz Worthing wasn't stupid enough to open himself up to libel suits on the basis of mere guesswork. But if he preferred not to tell, why push him? Then again, why not? Managers have some rights.

"Come on, Jazz. How did you know?"

"I'm a Swipe," Jazz answered.

Hop rolled his eyes and laughed. "All right then. Don't tell me. Protect your sources. But at least tell me why she tried!"

Jazz only smiled and looked over at the group gathered to commiserate with their offended hostess. She was looking weak and helpless, and Hop couldn't help but admire her technique. A brilliant actress—able to utterly hide every natural emotion, play a role every waking moment.

Fritz Kapock separated himself from the group around Arran Handully and began to walk toward where Hop and Jazz were sitting.

"You see," Jazz said, "they're persistent. They won't settle for one attempt."

"What?" Hop asked. "Not Kapock. He's—" but then Hop remembered the gossip sheet "—a damned good swordsman and has had more than a few formal duels. None to the death, but Jazz, be careful, you've got to keep yourself safe. The Empire needs you."

"Not as much as you need your twenty percent, my dear friend," Jason answered.

Fritz Kapock stopped about three meters away, and began talking loudly with a group that had gathered there. Jazz didn't take his eyes off Kapock. Hop was worried. "Jazz, you know a hell of a lot more than you've been telling me."

"Of course," Jazz said, patting Hop's wrist. "That's why you're a manager and I'm a starpilot."

Kapock's voice came loudly to them: "Only a bastard and a coward would make an accusation like that—especially at her own party."

People nearby began to edge nearer. Actresses frantically fiddled with their loop recorders, trying to get them to warm up again, though they knew it was hopeless for a few minutes more —suppressors always ruined recording for exactly ten minutes, no more, no less.

"Jazz, he's trying to provoke you," Hop said.

"Perhaps I shall let him succeed," Jazz answered, and Hop resigned himself to watching his meal ticket get killed on the end of Fritz Kapock's sword. It went like clockwork.

"That boor isn't fit company for civilized persons," said Fritz.

"Hold my hat," said Jazz.

"They should never allow these common soldiers in refined company," said Fritz Kapock.

"Fritz Kapock, I believe?" said Jazz.

"And you're the man who ruined our hostess's evening, aren't you?" Fritz snarled.

"I assume you were hoping I would overhear your insults."

69

"It's hardly my affair what you do and don't hear."

A woman whooped with glee as her loop recorder came on. Another breathed a sigh of relief.

"I heard, I take due note, and I assume you'll want choice of weapons."

Hop moaned. Jason hadn't even been clever. Hadn't even tried to get Kapock to make the challenge so that the starpilot would get the chance to choose peashooters or tennis or some other harmless duel weapon.

"Foils are effeminate," Kapock said. "And sabers are like meat axes. Rapier? Three edged?"

"Which, just by coincidence, you no doubt have nearby," Jason said. "I'll agree to that."

A servant went for the weapons, and Hop angrily volunteered to be Jason's second. "You irresponsible bastard," Hop muttered as he helped Jazz take off his jacket and shirt.

"True, true. It's been nice knowing you," Jazz said.

"Do you know how to fight with swords?" Hop asked, wondering how Jazz could be so calm about this.

"Sure. You just hold it by the dull end and stick the sharp end in the other fellow."

"Not funny," Hop said. And then the weapons arrived, the crowd cleared a space, and Fritz and Jason, stripped to the waist, took their weapons and went to opposite corners. As a volunteer referee went through the ritual of pleading with both parties to reconcile their differences peaceably, Jazz asked Hop Noyock, "Do you have your loop recorder?"

"Yes."

"Is it off?"

"Of course."

"Then here. Use this." And Jazz handed Hop a small suppressor. Hop looked at him in surprise.

"This is illegal."

"So is duelling. But I want you to have an exclusive. Your last chance to make money off me."

Hop grimaced at the implication of his own venality; at the same time he realized that having an exclusive of this duel would be immeasurably valuable whoever won. So he turned on the suppressor, and the moans and cries of outrage came from women and men all around the duelling square. Then, because his own loop recorder had not been on, Hop started it right up, ready to create another Noyock Productions masterpiece.

"All ready?" Jazz asked. Noyock, holding both suppressor and recorder in his pockets, nodded. "Wish me luck," Jazz said, and then he raised his sword to signal the start of the duel. Kapock raised his, and then leaped forward, swinging the sword in a dazzling display of control, putting the point exactly where he wanted it. Jazz merely held his sword in front of him, almost as if it were a foil, and stood half-crouched. No style at all.

Then Kapock came close enough to strike—and struck. But his sword met Jason's in mid-thrust. Kapock recovered, struck again and again found his blade parried. He backed off. Jason merely stood, waiting, his sword having varied only twice from its straight forward position. Kapock was embarrassed and angry. He had been made to look like a pompous show-off, who could be stopped with ease by a man not even bothering to observe proper form.

Kapock moved to attack again, this time with such quick movements that parrying seemed impossible. Feints could not be distinguished from attacks; but Jason was not drawn into parrying any of the false moves. Instead he moved only three times, each time throwing aside Kapock's whistling blade, and the third time twisting the blade, breaking it off near the hilt. The broken blade spun out toward the crowd, but hit the floor before it could do any damage.

Kapock stood looking at the broken sword in his hand, as amazed as Hop had ever seen a man. Hop could understand it—he had tried his hand at swordplay years ago, and he remembered enough to know that it was humiliating to be disarmed on only the fifth parry. He also knew that Jazz had blocked the attacks as perfectly as if he had known exactly where and when they were coming, before Kapock himself even knew. More grist for the Jazz Worthing legend mill.

The next step, of course, was for Jazz to step forward and magnanimously state that he was satisfied, and no further fighting was necessary. But at that moment a woman screamed, and all eyes whirled to Arran, who was standing, still naked, looking with horror at the large doors to her hall. They were open, and a group of laser-armed men in Space Service uniforms were marching in. And all at once everyone seemed to come to the same conclusion. Jazz Worthing, the great starpilot, had been under attack—poison, and then a duel. These soldiers would not stand for such an insult to the Service and to the Service's most successful fleet commander. And the guests, in the irrational manner of crowds, immediately began to head for the opposite exit. At the moment they started to move, however, *those* doors opened, too, and more soldiers came in. The crowd panicked, massed in a jumble in the middle of the hall, and began to shout and scream and scurry meaninglessly from place to place so that it was impossible to tell what was going on.

So Hop did what he always did. He stuck with Jason, following him as Jazz coolly walked to Arran Handully, who was looking dazed and vaguely depressed as the crowd whirled around her. Jazz picked her up and lifted her over his shoulder in a manner vaguely reminiscent of the worst excesses of the pornographic brutality plays. Hop had never seen Jazz treat a woman like that—but then, she had tried to kill him.

Fritz Kapock tried to interfere. Jason hit him, but the blow would only have slowed the artist down, hampered as Jason was by Arran's rather uncooperative bulk. Hop considered it his duty (and a pretty damn good idea for profits) to try to keep Jazz Worthing alive no matter what stupid things he was trying to do. So Hop used a few of the low blows he had learned in his childhood in the lowest corridor of Capitol, and Fritz was out for the duration. Perhaps longer. Hop didn't stop to check.

They headed for a service entrance, and Hop helped muscle a

path for Jason to follow through the crowd that was trying to get out that way. Once into the corridor beyond the door (carpeted, Hop noticed—Arran had spent a lot of money on her flat), Jason looked at the direction the crowd was heading, and went the other way. Hop Noyock tagged along, noting with pleasure that he was young enough to appreciate the way Arran Handully looked as she wriggled and jerked, trying to free herself from Jason's grasp. When she started digging fingernails into Jazz's back, Noyock swatted her sharply. "None of that," he said, and she seemed to realize for the first time that she and Jazz weren't alone. She stopped struggling.

"Why don't they have anybody in here guarding the halls?" Hop asked.

"Because they're Servicemen, not constables, and certainly not Mother's Little Boys," Jason answered. "Besides, we're heading farther in, not out."

"Why the hell are we doing that?" Noyock asked, making it a point to breathe heavily so that Jazz knew how tired he was getting as they wound up a ramp.

"Go the other way, if you want to get picked up by angry soldiers."

Hop doggedly followed as Jason went up the ramp, and saw, to his relief, that the starpilot was capable of getting tired. Jazz slowed at the top of the ramp, then swung Arran off his shoulder and slammed her a little harder than necessary against a wall. He held her right hand in his, with his forearm pressing against her throat, and his legs both to one side of hers—he wasn't giving her an opportunity for any action. Just to be sure, however, Hop held her left hand, too. She shot him a glare.

"Don't look at *me* like that, Arran," Hop said, using his wounded dignity voice. "I'm only holding you twenty percent against the wall. He's responsible for eighty percent."

She didn't answer. Jazz ignored Hop, too, and so he stood holding Arran's hand as Jazz asked her, "Which way from here?"

She didn't answer.

"I know you have a hiding place, Arran. The reason those sol-

73

diers were there is because the test on the poison came out positive and they got mad. Want me to take you down there to them?"

She shook her head.

"Then where's the hiding place?"

Hop watched as Jazz stared at her eyes, as if hoping to pluck the answers out of them. Apparently Arran saw a different intent, and she let her eyes fill up with tears. A play for sympathy, Hop knew, but it didn't stop him from feeling instant pity. The bitch. Actresses shouldn't be allowed to have private lives. They didn't know how to stop acting.

Abruptly Jazz jerked her away from the wall and slung her over his shoulder again. Sighing wearily, Hop followed him off down a corridor.

The halls were narrower up here, Hop noticed, and the floors and walls were made of wood. He touched one, and was surprised at the roughness. Not just wood, then. *Real* wood. He whistled.

"Shut up," Jazz said.

"Why so glum?" Hop asked. "A billion men would give their privates to have her over their shoulder wearing that costume. Though that would rather defeat the purpose, wouldn't it?"

Jazz didn't laugh, and so Hop shut up.

They stopped in front of a rather insignificant-looking door. "What's in here?" Jazz asked.

"A wardrobe," she said immediately.

"Can you break it open, Hop?"

"Me?"

"Forget it," Jazz said. He stepped back and, still burdened with Arran, kicked the door. It budged, but just barely.

"Let me," Hop said, now that he was sure there was no sentry planted in the door. No sense getting blown up unnecessarily. Jazz may be a meal ticket, but keeping him alive would be pointless to Hop if Hop weren't around to get his twenty percent. He stood facing the opposite wall of the narrow corridor, his hands firmly placed on the wall. Then he jumped up and

74

pushed off from the wall, slamming his feet into the door. It didn't quite break free, but all it took was another half-hearted kick from Noyock as he lay on the floor.

"Spectacular," Jazz said as he stepped over Noyock and walked into the room. "You're very agile for a fat man."

"Paunch covers muscle, it doesn't replace it," Hop commented, and got up. The "wardrobe" was a large library, with mirrors wherever there were no shelves, including the floor and ceiling. But the real attraction was the contents of the shelves—real *paper* books, not tapes, filling every available space. Noyock wasn't much of a reader, but he appreciated value in whatever form it took, and under his breath he mumbled, "The lady's literate, after all."

Jazz paid no attention. Instead he picked Arran off his shoulders and tossed her to the floor. She landed heavily.

"Where's the door?" he heard Jazz say. Arran shook her head, wincing with some pain she acquired in the fall to the floor. Jazz shook her, and she started to cry. Hop hated himself, but the crying made him want to say, "Hey, Jazz, go easy on the woman, huh?" He resisted the impulse, however.

So did Jazz, if indeed he felt such a charitable feeling. Instead, he doubled up his fist and plunged it sharply into Arran's stomach. Hop was sure he heard a rib break. She screamed in pain, and Hop wondered if it was the first honest emotion he had seen her use.

Jazz leaned down and put his ear by her lips. Hop was surprised she was conscious—but apparently she had been for at least a moment, for Jason got up and walked straight to a bookshelf and pulled off two books, reaching behind to find something. Immediately a mirror slid into the floor, and a little room was revealed behind. Jazz walked back to Arran, picked her up, and carried her limp unconscious body into the room. Noyock decided to follow.

As soon as they were inside, Jason lay Arran down on the floor. "Find a light switch," Jazz said, but before Noyock could even glance around, the door slid back up, cutting off all light.

75

"And I suppose you didn't think to bring a candle," Jason said.

"Next time I'll do better," Hop answered.

"A lighter?"

"You know I don't poison myself, Jazz, why would I carry fire with me?" Not that Hop hadn't once junked himself, but he had long since decided long life took precedence over fleeting pleasures, like smoking. That decision had made him feel like a puritan for months. Now he regretted it again.

They stood in the darkness for a while. Then Hop offered to prowl around and see what he could feel.

"Don't even twitch," Jazz said. "There may be some nasty surprises in here."

They waited awhile more. "Has it been three years yet, Jazz, or only two?" Hop asked.

"About four minutes. Give the lady a chance to wake up."

"I think you broke a rib."

"I hope so. The bitch deserved to lose her head."

"But she never did lose it, did she."

"Quiet. She's waking up."

Arran groaned, and Noyock wasn't even surprised that the moan was vaguely seductive. She could hardly be expected to lose lifetime habits all at once.

"Don't move around too much, Arran," Jazz said softly. "Your rib is broken, and you're in the secret room behind the mirror in the library."

"How did you find the door!"

"You told me."

"I never—"

Jazz slapped her, and she cried out. Hop began to feel a little bit disturbed at the way his meal ticket was acting. Cruelty should have some point, Hop firmly believed.

Jazz hissed at her, "You've lied every moment since we first met tonight. You tried to kill me. I want to know why."

Silence. Then another slap, another cry of pain.

76

"Dammit, Jazz, stop it!" Hop said.

"I've got to know what I'm up against, Hop. There's a lot she isn't telling me. Like the fact that she has a friend named Farl Baak, a Cabinet minister, who for some absurd reason wants me dead."

She gasped.

"I didn't come to your party ignorantly, Arran. Now you can start telling us things. For instance, you might start by telling me how to turn the lights on in here."

"Right by the door," she said.

Hop stepped in the direction he remembered the door was in, but Jazz's voice cut through the darkness. "Don't touch it! Stop where you are, Hop!" Hop stayed where he was. He heard Arran groan in fear—whatever Jazz was doing she didn't like. "Clever trap, Arran," Jason said. "But I'll start feeding you your fingers in small sections if you don't start cooperating."

Another groan of fear and pain, and Arran shouted, "Stop it! Stop it—the light's in the far right corner as you come in, at about knee height—"

The light went on. Jazz was still holding Arran's hand, tightly, while his other hand was extended to touch the spot she had described. Noyock turned from them to examine the door. "Where's the trap?" he asked.

"A metal plate under the wallcoat," Jazz said. "How many volts, Arran?"

"Enough," Arran answered. "I wish it had fried you."

"Hit her once for me," Noyock said. "Suddenly I'm not in love with her anymore."

"I'll be glad to oblige you," Jazz said, "in just about one second if Arran doesn't tell me why Farl Baak wants me dead."

She shook her head. "I never heard of Farl Baak."

"Just because nobody looped it doesn't mean it didn't happen," Jazz said.

"I didn't know the drink was poisoned," she said. Jazz slapped her hard, on the growing bruise at the bottom of her rib cage.

She cried out, swung her arm to try to hit him, but was stopped by the pain. He slapped her again. She cried out again in pain, and tears flowed out the corners of her eyes, dribbling down into her ears and hair. These tears, Hop realized in surprise, were involuntary.

"I don't know why you're persecuting me," she said. Jazz only waited. "All right," she said. "I know Farl Baak. But he didn't want you dead. He had nothing to do—"

Another slap, and this time the cry was louder, and she started to sob slightly afterward. Each sob took its toll in pain, and she stopped crying and only moaned. "Because," she grunted in agony, "you're in on the plot, you bastard."

"Plot?" Jazz asked.

"To control the somec. To take control of the Sleeproom."

Jazz chuckled. "And so you had to kill *me?* How could I be a threat to you, sleeping in a ship off between the stars?"

She shook her head slightly. "Too many of the wrong people were all timed to wake up when you arrived, Starpilot." She spat out his title. "Farl put two and two together."

"Ah."

"And you control the fleets and the armies. That's why we had to get rid of you before we acted against the others—"

"Jazz is just a starpilot," Hop said, wondering how such a sensible woman could believe such drivel.

"Go touch the doorframe," Jazz said. "Or shut up by yourself, Hop."

Hop shut up again.

"It's cold," Arran said, and her teeth *were* chattering.

Jazz looked at Hop, and Hop sighed. Jason was still stripped down for the duel, and only Hop's expensive topjacket was available. He took it off, emptied the loop recorder and suppressor out of the pockets, and handed it to Jazz, who wrapped it gently around her.

"Remind me never to trust a secret to her," Hop said to Jazz. "She didn't last very long under pressure."

78

Arran, despite the pain in her ribs, snarled back at him, "No one expected I'd have to deal with an animal."

Jason buttoned the jacket, and Hop noticed appreciatively that he had not bothered to put her arms into the sleeves—the coat would certainly keep her arms confined, if she should be tempted to try something. "The government," Jazz said, "has tricks that make me look like a lamb." Hop wondered vaguely what a lamb was.

"There are different kinds of pain," Arran said quietly. "Maybe you can take *this* kind without breaking. I'm sure of it."

"What kind of pain can *you* take?" Hop asked.

"I can keep smiling when I want to kill. I can seduce a man I loathe. I can spend six months without a single moment of privacy, waking, sleeping, or going to the bathroom. I can endure lovers who feel only contempt for me and pretend that I love every minute of it."

Hop didn't feel like making a clever answer, and Jazz patted her shoulder gently. "All right, and you held up pretty damned well when I was hitting you, too."

"What are you going to do with me now?" Arran asked.

"Sit and watch you, I suppose, until suppertime," Jazz said.

"She needs a doctor," Hop offered.

Jason shook his head. "If we try to take her out of here now, she'll need a mortician. Her whole flat's probably full of troops, searching for her everywhere. If they find her, the law lets them kill her. She did try to poison one of Mother's officers of the fleet."

"Does that mean we can *never* leave here?"

"It means we'll stay here awhile, Hop. Try to be patient. We'll be through with this before your waking's over. You won't lose any sleep."

"And when we leave, what'll we do? Report on this Farl Baak?"

"Whom do you report a Cabinet minister to? God?"

"What'll we do, then?"

"I want to find out what Baak is really up to. There is no

79

somec plot, and I'm certainly not part of one even if there is. So there must be some reason all those wakings were timed to my arrival. I mean to find out."

"She was probably lying."

"She wasn't."

"You sound pretty sure of that."

"I plan to find out who's behind the plot to kill me. And what his real reasons are. And then I'm going to kill the bastard."

"That's the Jason Worthing I've known and loved," Hop said.

Hours later, Jason decided it was safe for him to go look for Arran's private doctor. She told him how to get out, and to Hop's surprise he believed her immediately. Apparently he was a better judge of people than Hop.

The doctor confirmed that the rib was, indeed, broken. The shock was dangerous, the doctor said. They should have got immediate medical attention. Jason didn't bother explaining that it would have been impractical, and so Hop also kept quiet. And not even Arran hinted as to how she had broken the rib, or what she was doing naked in a secret room. Either the doctor was very good at hiding his curiosity, or he had done all this before. He left without asking for a credit card, either. Hop decided he had to look into the idea of getting a private physician.

Jason had picked up a full outfit of clothing for Arran. He had chosen from her wardrobe in the flat an outfit loose enough to fit over the bandages the doctor had told her she would have to wear for at least six hours until the growth hormone wore off. "Otherwise," he had said, "you'll have a very odd-shaped chest, which might hurt business." Jason had also found a shirt and jacket that made his military pants look a little less like a uniform.

And Hop got his topjacket back. "Well, dressed for the evening and nowhere to go," he said.

"Arran will tell us where to go," Jazz said.

"I don't know any hiding places outside my flat."

"I don't want a hiding place. I want you to take us to Farl Baak," Jazz said.

She gasped. "He'll kill you."

"He doesn't really care if I'm dead, Arran. He only wants to make sure I won't interfere with him. But what if I'm on his side in this little rebellion?"

She shook her head. "He won't believe you."

"Maybe not. Let's go see."

"I don't want you dead."

"Why the sudden change of heart?" Jason asked.

Arran suddenly made her face ugly. The woman can look downright natural, Hop realized. "Because even a bitch like me is capable of realizing that you had every right to kill me and instead you saved my life."

"Only in order to get information from you," Jazz said.

"If that were true," Arran answered, "I'd be dead now. You know how to get to Farl's place. You don't need me."

"I don't want to go in the front door."

She sighed. "Now that my ribs are healing, I don't want any interference with them. I'll take you. But it's none of my business what Farl does to you."

"Maybe it would be more to the point," Hop suggested, "if you worried about what we might do to Farl."

She glanced coolly at Hop. "Farl isn't a naked woman with a broken rib."

They walked out of the library and no one saw them. They walked down several ramps and corridors, and finally left Arran's flat through the delivery entrance, and in all that time they didn't see one soldier, one constable, or one human being.

"Why isn't there a guard?" Hop asked.

"Mother's Little Boys are asleep on the job," Jazz answered.

"Jazz, I think this is about the stupidest thing I ever saw you do."

Jason looked at him expressionlessly. "No one's making you come along."

81

Hop was surprised. "If no one's making me come along, then why the hell am I coming?"

"To protect your investment."

"Damn right."

Arran led them through a circuitous path of tubes, private cars, and corridors. Finally they found themselves ascending a long emergency stairway. After eight flights Hop suggested that they stop and rest.

As they sat on the steps, Jason looked intently at Arran's eyes. She gazed coldly back. Finally Jazz said, "You have one minute to tell me what's really at the top of these stairs."

Arran pursed her lips, then got up and started back down the steps. Jazz followed, and Hop muttered as he brought up the rear, "How come you only broke one rib, Jazz?"

They followed a different route and this time came to a very ordinary door labeled "Employees Only."

"I'm an employee," Arran said, with a nasty smile. Inside the door was a ladder, which they climbed. They came out in a storage closet with no lights. Arran confidently pushed open a door. From outside the closet they heard a man's voice say, "Who the hell—Arran, darling, I'll have you roasted if you ever come here again without an appointment—"

And then Farl Baak stopped talking because he saw Jason and Hop behind the woman.

"Take your hand away from the call button," Jazz said.

"Good morning, Starpilot," Baak said. "I must say, Arran, when you mess up an assignment it isn't necessary to bring the target back with you."

"Just a word of warning, Mr. Baak. I'm not very heavily armed—" not armed at all, Hop refrained from saying "—but the computer on my ship is watching us, and the full record of this conversation will be recorded in four different places. You don't pull the right strings to stop an investigation from finding you."

Baak pulled his hand away from the side of the bed he was lying on.

"The poison was rather direct," Jazz said. "And the duel was stupid."

"What duel?" Baak asked. He looked at Arran for an answer.

"Fritz Kapock," she said.

"That damned hero. And here I thought he was a honk." Baak laughed slightly. "What can I do for you, Mr. Worthing, since you're unfortunately still alive?"

Jason walked over to him, dragged him to an upright position, and slapped him three times. Blood ran from Farl's nose. Then the pilot slammed him against the wall. Farl slid down the wall to the floor.

Hop noticed that Arran seemed distressed by this turn of events, and so he took her hands and held them rather forcefully. "Don't strain any ribs trying to help your friend," Hop said. He didn't mention that he didn't know why the hell Jazz was hitting Baak right now. Was he beginning to believe his own image—tough guy and brawler? (I've created a monster.)

Arran didn't try to break away from him. She merely spat in his face. Because he was holding her hands, he couldn't wipe it away. "Jazz," he said. "I want a new contract for twenty-five percent. Twenty isn't enough for these special services."

Farl Baak was tipping his head backward to try to stop the nosebleed. "If you've broken my nose, you bastard, I'll see to it you're shredded."

Jazz laughed. "Baak, you've got a reputation as a jackass and a pervert. No need to try to maintain that reputation right now. *Why* did you want me killed, and who are you working for?"

"I'm a Cabinet minister, Worthing, and I don't work for anyone."

Jason took a step toward him. Farl slid away. "I meant it, Worthing. Until my last waking before this I *was* controlled, but I didn't know it. Now that I know it, I'm not controlled."

"By whom?" Jazz asked.

"I don't know," Farl Baak insisted, and Hop tended to believe him. "That's what I'm trying to find out. But you work for him, I know that. You're part of the plot."

"And how do you know that?"

Baak was silent.

Jason again menaced the man, but this time Baak didn't try to retreat. "If you touch me, Worthing, I'll have a civil suit on you, and criminal complaints for assault and battery, and you know I can make it stick, I'm a Cabinet minister, dammit."

Suddenly Arran spoke up. "Don't be stupid, Farl. Tell him. He doesn't give a damn about your silly office."

Farl looked at her angrily, but it was hard to take him very seriously with his nose bleeding down to his chin. "There are some things I'm willing to endure a lot of pain for, Worthing," Baak said.

Jason studied the man, then nodded. "All right, Baak. You're not what I thought you were. Not a jackass, anyway." Jazz reached for the man, and Baak flinched. But this time Jason only helped him to the bed. Baak sighed in relief, and lay down, tipping his head back to stop the bleeding. "Once my nose starts bleeding it goes off and on for a week," Farl complained.

"Baak, it was stupid to try to kill me. I'm on your side."

"And what side is that, Worthing?"

"Somebody's trying to take over the government, all right. Well, I don't like it any better than you do."

Suddenly Noyock felt lost. What the hell was going on? Jazz hadn't been on Capitol in decades, hadn't talked to anyone out of Hop's earshot since he got back, and suddenly he seemed deeply into plots and counterplots in the top levels of government.

Baak sniffed, then sputtered blood. "Dammit, why did you have to be so rough?"

"Sorry."

"It isn't a plot to take over the government, Jazz, and you know it. Somebody's already taken over. For eight hundred years or so, I'm pretty sure. Some bastard has been giving orders to the Cabinet."

Jason looked at the man intently. "Who?" he asked.

"Like I told you, my friend, I don't know. Until recently I didn't even know *I* was controlled. But I was. The man works through intermediaries. Blackmail, bribery, playing off old friendships and enmities—"

"You're being blackmailed?" Jazz asked.

"Hardly. Everybody knows every possible scandal about me. Actually I was controlled more subtly. Through an intermediary."

"Who?"

"Arran, of course," Farl answered.

Hop had let got of her when Jazz let Farl lie down. Now she cursed softly and walked toward the bed. "How can you say that, Farl, I've been with you since—"

"I didn't say you *knew* it, did I?" Baak waved her away. "Somebody keep the woman from interrupting. You know how it is, Jazz. You were born on Capitol. I came here from—well, it doesn't matter. Nowhere. There are certain social circles. Certain groups that dominate the lifeloops, that go to the same parties, that share all the interesting gossip. When I got to this somec level I began to think I belonged in those groups. But I was provincial, a boor. Utterly without manners. It was quite a coup when Arran let me into her life—the unlooped life—and started bringing me to parties, helping me learn what to do, what to say. For fifty wakings, now, I've listened to that group debate the great questions of the day—which is a laugh, since the great questions rarely come more than once in a century— and there was definitely an 'in' opinion and an 'out' opinion. I admit to you that I invariably voted with the ins. It got me a reputation for wisdom. Arran, here—she decides what the in opinion is to be."

"Ridiculous," Arran said. "I just think what I think."

"I traced it. I wish I could trace it further, but you were so obviously innocent of the plot that I didn't want to discover any—"

"Damn right I'm innocent," Arran interrupted.

85

"Jason, every single Cabinet minister is controlled some way or another. I didn't even discover it on my own. I was told. By a friend who shall remain nameless."

"You mean Shimon Rapth," Jazz said.

Forgetting his nose, Baak sat upright. "If you already know so damn much why did you come in and break my nose!"

"What did Rapth tell you, Farl?"

"Just what I told you. That the Cabinet is being controlled."

"And you nobly decided to try to put a stop to it by killing me."

"No, Worthing, not at all. I don't give a damn who controls the government. What I care about is who controls the somec—"

And then the conversation ended, because a half-dozen guards broke into the room, armed with lasers and ready to kill. Three of them took Jason and held him. Only one of them bothered to restrain Hop. Hop was a little offended at how little they feared him. Oh well.

"If you men worked for me," Jazz said, "I'd fire you all. He pushed the button ten minutes ago, and had to stall me this long."

Farl only set his lips and got up to get something to stanch the nosebleed. Arran also moved. She headed straight for Jason, who knew what was coming but couldn't do anything about it. She brought her knee up sharply into his groin. Jason cried out and went slack for a moment in the guard's arms. Then he pulled himself upright and she did it again, even harder. This time Hop cried out, too, and Farl said from the kitchen, where he was dampening a cloth, "That's enough, Arran." The Cabinet minister came back into the room with the cloth pressed to his nose. "Too bad you came along with Worthing on this one, Hop," he said. "We've had some pleasant dealings in the past, but this time Jazz is going to die, and I'm really not very afraid of the record on your ship, if there is one, Worthing."

Jazz didn't answer. He was still in pain from Arran's blows.

"Jason Worthing isn't any traitor, Baak," Noyock said.

"Oh, heavens, of course not," Baak answered. "How could

I think such a thing? Listen, Noyock, how would you feel if you knew that somebody was getting payoffs to promote wealthy people to high somec levels *on merit*—men and women who obviously *have* no merit?"

"I'd kill the bastard. But Jazz hasn't even been on Capitol in forty years!"

"People are getting those promotions, Hop. Somebody's controlling the somec review board the same way they're controlling the Cabinet. And Jazz Worthing *is* involved. Do you want to see the proof? I'd love to show you." Farl Baak walked to a looper—one of the incredibly expensive home models—and slipped in a loop. Immediately on a small viewing stage a half-size replica of Jason Worthing stood in full starpilot's uniform. Baak punched the start button and adjusted the volume.

"Fellow soldiers of the Empire," the holocene of Jazz began, and the speech went on, an eloquent reminder of all the ways that the troops and the fleets had been trodden on and ignored by those in high places in the government. The speech, if played before soldiers, would have had them ready to tear apart the entire civil service after only ten minutes. And then the holo of Jason Worthing dropped its voice and said, "But, brothers, none of this amounts to anything. It amounts to nothing at all. You haven't suffered a bit, compared to this one outrage:

"You are not on somec, my friends.

"Except when they dump you in the belly of a ship and send you off to die in some forgotten colony, somec never reaches the common soldier. These friends of ours in the civil service scramble in their petty departmental squabbles in order to get five years, ten years, twenty years on somec at a time. What do you get? How long does a soldier live?

"In this Empire there are men and women who live forever! And you—if you're lucky, you'll see a century. And you'll spend the last fifty years of it on a pension that isn't enough to buy a bottle once a month." And so on. Until any soldier seeing it would be ready to kill anyone who kept him from somec. And the speech ended when Jason Worthing raised both hands above his head and cried out, "But there's one man—no, not me—one man who can stop this, one man who can give you eternal life, if you'll only help him, if you'll only reach out with him and strike down the vipers who strangle you! And that man is here with me today!"

The holo of Jason Worthing turned and extended an arm, waiting for someone to appear.

And then the loop ended.

They all sat around the room in silence. Arran looked at Jason Worthing with loathing. Baak glanced at both the starpilot and his agent with an amused half-smile. Jason looked at Hop. Hop looked at Jason. "Jason, you're a bastard," Hop said.

4

"THE loop is a fake, Hop," Jazz said, with feeling.

Baak chuckled. "Should we enlarge the image for you? Show you the fingerprints? It's no fake. Jason Worthing is up to his ears in a plot to help someone—this mysterious person who controls the Cabinet—take over somec, and with it the government, not in the subtle way he now controls it, but openly, overtly, taking the reins of power himself. And I don't think I'm the only one who objects to someone playing around with my somec. I like the thought of being immortal. So does everybody else."

Jason said again, now sounding more tired. "The loop is a fraud."

Hop shook his head. "You can't fake a loop, Jazz. I know you. And that was you."

"You know me, but you don't know what that loop *means*," Jazz insisted.

Baak swung himself off the bed again, where he had reclined during the playback of the loop, and walked over to Jason. "Actually, Jazz, Arran's little cup didn't contain enough to kill you. Remember, the ritual she offered you required only a little sip. It would have put you to sleep long enough for us to get you here, where I can find out from you the one thing that nobody knows right now."

"I don't know anything that you don't know," Jason said wearily.

"You know one thing, Jazz. You know who is supposed to walk out when you hold out your arm in that loop. You know who our enemy is."

Jason shook his head.

"Don't worry, Jason. We don't expect you to volunteer the information. When the probe gets through with you, you'll have so little mind left that you won't even notice when we kill you." Baak waved to the guards and they pulled Jason out of the room.

Before the door slid closed behind them, though, Jason called out, "Don't believe it, Hop!" Then silence.

Farl Baak looked at Hop with raised eyebrows. "He must value your opinion very highly, Mr. Noyock, to want so badly for you to deny the evidence of your own eyes."

"Maybe," Hop said.

"Now we have a problem, Hop. What to do with you. You're a witness, unfortunately, and there could be serious legal repercussions to what happened today. Shimon Rapth and I have a lot left to accomplish, even after we find out from your ex-client who our enemy is."

"My enemy, too," Hop said.

"I'm glad you feel that way. Unfortunately, Hop, there's always the risk that you might suddenly feel a rush of loyalty to the bastard whom you've served so well during the last few centuries, and we can't afford to have you wandering around, able to tell people what you know. You understand?"

"I'd rather you didn't kill me," Hop said, amazed to discover that he could say that calmly. Baak laughed.

"Kill you! Of course not. You'll just be my guest here for a few days. *We* aren't animals, Hop. At least we try not to be. Arran will show you to your room. Unfortunately, we'll have to lock the door behind you, but that can't be helped. We happen to know that you're a wily old devil, and there's a strong risk of you sneaking out if we don't bar the door." Baak laughed again, but it was a friendly laugh, the kind of laugh that a good man laughs when he's been worried for days, but now knows that things are going to work out well for him. Hop found himself feeling almost at ease.

Arran led the way down a short hall to another room. It was almost as plush as Farl Baak's own. The guard waited outside as Arran went in with him. She touched his arm as he stood surveying his surroundings.

"Hop, I'm sorry I almost killed you there in the hiding place. I was fighting for my life."

"All in a day's work," Hop said. "You aren't the first."

"What I'm saying, Hop, is that we were both forced into doing things we usually wouldn't do. By Worthing. I don't think we have to hate each other."

"Are you looping this?" Hop asked.

"No," she said, looking a little angry.

"Well, I am," he said, and smiled. "I have an exclusive. I'll give it to you for your birthday."

She smiled back. "I was never born. Friends?"

Noyock shook his head. "Let's just say, temporarily not trying to kill each other. Let me decide what to believe about Jazz."

She looked ceilingward, but turned to leave. As she did, it occurred to Noyock that these people were basically decent. But, he reminded himself, they were also dangerous. (Never trust a woman who knows where to kick, my father always told me.)

"Can I ask you a question," he said.

She turned and faced him, and waited.

"What is a probe? What will it do to him?"

She shook her head. "It's fairly new and completely illegal and I don't know much about it. A scientist who is with us invented it."

"Who is *us*?"

"Just a few of us who believe that somec should be shared fairly. According to law. And this may not sound very plausible, coming from me, but we think it should be given only by merit. Not for money at all."

"Damned stupid idea," Noyock said. "I'd be dead now if that were the system when I came up out of the slime."

"Well, there are some advantages to the system now, that's true. But the main thing is that we've got to stop this man, whoever he is, from getting control of the Sleephouse. He'd have us all, then."

"So it does boil down to self-preservation, in the end."

"Who said it didn't?" she retorted. "But you may be surprised to learn that sometimes even the rich and famous have consciences."

"Jazz Worthing has a conscience, too," Hop mused.

She laughed at him.

"I know him," Hop said. "You don't. Something doesn't fit in all this."

"Well, believe what you want, Hop. All I know about Jazz Worthing is that he's sadistic and a traitor to humanity. Sorry if you like him, but when the probe finds out who the enemy is—"

"Jason won't tell it. He can take more pain than—"

"It isn't pain—"

"He's immune to all the drugs—they do that the week they enter the Service—"

"It's not drugs, either. The inventor told me that it's like bright, dazzling lights that suddenly come and go from many directions. Only instead of lights, it's brain waves, like the recorders in the Sleephouse. It's like pouring different mindsets into your brain, distracting you, driving you crazy, breaking down all will to resist. You tell anything. You respond to anything. It's just too many surprises inside your own head."

"And does anybody recover?"

"We're not altogether sure. We've only used it a few times, and nobody has, if they stayed under for very long. If Jazz Worthing resists for very long at all, then he'll lose his mind." She patted Noyock's arm. "Think of it this way. Your friend won't even notice when he's killed."

"Thanks a lot."

"Sorry, old man." It didn't even sound like an obscenity when she said it. She left, and the door was locked behind her.

Hop went to the bed and lay down. The probe worked by surprise. It really would have a tough go with Jason Worthing, then—Hop couldn't remember ever seeing Jazz surprised at all. It was the same in all the loops—whatever the enemy did, Jazz always seemed to know just a hair in advance. He always spotted the ambush at the last moment. It made for great loops.

Even today. Even last night. Jazz had known the drink was drugged. He even seemed to know without asking—

Hop got up and turned on the loop recorder's playback. It was an excellent model, and the figures were almost a quarter size— excellent for a portable. It started with the duel. Hop jumped it forward. The crowd, panicking. Jazz picking up Arran. Knocking Kapock aside. Hop stopping to pound Kapock into the ground, then following Jazz to the exit.

Noyock watched closely, then. He tried to see when Jazz heard the answer from Arran about where the hiding place was. He couldn't find it.

Breaking down the door. The library, and Jazz throwing Arran down and breaking her rib. Then. It had to be right then, and Hop took the action at tenth-speed, volume on full, close-up on the two heads, now larger than life-size. Jason, incredibly slowly, saying "Where's the door?" Hop moved around, stared at Arran's lips.

They did not move. She was nearly unconscious. She did not make a sound at all.

He shifted back to normal size when the holo showed Jazz walking away, straight to the two books. The door opened as Jazz pulled on something.

Arran hadn't told him a thing. Hop sat, numbed, as the loop went on; turned down the volume when it became annoying;

flipped off the machine when it finally stopped. Jazz knew things that hadn't been told to him. The only place he could have found out about that door was from Arran's mind.

(Be reasonable. If Jazz really is a traitor, he'd have sources of information.)

But he knew other things. The poison in the glass. How could he have learned about that forty years ago, before he left? And Hop knew for a fact that Jazz found out *nothing* after he came back to the planet. Unless he found it out in the ship before he disembarked. He might have. . . .

Jazz as a traitor or Jazz as a Swipe. If I can choose between them, Hop told himself, I'd rather he were a traitor.

Or would I? Hop remembered all his association with Jazz, from the beginning. The young starpilot, eager, enthusiastic, itching for battle. That couldn't have been an act. And what change had there been since then? A gradual maturing. There was no time that Jazz seemed to show any change at all. When did he turn traitor? When did he start to plot? Noyock couldn't believe it.

But Jason Worthing a Swipe? That was even harder to believe. But the glass, the door, the inside information he seemed to pluck from midair. Even the battle with Kapock, seeming to know every motion before he made it.

And Jazz had even told him he was a Swipe. Noyock had assumed he was joking. Wasn't he?

Back and forth, back and forth, like a tennis duel, Noyock thought, and eventually he slept.

He awakened to the sound of the door opening. His first thought: they've come for me. He stiffened on the bed, prepared to struggle, though he didn't know what he could hope to accomplish.

But the hands that touched him were gentle. Insistent, but gentle. And the voice saying, "Hop, wake up," was Arran's.

"Is it morning already?" he asked.

"Shut up. Come with me, fast. Don't talk."

She sounded frightened out of her wits. Hop got up and followed her as she led him out into the hall and through a large meeting-room. She stopped only long enough to say, in a barely audible whisper, "Do you know how to kill an armed man?"

"Sometimes," Hop answered, wondering if he still remembered how. It was one thing to take Fritz Kapock from behind and by surprise—quite another to face a man who was pointing a cockle at you.

"Now's the time," she said. She pushed a button and a door slid open. A guard was standing on the other side, already turning to see why the door behind him was opening. There was a laser in his hand. Hop didn't stop to wonder why Arran was having him kill one of the men on *her* side. He just let the reflexes from his boyhood take over.

He finished with the guard by breaking his neck. In retrospect, Hop had the sickening knowledge that he had won only by a hair. Oh well, he thought. Better close than not at all. Still, when this was over, he'd have to lose weight. Get back in shape. This could kill him.

"Come here!" Arran hissed at him, and he came.

"What's going on?" he asked.

"There's no time." He followed her down the corridor. They went into a bathroom and closed and locked the door.

"Who's chasing you?" Hop asked.

"We only have a couple of seconds," she said. "In the shower, the ceiling light. Can you reach it?"

He could reach it. She told him to push it up. It gave fairly easily, then swung back, out of the way. Arran immediately stepped into the shower and reached for the opening. Hop helped her up. When she was through the trap, she hissed down at him, "Come on up, quickly, they'll be here any minute, and I don't know how many people know about this way."

But Hop didn't go into the trap door. Instead he stepped to the bathroom door and unlocked it.

"Hop, don't!" she hissed, frightened. But he didn't leave. He just left the door unlocked and climbed back into the shower and, with a great deal of difficulty hoisted himself up into the opening in the ceiling. Once there, it was hard to find a way to get his legs up through the opening. He could hear shouting down the corridor the way they had come. Arran heard it, too, and started pulling and tugging at him. "You're not helping one damn little bit," Hop said impatiently, and she left him alone as he finally got his weight up far enough to let him turn around and pull his legs up.

The moment he was clear, sweating and panting from the exertion, Arran pushed down the trap. Now an innocent-looking lighting fixture hung over the shower again.

"Why did you unlock the door!" she whispered angrily.

"Because a bathroom door locked from the inside with no-body there is an advertisement that there's another way out."

Worklights here and there provided a dim light, and soon they could both see—a little. The crawlspace they were in was only a meter and a half high—neither of them could stand up. Structural beams were hard to tell from air conduits, wiring frames, and exhaust shafts. Hop leaned over from the catwalk they were sitting on and pushed on a ceiling tile. It gave easily.

"We can only walk on beams and catwalks," he said.

"Wonderful. Do you know your way around in here?" she asked.

He shrugged. "Not right here, anyway. Capitol isn't the same anywhere. Nobody planned the remodeling over the last few thousand years. Good luck to us. Now will you tell me who the hell we're running from?"

She nodded. But Hop noticed that she was breathing too heavily, and her hands were trembling. She didn't say anything.

"What's wrong?"

She just shook her head and started to cry. Hop had seen her cry several times before, in pain, for effect, a play for sympathy. But this looked like real honest-to-goodness little-girl tears. Nothing controlled. She wasn't even beautiful or seductive as she cried. Her fans would be shocked. Hop reached over and touched her arm. A little human contact, he decided, might help. It didn't. She recoiled, turned away from him.

96

"Go ahead and cry, then," he said. "Just do it quietly."

"I am, dammit," she said. "Farl is dead."

And that explained it, at least well enough for Hop, well enough for right now. Farl Baak was the one relationship that Arran Handully had never looped; therefore it wasn't for sale to the public; therefore it must be real. And now he was dead, and her grief was also real.

"I'm sorry," Hop said.

She nodded, acknowledging his sympathy, and began to get control of herself. "Sorry," she finally said. "Sometimes things actually happen that aren't in the day's scenario."

"Yeah. I'll spill a few tears for you sometime and we'll be even."

"Don't hurry," she said, and managed a faint smile. "From now on I promise to cope. I don't know where to go now, you know. I knew how to get here, but from here I have no idea."

"Who killed him?"

"A man, just one of the guards. I didn't know him. I went to watch the—questioning. With the probe. I couldn't believe it, Hop. Jazz Worthing lasted an hour and a half. No one has lasted fifteen minutes. An hour and a half. It was terrible. Like waiting for a deal to close in the other room, you know at first that it'll be simple, but when it takes longer, and longer, and longer, you begin to think that it's gone sour, that it'll never happen."

"But he finally broke?" Hop asked, not sure whether he was glad that Jazz had held out so long (the bastard traitor) or sick that he had suffered so much (I like him anyway, dammit).

"Yes. I was near the door. That's why I'm alive. The moment he named the man, the cockles went off, just like that. Farl didn't have a chance. Dead on the spot. A few others, too. As if it had been planned."

"But who was it? Who did Jazz name?"

"Didn't I tell you? Shimon Rapth."

Hop didn't know him, but remembered—"Hey, wasn't he the guy who was helping Baak figure all this stuff out?"

She nodded, and a flash of hatred crossed her face. "Looks like he was just trying to find out who his opposition would be. The guards were all his men, of course. They'll be rounding up the whole group, there are at least a hundred of us, maybe more—"

"You mean Jazz Worthing was working for this Shimon Rapth?"

"Looks like it, doesn't it?"

"But—that's impossible, I never even *heard* of him before. And why would he let them put Jazz through the probe, drive him insane like that—"

She shrugged. "Get rid of a possible future competitor, maybe. I don't know. I just ran."

"Why'd you come to me?"

"Farl was dead. I didn't trust anybody else in the group. I could have come here alone, I guess."

"I'm glad you didn't," Hop said. And then he got up—as far as he could, since the floor of the room above kept him from standing straight. He took Arran's hand. "Hang on. Let's not get separated in the dark. But if I suddenly fall down a hole, let go."

"Where are we going?"

"I told you, I don't know this area. I was born and raised—if you can call it raising—in the bottom levels of the stinkingest borough of Orem district, and we'd go into the crawlspace all the time. The only way we could stay out of the reach of the constables and Mother's Little Boys."

"Then there might be criminals here?"

"In *this* district?" Hop chuckled as they walked gingerly along the catwalk. "In this district all we'll meet is dust. Every district is absolutely sealed off from every other. Including the crawlspace."

"Oh," she said. They came to a ladder. Hop leaned on it, looked up. He could see light above—dim, but light.

"Up," he said. "You first."

She started to climb. When they got to the next level up, she stopped.

"What're you stopping for?" he asked.

"Don't we get off here?"

"No, of course not. Do you think we'd ditch them by just changing floors? If they're serious about rounding up everybody from your little group, they'll seal off this whole district. Check anybody coming and going, and spot you the first time you use your credit card. We've got to get out of this district."

"But you said they were all sealed off—"

"Just keep climbing. There's a way out, and it's up. This ladder's part of the exhaust system, and the exhaust system leads to the surface."

"And what then?"

"Maybe we'll think of something on the way."

And so they climbed. Following the exhaust vents meant hours of squeezing through narrow spaces, climbing ladders to dizzying heights before the great vents leveled off again, bellying through inches of dust in foot-high crawlspace. They were filthy and exhausted a few minutes after they started. They stopped three times to rest. Once they stayed long enough to sleep. And then they came to a place where huge steel girders stretched above them, and the vents plunged suddenly upward to a heavily girdered metal ceiling. For the first time, except on the ladders, they could stand up straight.

Arran looked around. The light was still dim, but it was obvious the space around them was huge—much larger than any hall they had ever been in, and interrupted only by the rising vents and the huge steel shafts that apparently supported the roof.

"It looks very strong," Arran said.

"You should see it where the ships cradle. Makes this look like foil."

"What's outside?"

"We'll soon see," Hop said. "Better lie down and rest again. The next part's going to be hard."

"As if it had been easy up to now," Arran said, lying down willingly enough. They lay on a large vent, and the rush of air pouring through it made the surface vibrate. "I heard," Arran said, after a while, "that you can't breathe the air out there."

"A myth," said Hop. "You can breathe it. You just can't breathe it for very *long*."

"What'll we do?"

"We'll go along here until we find the end of the district. The sealed-off wall. Then we'll go up the nearest vent and try to get across to a vent on the other side of the barrier. The air isn't really dangerous. The real danger is the sun."

Of course Arran knew what the sun was. It was the nearest star, and the source of all of Capitol's energy. She had never seen it. "Why is the sun dangerous?" she asked.

"You'll see," he said. "I can't describe it—just *don't* look at it! And whatever you do, don't let go of my hand. If the sun *isn't* up we're coming right back. At night we'd probably freeze to death in the winds and get lost to boot. So we'll wait for sunlight."

Silence for a few moments, and then Arran laughed softly. "Funny. I never think of Capitol as having winds. Just drafts. Just little breezes from the vents. Capitol is a planet after all."

"The surface is the worst desert you'll ever find, though. Any interference with our food supply or energy sources, and it'd be a desert down below, too. Sleep."

They both slept. When Hop woke, Arran wasn't beside him. He got up quickly, looked into the dimly-lighted distance for her. She wasn't too far away—sitting at the edge of the huge exhaust duct they had slept on, off toward the ladder they had climbed to reach it. Hop walked toward her. His steps were muffled by dust and the distance of the walls—no echoes here. But she heard him a few steps off, and turned to look at him. Wordlessly she waited until he came to the edge and sat down beside her.

"A long way down," he said. She nodded. "Ever been this close to the surface?" he asked.

She shook her head. "I woke just now without a toothbrush,"

she said. "I couldn't bathe. I couldn't go to the wardrobe and choose what I would wear for the day. Nobody's coming to call."

"*You've* got problems," Hop said. "I've already missed about fifteen appointments, and Jazz's latest tape isn't ready for distribution. It's costing me about a thousand a minute just to sit here."

"What will we do, even when we get to another district?"

"You're asking me?"

"We can't use our credit cards. They'd track us down in a moment."

Hop shrugged. "Maybe they aren't looking for me. Maybe I can use mine."

"And maybe not."

Suddenly there was an abrupt change of pitch in the hum of the air passing under them. "What was that?" asked Arran.

"Maybe eight thousand people flushed their toilets all at once in this district. Maybe fifteen thousand people turned down their thermostats. Maybe there's a fire."

"I wonder what Capitol looked like before," Arran mused.

"That's a strange thing to wonder."

"Is it? But there must have been a time before men came here. What did the first colonists see?"

Hop laughed. "A virgin world, ready for raping."

"Or perhaps a home."

"What is this, a lifeloop? Nobody talks about home in real life," Hop said.

"Nobody talks about home in lifeloops, Hop," she said, a little annoyed. "Nobody has used the word in thousands of years. But we keep it in the language. Why?"

Hop shrugged. "Everybody says, 'I'm going home'."

"But nobody says, 'This is my home. Come in.' We live in flats. We walk through corridors. We travel in tubes. What would it be like to live out under the sky?"

"I hear there are bugs."

"A huge park."

101

"Well," Hop said, "that's your solution. Go to a colony. Get on a colony ship, and your troubles are over."

Arran turned to him, horrified. "And go off somec? Are you crazy? I'd rather die."

She got up and walked back toward where they had slept, and Hop joined her. They looked around at the two patches where the dust had been largely cleared away by their sleep. "Nobody's ever going to believe this," Hop said. "Here I was, alone with Arran Handully for hours on end. We slept together, and not only did I not try to make love, lady, I didn't even have my loop recorder going."

"Thank God."

"Let's go."

They went to the opposite end of the duct, where it turned a ninety-degree angle and shot upward to the distant ceiling. A thin, spidery ladder crept up the shaft. They both stood and looked upward for a few moments, and then Arran said, "Me first?"

"Yeah. Try not to fall."

"Just don't tickle my feet."

And they began to climb. Their muscles were still cold from sleep; at first they climbed awkwardly, slowly, carefully. After a short while, though, they settled into a rather quick rhythm, hand-food-hand-foot, the motion carrying them endlessly upward. Once Arran spoke, saying, "How many kilometers to go?" The speech broke her rhythm, and she missed a step, and for a mad moment she felt herself fall. But her hands never left the side shafts of the ladder, and her foot caught on the next rung down. From then on neither of them spoke.

At last the rhythm slowed down again. There are only so many rungs of a ladder that untrained, weary bodies can climb. "Stop," Hop said. Arran took a few more steps and came to a halt.

"Tired?" Hop asked.

"Are you?"

"I think maybe yes."

"Can we rest?"

"Sure. Just lean back and doze off."

"Laugh laugh. I'm too tired to be amused."

"Keep on going."

It was not long after that, though, that they reached their destination. It was a small platform built onto the side of the duct. The ladder kept going up, but Hop told Arran to climb up only a little way and stop. She did, and Hop stepped onto the ledge. There was only one handhold, beside a door that was too short to use comfortably. It was latched shut, and a wheel had closed the seal.

Arran climbed back down until she was even with the ledge. "How do we know we can get out of the vent?"

"We don't. But I'm betting that Capitol's surface arrangement is the same everywhere. And even though I was raised on the other side of the world, I'm betting that I can get through the screens the way I used to."

"And what if there isn't a vent down to the other district?"

"They channel all the exhaust vents from the same prefecture into the same general area, so that other areas can be kept relatively clear of smoke. I say relatively, of course, because it gets pretty smoky. Now on the other side of the door the air is pure poison. All that comes out here is the absolute crap that the filters couldn't clean and recirculate. Poison means don't breathe."

"How long?"

"Till you get out of the duct. So take a good big breath before you go in here. And don't look down in the shaft. If you think it's bad here in the dim worklights, you ought to see how it looks with all the fires of hell sending smoke up a sunlit shaft."

"What if the sun isn't up?"

"Then we go back down and wait."

Arran cursed. "I hope the sun is up," she said.

"All right, count to ten after I go through. Then hold your

103

breath and come through. There'll be a ladder on the other side of this door. Stay on the ledge on the other side just long enough to close the door. We don't want to set off any alarms."

"Got it. Now let's hurry," she said.

"Let me have time to psych myself up, all right? Do a chicken middle-aged man a favor." Hop stood and counted to fifty, wondering why the hell he was counting. Then he took hold of the wheel and spun it until the seal was opened. A thin trail of smoke came in around the edges of the door. Hop flipped the two latches. The door slowly swung open, inward, and the smoke jumbled through the opening, falling mysteriously down toward the deep darkness they had climbed from. Through the door, sunlight made the smoke brightly gray, with black wisps here and there. Arran was immediately aware of a revolting stench. She looked at Hop with a disgusted expression, and Hop grinned back, took a deep breath, and swung through. She could hear the faint sound of his feet on the ladder.

Carefully, she stepped onto the ledge, took a deep breath, and then ducked into the smoke and passed through the door. She reached over and swung the door shut fastening only one latch (good enough for what we need, she decided) and then began to climb. She could hardly keep her eyes open—the smoke stung terribly, and tears flowed. I'm not even acting, she said in her mind. Tears without acting; pain without pretense. What an education in theater I've been getting these last few days.

She scrambled on up the ladder, and suddenly bumped into something with her head. It was Noyock, and she wondered what the hell he had stopped for. But a moment later, she heard a clanking sound, and Noyock was up and out of the way.

As she came out, almost totally blind from the smoke, she felt Noyock's hands on her shoulder, helping guide her. A moment later she was standing on the surface.

"Breathe now, but stay low," Hop ordered, and Arran breathed, then coughed. They were not in the thick smoke of the vent, but the atmosphere itself was thick as shower fog, and smelled hideous. She could open her eyes a little more now, however, and she watched as Hop swung the screen back down and latched it.

"Hold my hand," Hop said, taking her and starting to pull her along. "And stay low."

She noticed her feet were hot. "My feet are hot," she said.

"Be glad you're wearing shoes," Hop answered.

There was a constant breeze coming from the right. Abruptly the breeze turned into a tremendous gust that for a moment lifted them both off their feet. Hop landed standing; Arran did not. She skidded along the surface of the metal, knees and one hand holding her up, and Noyock hung onto the other hand and tried to keep her from sliding. The gust abated as quickly as it had come, and Noyock yanked Arran to her feet. She was gasping from the heat of the metal on her hand and knees, the scraping the metal seams had given her.

Just behind the gust, the air cleared noticeably. Suddenly the bright gray sky turned white, and the metal dazzled in sunlight. It completely blinded Arran. She closed her eyes, and tried to keep her balance as Noyock dragged her along. The heat of the sun on her head was intense; and then, just as quickly as the air had cleared, the smoke closed over them again, and Arran could open her eyes. She touched her hand to her hair—it was scalding hot.

And then they were at another exhaust vent, the smoke pouring up darkly. Noyock took Arran's hand and made her hold onto the mesh of the vent. "Hang on and don't put your head in the smoke," he shouted, and just then the wind came up, blowing the smoke mostly away from them, but almost tearing Arran's hand away from the screen. Noyock hung on with one hand, while with the other he fiddled with the latch. Just as the gust died, he tossed the door open.

"Count to ten, take a breath, and follow me!" he shouted, and Arran nodded. Then Noyock disappeared down into the smoke.

I'm too tired, Arran thought. Her feet were burning hot from the metal; her eyes were in agony from the smoke of the atmosphere; her knees and hand hurt terribly; and her side, where

105

the ribs hadn't had a chance to heal properly, ached deeply. Worst of all was the exhaustion, and she wondered why she was trying.

Can't think that way, she told herself, as she swung over the edge and began to climb down the ladder. But as she descended she thought of how restful it would be just to lean back into the smoke, falling out of sight into soft oblivion. She began to speed up her descent, stepping every other rung, her hands only skimming the sideshafts of the ladder.

"Arran!" somebody called from above her. "Arran, you passed me! Come back up!"

Air, she thought. I need air very badly.

"Arran, just five meters up. Climb up."

Have I stopped? I stopped. I must have stopped when he called me.

"Move, before you have to breathe! Move!"

I'm moving, aren't I? Aren't I still climbing?

"Can't you hear me? I've got the door open here! Just a few meters up."

Dammit, I'm climbing. I need air.

"Lift your right foot and put it on the next rung."

Foot. Yes.

"Come on, now the left foot! That's it, keep coming." And slowly Arran climbed up to where a strong hand grabbed her arm, pulled her slowly to the right. She couldn't see in the smoke. Who was it? She brought her face close to him. Noyock. Ah, yes. She opened her mouth to speak to him, took a deep breath, and then began to cough violently. Someone—must be Noyock—pulled her through a door, forced her hands to hold a thin handrail. Couldn't hold the handrail, she decided. Had to cover her mouth as she coughed. Impolite not to cover your mouth when you cough.

Inhale again? Clean. She sighed. Her lungs still stung, and her head ached painfully. She was flat against a metal wall, covering her mouth with her hands. Behind her she could feel Noyock's body, and arms around her on both sides, holding the handrail, keeping her from falling backward. She opened her eyes. They still smarted, but she could see. Beside them, an open door still let smoke pour into the dimly-lighted interior of the space under the ceiling.

"I won't go in there," she said.

"You don't have to. You just came out."

"I did?" Oh, yes, I did. "Am I safe?"

"You are if you'll only take hold of the handrail. I've got to close the door before the smoke alarms go off. Do you have it?"

"Yes."

"Both hands."

"Got it."

Noyock inched away from her and reached through, closed the door, spun the seal, latched the latches.

"How are you feeling?" he asked Arran.

"Really sick. My head aches."

"You breathed in the exhaust duct."

"Did I? Dumb. Dumb, that's all."

"Dead tired, that's all. But we've got to go down before you can rest. All right?"

"I don't want to go anywhere."

"You're going to, though."

And so he helped her to the ladder, and this time they went down virtually together, Noyock's feet only a few rungs below hers, so that his head was at the level of her waist as they slowly descended the ladder.

It took forever.

"Stay awake," he kept telling her.

"Sure," she kept answering. And finally something changed, and he wasn't behind her, and then his hands lifted her off the ladder and laid her gently down on the heating duct.

She woke in near darkness, the air cool and musty, but clean compared to the atmosphere outside. Her head still ached, her knees smarted, and her eyes were dully tired as she opened them. But she was breathing, and felt better. Than what? Than she thought she should.

107

"Awake?"

"Alive. I didn't worry about anything else."

"Head?"

"Aches. But I can breathe."

"Hungry?"

She hadn't thought of it until he asked. "I could eat a person."

"I'll stand back."

"What are we going to do?"

"Get something to eat. Stay here."

"I'm coming with you," she insisted, trying to get up. But a pain shot through her from her head down her spine and she changed her mind. "I'll keep the home fires burning," she said. After he left, the darkness became overwhelming and she slept again.

"It's morning," a cheerful male voice said, and for a moment Arran was confused, and began speaking in character. "Morning, already? How can it be morning, and we just barely went to bed?" Her voice was seductive. But when she rolled onto her side (enhances cleavage, her manager had always reminded her) she realized she was dressed, and on a hard metal surface; more important, she was stiff and sore, with a headache. But the worst of the pain had dissipated while she slept. Noyock leaned over her, holding a bag of ragaway and another bag, this one cold and filled with—"What?"

"Milk."

"Do they still make that?"

"The only place I could make a pull was in a school lunch room."

She nodded, and he helped her sit up. "It's hard to believe I worked that hard," she said, "and there wasn't even a loop of it."

Hop laughed and looked around as she put her mouth to the nipple on the milkbag and drank a little. He walked away as she ate the ragaway, and didn't return until after she had finished and was lying on her back, looking up into the darkness.

His footsteps were muffled by dust, of course, but she heard him long before he arrived. "How do you feel?" he asked softly.

"I feel like getting the hell out of here," she said.

"Which brings us to the next item of business," Hop said. "I'm pretty good at pulling a living out of Capitol without a credit card—but you get pretty damn hungry that way, and you're competing with a lot of other people."

"Thieves? I never knew there were thieves—"

"At your level? Not many. Thieves can only afford to prey on the poor, Arran. The rich have Mother's Little Boys to protect them. The thieves have to live in the walls in the foulest boroughs. And I learned my trade in childhood—I doubt you'd catch on fast enough to keep from getting caught on one of your first pulls."

Arran smiled wanly. "It didn't occur to me that if I couldn't live honestly, I'd actually have to live dishonestly."

"There's another alternative," Hop said. "You could hook."

"Hook?"

"Whore."

"Oh my. Not even looped, I assume?"

"It pays very badly. And I'm not in love with the idea of being a pimp."

Arran laughed. "Do it on a loop in front of billions of eyes and it's an art. Do it in a dirty little room with no audience and it's a filthy career."

"If it's any consolation, I'd see to it the room was clean."

Arran shook her head. "If it's the only way. But Hop, that's the part of my job I hated worst. Do you realize that in four hundred years the only time I ever made *love* was to Farl? And he even preferred little boys."

"Well, you know that leaves us with only two other alternatives. One is to turn ourselves in."

"Throw ourselves on the mercy of the court."

"Not renowned for being particularly clement, especially when someone in a position of power has a vested interest in a guilty verdict. The other alternative, Arran, won't sound much better. The colonies."

109

"Are you joking?"

"Was it funny?"

They sat in silence, Hop making little balls of dust by allowing the last dregs of milk from Arran's milkbag to drip slowly out.

"You can't take any money into the colonies, can you?" Arran asked.

"You can't take somec, either, which is more to the point," Hop said.

"But what would you do when things got boring?"

"Stay awake and be bored," Hop answered. "You actually wouldn't lose any real lifespan, of course. Somec doesn't add to your lifespan. Just stretches it out over a few centuries."

"I know, I know. But it means that only three wakings from now, I'd be dead."

"That *is* what it means."

They sat for a while longer, and then Arran slowly got up. "I feel very old right now," she said, trying to make stiff muscles respond. "Dance exercises just don't prepare you for climbing kilometers of ladders."

"Have you made up your mind?"

"Yes," she said. "But of course that has no bearing on *your* decision. You can stay alive as a thief."

"You're going to the colonies, then?"

Arran shrugged, moved away a little. "I really don't have any other choice." She laughed. "I was getting bored with the life of a looper, anyway."

"Then I'll go with you."

"To the colonies registrar?"

"Yes. And then to the colonies. If you don't mind, I'd like to petition to be sent on the same ship with you."

"But why? You may not even be wanted, Hop. The colonies are like suicide."

"Whither thou goest, I will go, and whither thou lodgest I will lodge. Thy people shall be my people, and thy god, my god."

"What in the world did that mean?"

Hop walked to her, put his arm around her waist, and began

110

leading her in the direction of the nearest ladder down. "My mother was a Christian. That's from the Bible."

"A Christian. How quaint. What world are you from?"

"Here. Capitol."

"A Christian on Capitol! How unusual! And what did it mean?"

"It's from an old story that Mother told us a lot. I got very bored with it. It's about a woman whose sons die and her daughter-in-law still won't leave her. She just figured, I supposed, that like it or not their fates were wrapped up together."

"Do you really think our fates are wrapped up together, Hop?" Arran said, awkwardly, no hint of the famous Arran Handully, Seductress.

"I'm not a fatalist. I *want* to go where you're going."

"So have a hundred billion other men," she said, and now the actress was in her voice again.

"I always thought you were a disgusting, cheap little tart," Hop said, mildly.

Arran stiffened, and stopped walking until Hop removed his arm. "Thank you," she said icily.

"Watch out for where this duct ends," Hop said, still calm. "It's a long drop."

"I can see perfectly well," Arran said.

"I was right, too, you know," Hop said. "That's all you've been for the last few centuries."

Arran didn't answer. They reached the edge, and Noyock swung easily down to the ladder. Arran followed.

"A pretty damn *good* cheap little tart," Noyock added, sounding very casual. "Very well worth the price of admission."

"Haven't you said enough?" Arran asked. But Noyock couldn't hear the famous Arran Handully anger. Only an unaccustomed tone. On another woman, it might be considered well-disguised pain.

"Have I?" Noyock said. "We get off the ladder here. It's just a step backward onto this catwalk."

"I can see it."

"I was just trying to tell you," Noyock said, lifting her down from the ladder by her waist, "that I didn't fall in love with what eight billion other men fell in love with."

"What a freethinker you are," Arran said, and they walked one behind the other along the catwalk.

"Watch your head," Noyock said, and they ducked as they passed under a floor. Now they had to walk stooped again, and below them the ceiling of a borough of flats stretched out for kilometers in either direction, until the dim worklights disappeared entirely in the dust and the distance.

"What I fell in love with," Noyock said, "was the kind of woman who could accept reality and decide to go to the colonies, giving up everything, without a qualm."

"I keep my qualms to myself."

"Three days ago I never would have believed someone who told me that Arran Handully would be capable of making the roof passage."

"Neither would I."

"And now it's discovery time, boys and girls," Hop said, imitating the nasal twang that always came on the daily school broadcasts. Arran laughed in spite of herself.

"What a cheerful sound," Hop said. "We get out here."

He knelt on the catwalk, reached over, and pulled up a section of ceiling tile. The room below was empty.

"Don't know how long it'll last," Hop said, "but this room is empty."

He dropped down through the hole, then helped Arran as she lowered her legs through. "Pull the tile back after you." Awkwardly, she did so, and when she was on the floor, Hop jumped up and adjusted it deftly with one swift pass of his hand, so that it set firmly into place.

"How can we get back in there?" she asked.

"You come *out* of the crawlspace through ceilings. You go *into* the crawlspace through exhaust ducts. What a sheltered childhood you must have had. Still want to find the nearest Department of Colonization?"

112

Arran nodded, then looked at her filthy clothing. "We look rather conspicuous."

"Not here," Hop said, and they opened the door and stepped into a corridor. Arran had never seen poverty before—now she had ample opportunity to look. Her clothing was the dirtiest she could see, but there were many shabbier costumes on the grim-faced people who passed. No one looked at them. They just threaded their way through the corridors until they reached a main passage.

Three ramps later, they saw the lighted sign of the Department of Colonization.

"Home sweet home," Hop said.

"Shut up," Arran answered, and they headed for the sign.

"Chatter!" said a newsboy, with a gossip sheet in his hand. "Buy *Chatter.*"

Hop brushed him aside, but Arran stopped and took a paper from his hand.

"Four and a half," said the boy.

"Wait a minute," said Arran, impatiently, using her can't-you-servants-ever-remember-your-place voice. "Look at this, Hop."

Hop looked. The item of interest was headlined: "Cabinet Minister Slain in Lover's Quarrel."

The subhead said, "Shimon Rapth jailed. Says he killed 'for love of Arran Handully'."

The story went on to tell how Shimon Rapth had confessed to murdering Farl Baak because he had alienated the affections of Arran Handully, who was even now secluded in her huge apartments, refusing all visitors.

"That doesn't look like very accurate reporting, does it?" Hop said.

"Shimon Rapth is *arrested,*" Arran said.

"You certainly have distilled the most interesting aspect, haven't you?" Hop said in his most congratulatory tone. "Now pay the boy for the paper."

"I don't have any money. Just a credit card."

"I take credit cards, ma'am," said the boy.

"Not hers, you don't," Hop said. "Nor mine, either. So here's your paper and good luck selling it to someone else."

The boy's curses followed them on their way to the Department of Colonization.

"If Shimon Rapth isn't the man who was behind the coup—"

"He has to be," Arran answered, disturbed. "The probe. Under the probe, Jazz Worthing said—"

"Jazz Worthing is a man of many gifts. Ignore what he said under the probe. If Shimon Rapth wasn't the man you were out to stop, then who is?"

"Does it matter?" Arran asked.

"A little bit. It might be a friend of ours. It especially matters because whoever it was, he won."

"We're here." They went into the reception room. They ignored the advertising and headed straight for the desk.

"Would you like to register for a colony?" asked the beaming receptionist.

"We would. An agricultural planet."

"A bit of the farming blood, eh?" she asked, cheerfully. "We have just the thing, a little planet called Humboldt."

"Put away Humboldt, lady, and show us something that didn't have to be terraformed."

A bit miffed, the receptionist pulled out another folder. "Before we go any further, sir and madam, I will have to have your credit cards in order to get your aptitudes from the computer. You may not be suited to agricultural work at all."

They gave her their credit cards, which she slid into the terminal on her desk. Then they discussed the merits of Cecily, a new colony 112 light-years away. They were still discussing it when a dozen of Mother's Little Boys came in from all the entrances to the reception area and put them under arrest.

"What for?" Hop demanded.

"Preventive detention," said the apparent leader of the faceless security men. Hop grimaced at Arran. "That means it's political. Confess to everything. It saves time."

114

She looked at him with frightened eyes. "Can they do this?"

"Can you stop them?" Hop asked, and then smiled at her, trying to give her confidence. As if he felt any himself. They were led away—but not out into the corridors. Instead they were taken into a door that said, "Employees Only," and Mother's Little Boys took them deeper into the Department of Colonization.

*I**T continues to amaze many people that the Doon Expeditions could have been set up and sent out in utter secrecy, right in the heart of Capitol. Those who understand Capitol society, however, find nothing surprising in this. Our present open society has almost nothing in common with the authoritarian, byzantine way of life in the corridors of Capitol. Doon, because he controlled the instruments of power—the Cabinet, the secret police ("Mother's Little Boys," as they were less-than-affectionately called), the Service, and above all, the Sleeproom—was able to construct, populate, and send a dozen colony ships, filled with the elite of the Empire, to destinations far beyond the pale of human settlement. It hardly needs repeating, of course, that the Doon Expeditions, conceived of by one man, and sent in spite of an empire, have done more to influence the post-Empire history of humanity than any other single event.*

Solomon Harding, *Abner
Doon: Worldmaker, 6690*
p. 145.

Hop Noyock was sitting in a tree. His legs dangled from the branch. His hands were touching wood, and a slight breeze

117

tousled his hair. Overhead, the imitation sun moved discernibly across the arch of an imitation blue sky.

Below him, the garden was populated with many dozens of men and women, who had been moving around aimlessly for the past several hours. Enough hours, in fact, that the sun had risen, set, and risen again in its hurried pattern. Hop had gathered very quickly that everyone in the overgrown park was one of the conspiracy. Each bit of news was eagerly seized on: this man dead, this woman yet uncaptured, this man probably a traitor, this woman seriously injured but accounted for. Hop knew none of the names, except in their more official roles. Here and there he recognized the name of an undersecretary of chamberpots or some other such meaningless title. But he personally knew no one, except Arran Handully, and he began to appreciate how important she had been in the conspiracy from the fact that practically everyone spoke to her and of her with respect.

But Hop gave up quickly on making any acquaintance. Many had already learned that Jazz Worthing was one of the chief manipulators of somec, and even though he had been mentally stripped under the probe, Hop Noyock was still his manager—worse, was not and never had been a part of the conspiracy—and worst of all, still felt that Jazz Worthing was a decent human being and made the mistake of saying so.

And now he sat on a branch of a tree. No one noticed him, because in the corridor society no one was used to looking up. He sat and thought, and grew more uncomfortable and miserable the more he thought.

He remembered Jason, and wondered what had happened to him.

He remembered that he was a prisoner (but of whom? And what was going to happen?).

Most of all, however, he thought of Arran. It was childish (and I am several centuries old, he reminded himself) but when suddenly Arran was embraced and wept over by so many friends, he felt left out (self-pity, dammit, I haven't let myself feel that in years), he felt used. He had been an escape route—but escape had proved impossible. He had thought himself a friend. Wrong again.

(I'm as bad as the other billions of gonad-dominated oafs who ogle the holos and dream of Arran Handully. I wish Jazz had broken another rib. Damn childish attitude, of course.)

And then the milling groups fell still. The sun did not set—it darkened, and no stars came out. In a short time the entire room was pitch dark. Hop wondered idly if this was the first step to execution—the garden, then darkness, then a gas. But it seemed unlikely. Why plant trees when a sterile room was all that was needed?

The silence, almost palpable when the darkness first came, was gradually nudged aside by whispers. But in the darkness, no one moved, and the conversations were soon exhausted.

Then, suddenly, a light. In the middle of the lake. A man standing on the surface of the water. Hop felt a sudden start, a quick memory of a story his mother had told him from the Bible; but he immediately recognized the brilliant colors of looped life, and relaxed again. Neither murder nor miracles today. Just a few doses of technology.

The man in the lake raised one hand, and silence fell again. Then came the voice, soft and gentle, but filling the entire garden. Hop had to admire the sound work—very well designed, giving an illusion of omnipresence without any obvious stereo effect.

"My name is Abner Doon. Welcome to my garden. I hope you've found it comfortable."

Impatiently Hop moved on the branch. Skip the trash, buddy, and get on with the meat.

"You have all been arrested in the last forty-eight hours, ever since the unfortunate death of Farl Baak. May I assure you that Shimon Rapth did not kill his friend in deliberate betrayal—he was, himself, the victim of a rather elaborate illusion. However, that unfortunate incident did have a fortunate side effect. Every member of your sincere but amateurish plot exposed him-

119

self in one way or another. Hundreds reacted by immediately betraying their fellow-conspirators. No, don't look around at one another—all such have been held somewhere else. All of you are the ones who tried to hide, or who surrendered in order to shield someone else, and so forth. There were many others, of course, equally loyal as you were, who are not here. That is because I have selected, from the group most loyal to the conspiracy, those with the most intellect, the most creativity, the most ingenuity, the most impressive record of achievement. The elite, if you will."

Well. What a clever bunch we are. Hop sneered inwardly. Congratulate us, and then what? And who the hell is Abner Doon?

"I think the rest of your questions will be answered if I tell you two more facts. First, there are exactly 333 of you here in my garden."

A pause, while that sank in. Three hundred thirty-three. The number of colonists in the standard colony ship: three passenger tubes, each with a mayor, ten aldermen, and ten more groups of ten citizens—111 per tube, three tubes per ship, deliberately set up so that no one leader under the captain could possibly get a majority of colonists to rebel. Three hundred thirty-three. It meant that every man and woman in the group would lose somec privileges once the voyage was over. It meant that they would be irrevocably exiled from Capitol, from civilization, and be forced to rush through the rest of their lives in a mere handful of decades.

Hop smiled when he realized what the numbers meant. He and Arran had signed up for a colony, nearly—and had been interrupted. Now it looked as though they would go out into deep space after all. Like it or not. Hop didn't like it—but since he had already made up his mind to do it before, it came as less of a shock to him than it did to the others.

Only one thorn in his side: He had decided to go before in order to stay with Arran Handully, in a dramatic, chivalric gesture of love. (I've seen too many tapes.) Now he would be just an-

120

other man along for the trip. And worse—another man who had never belonged in the conspiracy, an outsider untrusted and unwanted.

Bon voyage, he wished himself.

"Second," said the man in the middle of the lake. "Second, I must tell you that because you have all been convicted of treason against our most perfect and majestic Empress, the Mother of all mankind, your last memory tapes have been removed from the Sleeproom and will accompany you on your colonizing voyage. You will make no new tapes. That is all. Try to get used to the idea quickly—we have little time to waste, and there's no point in awakening at your destination with bruises and broken arms and legs. In other words, for your own sakes, cooperate, my friends. Good night."

And now the murmurs turned into shouts; of dismay, of fear, of protest. The darkness didn't hear, and the man on the lake disappeared, leaving the night complete again. Some panicked and ran—a few splashes indicated that some of them had quickly run into the major obstacle in the garden. Hop didn't laugh when someone ran into the tree he was sitting on.

Convicted of treason meant that all laws and rights were suspended.

The use of a previous memory tape and the failure to make a new one meant that all memory of their latest waking would be utterly erased. Once somec had drained all but the most basic brain activity, everything would vanish. They would awaken on their new planet remembering only what had happened up to the time they last went under somec. They would know that something was missing—that would be enough to tell them that they had been convicted of treason. They would all assume that their conspiracy had been launched, that they had been defeated. But they wouldn't know how. They wouldn't know who had been cowardly or courageous, loyal or treasonous.

But at least they would know that they were conspirators. Hop laughed at what he would think when he woke on the colony planet. For he had known nothing of a conspiracy before

121

he went to sleep. And this time there wouldn't even be a note between his buttocks to hint that something was wrong. He alone, of all of them, would understand nothing. Oh well, Noyock decided, what the hell. I'll survive.

And then he realized that he would remember nothing of Arran Handully beyond the actress he had seen in the lifeloops. A shallow, seductive, empty woman who mouthed insincere words and made phony love to paying lovers. Not the woman who had come to him in his prison and asked for his help in escaping her (suddenly their) enemies. He wouldn't remember the heart-stopping moment when she had descended past him on the ladder, hysterically closing her eyes and plunging deeper into the smoke of the exhaust duct. She wouldn't remember, either, nor would she recall whose voice had called her to come back up. Whose hand had led her to safety.

It was a little harder to say What the hell now.

As abruptly as it had gone out, the sun lit up again, and the light was dazzling. Hop closed his eyes entirely, as all around him he could hear people beginning to call out to each other again. Given their vision, they found their voices, and began calling out names.

Hop left his eyes closed. He would have closed his ears, too, since he wished very much to be alone, but the sounds of the crowd wouldn't leave him alone. Snatches of grief, worry, anger —"What right do they have!" said one, and the answer, "We *are* traitors, after all." (How philosophical.)

"I have three children! Do they ever think of that?" (Do you? Hop thought. Doubtless she was on somec—it was unlikely that a conspiracy made up of somec users would include a non-sleeper. How much did she think of her children as the drug took her away from them for years at a time?)

And then a voice calling, from a distance, "Hop!" and then closer, saying, "Hop, there you are, I've looked everywhere."

He opened his eyes. Arran was at the foot of the tree.

"Hi," he said stupidly.

122

"What are you doing up there, Hop? I couldn't find you. I walked by here a dozen times at least—"

"I think I was hiding," Hop said. He pushed off and jumped to the ground, landing awkwardly on all fours.

"Hop," Arran was saying, as he got to his feet, "Hop, I had to find you, I had to talk to you—why didn't you stay with me? —never mind, nobody could expect you to follow along like a pet or a husband or something—Hop, they've posted a roster at the doors. All the colonists, in their groups of ten and hundred."

"And?"

"Well, for one thing, you're a mayor of three hundred, Hop."

"Me?" Hop laughed. "What a joke! Just what I was cut out for."

"Well, I'm an alderman, which is just as funny. In your group, for luck! But Hop—it's the captain."

"Who is it? Anybody I know?" As if it would be.

"It's Jazz Worthing, Hop. Jason Harper Worthing."

And Hop couldn't think of anything to say to that.

"Hop, he's supposed to be crazy."

"That's all right. We're supposed to be sane."

"Don't you see, Hop? He's your friend. The notice said that anyone with a question could sign up for an appointment to see him. I signed us up, and it's only fifteen minutes or so from now."

"What do you want to see him for?"

"Us, Hop! We've *got* to see him. He's got to arrange it for us."

"Arrange what?"

"To keep our memories, Hop! If they take away my memory of this waking, I won't love you. I won't even *know* you. You'll just be the manager of that despicable bastard Jazz Worthing, and I'll be a disgusting, cheap little tart."

And suddenly Hop felt very good. She wanted to remember him. He took Arran's hand, and she led him along to the door. On the way it occurred to him that he would see Jazz again— that it had been two days since he last saw him—that the world

123

had changed since then—that he and Jazz were now on opposite sides of a very high fence. Would they be friends? Had they ever been? (Is there anything that can't be called into question, eventually?)

It is ironic that science itself, so long the graverobber of all the gods, should have proved conclusively the existence of the soul. It was certainly not intended, and judging from the acute embarrassment of the team the developed somec when they subsequently discovered the soul effect, they would have avoided discovery at all, if that had been possible. But somec had first been used to prolong the lives of the mortally ill in hopes of a cure for them. It was only afterward that somec's memory-erasing effect was noticed, leaving the first somec sleepers as mindless vegetables. George Rines was the first to make the connection between the new braintaping techniques and the disaster of ignorant and premature use of somec. When he tried to resurrect the sleepers by playing someone else's tape into their heads, the result was madness within a few days. There is something not part of memory (and therefore not learned but rather innate in the individual) that remains even after the somec has taken everything else, something that refuses to accept the implanted memories of another person for the simple reason that the new memories are of actions and decisions that the wakened sleeper himself would never have done or made. Rines reported that as an inevitable reaction: The wakened sleepers invariably said, "I remember doing it, but I *would never have done it." They could not accept memories that they had no way of knowing were not their own. For lack of a better word, Rines whimsically named this property of the human individual the* soul. *Doubtless he meant to be ironic. But further research has borne out the fact that his irony was really accuracy.*

The Soul: Awake in the Age
of Sleep, 2433, preface *ii.*

The woman was crying, and, as she left, Jazz wondered why he was doing all this. As Doon had so aptly pointed out, any

124

comfort Jazz might give them, any answers to questions he might offer would all be swept away by somec. They'd remember nothing so why waste time trying to help them?

But Jazz didn't see it that way. Though the memory would be gone, these people were still people. They deserved to be treated humanely. "Memory disappears with death, too," Jazz had pointed out to Doon, "but we still let old people ask questions." So Doon had consented, laughing, and now Jazz found himself unable to help after all. His gift to see into people's minds was no particular boon—in this extremity, they willingly unfolded all their thoughts to him, and he could give them no comfort. The decision was made to wipe out their knowledge of this waking; that decision would stand. Yet that decision was the cause of their distress.

"Next," Jazz said, bracing himself for another ordeal. But this time, he heard a familiar voice. "Jazz, you hunk of cooler grease! How the hell are you doing?" and then Hop's arms were around him, and Jazz hugged him back, not the artificial, is-everybody-watching kind of hug they had shared at every docking of Jazz's ship, but a sincere embrace of friendship. Out of a long-standing habit, Jazz looked into Hop's mind, and heard there an absurd quotation: "For this my son was dead, and is alive again; he was lost, and is found." Jazz found the quotation in his memory —a snatch from an old religious book that still haunted Noyock from the time his mother had drummed it into his head in childhood.

Jazz smiled, and finished the passage, though Noyock hadn't spoken it aloud. "And they began to be merry."

Noyock looked at him, startled, and then suddenly stepped back. Jazz was still listening to Hop's mind; he heard Noyock's final, sure realization of what he had come to suspect: Jazz is a Swipe.

"Of course," Jazz answered. "Didn't I tell you so?"

Hop's boisterous confidence disappeared. He stepped back, unsure what he should do now. If Jazz could so easily read his thoughts now, that meant that Jazz could have heard every other thought he'd had before. He was embarrassed. He turned to Arran, mumbled something. What he wanted to say was, Let's get out of here.

"Arran Handully," Jazz said. "With clothes."

"And Jazz Worthing, with his mind intact," she said. "It looks as though the tables have turned back again, doesn't it?"

"I try to be a graceful winner," Jazz said. "And I see you have lost none of your grace in losing."

"It's losing that we've come to talk about," Arran said, and Jazz heard in her mind a puzzlement as to why Hop had suddenly become so reticent. Wasn't it his job to try to influence his friend? "Captain Worthing, Hop and I have found something that we don't want to lose—"

"That we don't believe we *have* to lose—" Hop said, fumbling for words.

"If you can help us."

"If you're willing—you see, we—" and Hop gave up the struggle for the right words, quit trying to make sure his words matched the thoughts he knew Jazz was hearing anyway. "Dammit, Jason, you know what I'm trying to say. Save me the pain."

"You two have decided you love each other," Jazz said, "and in a sudden burst of domesticity you want me to have your memories taped so you can remember."

"That's it," Arran said, but Hop only turned away, his face red. "Hop," she said, "what's wrong?"

"He can hear us, dammit. He can hear every word we're thinking. He's a Swipe!"

Arran half-laughed, turned to look at Jazz, saw a beatific smile on his face, and whirled back to look at Hop. "How do you know!" she demanded.

"He's been reading my thoughts since we came in here. And for a dozen wakings before—it all fits together—"

"A Swipe!" Arran said, then laughed again, nervously. "You can read my—"

"Yes," Jason answered, quietly. "When I want to. If you had

126

known that about me, you would have known the probe wouldn't work on me. I'm used to having other people's thought patterns imposed on my own. I almost fell asleep under the probe."

Arran fumbled for the chair. Sat down. Jazz listened as she tried to drain her mind of all the thoughts she didn't want Jazz to hear.

"You know," he said, "the more you think about what you don't want me to know, the better I can hear it."

It had taken only thirty seconds, and with that comment Arran was reduced to near-hysteria. "Hop!" she cried out. "Make him stop! Make him get out of my mind!" She was crying. Hop himself was trembling, but he understood what she felt, the insecurity of having no secrets.

"Jazz, please."

"I'm not listening right now, if that's all you're worried about," Jazz said. "But you see, don't you, why I never told you I was a Swipe until this waking. It makes other people very nervous. It makes them, in fact, want to kill me."

"I don't want to kill you," Arran said, regaining some control over her voice. "I just want to get out of here."

"I'm sorry, Arran," Jazz said. "You won't be able to rejoin the others now. If they knew I was a Swipe, they'd never go under somec at all."

"We'll promise not to tell," she said, and then she turned back and faced Jazz squarely. "Oh," she said. "You've already answered us, haven't you?"

"What do you mean?" Hop asked.

"You stinking Swipe bastard!" she shouted. "Why did you tell us *that!*"

Hop stood up, put his arm around her. "Arran, you aren't helping anything—"

"She's right, Hop," Jazz said, maintaining his calm. "If there were any chance that Abner Doon would let any of you have a memory tape, even you, Hop, I would never have let you know I was a telepath."

"So now that we know—"

127

"I'm sorry. Maybe you'll fall in love again, if that's what you want."

And now it was Hop's turn to be angry. "Jazz! My friend!" he said, spitting out the words bitterly. "It's not being in love that I want. It's the last forty-eight hours that I want! It's every damned hideous thing we've gone through together! You don't have a right to take that away from me!"

"I'm sorry," Jazz said. "But I can't change it."

Hop tried to shout something else, but the words found no articulation, just a roar of fury and grief and loss as he scrambled around the table, striking at Jazz as he had struck at members of rival gangs in the deep slums of Capitol. Go for the eyes, the throat, the testicles, said his reflexes. You can't do this to me, shouted his mind. Weep, said the tears in his eyes, and Jazz overpowered him easily, had him sitting in a chair, sobbing like a child before he was sure what was happening.

Now it was Arran's turn to offer a comforting arm, and she softly whispered to him, "Hop, all we can do is think of it as death. We're being murdered, and in our place they'll be resurrecting a new person, the person we were at the beginning of this waking. We're just going to die."

"That's comfort?" asked Noyock, unable to resist seeing the irony. Jazz chuckled softly. "You can shut up," Arran snapped.

"You came in to ask me the impossible. When I denied it you hated me."

"Listen in our minds," said Arran, "and see how much."

"I was wrong," Jason said, "to give these interviews. False hopes are worse than no hope at all. I'm sorry." He stepped to the door, opened it, said to the guards outside, who were supervising the line of colonists-to-be waiting to plead for their past. "You can all leave," he said. "No more interviews today. Sorry." The people grumbled, cried out in frustration, muttered epithets. But they got up from the chairs where they had been sitting, and left.

Jazz came back in, closed the door. "I'm sorry," he said again.

128

He heard both Arran and Hop think, "A lot of good that does," and then think again, "What else can he do, either?"

Aloud, Arran said, "We're all trapped, then, aren't we?"

"Who is this Abner Doon, anyway?" Hop asked.

"Just a man who collects people," Jazz answered. "Hundreds were collected today. You were collected centuries ago, Hop. He found out you were brilliant. And you lived to be sixteen years old as the most prominent member of the most prominent gang in the lower corridors. You're a born survivor. So he collected you—and you've been my agent ever since."

"A puppet master," Arran said, bitterly. "And what does he do with his collection?"

"He has a vision," Jazz said. "He saw in his childhood that nothing important had happened to the human race since somec taught us to fear death and sleep through the centuries. He, and those of us who have seen his vision—we're out to wake the sleepers up. Destroy somec. Make people live out their normal threescore and ten, so that perhaps the human race can get back about its business."

"Destroy somec!" Arran scoffed. "Do you think the sleepers will ever part with it?"

"No. But we know that those who are denied it will come to the point where they will either have it, or destroy all those who do."

"Insane," said Arran.

"And for that you manipulated a thousand of the best people of Capitol, so you could throw them out into space and let them rot," Hop said.

"Manipulate? Who isn't manipulated? Even you, Arran—you were manipulating Farl Baak. And who was manipulating you? A person who believes with all his heart in Doon's vision, who is willing to go to the colonies, willing to lose his last waking for it—"

"Fritz Kapock," Arran whispered.

"There, you see?" Jazz said. "We all know who our manipulators are, once we're willing to admit that we're not really free."

"But Fritz is such a good, honest man—"

"So are we all," Jazz said. "Even me."

They left him then, and the guards took them directly to the tape and tap, so that they could see no other colonist and tell what they had learned. In the tape and tap, however, the attendant was called to the phone, and when he came back, he led Hop and Arran away from the somec table, and sat them in the taping chairs, and put the sleep helmets on their heads. "What does this mean?" Hop asked, knowing what it meant. "Captain Worthing told me to do this," the attendant said, and Hop and Arran wept with joy as they lay back and gave their memories to the whirring film. And when the helmets came off, and they were led to the somec beds, they embraced, and wept again, and smiled and laughed and kept thanking the attendant, who nodded, promising to offer their thanks to Captain Worthing. And then they were put to sleep, and laid in their coffins, and the attendant took the tapes to the colony ship, and gave them to the starpilot, who also thanked him, and paid him the money he had promised.

Colonists traveled nude, of course, in special boxes that were linked to the life-system of the ship. Because of their shape, these boxes were called coffins, though their purpose was exactly opposite. Instead of guarding a body as it rotted and decomposed, the colony ship coffins kept colonists alive, so that they didn't age a day as somec helped them sleep their way across the galaxy. As long as the coffins remained absolutely, perfectly sealed, and as long as the ship's life-system kept functioning, human beings placed inside them under somec sleep could, in theory, live forever.

Peopling the Planets: The Colonies, 6559, II:33

The last of the coffins was wheeled through the lock, down

130

through the storage compartments (which, on a military ship, would have held armaments) and on to the passenger section. The *A* and *B* tubes were full, sealed, locked, the dials and registers on the doors monitoring the almost infinitesimal but still detectable life-signs of the sleepers. Jazz Worthing and Abner Doon watched as the coffin was wheeled through into the tube. Watched as the silent workmen connected the tubes, wires, and drains that kept the sleepers alive.

"Back to the womb, back to the placenta," said Doon, and Jason laughed. And as they had done a dozen times before, stretched out in front of the highly illegal and therefore very expensive fireplace in Doon's flat, they began to play their game of archaism. "Western Airlines, the *only* way to fly," Jazz said. Doon blandly responded, "Go Greyhound, and leave the driving to us." And so it went as they followed the workmen back through the ship. In the storage compartment, Doon paused to pat the oversized coffin that held an ox. "For years," he said, and the joking tone left his voice, "these people have known no other animal, except the rats. For the first time they're going to have to deal with an animal that's guaranteed to be stupider than they are."

"The sudden proof of superiority will probably bring back a belief in God, don't you think?" Jazz asked.

"God?" Doon asked. "There's only one God on this ship, and he's already playing his role."

"I thought you said you didn't claim that title."

"I don't. But you do."

"I? I'm part of your collection, remember?"

"Playing God with your colony, Jason, can be dangerous. Especially when you aren't following a plan. Doing things for sentimental reasons will destroy you and your colony. Sentiment has no place in a man of vision."

"I'm not a man of vision," Jazz said, shrugging.

"Then you'll die as fruitlessly as your father did. In the meantime, I advise you to destroy the memory tapes you had made of Hop Noyock and Arran Handully."

Jazz chuckled. "I knew I should have paid that attendant more."

"It would have made no difference. He has instructions to accept all bribes and do everything he's bribed to do. As long as he reports it to me. Destroy the tapes."

"I don't think it will do any harm to have two that remember their waking."

"No harm? A man with full knowledge will spread even more poison than a man with no knowledge. Hop and Arran would have you in their power. You'd have to ask their advice before you did something, and before long asking advice always turns into asking permission. It's up to you, though, Jazz. Be a fool if you like."

"Hop's my friend," Jazz said.

"And you're my friend," Doon said. "But of course, I'm a megalomaniac, as you love to remind me. A man with a eugenics program for the universe. The other ships are all gone."

"Eleven others?"

"And no, I won't tell you where the others are going. If you want to find them, you'll have to look."

"You told my colony that they were the best of the conspirators. Was that true?"

"For once, Jazz, I wasn't lying."

"Why are you giving me the best?"

"The others all have excellent colonies, too. I want the gene pool and the intellectual climate to be superb. The best start I can give my little projects."

"But why the best for me?" Jazz insisted.

"Because I love you so dearly," Doon said, reaching up to pat the starpilot's head. "But mostly, I'm afraid, because I believe that you, of all the captains I've sent, are best equipped to create what I want to have created."

"And what is that?"

"A better human race than the one we've had since men began killing each other and cooking the meat."

132

"And what improvement could the human race possibly make?"

"Perhaps," Doon said, "you might be able to develop a branch of the human family that could know and understand what other human beings are—and love them anyway. Hmmm?"

"Impossible. And I should know."

"You should know," Doon said. They left the storage room and went back to the pilot's cabin, where a soldier was waiting, out of breath. "Captain Worthing," the soldier said, saluting. Jazz returned the salute. "Yes?" And then the boy noticed Abner Doon, and saluted again, his face showing even more awe. "Abner Doon, sir," he said.

"I take it this means the tape has been played," Jason said.

"It has, sir, and we're waiting for orders. The fleet is with you."

"Then tell the fleet," Jazz said, "that I have done all that I can do, and am leaving on an important expedition. Tell them that Abner Doon will give them somec. Tell them to follow Abner Doon."

The soldier nodded, saluted, and then said, "Sir," looking at Doon. "Sir, will you come with me? Admiral Pushkin is waiting."

Doon smiled at Jason. "See you again."

"Where?" asked Jason. "In heaven?"

"Unlikely," Doon said. "Give me three hundred years, and I'll have this Empire where it should be."

"And where is that?" Jazz asked.

"Please hurry, sir," the soldier insisted.

"In a gutter, bleeding to death," Doon said. And then he walked out of the ship. The door closed behind him, and he followed the soldier to the hall where the representatives of the Fleet were gathered.

Inside the control room, Jazz began working immediately. He didn't know his final destination—only the official destination, Siis III, was known to him. The computer would tell him where Doon wanted him to go only after he got the ship to Siis. But

Jason knew enough—that the ultimate destination would be deep in the galaxy, far toward the center, far from the human pale. He knew that it would be hundreds of years of sleep, traveling all the while at many times the speed of light (using the drive that he himself had made possible in childhood). He knew that there was no record in the Empire, save in Abner Doon's head, that clearly told that Jazz Worthing and the other eleven ship captains were going anywhere but to their official destinations.

All in the hope, as Doon had often explained, that once isolated, these little colonies of humanity might actually develop something new. Something better than the decaying remnant of the Empire. "All we are," Doon had often said, "all we are is that last relic of the European civilization that was born in England with the industrial revolution. All we are is the fading shadow of the Technical Age. We're ripe for something new. Either for regeneration of the human race, or for replacement." And Jazz had cast his vote for regeneration, as had dozens of others who, though at first coerced into Doon's collection, had later been willing servants of Doon's vision.

Vision, thought Jazz, and as he settled down to maneuver the ship out of the cradle and out of Capitol's system, the idea of vision kept nagging at him. Vision of what? Do I have anything I want so badly that I'd sacrifice anything to have it? Is there anything that I am so sure is right that I would fight for it?

My own life, Jazz thought, but that isn't vision—every animal instinctively fights for that.

And then the go-ahead signal came, Jazz opened the view walls of the control pod, and the cradle slowly lifted him into the smoky sunlight of Capitol's surface. Around him the winds eddied and whirled, and from where Jazz sat in the retractable bubble at the front of the needlelike payload section of the ship, it seemed that the winds were dancing for him. Far below him, the vast doors of the ship cradle slowly closed, sliding under the massive landing gear that now bore the weight of the barrellike stardrive section of the ship.

When the door was closed, Jazz sat for a moment, waiting for clearance from the deeply buried traffic controllers, whose communications complex was called, for some nonsensical reason, the "tower." As he sat, he mentally said good-bye to Capitol. To the teeming crowds who had cheered on the exploits of Jazz Worthing, hero. To the men and women who had offered their bodies to him; to the incredible wealth and equally incredible poverty; to the oppression and the heady liberty that lived side-by-side in the corridors of Capitol. He also said good-bye to somec, and found that it was somec he would miss most of all.

"I'm a bloody hypocrite," Jazz said, laughing nastily at himself. "Out to destroy somec, when I crave it as much as anyone else."

And then the clearance came, and Jazz punched in the preset program alert, specified the route they had been cleared for, and then retracted the bubble so it wouldn't be shredded in the stresses of takeoff.

Days later, as the starship drifted lazily out of the Capitol system at a mere 1.35 gravities, and as the computers lavishly checked, double-checked, triple-checked, and then reported to Jason Worthing, Jazz realized the mistake he was making. Would Hop love him when they reached their colony, knowing he was a Swipe? Of course Hop and Arran would be grateful at first. But gratitude is the least dependable of human emotions, Jazz reminded himself. And I should know. I should know.

He confirmed the computer's verdict that the ship was ready for starflight. The readout warned him that he had thirty minutes before the ship would make its turn, putting the full thrust toward Capitol's sun, and accelerating to five, fifteen, twenty light-years per year. As always, Jazz had the whimsical thought that all the electromagnetic radiation in the universe was envious of him for the speed he could muster.

"Gratitude is the least dependable emotion," Jazz said aloud, and he went to the storage cabinet where the papers and rosters of the colonists were stored. There he found the two memory tapes that the Sleeproom attendant had brought him. On the one, the words *Arran Handully,* on the other the words *Willard Noy-*

135

ock. Jazz felt a momentary longing to go and wake them, play the tapes into their heads, *talk* to them for a moment or two, plead for their reassurance that he was, after all, *right* in the choices he had made. But he squelched the desire. Who in the universe has ever been sure he was right?

Except Abner Doon, of course.

And thinking of the man who had collected him, and remembering his advice, Jazz confidently walked to the garbage recycler and tossed the two memory tapes inside. Within ten seconds they had been stripped to their basic molecules, and those had been simplified to uncombined elemental atoms, which hung in a static field, available for use later. "So easily we murder," he told himself, and then went to the coffin that waited for him in the control room—the only coffin in the ship that was not in the control room—the only coffin that was not in the hindmost compartment of the ship, the only one that would waken its occupant automatically, at the command of the ship's computer.

Jazz stripped off his clothing and laid it aside. Then he climbed into the coffin, eased himself down, and pulled the sleep helmet over his head. It recorded his brainwave pattern. A small amber light flashed on just outside Jazz's range of vision, and he said, "Jason Worthing, XX56N, sleep OK." That was the code; but he added, "Good night."

The cover slid over him, and he watched as the sealer oozed upward from the edges of the coffin and made the space airtight. And then a green light flashed on, and a needle entered his scalp from the sleep helmet, and the somec flowed hotly into his veins.

The somec burned, the somec was agony, the somec felt like death—or worse, like the fear of death. Jason panicked, afraid that something was terribly wrong, afraid that somehow the somec was burning him up from the inside out, destroying him.

He didn't know that somec was always like that; it had always happened after the taping, and he had no memory of it.

But after a fifteen-second eternity the somec emptied his brain and Jason slept.

As soon as he was unconscious, the great stardrive silently fired, and the tremendous acceleration began. Jason's coffin, and each of the coffins in the passenger compartment, filled with a clear gel. As the acceleration reached 2.7 gravities, the gel solidified, formed a rigid supporting structure that kept the bodies from breaking under the strain of three gravities, four, five.

And the ship shoved its way relentlessly through the empty space with three hundred thirty-four bodies inside it, all of them alive, all of them on fire, though they didn't know it, with an agony that would make even life worth enduring by contrast.

6

S*OME revolutions happen overnight. Some are years in the
making. But no other took so long to foment as the Somec
Revolution. The first step of the revolution was Abner Doon's
seizing of control of the overt organs of Imperial power. With
the Service and the secret police behind him, he ousted the Cabinet, and assumed tyrannical control of every aspect of the Empire. At first this seemed to be merely a coup—and one long
overdue. But Doon was subtle.*

*He began to make his tyranny oppressive in the colonies first.
Had Capitol come to hate him from the beginning, its inhabi-
tants might have ousted him, put another more clement man in
his place, and the Somec Revolution might never have happened. As it was, minor rebellions began to occur on planet after
planet, as the privilege of somec sleep became whimsical in its
bestowal, corrupt in its administration. Acting on Doon's intruc-
tions, totally undeserving people were put on somec, while those
long accustomed to it were abruptly removed. And in every case,
the rebellions were begun, not by the masses who had never had
any hope of somec sleep, but by the wakened sleepers, whose
fear of death was irrational, whose hatred for those who stole
immortality from them was implacable.*

Each rebellion was put down, as cruelly and bloodily as possible—and yet each time, some of the key leaders were left alive, allowed to leave prison as magnanimously pardoned "friends of the state." These freed rebels invariably became the seeds of still further revolt.

Besides its tremendous length of time in fomenting and the devastating effects it had on humanity, the Somec Revolution was remarkable for one other aspect: it is probably the only revolution that was completely planned, from the outset, by the very tyrant against whom the rebels revolted. Many theories have been advanced for Abner Doon's actions, but examination of all the most recently available documents suggests this inescapable conclusion: for some reason of his own, Abner Doon wanted somec to be removed from consideration in the affairs of humankind; wanted, perhaps, the terrible collapse of technology that followed; perhaps wanted, though this is doubtful, the death of interstellar travel for more than a millennium and a half; and some even suggest that Doon planned and even desired the diversity in humanity that occurred when technology could no longer sustain the "business-as-usual" way of life that humans had enjoyed on planets utterly unsuitable for human life. This last is doubtful. What is most likely is that Doon was exactly what he has always been thought to be: a madman bent on destruction as the ultimate demonstration of his power.

Certainly when Capitol was at last provoked and mobs stormed the Sleeprooms, smashing the coffins and killing every sleeper, his mad dreams must have been realized. And though for centuries it has been supposed that Doon died in that holocaust, recently discovered evidence suggests quite the contrary. One eyewitness account seems typical of many, which all agree on the general outline of events:

"We went to the Dictator's private apartments, and by threatening his servants with death, we were led to the sleeproom he had privately used. It was empty. I myself checked the instruments, and determined that he had been awakened only three

140

hours before we reached the coffin. Inside the coffin was a note, which said, 'Dear Rebels: I give you my best.' Of course we killed all his servants as traitors to the People. Where Doon went, we do not know."

And we must echo that statement: Where Doon went, we do not know. After all, we have only recently been able to visit the ruins of Capitol and search for old records. That we have already found this much is to the credit of many dedicated researchers. . . .

It seems to be a pattern in revolutions against individual tyrants, that as often as not they are never found. Perhaps it is a subtle, hidden element of the human psyche (if one may speak of that entity as being even vaguely uniform) that the object of mankind's most virulent hatred must be allowed to continue to live. Let us call this the "devil syndrome," for we shall find it repeated in dozens of other revolutions. . . .

After the sleepers were slain on Capitol, the economy ground to a halt, not the least because all incoming starship pilots were dragged from the landing platform and tossed to their death at the bottom of the ship's cradles, which in the days of oversized starships were invariably at least a kilometer below the door of the payload section of the ship. Naturally, starships stopped arriving at Capitol, and deprived of the essential influx of raw materials, the seemingly eternal city of Capitol died; food ran out first, and then, with maintenance abandoned, the air cleaning system stopped working, and oxygen was no longer electrolyzed from the sea; the smoke of three thousand years of exhaust seeped down into the corridors; the hydrogen that had stored the sun's power for use all over the planet stopped coming from the sea; and within a year of the revolution, all life on Capitol was dead.

With the centers of power gone, the rebellions on the other planets could not be put down, and soon the entire Empire was in chaos, though few planets died as completely as Capitol. And it took only a hundred years after the Empire's death for the

141

Enemy, poisoned by the rebel planets it took over in a quick grab for power, to also fall victim to the general destruction, thus setting the stage for our own age—the Age of Diversity.

Hunter and Halleck, *Revolution in the Age of Diversity, 6601,* pp. 5–8.

7

JAZZ wakened to see the lid of the coffin sliding back, the amber light winking at the edge of his vision. The memory tape must have just finished, he thought, though of course he had no memory of it happening. His body was hot and sweating —like all somec users, he believed the warmth was caused by the drugs used for waking.

He sat up abruptly, rolled himself over the edge of the coffin, and dropped to the floor in push-up position. Twenty push-ups and thirty sit-ups later, he got to his feet, the blood flowing, feeling refreshed from the long sleep.

Only then did he notice that it was not the amber light flashing in the coffin. It was the red.

He had been reaching into the cupboard for the packet of clothing that would have been prepared by the ship for his waking. But the red flashing light sent him immediately to the control board.

QUERY.

RESPONSE: ENEMY SHIP ROUNDED SIIS III SEVEN MINUTES AGO.

QUERY HOSTILE ACTS.

Response: Two projectiles launched, impact 1.7, impact 3.4.

Query attack path.

Response: Random unpredictable.

That meant that the enemy pilot was still guiding the projectiles. Jason immediately began searching through space for the enemy captain's mind, even as his fingers automatically sent half of his projectiles—a pitiful two on a virtually unarmed colony ship—and he found, yes, the mind controlling the projectiles. Found in the mind the path the projectiles would follow. And then maneuvered his own ship, just slightly, in a feint. The other captain followed the feint, committed the first projectile, and then when it was too late for the enemy to alter course in time to strike him, Jason shifted again, just enough to keep his ship out of reach.

The second enemy projectile was easier to dodge. And now it was time for the opposite maneuver as Jason controlled his own weapons, seeing in the enemy's mind his evasion plans, countering them just in time each time, until his first projectile made contact with the giant stardrive of the enemy ship, and its image on the holomap became an ever fainter, ever expanding globe.

Just before the contact, Jazz had heard the enemy captain crying out for help, had felt him fumbling with a microphone, had heard in his mind the faintest wisp of a prayer as he realized that contact would be made, and then had heard for an infinitesimal moment the agony of death, and then felt the peace of death, the absence of mind.

Jazz leaned back on the upholstered chair, noticed how cold it felt on his naked, sweating back.

The red light was still flashing. Jazz was puzzled, leaned forward again.

Query.

Response: Second enemy ship, rounded Siis III four minutes ago.

Query hostile acts.

144

RESPONSE: TWO PROJECTILES LAUNCHED, IMPACT 0.2, IMPACT 1.9.

Impact 0.2! Jason shouted at himself. And even as his fingers played along the control board and his mind sought the enemy captain's mind, his intellectually unfazeable mind was saying to him, "You fool, he would never have called for help *by radio* unless he had someone else nearby."

The other mind found; the flight path of the projectile mapped; contact inevitable; and by reflex Jazz did the only possible maneuver that would ensure survival: he swung the starship very slightly—and intercepted the projectile with the payload section of the ship, catching it deftly with the only portion of the ship the weapon could strike without causing a nuclear explosion.

At the same moment, Jazz released his last two projectiles, hoping that there would be no more enemy ships.

And his control room shuddered with the shock of impact. The enemy projectile was not nuclear, of course—on the surface of the stardrive, a nuclear explosion would not penetrate through the shielding. Instead, it was equipped with high intensity fusion-source lasers, and it melted a path ahead of itself for a critical number of seconds. Just long enough, with a few meters to spare, to penetrate the shielding of a stardrive.

Jazz didn't bother to wonder whether the projectile had had to force its way through enough payload that it would run out of fuel before penetrating to the stardrive core. He was too busy moving his ship (the controls still respond, good) to avoid the second enemy missile; and then he immediately shifted his attention to guiding his own projectiles as they homed in on the enemy ship.

He saw the enemy captain's disbelief as he realized that he had made contact—and yet Jason's ship had not exploded. And then the panic as the enemy captain tried to dodge Jason's projectiles, couldn't, and realized horribly that he would die as his fellow captain had just died.

And then the globe of fading light on the holomap.

QUERY.

RESPONSE: NO ENEMY ACTIVITY.

QUERY LOCATION.

RESPONSE: SIIS III.

So Jazz had reached his destination; as was often the case, the Enemy had dispatched warships to intercept the colony ship before it could land. Those Enemy craft might have been orbiting Siis III for as much as a century, waking their captains only when Jazz's ship was sensed as it decelerated to subluminous speeds. Traditional pattern, except that there were two ships instead of one.

The tension of battle fading, he remembered how he had stopped the enemy projectile, and felt a horrible burning sensation in his stomach and groin.

He got up from the chair and went to the cupboard, dressed, and then for safety put on a pressure suit with a field helmet. He adjusted it for transparent and semipermeable, and then turned the wheel on the seal lock of the door leading to the back of the payload section.

The storage compartment was completely undamaged—none of the animal coffins had even come loose. Which left only one conclusion: the projectile had entered the payload section in the passenger tubes.

Jazz readjusted for impermeable, and opened the door at the back of the storage section. No rush of air into space—the monitor area was also undamaged.

Jazz looked at the dials that told the condition of all the passengers in each of the tubes. The *A* section dials were all functioning, and their message was uniform: no life in any of the coffins. The *C* section was worse: the dials were all dark, meaning that the life-support system was out. Only *B* section was intact, showing no damage. Jazz wasn't sure whether to be horrified at losing two-thirds of his colony, or relieved at still having one-third.

146

He opened the door to *B* tube and walked down the rows, inspecting each coffin for damage. There was none that he could detect, not even a shifting of the bodies. Noticing who was still alive also told him who was not. But among the survivors was Hop Noyock, and Jazz felt an unreasonable gladness, as if Hop's survival insured the success of the colony after all.

At the end of the tube was another door, which led to the schoolroom, where all the memory tapes of the colonists were stored, and where at the end of the voyage Jason would waken each of the passengers.

Beside the door a warning light was flashing red.

Jazz punched in the code on the doorbutton that flushed all atmosphere out of the tube. When the green light flashed on, he opened the door and found chaos.

The schoolroom had been directly hit, and from that vantage point he could see the gaping hole left by the projectiles. It had entered near the front of the passenger tubes, cutting a swath between the life-support system of *C* tube and the coffin racks of *A* tube, destroying every coffin and every life-support complex on its way down the length of the tubes. Then it had bored through the end, struck the schoolroom, passed right through a corner of the tape rack, and passed on into the shielding in front of the stardrive. Looking down into the hole, Jazz could see the back of the projectile, stopped where it had gone cold, unable to penetrate further. He quickly guessed that two more meters and it would have exploded the ship.

I should feel grateful, he told himself. But when he looked at the tape rack, he couldn't. The left section of the rack, where the projectile had passed, was utterly destroyed—where it wasn't cut away by the projectile's passage, the tapes were melted by the heat. The *B* section of the rack, in the middle, was also mostly melted. Only a few of the *C* rack tapes were still usable.

And everybody in *C* tube was dead.

Jazz knelt down and pulled out every tape in the bottom part of *B* rack, where the heat was least intense. But tape after tape showed damage—and even the slightest melting made the entire tape unusable. Out of all the tapes, only one was undamaged, the one in the bottom right-hand corner. It belonged to Garol Stipock.

Only one tape.

Which meant that only one single passenger could be revived with his full memory. With any memory at all. Only one that could be revived as an adult human being. If anyone else was revived at all, it would be as empty-minded as an infant, a creature of reflex, unable to walk, speak, even control bodily functions.

Jazz left the schoolroom, clutching the one usable tape, and walked back through *B* tube. This time as he passed the coffins he didn't see adults whom he knew—he saw huge infants, impossible to care for, utterly cut off from their own life history in the Empire.

Except Garol Stipock. And as Jason looked down at the reposed face of the man who had invented the Stipock geologer and a dozen other devices, he said, "Gadgetry. Gimmicks and games. What a wonderful colony we'll make together. And what wonderful children we'll raise."

He left *B* tube, sealing the door behind him, and wandered listlessly back into the control cabin. He passed the roster compartment and remembered, bitterly, the two tapes that had been in there, tapes which he had destroyed for a purpose—some purpose—what purpose could possibly compare with the terrible need he had now? He longed for a way to reverse the garbage process, bring back the lost fragments of Hop's and Arran's memory tapes, restore them and waken those two people whom he at least *knew*. Garol Stipock. Who the hell was Garol Stipock?

A colony of infants.

Here it is, Doon. The perfect society. One you could teach to be anything you wanted. As long as you enjoy changing the diapers of adults who kick like infants with grown-up strength.

He sat down in the control room, and the computer, sensing

148

that he had returned, began readouts on the information that had been kept from him back on Capitol—where the colony ship was supposed to go.

Jazz was past caring, but by reflex he looked, and by reflex he fed back into the computer his confirming orders, his explicit instructions. Mechanically he carried out his part of the mission, as if there were a mission to perform.

Something was gnawing at his stomach, and it churned within him. But he finished the calculations in only seven hours, and then, exhausted, threw himself on the cot provided for the star-pilot.

He dreamed of the Estorian twick, staring at him from a meter away. It just sat and stared, and Jason knew that if he moved, if he made any move at all, the twick would leap, would carve him with its razor teeth, would devour him if it could. How long can I stand without moving, he kept wondering, and the twick only watched, and waited. And then suddenly he heard Doon's voice saying, "You're a survivor. You're a survivor." And then he felt himself swimming in the lake, the twick's body floating beside him, feeling exultant. Survival. That is enough grounds for joy.

He woke needing badly to go to the toilet. He got up, un-accustomedly groggy with sleep. It had not been a restful nap. He closed the toilet stall and showered. Then he stepped out of the toilet and looked at the computer.

The readout board said, "Ready for execute."

Why bother? Jason wondered.

"Why bother?" Jason asked aloud.

But he knew he would bother. He would push the buttons on the computer, and then would climb into his coffin and sleep the years until his new destination. He would waken after 900 years, farther by a dozen times than any starship had ever gone from the human pale. And he would revive, one by one, the huge infants that slept in the back of the ship.

And as he resigned himself to survival, because he really had no other choice, it occurred to him how ignorant his colonists would be. Except for Garol Stipock, they would know only what he told them.

They would have no memory of Capitol, and therefore no memory of any particular system of law or government.

They would not know the technology that would never be possible to them.

They would not remember that they had been arrested as traitors; they would not remember that Jason Worthing had been an enemy to them.

The word *Swipe* would be meaningless to them.

Except Garol Stipock.

I can make the world the way it ought to be, he thought. A clean slate, Doon. If I can survive the first years, I can make a decent world.

And how ought the world to be? Jason laughed at himself. A chance to make a utopia, and he had no idea where to begin. Well, plenty of time for that later. Plenty of time to work out the details. I have a vision now, at least, Doon. Pat me on the back for that.

Jason Worthing locked the solitary memory tape in the cupboard, punched out the execute code, and climbed into the coffin. He was excited, exultant, and a little mad when the sleep helmet recorded his mind. He would waken with that excitement and madness when the ship woke him a millennium from now.

A needle in his scalp. The hot rush of somec in his veins. The agony, the panic. And then the oblivion.

And the gutted starship turned, fired, and accelerated madly, racing with the light of the star Siis toward another star an unfathomable depth into the broad white lake of the galaxy.

8

J has told me I must write, though my writing is slow and not always good, and so I write. I am Kapock, and I am called the Eldest of the Ice People, though there is no time when I do not remember the other five who are also the Other Eldest. J is gone now for the first time in memory, and I am Warden, and I am afraid.

J has told me I must write what is most important. Most important to me? I asked J. He said, Most important to Heaven City, which is what we call our place where we all live. J has gone up into the Star Tower and I cannot ask him what is important, but I will obey him the best I can which is not always good.

J has told me I am writing to my children. I do not understand this, for my children are both very small, and even though one of them can now walk, which he could not do at first, he cannot even speak. Does this mean that J promises that someday my children will not only speak, but also will read? This is a great promise, if it is true, but I am not sure and so I tell it to no one yet. I tell no one that I write.

I live apart from all the others with Sara my wife. This is

our way now. When Sara and I chose each other and first coupled we were afraid, for this thing had not been taught to us by J, but rather by the oxen. Nevertheless J was not angry and only said that now we must live apart. He said words that declared us to be married and said that once married a man and a woman must live only together and never with any other man or woman, so that children could be born. This we have done, and it is a good way, for I am happy. And also Sara.

This is the first thing that is important. When I was a man alone I was often afraid and would always ask J before I did anything. Now I ask Sara, and she answers me, but I do not always do what she says. This is not because I do not respect her, but because we do not always agree. Many times I have thought one way and she has thought another way but we have done still another way between the two. This is a good way to decide, and now I do not need to ask J before I do things. I am not alone and I am almost never afraid anymore.

Until now that I am Warden, and I am afraid again, because now I do not decide just the things of a man and a wife, the things of my sheep and my house. Now I must also decide the arguments of the other people, and name the day of planting and plowing and hoeing and reaping and all other days, and this makes me afraid, for only J has decided these things before.

Will the others obey me as they have obeyed J? I do not know, for J is always wise, and I am always foolish and this is known to all the men and women of Heaven City. Yet J has told them to obey me, and so they must do it.

But J has also told me to give commandments as he would give them. But I am not wise, and so I cannot obey. Does he not know this? I am afraid.

If I did not have Sara with me I would run from Heaven City and build a far house. But Sara has read what I am writing and has told me I am not foolish. Even now she touches my hair and I am not so afraid. I make an end of writing for this time.

Linkeree and the ax.

Now I will tell you of Linkeree and the ax, for Sara says to me all day that this is important, and now I agree with her. J left at the seventh day of the harvest moon, and now it is the third day of the leaf-falling moon. Soon there will be first snow. I remember this from two other winters. Our main work at this time is building a new house for Wien and Miott, who have coupled. Also this is the time for making new thatch to cover the roofs of our wooden houses, and this we also are doing.

Yesterday was the time of walls, and Linkeree is the best at walls. He is also the best at much other things working with wood, and so we listen most to him in the making of houses and other things of wood. Linkeree worked very hard, and the walls were ready with four hours of light left.

At that time Linkeree said to me, Kapock. Can I take an ax?

And I said to Linkeree, Where will you take the ax and to what purpose? This I said because J has told us the metal tools are precious and cannot be made again as well, and so we keep them carefully and do not leave them lying around in the fields to be lost or broken.

Linkeree said to me, Kapock, I will take the ax to a place I know and there I will cut trees for a special purpose, and I will bring the ax to you at dark, and you will have it again.

Now I am not a fool, though I am sometimes foolish, and I knew that Linkeree had not answered me at all. But I also knew that Linkeree was not lazy and that he had several times thought of ideas that J said were very good. Linkeree thought of the way to catch fish with a cloth with holes cut in it, giving us a good change from bread and potatoes and radishes and cream and other such quiet food. Linkeree also thought of the stool with three legs that sits steady no matter what the ground. So he is one to treat with respect. So I did not argue with him, but decided that I would let him take the ax this once, but that if any harm came to it he could not have it again. I thought that this is the way J would have decided.

153

To my anger Wien and Hux were standing near, and Hux said, Why did you say yes, Kapock? He did not answer you.

And Wien said to Linkeree, Where are you taking the ax and what will you do with it?

I do not answer quickly when I am angry, but Linkeree is always quick to speak his anger. He said to them, It is Kapock who is Warden, not you, and I do not have to answer you.

This made Hux and Wien very angry, so angry that I thought Wien might try to take the ax from Linkeree by strength, which Wien could surely do, being very large and strong, while Linkeree is slight, though also tall.

This is what I said to Hux and Wien: Linkeree is a good man and I will let him take the ax. But if he does not keep his word and return it at dark, then I will require that he tell us where and to what purpose he would take the ax.

Then it will be too late, said Hux.

But I was angry now, and told Hux that tomorrow he would have to bury all the nightsoil of Heaven City himself. Hux said no more because he knew that his punishment was just. Wien also said nothing more. But I knew they were angry at Linkeree and angry at me.

Then Linkeree left. He brought back the ax at dark, as I had said, and no more was said on the matter.

I did not think this was important yesterday, but today Sara told me that it was very important. This is the reason she told me: It is important because never before have any of the Ice People spoken against my decision after I had made it. I had not thought of that at the time, but now that I think of it it makes me afraid again, for it means they do not think of me as if I were J, because they would never have spoken against J.

J promised that he would return at harvest next year. Will he then find that I have failed and not been a good Warden? If he does, I will not want to live anymore. I will want to die like the squirrels who are crushed at the falling of a tree.

Sara is reading this and she tells me that I am now being foolish.

There is another reason why this thing that happened yesterday is important. This is the first time that any person has ever done something and not told all the people what he does, and yet has told them that he is doing it. I write this, and have not told others, but they do not know that I am not telling. It is as if Linkeree wanted us all to know that there is something he will not tell us. Why does he do this? It only causes pain and anger, as Hux and Wien and many others are angry.

They fear that Linkeree does not think himself equal to us all, but better, and J has told us that though each of us is better at some things than others are, yet all of us, added together, are equal.

This is why we have equal food, unless we are lazy, and why we have equal houses and equal portions of all things, good and bad. This is why when one house is cold, all must help to fix it, or all must take turns sleeping in the cold house until it is warm again. This is good and right, because one should not have less than another when both work as hard.

But if Linkeree thinks himself better than others, will he not want more for himself than for others? This would not be right.

I want to know what he does. But I will not force him to tell me—nor will I follow him or allow others to follow him. For as J said to me on one day, If a man does something that you do not understand, do not stop him. Rather wait until you do understand, for then you may learn something for your good. These are the words of J.

This is what has happened with Linkeree and the ax, and I make an end of writing at this time.

My house.

Sara says I should write of my house. I do not think so. But because Sara is often wiser than I, and because it will do no harm for me to write, I write:

My house was built like all other houses of Heaven City, except that I am on this side of the Star River and all the other houses are on the other side with the Star Tower. But my house is now different, and this is because I am a foolish man. Sara now laughs at me. But it is true.

I looked at the house and it did not look right to me. It was solid like all other houses, but it did not look right to me. Now do you see why I call myself foolish?

So on a night with nothing to do, I took some of the scraps of wool that we had not needed for cloth, and I began to work the loom. After several nights I had good lengths of cloth. I sewed them together like a blanket, only tighter and stronger, and I fastened the cloth to the front of my house above the door, and then tied the two far corners to ropes and tied the other ends of the ropes to posts I put in the ground fifteen paces off. Now the sun never shines through our door, which means that all through the summer our door is open and yet the house is cool.

This is a good reason to do the thing I did. But that was not the reason I did it. I did it because the house did not look right until I did that.

And now I will write something that will surely make Sara laugh. I looked at the house tonight and once again, to me, it does not look right.

Sara is laughing at me. I will make an end of writing for this time.

Linkeree and days of work.

Today was a bad day again, and once again the trouble was about Linkeree. What does he do in the far forest with the ax?

Today Linkeree took the ax early in the morning. With my consent he took the ax. But then later in the morning Hux told me that the firewood was not as deep as it had been last winter, and I went to see. Sure enough, the firewood did not rise as high as the mark in the wall. I felt bad that I had not checked this sooner. But I told Hux and three other men to take axes and cut wood all day instead of doing work on the thatch. This is because thatch can be made even inside a house, but wood cannot be cut easily after the snow is deep.

156

I forgot that Linkeree had one of the axes. There would not have been a problem except that I forgot.

Hux and Wien came to me and said, We have not got all four axes.

Linkeree has the other, I said.

Then they became angry and said loudly, Why does Linkeree have the ax doing things he will not tell when all of us need the ax to cut wood? It is not right for him to have the ax alone when it is needed for all of us.

They were right, for this is J's law: No man or woman may use a tool when it is needed for another purpose by more people.

But to answer them I had to say, Linkeree did not know our need, and we do not know where he is to fetch it back.

Then they said, It is not right for us not to know, for the ax does not belong to him alone, and yet he has it where none but him can use it.

I said to them, Let three of you cut wood, and the other will make thatch.

But they would not listen, and Hux said loudly, so all in Heaven City would hear him, that he would go and follow Linkeree's trail in the forest so he could find him and fetch the ax.

Then I became angry and said just as loudly, so all could hear: You will not follow Linkeree. I am the man that J left as Warden, and I command you as J would command you, not to follow Linkeree, but to wait for his return, and then we will consider what to do.

Then Hux grew very angry, and so did Wien. They said many things. The worst thing they said was this:

Kapock, they said to me, you are not a good Warden, for J treats all of us the same, but you give Linkeree special treatment. You do not make him work as much as us.

And I held my tongue and did not speak, for they were right, and yet they were wrong, and I could not explain. It is true that Linkeree is not working at our tasks as much as the others are. This is because I let him go into the forest to do his unknown thing.

But Linkeree never goes into the forest until he has done as much work as others do. Linkeree is very fast and clever with his hands. He can make good thatch, the best that is made in Heaven City, faster than any other man or woman. When he works the same time as the others, his pile is twice as big. Likewise working with wood and even plowing and other things. Linkeree is not as strong as Wien, but he is clever and works fastest of all.

Thus I do not think it is unfair for him to not work as long as the others, for if he worked as long, would he not be doing more than others?

And yet all men are equal, and Linkeree cannot be given more than others are given. I do not give him more food. I do not give him more clothing, or more of any good or bad things we have.

But I do give him more hours when he is not told what to do. The others now tell me that this is not fair. They say that Linkeree should be in all things equal. Their words sound just.

But this is the question, I think, for Sara and I have talked many hours tonight about this: Does a man's or woman's time belong to all the people, or does his time belong to himself? His body belongs to himself, because no other man or woman can use it, except his wife, which he has not got. Speaking of Linkeree.

But does his time belong to himself? If yes, then when he has done an equal share of all the tasks, the time that remains is surely his own to spend as he wishes, and then I am right to let Linkeree go deep into the forest.

But if his time belongs to all of us, then it is not right for him to go into the forest, but he must work alongside us all, giving his time equally, even if he does more work during the time.

Which is right? I do not know. In my own mind, I think that a man's time is his own, for does not J give us all time alone, not telling us what to do? And I like best the things I do in those times. But the others say that such time is only a gift from J, and that J gave it equally, which is true.

I do not know which is right. I only know that I must do something to stop the others from being angry at Linkeree and at me. And yet it does not seem right to me that Linkeree should be stopped from what he is doing. If he would only tell us what it is he does in the forest.

Tomorrow all must work to build a good large fence and roof for the sheep for the winter, for there are many more sheep this year than last, and the old fence and roof are too small for them all. This will stop the argument for a day.

This is another important thing: My son Ciel has spoken a word today. He said, Sara, which is his mother's name. Sara was so happy that she sang all day, and Ciel said the word again tonight. Sara is happy because it means that maybe our child will be as clever as J's children which he brings from the Star Tower. I do not hope for this, for our children are weak and small. But I am happy because J's promise is going to be fulfilled: my children will speak, and then will read someday.

From now on Ciel and Mun I write to you, my son and daughter. And now I make an end of writing for this time.

Linkeree is a good man.

I write this because Linkeree is a good man and will not cause trouble anymore. I told him of yesterday's trouble with Hux and Wien. Linkeree was quiet for a little time, and then he said to me, Kapock, I will not cause trouble in Heaven City. I will work many hours like all the others, and will not go into the forest again at all during this time until the moon of the thaw. Maybe they will forget during the winter when there is deep snow.

This way we will not have the trouble, for Linkeree will no more take the ax.

Linkeree is lost.

I did not finish my writing of yesterday because there was a trouble after all. Linkeree went away during the night, and I stopped writing when Batta, one of the women who only a few months ago learned speech, came to me to tell me that Linkeree was not in his bed in the house with other unmarried people.

We called for him, but he did not answer. Batta said, We must look for him.

But I would not, because there is now snow on the ground, and if anyone got lost in the night he would die of cold before the morning.

Then in the morning before we could leave to search for Linkeree, he came to us of his own will.

I am ready to work, he said.

Everyone said, Where were you all night, and why are you not frozen in the snow.

But Linkeree would not say. He only said, I am ready to work. What more can you want from me?

And this is true. For J never commanded us to tell all things, but only to do all work in common. Our thoughts belong to ourselves: this J has always said. We can make no man or woman tell us her thoughts.

But Hux and Wien were very angry. I do not understand why Hux and Wien are always angry at Linkeree, for he does not make them hungry, and he does not make them cold; he hurts them in no way, but they do not like for him to do things they do not know about. They say it is not fair, but I do not think fairness is the question. I think that Linkeree makes them afraid.

Why are they afraid of Linkeree? Why does he make them angry doing this thing? I do not understand. For I, like Linkeree, look for time to be alone. I have found out that the hours I spend writing this are some of my happiest hours, like the hours I spent at the loom, making cloth, for no one takes my thoughts away from me during those times, except Sara, and when she talks my thoughts are not taken away, for I can tell my thoughts to her, and so I keep them.

And now, tonight, Linkeree is gone again, and the snow is falling. I am afraid that some danger will come to him. But at least now I know what he has done in the forest. All alone he has built a house. This must be so because there is no other way that he could have come to us warm and dry in the morning.

Linkeree with his fist, also. But I went to Wien and put my hand on his arm, and he did not strike Linkeree.

I did not know what to do, for such a thing had never happened before. This is what I said, and I fear it was not wise: Hux took that which he did not have a right to take—another man's bread. For this a good and just punishment is for him to lose his own dinner, which he has done. Therefore I will give no more punishment to Hux.

Then I said to Linkeree: You have built yourself a house, but this does not mean that you are not one of us, equal to all of us. When we have a problem we have always gone to the Warden or to J to have an answer. But this time you did not wait. You decided for yourself what the punishment should be, as if you were the Warden. You are not the Warden. You did not have the right to cause pain to Hux.

Linkeree could see that I was very angry, because he said, I am sorry you are angry, Kapock, and I am sorry that I struck Hux. I was angry, and I did not think first.

But this could not be enough. For if a man can make another man do his will by striking him hard, then Wien would soon be the Warden, for he is the strongest. And those who are not strong would soon be ruled not by justice, but by the desires of the strong. And did J not say, The strong man and the clever man and the kind man have equal gifts, and shall not rule over each other?

So I said that Linkeree must be punished, and his punishment must be like what he did to Hux. Therefore I said that Linkeree must stand while another man struck him as he had struck Hux.

Everyone thought that this was a just punishment, even Linkeree, though he looked afraid. But then, even though the punishment was just, no one was willing to strike Linkeree. Not even I, for it is too hard a thing to cause someone pain, even when they have caused it to someone else.

Then Sara said, I will do this, because the punishment must be carried out.

I forbade her.

But she said, I will do it because it must be done, but Linkeree must understand that I am not angry at him, but love him like everyone else here, or I will not do it.

I understand, Linkeree said.

Then Sara went to Linkeree and struck him very hard in the stomach. Sara is very strong, stronger than Linkeree, but because she was not angry she did not strike him with the same force that Linkeree had used with Hux. But Linkeree still bent in half with the pain, and cried out loudly, and all of us agreed that justice had been done.

But I am still afraid. For Linkeree and Hux now hate each other and are angry deep down inside them, where it does not heal, and I fear that other bad things will happen. Why did J make me Warden? I would rather be just Kapock who tends the sheep and works the loom. For if I stand between Linkeree and Hux they will hate me also. I am afraid that they already do. And yet I have only tried to be fair. But sometimes what is fair to the one person and what is fair to all persons are not the same fairness, and then how can I judge when I do not have J's wisdom?

I have written many hours into the night, but I cannot sleep even now. But I will make an end of writing at this time. My hand is tired.

Kapocks gonn and Im alone here at the house and so Im writing wat Kapock would write but hes not here. Im Sara and wats happend is worse than any of us thought. For Hux has hatid Linkeree bad for days, and so hes gonn and made things worst they can be.

Hux he hatid Linkeree even after I hit that good man as punishment for hitting Hux who deservd it. So he got the plan to marry Ryanno now instead of wait for spring when we can bild a house.

Hux he said how he and Ryanno did not have to wait to marry because already theres a house that is fine for them, a fine house

166

he said over and over. No need he said to bild a new house and so he and Ryanno did not have to wait for the snow to melt.

This was the hardist thing Kapock my dear husbind has ever decidid but he did his best. Wat could he do? For it was winter and we could not bild a house and the snow was deep, like it is today. Last year when Ally and Jobbin married they had to wait for spring and it was hard for them all winter not to couple when they wantid to so bad but that was the law.

Now there is a house why should they wait? But the house was bilt by Linkeree he did all the work. And yet never has any man or woman in Heaven City said to any other man or woman in need of his thing, No. Always we have said Yes what I have is yours all of it take wat you need.

If Jason was here he would have decidid but Kapock is Warden and whatever he decidid would make somebody angry. So he said to all people Wat do you think? And many said Linkeree should have the house but many more said It is not right for Hux and Ryanno to wait when there is a house.

And so Kapock did the thing that would anger the less people because he did not know wat is right.

And now all things are bad and I am afraid for Kapock is gonn like Linkeree into the night and it snows hard so I cannot even see the sheep behind the fense.

Hux is stupid and stubborn like the ox that does not move unless it is hit. I would want to hit him five or eight times but he would still be stupid.

Kapock said Hux could have the house and Linkeree got tears in his eys but he said If you think thats right Kapock I will do wat you say. Kapock he said thank you.

Then Kapock said In a week weel do all this like I said. But Hux was not happy yet, he said I want the house tonight and marry tonight. Ryanno she said Wait a week Hux we have no hurry. But Hux he got angry and said Tonight or youll all be sorry.

Kapock he said This is not fair Hux. Youll wait a week.

167

In the night Hux like an ox took Ryanno and his clothes and things and went in the darkness for there was a moon. They came into Linkerees house where Linkeree was sleeping and said Make room.

Linkeree he was very angry, but still he would not hit again for he promist.

So Linkeree came in the night to Kapock and said all that had happind and that Hux and Ryanno were in his Linkerees house.

Many people then went in the night to Linkerees house where Hux and Ryanno slept and Kapock said Why did you do this when I commanded you to wait?

It was not fair said Hux.

Jason said you should obey me like I am Jason said Kapock.

Then Hux he said When you decide wise like Jason I will obey like youre Jason.

Then my husbind Kapock got angry and when he gets angry he will not speak but instead is silent because he says When I am angry I am foolish.

And then Kapock said to all the people, Lets go home and sleep in Heaven City and decide what is right and wrong in the morning. But Linkeree said No, for Ive dunn all things like you said even giving up my house like you said now make Hux this ox do like you said, for Ive obeyd and hes broken all your words.

Then Hux he shoutid I will never leave this house unless you kill me to get me out.

And so Kapock said Please Linkeree lets not have more of this fighting this is so bad:

But Linkeree said I have dunn right and Hux has dunn wrong take him out. When Linkeree saw that Kapock would not do it because he wants no more fighting, Linkeree went to the door of the house he bilt and opend it to go in and fight with Hux. But Hux struck Linkeree with the little door that Linkeree had bilt for the other end of the house and Linkeree fell down with bleeding from his head and he didint get up we thought he was dead.

168

Then Kapock said to Hux, You are not one of us Hux. You are alone. You may not marry Ryanno I forbid it. Ryanno come to me.

And Ryanno who is a good woman came out of Linkerees house and came to Kapock. Hux he stood looking at Linkeree who lay so quiet and he said Im sorry I just wantid to keep him out of this house I was so angry but I didint mean to hurt him so bad.

But Kapock he just said You have killd a man and you will have no more food in Heaven City and no more friends in Heaven City. Live however you want but come to us no more.

Then Kapock had the men carry Linkeree back home.

But Linkeree he was not dead he was still alive and when Kapock saw this he cried and said Linkeree my friend youre alive youre alive and many others of us cried. Then we all went to sleep. I askt Kapock What about Hux? He didint kill Linkeree after all.

Kapock he said to me, Sara he didint care if he killd Linkeree or not. So let him go a night thinking that Linkeree is dead and then weel see how much he hits a man or woman again, I think never.

But this was again a wrong thing, yet how could my Kapock know? How could he know what Linkeree would do? Can he look into other mens hearts like Jason can and see the real truth inside them? No he cant. So he did the best he could and Jason if you read this Im saying to you Dont you blame Kapock because hes a good man and its not fair to tell a Warden he must be as wise as you because no man can be so wise and if you say he did bad and make Kapock feel bad I promise you Ill never love you again Ill always hate you and never do wat you say. Jason my husbind is a good man, he is the best man in all of Heaven City. Wat could he do?

Linkeree he took a burning branch from the fire and went in the dark morning before the sun and lit on fire the house he bilt. Hux he heard the flames and he run out of the house into the snow but all that he had except his own sleeping cloths burnd up in the house which is nothing but ashes and burnt up poles now.

All day we lookt for Linkeree we did not work because it was about to snow and we did not want Linkeree lost in the woods. But we did not find him and when we get back wat do we find? Batta is gonn too and with her much food and one ax and much cloths enouf for two people and so we know she is gonn to Linkeree. Did Linkeree come to her or is she also lost in the forest? We do not know.

And when the snow fell nobody would go looking any more except Kapock and he promist me he would not go eather but he is gonn and I know he is in the snow. This is the worst storm so far this winter it is very bad and I am afraid for Linkeree and Batta but most of all I am afraid for my Kapock. But he is full of darkness he said to me, he said Sara even you cant take this dark out of me.

Before Kapock went out alone I said Here is Hux who has dunn all these stupid things. I say lets put him out in the snow till Linkeree and Batta come back.

But Kapock he said No. He said, Hux did not mean to hurt Linkeree so bad he is just stupid and thinking only of hiself not of all of us. Hux he usd the laws to do a thing for himself just like he said Linkeree was doing, and now we know which of them both is trying to be better than others it is Hux.

This made Hux to cry.

But Kapock said We will not punish Hux any more now, we will wait for Jason to come back to us and Jason will say what Hux shall do. But I command this one thing. Hux will not marry for five years. As long as I have lived since Jason took me down from the Star Tower, Kapock said, that long will Hux not marry and not couple with a woman. This is my commandment in the name of Jason.

This time Ryanno cried and Kapock said Im sorry Ryanno this punishes you as bad as Hux, so I say you have no more promise to Hux but you can marry any man who wants you because you can see that Hux is not a good man right now he would not be good to you and a man must be good to his wife.

Ryanno said Its not fair.

And Kapock said There is no way to be fair Im not trying to be fair. Im trying to stop all of us from hurting each other any more and I dont care about fair I care about right. And it is right that Hux is treatid like one of the Ice People who comes down from the Star Tower knowing nothing saying nothing just crying and making nightsoil and eating and sleeping. Hux must be punisht so no other person will do like he has dunn. And besides, Ryanno, Kapock said, you did much things with Hux like going to Linkerees house early and you knew it was not right.

Then Kapock said to everybody Im going now to find Linkeree and Batta. While I am gonn you will obey Sara as if she were Jason or me. If I dont come back at all then you obey her until Jason comes back.

And he made all people promise but I said Dont go Kapock but he didint anser just went out of the door and into the snow which falls so fast.

Im writing all these things so that Jason will know the truth of wat has happind no matter what lies Hux and Ryanno try to tell.

Wat has happind to us it is not three moons yet since Jason left us and went into the Star Tower and now there has been much wrong and Linkeree and Batta and maybe Kapock are surely dead tonight who can live in this snow? It breaks branchis. It breaks even roofs tonight sometimes when it is so bad.

And I have not said to Kapock yet because he has been so worried but I am about to have another baby will this baby ever see his father? Even now in the early morning Ciel cries in his bed saying Kack, Kack, which is all he can say of Kapocks name I would suffer any pain if it only meant I could see Kapock at the door smiling at me Im so afraid Ill never see my husbind again.

Now has been three days Kapock and Linkeree and Batta they are gonn and nobody thinks theyll come back not even me. Jason why did you go away and leave us like this? If you were here Kapock would not be dead.

Now at last with three of our best people dead even my husbind now Hux and Wien and everybody they are being good and doing wat I say and not causing argumints. Hux does not even speak to anybody he is so ashamed but I want to spit on him everytime. I stay away from him because I would spit on him every time I see him. Today we are fix three roofs that broke in places during the bad storm it was so bad that one of the yung sheep it died of the cold. Even with its wool it died oh Kapock I cant write anymore now I am Warden but I want Kapock to be Warden and hell never be.

It is five days and today Hux wont eat. I hate him but I dont want him to die we made him eat anyway. I said Hux only the good people have died and I wont let you be like them. Then he cried but he did not try to not eat or to die any other way eather.

The snow meltid a little today the sun is up and hot for winter. Today we went out looking for them to find the bodies maybe but we couldint find any tracks for the snow had coverd all of it. I do not let myself cry at night anymore because it makes Ciel and Mun wake up and cry too and it is not good for these little ones to be unhappy when they do not even understand why.

Where Linkeree and Batta are and how we built a house.

I am Kapock and I have come back from my time in the forest with Linkeree and Batta. I have read all that my wife Sara has written, and she has written well, for the things she wrote are mostly important. She even now holds to me and cries because she is happy and tells me, Kapock, do not write that for I will seem foolish.

I said, Sara, you are foolish. It is why I love you, because I am foolish too. I cried when I came home. Ciel now says my name.

172

Sara has already written all things before I left and there is no need for me to add to this because she has written it well, though her writings are not always the way J has taught us to write.

I, Kapock, went into the forest and I was afraid because the snow was falling very fast and covering all the ground deeper than before and there was a wind that moved the snow so that the deep places looked like smooth ground. I called often in the darkness and the snow, but no one answered me. Then I thought to come back but I could not find the way, and as I searched I fell into a deep place and when I got out I was wet all over and very cold, and I knew I would die.

Then it was that Linkeree and Batta came to me, for they had heard my cries and by chance I was not far from the place where they were hiding. They had been afraid that I was coming to do them harm because they had burned the new house, but then they remembered that even though I was not always wise I had never tried to do them harm and they came to me.

Now this was how they had built a house: They found a place where two trees grew close to a steep hill. They cut long branches and put them between the low branches of the trees and between the trees and the hill making a roof. Then they covered it with many branches and dead leaves that they uncovered from the early snows. This way when the snow began to fall they already had a roof, and as the snow was falling they made walls out of branches leaning against the roof and they were dry. They made a small fire at the door of this house, and the wind blew the smoke away but also the heat, and even in blankets it was cold all that night.

In the day the snow still fell, but Linkeree and Batta and I decided that waiting would only make us freeze like the water of the Star River, and we must work to be warm. So Linkeree cut trees while Batta and I brushed snow from a place on the ground, even though the snow still fell, and then we moved the logs to the place and began to build walls. Linkeree and I built the walls as Batta kept sweeping out the snow. During the day the little house by the hill fell in from the snow on it, and so we hurried to finish the new house by dark, but we could not. So once again we only used the walls of the house which were about shoulder high to stop the wind, and we built a fire, and snow fell on our blankets and we were cold but the snow was not as bad as the wind, and so it was better that night and I did not freeze and neither did they.

Then the next day the snow was less, and we finished the walls, even with a door and a little door. Then we all made the roof frame out of logs and long, thin branches but we had no straw for thatch and so we used only leaves and this did well enough for this time, though water drips in many places. Also we made a door and a little door frame to cover the holes and on the third night we were warm and mostly dry.

Then I said to Linkeree, Who built this house?

You and Batta and I built it, he said to me.

Then who owns this house? I asked.

All of us, for we built it. If all of them had helped us build it, then it would belong to all of them.

This is true, I said. And now, Linkeree, I give you and Batta this house. It is no more mine, just yours and Batta's. But you must also give me something.

What can be as much as a house? asked Linkeree.

You must promise me, I said to them. You have to promise me that even though you will live just the two of you here, and will surely plant seed here and make a field just like the field at Heaven City, you will always be a part of Heaven City.

No, said Linkeree. I do not want to be a part of them.

But I said to him, This is a new thing you have done, and we did not know what to do. When you made the cloth for catching fish, none of us knew what it was for, did we?

No, he said to me.

But still it was good, and when we understood we all were made stronger and better by it. Now you also have learned from me and others. Is my woollen cloth not warm? Do you not put cloth in front of your door like I do in the summer?

174

But Linkeree said nothing. Then I said to him, Linkeree, my friend, you are wise like J, you think of things that no man has thought of before. We need you. But you also need us. How will you plow and plant without an ox? How will you do it without seeds? And we need you to help us make straight walls and to teach us the things you think of that have never been done before. You are part of us, and we are part of you. I said this to Linkeree.

Then he said to me, If I promise you to be part of Heaven City always, and obey, you must promise me that what I make with my own hands will belong to me and what Batta and I make together will belong to us.

And so I promised him this, even though it will surely make J angry, because I think it is more important for us to be together than it is for us to have all things equally. Yet it hurts me to write this, because it seems good to me that all men and women have things the same as each other. For now that Linkeree has his own field to plow and care for, we will be weaker, and he will be weaker, for we will not take care to put food in the mouth of our friend, but only in our own mouth. This is ugly to me.

When J comes again he will see what has happened and he will know that it is bad and he will not make me Warden anymore. I will be glad. And now I make an end of writing and I will write no more, because I do not want my children to read even this much, for it tells only of my foolishness and my children will be ashamed that I am their father, and J will be ashamed that I am his son. I make an end.

J comes in the night.

I thought never to write again, and for several moons I did not. But it is now the moon which at its end means we will plant, and tonight J came to my house in the night.

He came quietly and commanded Sara and me to wake no one. This is what he said:

Kapock, I come to see what has happened while I was in the Star Tower. But I do not want the others to know I came, for they must expect me only in the harvest moon, and not look for me at other times.

And so Sara and I promised.

Then J read all we had written. He cried twice. Once when he read what Sara wrote about J himself, and once at the end of it when I wrote. He said to me: Oh Kapock, you have done wisely, not foolishly. It was a hard choice and no one could have done better, not even me.

But I said, You could have done better, for you see into men's hearts and you would have known that Linkeree planned to burn the house, and that Hux planned to take it away from him.

And J said to me: That is true. But my power is not the power of a man, and you did all that a man could do.

And you, too, Sara, he said. You did wisely and well, and I will say the same punishment on Hux that you said, for there is nothing a man can do that is worse than what Hux did, which is to make another man do your will by striking him without thought for his life. And if a man kills another man, or a woman kills, either one, then the man or woman who has killed man or woman, he will also be killed.

And who will kill him? Sara asked.

All the people will kill him, Jason answered. This is an ugly thing, but it is the only way to keep a strong man from killing the weak who will not do his way.

I will never do it, Sara said.

But others will, J said. And I thought he looked sad as he said it.

Then J went out of the house and took me with him. The moon was not full, but it still was bright and so were the stars, and we could see for a long way. We could see even the mountains to the south, which are so far that we could never go to them.

J said to me, All of this that you can see, it is not even the hundredth part of the world.

I asked him what is the world.

He said to me, The world is round like a berry and we stand on its face. And it flies through the air.

I said to him, Is this why there is wind?

But he looked sad and said, No Kapock, for we move with it and do not feel its motion. But this I did not understand, for how can a thing move and not know that he moves?

But I asked him a question because he seemed to be ready to answer questions, and I asked him a question I had thought of often.

I asked him Who makes all these things? When you bring the Ice People from the Star Tower every year at harvest time and we feed them and teach them to walk and talk, where do they come from? And who made the Star Tower? And the forests? For I know who made the houses and the fields, for I make them myself. And I know who makes the children and the new lambs and the calf oxen, but I do not know what makes the Ice People.

Then he said to me a story, and I try to write it as I remember it.

Once J was in the sky with 333 of the Ice People, and the Star Tower flew like a bird only faster. Then an enemy came and with one hand killed 111 of the Ice People and with the other hand made 111 more of the Ice People sleep so they could never wake up, and then with his spit the enemy made even the last 111 Ice People forget all things.

Then J killed the enemy and brought the Star Tower to this world. There are many worlds, with many people, but this world was empty, and he brought the 111 Ice People who could waken out of the Star Tower and J said that Sara and I and all the others are these Ice People.

But there are not 111 of us, I said.

There will be, he said.

But I am foolish and I asked him, J, who made the Ice People, then? And who made this world if you only found it?

Then J shook his head and laughed softly and said, God did, Kapock.

177

But this is not an answer, because what is God? I asked him this, but he would say no more, except this: I have told you the truth, but you cannot understand it, neither can any of the others. I will tell you only the truth that you can understand.

This is why I have written all that J said, for somewhere in what he said must be the answer to my question of who made all these things, or of what this god is.

Then J and I went inside, and he said to me that the promise I made to Linkeree and that Linkeree made to me is a good promise, and that this will be the law of all men and women: What a man makes with his own hands is his own; what many men make together belongs to all who worked. When a man owns a thing that another needs, the other must give the man something that he needs in trade for this thing, and the trade must be fair, or it is a crime.

This is a new word, which I shall teach the people. Crime. J said it means those things which if all people did them would make a man want not to live among men.

J said many other things which I will not write because he said not to. I write these things because he did not say not to, and they are important.

After many hours in the darkness J left us, and after he left Sara and I could not sleep, and so I write. But now Sara sleeps and I too can sleep, and so I make an end of writing for this time.

We plow three fields.

The plowing is done and we have plowed three fields. First the field at Heaven City, which is the first and the largest. Then the field where Linkeree and Batta now live, which is not large, but which has black soil that feels warm and that will grow much food, I think.

The third field is at the place where Linkeree built the house that later he burned. We have all built a new house there, and into it Hux has moved. And we have plowed a field with Hux, and he will live alone.

But not alone. Rather only apart from the most of us. For I saw that Hux was truly sorry for all he had done wrong, and I believe that he will not let anger make him do such bad things anymore. So I called all the people of Heaven City together and asked them, one by one, saving only Linkeree and Batta, if they had any thing bad to think of Hux for anything he had done to them. And not one of them said anything bad except Sara, and she would not speak. Then I said to Hux, Neither do I have anything bad to say of you, Hux. Yet that is because no harm has been done to me.

I said to him, Linkeree and Batta are the only ones who can speak bad of you. And so I say this: Hux will be allowed to marry Ryanno and live in a new house which we all will build, but only if he asks permission of Linkeree. Then it will be Linkeree who gives Hux a house if he is to have a house. This is only right, for Hux took a house from Linkeree.

Then Hux went to Linkeree and asked him for a house, and Linkeree and Batta said, We will work with our own hands to help build you a house.

That is the house that Hux lives in now, and it has the little door just as Linkeree's own house has, and it is a good house, and when Hux and Ryanno moved into it all of us sang and there was dancing and laughing and we caught many fish and ate them because it was a good day, for even though we live in three places instead of two, we are one people.

And now tonight I thought of what J said to me that night and I think this: When J said, God made all this, he was laughing because I did not know that J made all these things, so he made up a name and said this person did it. Or maybe God is J's other name. But this I am now sure of: J brings the Ice People from the Star Tower, and he is thus the maker of the Ice People. He must also be the maker of other things, for if he can make a man whole, without it growing from a woman, he could surely make all other things. This is what I think. If I am wrong then J will think I am foolish. But then, I am foolish. Why should he not think it?

We have found another thing. The Star River is large, but it goes only a little way from Heaven City and then it flows into a great river, a river so wide that the other side looks as far away as the mountains, and the water is muddy and not good to drink. It is also deep, and a man or woman can only walk a little way and the water is up to the shoulders and the river pulls as if to sweep you away.

Now I see something that I did not know before. There are small rivers and large rivers. Alone, the small rivers are not strong, like the Star River that we can walk across. But when the small rivers flow into the large ones, then the large ones are stronger.

This is like Heaven City, for Linkeree and Hux live apart, yet they flow into the Heaven City like the Star River flows into this big river. And so I have named the big river Heaven River, and said to the people:

Flow always into Heaven City as you see the Star River flow into the Heaven River. Then Heaven City will always be as strong as you see this great river to be.

But if you flow in different ways, like the Star River does when it splits upstream into two rivers that pass on both sides of the hill I live on, then you become weak.

Not all the people understood me, but many did.

I did not tell them that J is God who made all these things. This is a thing I will keep without telling, for it is a hard thing, and I do not understand it yet.

I am no longer afraid to be Warden. For I know that J does not expect me to act always as he would act. Rather he expects only that I act in the best way I know how to act. And this I can do. And I make an end of writing for this time.

I have thought of J as a father.

Today Ciel spoke to me and said, Father let me come. I was going to shear the sheep and he said, Father let me come.

When he said this I knew that he would someday say other

180

things, and I felt then that someday Ciel will grow wise like the Ice People, and a son of my body may speak to me as my friends speak to me.

And then as I sheared the sheep I thought of J and knew that he is to us as I am to my son Ciel. He is wise and knows many things, all the words and all the names, what to do, when to do it, why it must be done, and what will happen if it is not. None of us knows these things, and we only say to him the things he has taught us to say. Even as I do with Ciel who cannot say all that we can say, J must long to speak to us about things that we could not understand.

I tried to tell Ciel why he could not play among the sheep, for they might hurt him for he is small, but he did not understand.

I laughed and shook my head. This is also what J did when I did not understand. Laughed and shook his head.

J is a father with all the children. He has no one he can talk to as I talk to Sara. He can only talk as I talk to Ciel, in simple words that even then are not always understood.

J is like a father, but he has neither wife nor friends nor father of his own. Or is that where he goes when he leaves us? Is there a father for him inside the Star Tower? I do not think so, for now I realize that J always looks sad and alone, not happy like I am with my son Ciel. I think J has no one but us to talk to, and we do not understand.

But I will try to understand, so that someday when J speaks to me I will be able to answer.

Then maybe he will take me into the Star Tower and show me all the secrets there and he will teach me how to make Ice People and all the other things he has made.

Sara is reading this and she is angry. She says that I am truly foolish to think that I will ever know all that J knows. She is surely right.

But still I hope. If the Star Tower can fly like a bird, will J not take me with him into the sky? When Ciel is old enough and wise enough I will take him with me everywhere I go, and teach him everything I know. Is this surely not what J intends for us as well? And so I say to J as Ciel said to me, Father let me come.

But for now I will only try to be wise and will study how to not be foolish like a child anymore. J will know when I am ready. And I make an end of writing for this time.

9

STIPOCK woke with the sleep helmet still on his head, and as he moved his arms to the sides, he realized to his surprise that he was still in his coffin. It had never happened before. His body was soaked in sweat from the waking drugs, and his mind refused to clear. Bright spots appeared in front of his eyes. He blinked. The spots went away.

He reached up to the sides of the coffin, pulled himself to a sitting position, and looked around.

Not a Sleeproom at all, he knew instantly. The mass of controls placed within arm's reach of a chair could only be a ship's control board. The space was cramped. Garol Stipock had never been in a warship before, but he had seen loops, and he recognized quickly that this had to be the control cabin of a ship of the fleet.

He also recognized the man standing at the head of the coffin, who said softly, "Is everything all right, Dr. Stipock?"

"Jazz Worthing," Stipock said, and his body flushed with heat as everything fit together—waking in a starship, and Jazz Worthing, one of the prime enemies of the people of Capitol, standing by his side.

183

"I'm in a colony ship," he breathed, the words not sounding real.

"Very quick," said Jazz Worthing.

"Why? I never volunteered—"

"Not so quick, then?"

"No," Stipock said. "We must have launched our little coup attempt. We must have lost."

"In a nutshell," Jazz said, "that's so. There are more ramifications, of course. But I doubt they'd interest you."

"They interest me very much. Who else was caught?"

"Everyone."

Stipock turned away, suddenly conscious of his nakedness, suddenly aware of how vulnerable he was. "Can I have some clothing?"

"The ship has it ready for you." The clothing landed in a pile in the foot of the coffin. Stipock clambered out of the box.

"Is there a shower first?"

The starpilot pointed, and Stipock went in, showered, urinated, and came back out and dressed. His thoughts began to settle down in the process. Colonies. Death. No more somec. The raw emotions never reached panic; instead he began to think: Adjust. Fit in. Get along. Survive.

"What kind of planet is this?"

"Agricultural," Jazz answered.

"Most are," Stipock retorted, "at first."

"This one always will be," Jazz said. "Fossil fuels are buried too deep to get to without metal tools. Copper and tin are extractable with wooden tools. Iron is only within three kilometers of the surface at one place, the middle of an uninhabitable desert. This planet will have a very hard time getting out of the bronze age."

Stipock was surprised at Worthing's attitude. "Don't you have any heavy equipment?"

"Yes," Jazz said.

"Then what's this about the bronze age?"

Jazz smiled. "Awake for three minutes, and already you know more than the captain."

Stipock flushed with anger, and grew angrier at himself because he knew that his pale skin always turned red when he was angry, making it impossible for him to hide his emotions.

"What am I supposed to do? Where are the others?"

"The others are all outside. You're the last."

Stipock didn't know how to take that. "Why last? Why in here, for that matter? I thought colony ships had a tape-and-tap."

"They do," Jazz said. "Ours isn't working."

"Why am I in here alone?"

"Your situation is unique, Dr. Stipock."

"Why? I wasn't even one of the leaders of the coup. I'm not about to cause any problems."

Jazz laughed. "Your existence at this moment is a problem. One which I created myself, I know, but I have to see what'll happen. Experimenting, you know?"

Stipock felt sick. He had seen the stolen loop, knew that Jazz Worthing was set to lead a rebellion of the Fleet to seize control of somec. But if Jazz's rebellion had succeeded—

"What are *you* doing here? I didn't think top level starpilots were exactly thrilled with colony assignments."

Jazz sighed. "That's the problem with using old tapes to wake you up with. You don't know a damn thing. Follow me." And Jazz turned on his heel and walked to the back of the control room, opened a door, and stepped through. Stipock followed, telling himself that he'd have to humor this man, but knowing that whatever his situation turned out to be, he'd hate it.

They went through a large storage compartment, with many large and small coffins, most of them empty and stacked out of the way. A few were still connected. "Ocelots just aren't needed in the ecology," Jazz explained casually, "and I decided skunks had no useful purpose either, just now. Avoid the nuisance, you know."

185

Stipock followed the starpilot to the end of the storage room, where he opened a door. Jazz Worthing watched him as he stepped through the door. Stipock looked around—there were three sets of gauges and dials grouped around three doors. He resisted the impulse to ask questions, though he could think of no good reason not to. He just didn't want to converse with a man whom he had long hated (from a distance) and who now had a great deal of power over him (from close up).

Jazz parted the seal on the door marked *A*, opened it, and stepped back. Stipock moved to the door and looked through.

Dazzling sunlight poured in through a long oval slit in the roof. It took a moment for Stipock to adjust to the light. When he could see clearly, he gasped. The long tube, which had been lined with coffins, was a ruin. All the metal was melted down, and a clear swath had been cut through. There was no way a single passenger in that section could have survived. "What happened?" Stipock whispered.

"An enemy ship. Two of them, as a matter of fact. I had a choice between letting a projectile hit the stardrive and vaporize us all, or letting it hit here, in the hope that some would survive."

"What a choice," Stipock said. "Were either of the other two tubes hit?"

"All the life support in *C* tube was destroyed by the heat of the projectile's passage," Jazz said. Stipock noticed that the starpilot formed some of the words and sentences with difficulty, as if he were unaccustomed to saying them.

"I was in *B* tube?"

Jazz smiled patiently. "Isn't that obvious?"

Then Worthing stepped into the ruined tube, and Stipock followed. They walked carefully along the tube. Stipock looked up as he passed under the tear in the roof. The sun was blinding. He looked away, covering his eyes. A purple spot blocked some of his vision. "Don't look at the sun," Jazz said.

"Thanks for the warning," said Garol Stipock.

They made their way to the end of the tube and didn't have to open a door, because the hole left by the projectile was ample.

They clambered through, and Stipock was horrified by what he saw—the tape rack mostly fused and melted by heat. "The memory tapes," he said. "Look at this—this is terrible."

Jazz reached out with his toe, and showed Stipock an empty slot in the lower right-hand corner of the B-tube tape rack. "That's where the only *B* tube tape that was usable was."

"Mine."

"Again, obvious."

Stipock leaned against the wall. "But what about the others? They won't have any memory at all, no training, no education. They'll be like infants. What are we going to do?"

"It's all been done."

Stipock was puzzled. "But how? If you didn't have the tapes —you said I was the last one wakened! Why? How long did you leave me asleep after landing?"

"Fifty-eight years."

It was too much to understand all at once. Bad enough to wake up from somec and find that your last waking had been wiped and you were in the colonies, irrevocably off somec until you died—that much he had bargained for, had known the risks when he joined the conspiracy. But the deaths of two-thirds of the colonists in a battle in space, and then the loss of every survivor's tape except his own—

And why had he been left asleep for fifty-eight years?

"It wasn't an easy decision," Jazz said, answering Stipock's unspoken question. "A dozen times that first year I headed for the Star Tower—for the ship—to waken you. I needed your help."

"Then why didn't you? Because I was a rebel against your conspiracy? In a case like this, you forget political differences. Captain Worthing, I would have helped you."

Jazz smiled slightly. "Would you?"

"Damn right!" Stipock said. "Damn right! Of course I would!"

"Well, that's the question, isn't it? Whether you'll help me, or whether you'll work against me."

"Now? Aren't they all functioning adults by now?"

Jazz nodded, then went to the door from the schoolroom to *B* tube, opened it, went in. Stipock followed. Most of the coffins were empty, standing open. But twenty of them were occupied. Jazz touched each one as he passed, said a name. Most of them Stipock recognized—Fritz Kapock, the designer; Sara Hamilton, a wholesaler who had been one of the foremost leaders in the rebellion; Arran Handully, the best-known actress in the Empire and a primary financial backer of the rebellion. Others he didn't know, of course—he hadn't been that high in the ranks of the rebellion, to know everyone.

"Why are they still here? I thought you said I was last?"

"They aren't *still* here," Jazz answered. "They're back here. These are the ones who have proved themselves—the most creative, the most capable, those best able to lead. I bring them back here to sleep, so I can use them again."

"You still have people on somec," Stipock said. "But that's absolutely forbidden in the colonies."

"You worry about law?" Jazz asked. "You're the man who invented the probe, Garol Stipock."

Stipock flushed again, was embarrassed again that his anger showed so obviously. "I also invented the geologer, which you no doubt used for your planetary survey."

"Of course. I'm just pointing out that in special circumstances, law-abiding people break laws. You must admit these circumstances are special."

"When the next Empire ship comes, let's see what they say about it."

"There won't be any Empire ship," Jazz said. "We left Capitol more than a thousand years ago."

Another piece of unassimilatable information. "A thousand years! Then we must be—"

"Very, very far from the pale of human settlement. And the Empire doesn't know we're here."

"Why!"

"Does it matter? Here we are. Now I'll explain this carefully,

188

and you'll listen carefully, and we shall see what happens next. Dr. Stipock, these people all had empty minds, like infants. No conditioning from Capitol culture. No knowledge of somec."

"They know *now,* anyway," Stipock interrupted.

"I said listen. They know nothing about the universe except what I could teach them. They know nothing about law except what I have taught them. And in all of this, I was limited by what they could understand. On Capitol, children were surrounded by the artifacts of civilization. All the little gadgets that kept us alive and made life fun. How many people on Capitol actually know how those things work?"

Stipock snorted. "Almost no one."

"Only the specialists. Now if people who see these things and use them every day have no idea how they work, how could I explain, say, a laser to these colonists, who have never seen one?"

"I never thought of that. They don't have a fragment of the science of the last four thousand years, then," Stipock said. "What have you done?"

"I haven't tried to teach them."

"But they should know! They have to know—"

"Why? On a planet where the technology they and their children will have can't possibly extract iron or aluminum from the earth? On a planet where coal is inaccessible and oil even harder to get? Should I tell them about star travel and telephones and loops and food processors and tubes and toilets? Should I tell them that they're living in squalor and ignorance and make them hate their lives?"

Stipock shook his head. He sat on an empty coffin, looked at his hands. "But not to tell them *anything.* Captain Worthing, I couldn't do it."

"Yes you could," Jazz said. "I even tried to tell them. But they didn't understand. I told them I brought them down from the sky in the ship, and they decided that I must be superhuman. How could I explain the science of the stardrive? They have no need for higher mathematics—it would just be a game to them,

189

and a pretty damned hard one. None of them has time to learn things that can't be used—it takes all their time from dawn to dark just to stay alive."

"It sounds like hell."

"They're completely happy."

"That's hard to believe."

"Only because you remember the Empire, Stipock. If you forgot the Empire, you'd live like them and be happy, too."

"What do they make of things like the starship, then?" Stipock asked. "If they don't know about technology, what do they think of the fact that you're still young after fifty years or so, that these people you've got in here don't get any older?"

"They think," Jason said, "that I'm God."

Stipock laughed uproariously. "Well, I hope you set them straight on that!"

"I never tried," Jason answered, shrugging.

"You're joking," Stipock said, and then saw that he was not. "What are you doing, setting yourself up here as the local deity? What right do you have to force them into superstition and ignorance?"

"The ignorance is unavoidable. And they made up the idea that I was God all by themselves."

"You could have told them it wasn't true."

"And accomplished what? You've been pampered all your life, Stipock, just like everybody else in the Empire. Well, they've got a hard life out there, and no precedents, no parents, no one to teach them. Except me. I'm their parents and their teachers and their ties with the past. They needed a foundation, and I'm that foundation. Why else do you think people believe in God? They can't live without faith."

Stipock was silent, said nothing, but told himself, This man is insane. This man is playing God with people's lives. I've got to stop him somehow.

"Garol Stipock," Jazz said, "you can try to stop me all you like. As long as all you do is talk, and as long as you obey the laws."

"The laws? You're the laws, aren't you?"

190

"I wrote them. But they stand alone now. The government is entirely in their hands. I visit now and then, to install a new Warden, to take people who've excelled into the ship to sleep. You won't find it oppressive."

Stipock got up and walked out of the tube. He didn't look back to see if Jazz was following or not—the footsteps behind him soon told him that. He went back to the control room, and went to the door that led outside. He began unlocking it, but when it came to unfastening the seal, it wouldn't budge.

"Sorry, Stipock. Keyed to my thumbprint. And in case you get any ideas, it's keyed to my *living* thumbprint. Wrong temperature, no pulse, and no electric current, and the door won't open. In fact, if I'm dead and I touch the button, the control room blows up. The Fleet's little anticapture system."

"Are you keeping me a prisoner here?"

"It depends on what you plan to do when you go out there."

"I plan," Stipock said grimly, "to tell them all what a lying crazy bastard you are."

"Still a rebel," Jazz said. "Do you think they'd believe you?"

And Stipock calmed down, slumped as he realized how stupid his impulse had been. He would be a stranger to them all. Why should they believe him?

"Garol," Jazz said, "strange as it may seem, I know how you feel. A man once played God with my life, and I hated him for it for a while. But eventually I realized that what he was planning was good. I still had no choice but to obey him—but I didn't *want* another choice. The vision was good.

"I have a vision of this world, Garol. I imagine it being a simple, peaceful place, where people are *happy,* by and large. I at least want to give it a good start. And if that means giving them a deity to worship until they no longer need one, then I'll give them a deity."

"Why did you even wake me?" Stipock said. "Why did you even use that tape?"

"Well, as for that, if you don't cooperate, I'll simply put you back to sleep and wake you as I woke the others, with no tape at all. So in the long run you'll be part of the colony one way or another."

Stipock laughed bitterly. "Then put me under, because the way I feel right now, I'm sure as hell not going to cooperate."

"You're a brilliant man, Stipock," Jazz said. "There have been only eleven significant advances in Empire technology since the beginning of the somec. Four of them were yours."

"Four?"

"I count the probe. Stipock, I don't think the way you do. I can help people solve their human problems, and I've taught them everything I could learn out of the ship's library. But I can't *invent*. And in a world with no metal, they need invention. *We* need it. Now if I put you under and woke you up mindless, maybe you'd still become an inventor and maybe not. Kapock was a designer and he still has great sensitivity—but Linkeree was a businessman and now he carves in wood. You see?"

"So you do need me."

"We can survive just fine without you. But I want your help."

"I won't help you as long as you're playing God, Captain Worthing."

Jazz shrugged. "It's your choice. I'm walking out of here in three days. They expect me then. Either you'll come with me as you are now, or you'll come with me as an infant in a box. Up to you."

Stipock shouted, "You really believe you're God, don't you, juggling with people's lives as if they didn't have anything to say about it!"

Jason sat down at the control board, swiveled the chair around to face Stipock. "People never decide the major events in their lives, Dr. Stipock. The major decisions are made for them. The only things that people decide are the minor things. Whether they'll be happy or not, for instance; whom they'll love and whom they'll hate; how trusting they intend to be. You can decide to trust me, and I'll decide to trust you, and then maybe you can be happy, if you've got guts enough to be."

Stipock, bright red with rage, leaped for Jazz Worthing—no

192

clear plan in mind, of course. Just a vague but overpowering urge to cause pain. And pain was, indeed, caused. Stipock lay on the floor, holding his arm.

"That'll be a nasty bruise, Dr. Stipock. Remember—you may have won a few duels on Capitol, but the Fleet trains its soldiers to win. And I always will."

A gross misappropriation of funds. Stipock thought humorlessly. He felt the anger and humiliation of a cripple—unable to control his own fate, hopelessly trapped and yet capable, completely capable, if only he could set himself free of his handicap.

Jazz stayed busy the rest of the day, and Stipock began looking over his shoulder. He began wondering, from time to time, why Jazz was so calm and easy about having him loose in the control cabin, as if he posed no threat at all. But from time to time—in fact, whenever it occurred to him to try to attack the starpilot—Jazz would almost playfully, absentmindedly flash out a hand and bruise Stipock, a sharp, quick pain somewhere on his body. A reminder. And Stipock would put down any idea of resistance.

What Jazz was studying, and what Stipock read over his shoulder, were charts and readouts from the computer on probable population figures, depending on different variables. Now and then, curiosity aroused, Stipock would ask a question. "Which of these is accurate?"

"All of them. But the best predictor seems to be the max-max-mini figures—maximum fertility, maximum available resources, minimum environmental hostility. The people out there seem to like having babies. At least, they don't want to quit having them bad enough to invent twin beds," Jason answered, and Stipock couldn't help laughing.

And reports, all written by Jason himself, on the progress of the colony under each Warden. The names were all familiar—Kapock, Steve Wien, others that he had known or heard of. "Who's this Ciel?"

"Kapock's oldest son. Second generation. The first native-born that I appointed as Warden."

193

"Why do you call them Wardens?"

"I like the word."

"And why call it Heaven City, and the Star River, and all this other mumbo-jumbo."

"I like mumbo-jumbo."

Angry again, Stipock went away from the control and fumed quietly in a corner for a few minutes. He and Jazz spoke no more that day, until Jason yawned, looked at his watch, and said, "Time to sleep."

"Not for me," Stipock said.

"When I sleep," Jazz said, "you sleep."

And Jazz had a needle in his hand. Stipock leaped to his feet, bounded away to comparative safety by the door to the storage room. "Don't come near me with that."

"You're afraid," Jazz said, "that once I have you asleep normally, I'll put you under somec. Well, I won't. When I put you under somec, you'll know it."

"I'm supposed to believe that?"

"Got any choice?"

There was a struggle anyway, a brief scuffle that Jazz won handily, and Stipock soon slept.

Lights up. Stipock opened his eyes. Jazz Worthing was leaning over the bed, and Stipock sighed in relief. Awake another day, with memory intact.

Breakfast out of the ship's paste. Tasted foul. "Well, the ship has been out for over a thousand years," Jazz said, smiling pleasantly as Stipock grimaced and forced it down. "Usually they're refitted within a century. Time does things to flavor."

After breakfast, more reports, and Stipock began to get a feel for the community outside the starship. By lunchtime he had even conceded to himself that Jason had really done remarkably well, turning mindless infants into a functional, working society in only five decades—and without being there much of the time.

"I can see," he finally said, "that their worship of you served

194

a real purpose for a time. Continuity. Their awe of you lent authority to the Warden, kept them together."

Jazz turned around in amazement. "Do I hear *you,* Garol Stipock, the perfect judge of right and wrong, actually commending *me,* the man who plays God, of doing something right?"

Stipock turned red and Jazz laughed. "I told you that before. But you wouldn't believe me. Just like a scientist. Perfectly willing to decide what's right and wrong without recourse to the evidence."

"When I saw the evidence," Stipock said grimly, "I changed my mind."

Suddenly more mild, Jazz said, "Sorry. I didn't mean to mock. And I'm glad you saw my point."

"Then I hope you'll see mine," Stipock said. "This God thing can't be forever. Let's make a bargain. Let me go out there, let me live there for at least a year. I'll be 'inventive' or whatever you expect of me—I'll try to find ways to improve their lives with the limited resources. I'll help build up your colony. I'll obey all the laws."

"Bargain?" Jason asked. "And what will I do for you in this bargain?"

"You'll simply let me teach. I won't undermine the Warden's authority. I'll just try to wean them away from their belief in this God you've become to them."

"By teaching?"

"Persuading."

"You realize that if you try to teach them that I was a traitor to the Empire, which your little conspiracy believed, they'll either not understand, or they'll get very upset at you."

"I'm not a fool," Stipock said, "at least not usually. I know enough to avoid getting people angry. Peaceful means. Let me try to change their minds. Or do you like being God so much you won't even take a chance?"

Jazz cocked his head and looked intently at Stipock's eyes. "You mean you'd promise to obey all the laws, to build up the community in every possible way, in exchange for my allowing you to teach people that I'm not God?"

"I promise it now."

"It must be worth a lot to you to unthrone God," Jazz said.

"If there were a God," Stipock said, "I wouldn't fight it. But when a normal man acts the role, then I'll unmake him the best I can."

"Well, then," Jazz said, "I think that's a fair enough bargain. If you can persuade them, then fine. But I warn you—I'll give the Warden power to imprison you if you incite or perform one act of violence. Even one. Agreed?"

Stipock hesitated, then nodded. "But I won't be responsible if some crazy person takes an idea into his own head—"

Jazz laughed. "This isn't the Empire, Stipock. The Wardens are all just. They try to be fair. And usually succeed."

"Who's the Warden right now?"

"Hop Noyock," Jazz said.

"Your agent?"

"Was. But since I don't have any more income, his ten percent is gone, too."

Jazz held out his hand. Stipock took it, and they struck the bargain. Afterward Stipock laughed. "I can't believe making a bargain without lawyers and contracts."

"This isn't the Empire."

"Why are you trusting me?"

"Because," Jason said, "I have the foolish belief that I can see into people's hearts. I've looked into yours."

"A rather dismal place, wasn't it?" Stipock said, playing along with the joke.

"No more so than normal," Jazz said, smiling. "You still hate me. But I can trust you to keep your part of the bargain.

"And," Jason added, "you can trust me to keep mine."

10

NOYOCK laid down the pen on the table and rubbed his eyes. He shouldn't have left the writing until the last minute. But the History had to be kept. Not since the first day of the first Warden, Kapock the Eldest, had any Warden failed to keep the History, and Noyock prided himself on being more thorough than any of them.

A rooster crowed, and then another, as if in answer. Noyock reached over and opened the shutter slightly. Still dark—someone must be walking the chickenyards, then. But perhaps it was nearly morning. Was the sky a little lighter? Had to sleep. Jason coming today, he muttered to himself. Yawned again. Jason today, and the History is ready.

Noyock stretched, and left the room he had set aside for his duties as Warden—his planning, the History, meetings with individuals and couples, when the problems or questions weren't appropriate for open discussion. This, too, was new, since Jason had left. He will be pleased, Noyock told himself. I hope he's pleased.

Below him, he could hear the clank of tin pans, the dull sound of a wooden spoon stirring rapidly in a clay pot. Who this morning? Riavain, Noyock's own wife? Or his daughter-in-

197

law, Esten, Wien's eldest daughter, who had married Aven in a joyful ceremony—how many years ago? Thirty. Noyock chuckled. Poor Aven, he thought. My poor son, now more than fifty years old, while I look scarcely older than I did the day Jason brought me down from the Star Tower, they all tell me.

And Noyock paused to think about Jason for a moment, to think of the miracle of dwelling in the Star Tower, because no one who dwelt there with Jason ever aged. They could go in, as Noyock had done, leaving their children in their twenties, and come out to find that their children seemed to be older than they. Poor Aven. But no, aging was a part of life, the natural pattern of things. Like the cows and horses that grew old and died. It was not poor Aven. It was blessed, lucky, favored Noyock and Riavain and all the others who had been taken into the Star Tower; and thinking of Jason's goodness to everyone in Heaven City, Noyock's eyes filled with tears, and he wondered if he wasn't getting old after all, and just as he thought that, he heard a roar from downstairs.

"Lying to your father on top of disobedience! What kind of child have I brought forth!"

Aven, Noyock thought to himself, and doubtless poor Hoom was the object of Aven's wrath. Aven had always been obedient, deferent, careful. And now the poor man was cursed with a son who was wilful, forgetful, prone to disobey. But, Noyock remembered with a chuckle, the boy was a hell of a lot more fun to have around than his father had been. And Noyock had often spent hours with Hoom as he was growing up, teaching him, answering the boy's questions, asking his own. Bright boy.

The slapping sound of a leather strap. Ah, thought Noyock. This is a bad one, then. Noyock debated whether to go, for though he tried not to intervene in the way Aven raised the boy, he had often found that by simply appearing on the scene, Aven's anger was tempered, and Hoom was spared the worst.

Noyock went down the stairs to the second floor (remembering, proudly, that his farm and cattlefields had been so successful that he was the first in the whole of Heaven City to have a house with *three* floors. *And* a basement) and then turned, going up the hall to the small room that was Hoom's own, unshared with his sisters or his brothers.

"And that," said Aven's voice, now low and fierce with the exertion of the whipping, "is what happens to boys who disobey. And that," with the fall of the strap again, "is what happens to boys who lie!"

Noyock stood in the door. Hoom was kneeling at his bed, soundless as his father brought the strap down again on his naked back. Large welts were rising, but Noyock calculated that Aven could be hitting a good deal harder, and so didn't intervene, only walked in a little farther and cheerfully said, "That brings the count to eleven."

Aven brought the strap down again. "Let's make it an even dozen then, and be done."

He took the strap and hooked it through his belt, then faced his father. "Well, father," Aven said, "you see how my patience has finally been pushed too far."

"I do indeed," said Noyock. "And what did the boy do this time?"

"I come here in the morning to wake him, and find him in here half-dressed. I think, 'The boy's getting up early to help,' and come in to give him a hug and clap him a good-morning, and by damn his clothes are wet! Been down by the river again! Down playing water games with that little bastard Wix, no doubt. But I says to him, 'Did you sleep well?' And he says to me, 'Very well, father. Didn't stir all the night long.' And I'll not put up with being disobeyed and lied to on top of it all!"

"So I see. Well, the boy's strapped well, now, isn't he?"

"And I hope it hurts him long enough that he learns to obey his father." And with that Aven stalked righteously out of the room.

Now, in the silence that followed, Noyock could hear the boy's labored breathing. Crying? Either that or trying very hard not to, which amounts to the same, Noyock decided. But no need to let the boy wallow in it. Good cheer: "Well, Hoom, my boy, today's Jason's homecoming."

Grunt from the face in the blankets.

"And today your grandfather's been Warden for one solid year. Four to go. Better this time than the first. What do you think, will Jason have me out, or keep me on?"

No answer at all.

"I suppose that's a trivial question to you right now, Hoom. But it plagues me a far sight more than anything else right now. What's troubling you? I know the pain's a trifle to you—what's your sorrow?"

Mumbles.

"And only God heard that remark. Have you nothing to say to me?"

Hoom lifted his face from the blanket. His cheeks were tear-streaked, but his eyes were aflame with hatred. "I want to kill him," the boy hissed. "I want to kill him!"

The words were like knives to Noyock, who couldn't bear such words being said within his family. But he only smiled. "Ah, it isn't the pain at all, then, is it, because if it was the blows, you'd only want to thrash him. It's the shame, isn't it, of being beaten."

Hoom started to argue, then thought better of it, and Noyock took note of the boy's increasing maturity, that he'd change his mind so readily when he knew the other side had the truth. "Yes," Hoom said. "It's the shame."

"Well, Jason's coming today, and all shames are forgotten."

"Not all," Hoom said. "He forbids me to spend time with Wix."

"He's your father."

"Father or not, Wix is my friend! I didn't choose my own damn father! And I did choose my friend!"

"Well, you're thirteen," said Noyock. "In only eleven months you'll be fourteen, and come of age, and no father or mother can tell you what to do or not to do."

"But by then Wix'll have it done! And I won't have had a part in it!"

"In what?"

"Logs on the river!"

"Ah," Noyock said. "That again. But Wix is so impractical! Why go out playing on the river, with the current as dangerous and swift as it is, when we have no need to travel on it?"

"But the city'll grow, grandfather! Wix says there'll come a time when a floor of logs on the river will carry cargo from one end of Heaven City to another!"

"You can't even guide your silly logs," Noyock said. "The river isn't an ox, to be tamed by men."

Hoom turned away in ill-hidden disgust. "No, you're as bad as father."

"Probably worse," Noyock said. "I love you like he does, but I haven't the courage to try to stop you from drowning yourself. If it was up to me, I'd say, 'Let the boys experiment. Let them learn the only way they ever will'."

"I wish you were my father!" Hoom said.

"Too late to arrange that," Noyock answered, laughing. "But go on down to breakfast. Jason's coming today."

Suddenly concerned, Hoom said, "Are my eyes red? Does it show that I was crying?"

"Not a bit. But I'd advise you to put on some clothes, boy. Your mother's likely to belt you a good one if you come naked to breakfast." Hoom laughed, and so did Noyock; and the Warden left the room, wishing that all the unhappy people in Heaven City could be so easily comforted.

Breakfast was placid, except when Aven started telling how Niggo the tailor had nearly beaten Wix within an inch of his life, because the boy had been teaching Niggo's nine-year-old daughter to swim. "That'll teach young hooligans to keep their hands off young children."

The point of the remark was too sharp to miss, and Hoom piped up in his changing voice, "She asked him to teach her. He didn't want to, but she pestered him until he did."

201

"Nevertheless," Aven pontificated, "if Jason had meant for human beings to swim, he'd have given us scales and fins."

Hoom's eyes flashed with anger, and he said sarcastically, "And if God had meant for men to plow, he'd have given you blades for feet."

Aven grew furious immediately, and a crisis was averted by the arrival of the bacon and Noyock's loud laughter. "My son and my grandson, both prizes for their wit!" The desire for a quarrel passed quickly, and overzealous mouths were soon filled with dripping fat. "I say that even if hogs are disgusting creatures," Aven commented with his mouth full, "they're certainly good once they're dead!"

And Noyock answered, his mouth even fuller, "And let us say the same for fat men, too!" and everyone laughed, for they had nothing but contempt for the tailors and weavers and woodcarvers who sat all day at their tasks, while Noyock and Aven and all their family, keepers of cattle and tillers of fields, considered loose skin at their waist to be a sign that they'd been slacking.

The breakfast over, they gathered cloaks against the wind and headed out of the house, down the dirt road, and joined the crowd trickling along the new road that was generally called Noyock's Road. Noyock was justly proud of it—for though Cooter the wagonmaster had suggested the idea to two other Wardens, only Noyock had caught the vision of it, and found a way to do it.

The trouble had been that no one wanted to donate time just to spread small rocks over the surface of the road. So Noyock had assessed, not time, but goods from the older, wealthier people, and had paid those goods to younger men whose farms were not yet producing, or who were still learning the trade. That way the older men didn't have to waste their time on a public job, while the younger men could work for the general good—and not starve in the process.

The result was good. A summer of frequent rain had proved it: while every other road in Heaven City was a morass of mud,

202

Noyock's Road, which led from the Main Town, past Noyock's Town, over the crest of the hill, and down to Linkeree's Bay —the water ran right off or soaked right through, and not a wagon was stuck all summer. And now, with the evidence before their eyes, there'd been no trouble persuading the people to spread the small stones on all the streets of Main Town, and much of Wienway Road—clear to the forge. Jason would be pleased.

Firstfield was full already. The census last winter had brought a total of 1,394 people in Heaven City. Twenty had been taken into the Star Tower. Eight had died in all the history of Heaven City, of accidents or, in the case of a few of the Ice People, of the strange, inexplicable maladies of old age. Noyock had no hope of counting how many babies had been born since winter— these days it seemed that every woman was pregnant, and Linkeree's son Torrel had told Noyock, "Every third person wants a cradle these days."

Noyock came and stood on the Warden's place, and watched to see when the rising sun would be completely hidden behind the slender shaft that stuck out from the front of the Star Tower—the place where Jason lived. It was only a few minutes' wait, and then the citizens of Heaven City sighed with pleasure and fulfilled expectation when the dark place appeared at the front of the Star Tower, and the slender line descended slowly to the ground.

But Noyock's pleasure turned quickly to dismay. Jason was not alone. And the only time he ever brought an adult from the Star Tower was to put one of the sleepers into office as Warden. Have I done so badly this year, Noyock wondered, that Jason is already replacing me? But that would be unfair—he hasn't even inspected my work! And I did very well the first time I was Warden—not fair!

But as the line descended more and came closer, Noyock realized that the man with Jason was a stranger. Blond and pale, he had obviously never been in the sun; but he looked strong enough, and intelligent—but who was he? Noyock knew all the Ice People, and recognized by sight everybody over ten years of age in the whole city. This one was new.

Jason and the stranger touched the ground, and Jason strode from the chair he rode in, holding out his arms, greeting all his people. They leaped to their feet. They cheered. They cried out. They wept and laughed and some sang. And, representing all of them, Noyock came forward to embrace Jason. But Noyock couldn't conceal his uneasiness, and Jason, as always, saw into his heart. As they embraced, Jason whispered, "Noyock, my friend, this man isn't here to replace you. You're doing well, and you are still Warden with all my confidence."

And so Noyock was free to be curious rather than concerned about the stranger. Until it occurred to him that this man must be—

"The hundred eleventh Ice Person!" Noyock called out in realization.

"What?" Jason asked. But Noyock had already turned around to face the crowd. "Jason has brought with him the hundred eleventh Ice Person. The last of the Ice People! As Kapock prophesied in the History! The last of the Ice People has come!"

The people were awestruck, and Noyock barely noticed the helpless expression on Jason's face as he beckoned the stranger to come forward. "You see?" Noyock heard Jason say, but he didn't understand why. Jason stepped forward, bringing the stranger with him, and he raised his hand for silence.

"Your Warden is right," Jason said. "This is the last of the Ice People. And he is uniquely gifted! Of all the Ice People, only Stipock has come from the Star Tower with the power of speech. He is a wise man in many things—but he is like an infant in other things, and you must be patient with him!"

(Did I see the stranger glare at Jason? Noyock wondered. Why should he be angry?)

"His name is Stipock. Will you build him a house?"

Of course the people shouted, "Yes," and the meeting broke up immediately—it had lasted longer than any other Greeting in the History, and because of the stranger it seemed that the tumult

204

afterward lasted longer, too. Everyone had to touch Jason, talk to him, see if he remembered them, show him the new children, ask him a question, tell him how well things were going. And then the more curious—and the majority were very curious— had to come meet the new Ice Person.

"Stipock," they all said, trying out the name. "Welcome to Heaven City."

Noyock watched as Wix (the problem! The thorn in everyone's side!) came to Stipock and fixed him with that cold, painful stare, and asked, "Why are you able to talk, when all the others who came from the Star Tower were like babies?"

Stipock glanced at Jason (Why do I keep thinking they're adversaries? Noyock asked himself), saw that he wasn't looking, and said, "Because my memory tape was the only one that survived the wreck of the ship in space."

Dead silence fell over the group. Someone muttered, "He makes words, too, just like Jason." But Wix only sneered and said to everyone and to no one, "Anyone can make up words." And then to prove his point, the fifteen-year-old man said, "Because my memory glibbit was the only one that survived the wreck of the mumblebunk in tiddiewart." Though Wix was irritating to practically everyone, they couldn't keep from laughing.

And Noyock wondered why the stranger was turning red. Embarrassment? Anger? Ah well. He'd need a place to stay until the new house could be built—so Noyock went to him and said, "I'm Noyock, the Warden. Would you be willing to live with me until we can build you a house?"

"I don't want to put you out," said Stipock.

"We won't *leave*," Noyock said hurriedly. "We'd stay there, too. It's a big house."

Stipock seemed as if he wanted to explain something, then thought better of it, and followed as Noyock led him out of the crowd.

Several people followed them up Noyock's Road toward Noyock's Town, the cluster of houses mostly belonging to Noyock's children and grandchildren that fringed the road near the crest of the hill. They wanted to hear Stipock speak—he had a different way of saying things that was very amusing, and no one was sure what to make of Jason's latest miracle.

The farther they walked up the hill toward Noyock's house, the stronger the smell of the cattle pens became. To Noyock it was the smell of home; the smell of prosperity. But Stipock wrinkled up his nose and said, "Can't you do something with the smell?"

Noyock was startled, then laughed. "And what can you do with a smell, when no one knows what it looks like, or how to take hold of it?"

Stipock didn't answer, and Noyock wondered if the man had a sense of humor. A person who can't laugh is only half a human, Noyock firmly believed. Why had Jason created this half-man, and brought him here?

Stipock stepped in a pile of fresh cow manure that was sitting in the middle of the road. He lifted his foot and asked, "What's that?" He sounded irritated.

"Cow manure," Noyock said, puzzled that the man wouldn't know.

Stipock walked from the road to the thick grass and hurriedly rubbed it off his shoes.

"If you didn't want it on your feet," Noyock asked, genuinely confused at the man's actions, "why did you step in it?" Stipock only shook his head, and wiped his feet some more.

Late that night, Noyock retreated to the room where he worked on the History. But tonight he couldn't bring himself to write anything. He just stared at the paper, and at last passed the time by drawing maps of his farm as it was, and as it should be within a year, five years, ten. Meaningless. He was tired—he had only managed a two-hour nap in the afternoon. But he couldn't sleep.

All day Jason had been going through Heaven City, visiting with people, talking to them, asking what they thought about this, what they felt about that. As always the Warden was forbidden to come along. So instead, Noyock had had the increasingly odious task of dealing with this creature Stipock. He wasn't sure how he was going to broach the subject with Jason, but he certainly wished Jason would take the man back into the Star Tower with him.

Questions. "Why do you do this? Why do you do that?" When Stipock asked Aven, "Why do you let your wife do all this cooking while you just come in and sit at the table, expecting to be fed?" Noyock didn't even try to stem the outburst. Aven was at his furious best. "Because, by damn, I spend the day from an hour before dawn until an hour after dark tending cattle, hoeing fields, reaping, plowing, sowing and every other damn thing that keeps this family alive, including producing every damn thing you've put in your damn mouth today, Stipock! And if I expect my wife to cook the damn food and clean up the dishes after it seems only fair considering that there'd be no food and be no dishes and be no house and be no table if I didn't work to get them!"

Stipock had turned very, very red, and Noyock couldn't help it—he laughed outright. Now, drawing maps on the paper, he wondered what Jason intended to do with Stipock. Please, Noyock wished fervently, please explain at least what the fellow is *for*.

A knock on the door, and Noyock got up, startled. Everyone knew that after dark Noyock was not to be disturbed in this room. He opened the door—and it was the hundred-eleventh Ice Person. "What do you want?" Noyock asked.

"I just want to ask some questions," Stipock answered. And because Jason had, after all, said that he should be treated as carefully as an infant, Noyock invited him to come in and sit down. He did not, however, say to Stipock, "Be welcome." There were limits.

"Questions?" Noyock asked.

"I've been talking to Hoom," Stipock said. "Your grandson, right?"

Noyock nodded.

"He tells me that as Warden you tell everybody what to do."

Noyock shrugged. "When it needs telling, I tell it. Mostly people do what they want."

207

"But there are laws?"

Noyock nodded, wondering what Stipock was getting at. "Of course. Jason gave us those laws."

"And according to those laws a man has a right to beat his son?"

Ah. Another criticism. Noyock suddenly felt very tired and wanted to go to bed. "Within reason," Noyock said, "a man has power over his children."

Stipock laughed and shook his head. "I just can't believe how crude it all is."

Noyock stood up and stepped to the door. "Good night, Stipock. Let's talk in the morning, if you wish."

"No, I'm sorry," Stipock hurriedly said. "I didn't mean—I just meant that everything is so primitive." The word meant nothing to Noyock. Stipock went on: "I just wondered if you ever voted on anything. If you voted about the laws."

"We vote," Noyock said, "when there is no law. When Jason has given us a law, why should we vote?"

"Why shouldn't you?"

"Because if Jason says it, only a fool would disagree."

"It might as well be the Empire all over again," Stipock said, more to himself than to Noyock. "It hasn't occurred to anyone that the laws ought to come from the people, not from a man who comes out of the starship once every few years?"

"People are often very stupid," Noyock said.

"Including Jason, just like anyone else," Stipock said.

Noyock fixed a cold glare on him. "Good night, Stipock," Noyock said. "Sleep well."

Stipock shrugged, said, "Thanks for answering my questions," and left. Noyock closed the door after him, but his shaking fingers could hardly control the string to loop it on the bolt. He walked back to the table, sat down, and put his hands to his face.

It is very clear now what Jason wants, Noyock told himself. Stipock is here to test us, to try us. Jason has created an enemy, so that our love for him and our obedience to law will have its trial.

But we will overcome, Noyock vowed. We can and will be strong.

And then he remembered that Stipock had spoken with Hoom. With young, restless, easily influenced Hoom. And the spectre of the stranger stealing away the hearts of the children came up before Noyock's eyes for the first time, and he was afraid.

11

HOOM sat at the table, the tallow lamp casting a circle of light that included the paper and the pen. Except for the scratching of the point on the paper, the room was silent, until Hoom laid down the pen, sat up straight, and stretched, sighing softly.

He got up and walked to the window, which was barred. His fingers played along the bar, but he didn't lift it. He was confined to his room for a week, except for labor with his father on the farm. And Aven had gone so far, this time, as to insist that the window remain closed. Of course Aven would never know, this late at night, whether he was obeyed or not—but Hoom suspected that his father was so angry, this time, that he'd at least consider watching one night outside Hoom's room, just to see if he was obeyed.

Not worth a chance, Hoom decided. His back was still stiff from the last beating—the tenth in as many months. I will be fourteen next month, he reminded himself. Then I can move out of here and never see my father again.

Today his oldest brother, Grannit, at the age of thirty-two already a grandfather, had talked to him. "Why build a fire between father and yourself, so that neither of you can ever cross?" he had said, and Hoom had no answer. Except the silent one: "I'm not building the fire." He couldn't say that, though, because all the old people in Heaven City seemed to be on his father's side. They all distrusted Stipock, even though not a house in Heaven City lacked at least one of the tallow lamps Stipock had taught them to make. They all resented Wix, even though Jason himself had commended Wix for finding ways to travel on the water—even though Noyock (thank Jason for grandfather, Hoom thought) had ridden in the newest boat, which Stipock had helped Wix design. And they all had nothing but contempt for Hoom, who was "a disobedient child," as the phrase had so often been said. Hoom sat down and tried to write again. But the words were hard to come by. And would Jason even care to read what a thirteen-year-old boy had written? No, it was pointless. Noyock wouldn't change the law to set him free; Stipock hadn't the power; and Aven was determined that until the last moment that his authority lasted, Hoom would obey.

"I'll do all in my power to make him a decent man," Aven had said, loudly, when the cattlekeepers' council met tonight, "so that when he turns to rubbish next year, no man can say it was Aven's fault."

And while I rot this year, Hoom thought bitterly, no man says any fault to Aven, either.

A loud knock. Hoom got up, guiltily, as if his thoughts could be heard and he was going to be held to account. He turned the paper over, so the writing couldn't be read, and went to the door. No one was there. He wondered—who could be walking the halls tonight? And then the knock came again, louder, and Hoom realized that someone was knocking at the window. At a second-story window? No matter—someone *was* there, as a third knock testified. Hoom rushed to the window, opened it, and Wix tumbled into the room.

Surprise turned to dismay. Hoom quickly closed the window again, then rushed and closed the door. Returning to Wix, who

212

was now lying on his back on the floor, flexing his arms, Hoom whispered, "What are you doing, coming here when I'm confined? Are you trying to get me killed?"

"*You* killed!" Wix whispered back, laughing silently. "And there I was hanging by my elbows, trying to butt my head against the window loud enough that you'd hear me! Were you asleep?"

Hoom shook his head. "I was writing. As Stipock said to do."

"Writing'll never do any damn good," Wix said.

"I think Stipock's right," Hoom said. "Why should the Wardens be the only ones to write the History? Then it's all written down the way *they* think it happened.

"Well, it's your grandfather," Wix said.

"Why did you come here? I've been beaten too much already!"

"I came because you'd've killed me if I hadn't. We finished the new boat today, and Stipock says we're to try it out tonight."

"Tonight? In the dark?"

"There's a moon. And Stipock says that the night wind is from the southwest and will help us fight the current. We're going to cross the river."

Hoom immediately began pulling trousers over his naked legs. "Cross the river, and doing it tonight!"

"Coming then?" Wix asked, laughing silently again.

"Think I'd miss it?"

"What about your father?" Wix's eyes taunted him.

"This one's worth another beating," Hoom said. "And maybe he won't know." Hoom opened the window and Wix climbed out, falling lightly on his feet in the soft earth below. Hoom paused a moment in the window, dreading another huge quarrel with his father, wondering if taking this jump was worth it. But the thought of taking the *big* boat out into the river—*across* the river—ended his inward debate, and he jumped, landing on all fours and rolling.

Wix scrambled back up the wall enough to close the window,

213

so that discovery wouldn't be easy, while Hoom smoothed the dirt where they had landed. A few meters out from the house the dirt was covered by a thick mat of grass—no tracks there. And the dew was cold on their feet as they ran. A cow lowed as they sped through the pasture, almost three kilometers before they reached the forest's edge. There they rested, panting, out of breath, until their eyes got used to the denser darkness under the thick leaves. They followed a path known only to children's feet, a narrow winding that seemed deliberately to take the most dangerous descents, the steepest slopes, and it took almost a half hour for them to reach the edge of the river, in a little bay protected by a finger of rock that protruded into the river, blocking the current. There the boat lay rocking on the water; there a half-dozen shadowy people were busy at a half-dozen nameless, invisible tasks in the darkness.

"Who's that?" hissed a voice, and Wix answered, aloud, "Me, of course."

"Hurry, then, we're nearly done. Did you get Hoom?"

"I'm here," Hoom said, clambering down the slope after Wix. Closer, he could distinguish the features of the people there, and he immediately sought out Dilna, who smiled at him and let him help her with her task, which was folding and loading on the extra sail.

A few minutes later, Wix and Stipock pushed the boat out of the tiny cove and then were helped aboard as Hoom held the tiller. He had been tillerman on the last two boats, too, and as the boat hit the first currents (still not as strong as the main current a kilometer farther out—they had never tried to cross that before) he laughed with pleasure at how lightly and easily the boat responded to his touch.

Wix, in the meantime, with Dilna and Cirith, was putting up the sail, and the wind from the southwest caught it, pulling the boat forward, making it dance across the water.

There were four oars on the boat, just in case the sail didn't work, but Hoom laughed and said, "Won't be needing to row, now, will we?" and Wix laughed and said, "We could sleep our way across in this boat," and Stipock said, "Shut up and mind the tiller and the sail. The real current's still ahead."

When they reached the main stream, the bow of the boat yawed widely to the left, and for a moment there was a flurry of activity until the sail was turned to take the boat virtually into the current. Hoom plied the tiller vigorously, and kept the boat on course, and when they finally passed out of the main current and into the gentle eddies of the opposite side of the river, they gave a quiet cheer. Quiet, because Stipock had warned them that sound flew across water better than through forest.

Ahead loomed the highest hill of the opposite shore, and just to the west of it there was a beach. They unshipped the oars now, and pulled down the sail, rowing gently in to the shore. This time everyone but Hoom jumped out of the boat into the water, pulling it ashore. Hoom got out then, patting the firm structure of the boat as he swung from the bow.

"Well," said Dilna, "it doesn't feel much different from the sand on the other side."

"What did you expect?" Stipock asked. "Gold?"

"What's gold?" Hoom asked, and Stipock shook his head and laughed. "Never mind. Let's climb that hill, and see how the world looks from this side of the water."

So they climbed up the hill, Wix pointedly taking the shorter, steeper way, and Hoom following him. At the top, they waited for the others to come. Stipock was smiling when he reached them, and as they stood together in the wind, he laughed and said, "It's not too many years off, my friends, when you'll be as glad as I am to find a way that's not so steep!"

"The hill's high enough," Hoom said, looking at how small their boat seemed down on the shore. The moon was full and high, and without trees around them, it seemed they could see forever.

"Well," said Stipock, after they had all had ample time to look around, "what do you see over there?" And he pointed toward the shore they had come from.

"I can see my house," Hoom said immediately, because his

215

house crowned the bald hill of the Pasture. There were others near it, of course, but his grandfather's house, where he lived, was highest.

"There's a light in my father's house," Wix said, pointing to the many houses that skirted Linkeree's Bay, where Wix's father, Ross, still lived in the house that *his* father, Linkeree, had built.

"My family lives in the Main Town," Dilna said. "I can't see it from here."

Stipock chuckled softly behind them. "And is that all you see?"

Cirith said, "What I mostly see is trees. The houses look pretty damn small when you compare them to the forest." Stipock patted her arm.

Hoom wondered what in the world he was supposed to see as he looked across the river. Sure enough, everything did look smaller from farther away, but everyone knew that. What did Stipock *want* them to see?

Wix finally kicked a rock off the hill and turned back to Stipock. "Quit the guessing game. You want to show us something, show us."

"Right," Hoom said. "All that we can see from here is forest and Heaven City."

"And there's the answer," Stipock said, clapping Hoom on the back. "That's Heaven City. Over there, isn't it?"

"Where else would it be?" Cirith asked.

"Look down on this side. Is Heaven City here?"

No, of course not, they said.

"Well then. What if a man crossed the river with his wife, and they built a house here. Would that house be in Heaven City or not?"

And now they began to catch a glimmer of the idea. "It wouldn't have to be, would it?" Dilna said.

And Hoom added, "And if the people who lived here had the boats, they could pretty much decide who came and who didn't."

216

"They could even keep the damned Warden and his stupid laws on the other side," Wix said. "We could vote on everything, like you've been saying!"

But the excitement was dampened when Stipock said, "And could you keep Jason on the other side?"

They shrugged. They shuffled. They didn't know. After all, you never knew what Jason could do.

"Let me tell you, then," Stipock said. "You can't keep Jason away. Because Jason has machines that let him fly."

Fly! Hoom stared in wonderment at Stipock. The man strange—for hours he would talk to them about how Jason was just a man, like any other; and then he would say things like this, or talk about Jason piloting a great ship between the stars. Who could know? Even Stipock himself couldn't seem to make up his mind as to whether Jason was God, as the old people said, or whether he was just a man.

"And not just Jason. Which of you owns a cow?"

None of them did.

"Or an ax? Or anything at all?"

"I have *my* tools," Wix said, but he was the oldest of those who followed Stipock, and few of the others had turned fourteen and reached adulthood.

"Are your tools enough to build a town?"

Wix shook his head.

"Then we're back where we started, aren't we? Because you can't be free from Heaven City until you don't need Heaven City anymore. But it's still worth thinking about, isn't it? Still worth, perhaps, planning for. Perhaps?"

"Perhaps," Hoom said, so solemnly that he earned several punches and jests from the others all the way down the hill. But as he sat at the tiller on the way back, he couldn't keep from looking back often at the shore they had left. Land as good as any at Heaven City. But perhaps there the young, who, like Hoom and Wix, cared little for the old people's single-minded attention to every word that dropped from Jason's mouth, might

217

be able to set up another city, one that depended on the will of those governed, as Stipock had so often said, rather than the will of those governing.

Now as they crossed the river, the current was trickier. They had to steer into it again, though it took them far from the direction they wanted to go, because the wind was directly against them returning. Once they had crossed the main stream, though, they let the eddies carry them lazily back across Linkeree Bay, around the point, and into the shallow cove where they had built the boat.

They splashed to shore (except Hoom at the tiller) and tied the boat to three trees, and then they all laughed with each other and made funny remarks about having to go back to the old people again, and then they parted.

Because Dilna lived in the Main Town, she and Hoom had to go back in the same direction, which was perfectly all right with Hoom. He wanted to talk to her anyway, had wanted to ever since he had met her in the group that met to listen to Stipock months ago, while he was still talking about the stars and planets and billions of people on other worlds (as if anyone much cared what really existed in heaven). As they wound their way through the forest toward the Pasture, Hoom held her hand, and she only held the tighter when he tried to do the courteous thing, and let go as they reached level, open ground.

That was encouragement enough for Hoom. "Dilna," he whispered as they walked through the Pasture. "Dilna, in a month I'll be fourteen."

"And I'll be fourteen in two weeks," she said.

"I'm moving out of my father's house that day," Hoom said.

"I'd move, too," she answered, "if only I had a place to go."

Hoom swallowed. "I'll build you a house, if you'll come to live in it with me."

She tossed back her head and laughed softly. "Yes, I'll marry you, Hoom! What did you think I was hinting at so much all these months?"

And then they kissed each other, clumsily, but with enough fervor to make the experience all they had hoped it would be.

"How long will I have to wait?" Dilna asked.

"I'll have it built before Jason's Day."

"Will he come back, do you think?"

"This year?" Hoom shook his head. "This year he won't come. Not with grandfather as Warden."

"I was hoping he would be able to marry us himself," Dilna said, and then they kissed again and she took off running, heading for Noyock's Road, which would take her down into the Main Town. Neither of them noticed the incongruity of wanting Jason himself to perform their marriage, even as they planned and worked to remove themselves from the city he governed. After all, Jason may not be God, as Stipock always told them. But that didn't mean he wasn't Jason. And everyone knew that Jason could read what was in people's hearts, and that made him more than anybody else. God or no God, Jason still wasn't, in any way, ordinary.

Hoom reached the house and quickly scrambled up the horizontal logs to his window. He pulled it easily ajar, and slipped through, barring the window behind him.

His tallow lamp was sputtering, but hadn't gone out. He doused it, and undressed in the darkness. The room was cold, and his blankets were colder still. He shivered and he slid his naked body under the wool—but he was tired enough, and he was quickly asleep.

He woke when his door crashed open violently and his father shouted, "Hoom!" The boy sat up in bed, holding his blankets around him as if they would offer some protection. "Father——I—"

"*Fa*ther!" Aven said in a high voice, mocking him cruelly. "*Fa*ther." And then he roared. "Don't you call me father, boy! Never again!"

"What is it? What have I done?"

"Oh, are we innocent this morning? Didn't I tell you not even to unbar the window? And certainly not to leave this room for a week! Do you remember *why* I told you that?"

"Because," Hoom said, "because I disobeyed you and went on the river—"

"And have you obeyed me when I told you to stay here as punishment?"

Hoom knew then that the beating was coming. He had long since learned that when he was caught, it was better not to lie. The beating was easier then, and the shouting was over sooner.

"I have not obeyed you," Hoom said.

"Come to the window, boy," Aven said, his voice lower and so all the more frightening. Hoom climbed uncertainly out of bed. The early autumn air was chilly, and when his father unbarred the window and flung it open, it became freezing cold on Hoom's naked and sleep-slowed body. "Look out the window!" Aven commanded, and Hoom became really afraid—he had never seen his father so furious.

Down at the foot of the wall of the house, the dirt showed clearly Hoom's footprints leading from the grass to the wall. In two hours, they would not have showed—but the slantwise morning sun made the prints black on the dark brown soil.

"Where did you go?" Aven asked, softly, menacingly.

"I went—I went—" and Hoom saw some of his brothers and uncles and cousins, passing by with tools for mending fences. They had stopped. They were staring at the window. Had they heard Aven's shouting?

"You went to the river?" Aven prompted. Hoom nodded, and Aven roared again. "This is how I'm obeyed! You're not my son! You're an untrainable animal I've been cursed with! I won't have you in my house anymore! You won't live here anymore!"

Hoom could see some of his cousins, and he thought he could see them pointing, laughing, mocking. He whirled on his father and shouted back, as loudly as he could, though his young voice cracked twice, "That's no punishment at all, you old hog! I've been wishing for the day that I could get out of here, and you've set me free all the sooner!" With that, Hoom started for the chair where his clothes were piled. But his father caught his arm in a tight, savage grip, and pulled him back.

"Want your clothes, is it? Well, none of that. My sweat earned those clothes for you, and your mother's."

"I've worked too," Hoom said, defiant but terribly afraid as his father's fingers dug viciously into his arm.

"You've worked too!" Aven shouted. "You've worked! Well, you've been paid for it. You've eaten my food and slept in my house! But I swear when you leave me you'll leave as naked as you came! Now get out, and never come back!"

"Then let go of me, so I can," said Hoom, sick with embarrassment at the thought of having to go out naked in front of everyone, wondering where he would go.

"I'll let go of you," Aven said, "but you won't use the door, boy. You'll go out the way you snuck out last night, hoping to deceive your father! You'll dance out that window, boy." And Aven flung him toward the open window again.

Hoom stood at the window, looking at the ground below him. It suddenly looked farther than it had last night, and his cousins had come closer, were no more than twenty meters off now, could hear every word, would watch him jump, naked, with nothing to cover his shame.

"I said jump!" Aven said. "Now climb up on the sill and jump!"

Hoom climbed on the sill, trying to cover himself with his hand, his mind an agony of humiliation and indecision and hatred.

"Jump, dammit!" Aven bellowed.

"I can't," Hoom whispered. "Please!"

"You could damn well jump last night!" his father shouted; and just at that moment Hoom heard his grandfather's voice, from back by the door, saying, "Aven, be careful with the boy," and Hoom turned to call out to his grandfather, to cry for help, for relief from the intolerable. But at the moment he turned,

221

Aven finished the gesture he had begun, and struck Hoom hard. If Hoom hadn't been turning, it would have struck him on the back and stung bitterly; instead it struck him in the ribs, crushingly, and because he was off-balance Hoom teetered for a moment on the sill and then fell from the window.

He wasn't prepared for the fall. He landed with his right leg only, and the knee popped somehow, and with an agonizing grinding the leg buckled under him. He lay there, terribly, acutely, sharply conscious, though the only reality was the vast pain that pressed on him and shortened his breath and threatened to suffocate him utterly. He heard a distant scream. It was his mother. She ran to him, screamed again, crying, "Hoom, my boy, my son," and then in the distance (far up in the sky) he heard his father's voice call out, "Stay away from him, woman!"

"My name is Esten, *man!*" shouted his mother in fury. "Don't you see the boy's leg is broken?"

Broken? Hoom looked down and nearly vomited. His right leg was bent backward at a ninety-degree angle at the knee. Only a little below the knee, a new joint, from which a strange white-and-bloody bone protruded, bent his leg back again the other way.

"Jason!" he heard his father cry out, as if the call would bring God from his tower. "What have I done to the boy?" And then the pain subsided for a second, Hoom gasped his breath, and the pain washed back, twice as powerfully as before. The wave of agony swept him away; everything went bright purple; the world disappeared.

Hoom woke to hear a knocking at a door. He was immediately conscious of being hot; sweat dripped from him, and the wool of the blankets over him prickled in the heat. He tried to push the blankets off, but the movement was pain, and he moaned.

Someone had come in, and he heard, in the distance (a couple of meters away), an argument.

"You'll stay away from my boy, damn you," said Aven's voice.

"I can heal his leg, Aven," said another voice, "and you have no right to stop me."

"Jason knows you've done enough!" Aven said, his voice rising.

"And you've done more than enough!" came back the savage retort. "At least let someone who really loves the boy care for him now!"

Hoom recognized the other voice. It was Stipock. But now Grandfather Noyock's voice came, soothing, gentling. "Aven, the law is the law. And if a man injures his child, the child is no longer in his care."

A moan, a cry. "I didn't mean to hurt him!" Aven said, his voice twisted and bent with weeping. Father, weeping! The thought was incomprehensible to Hoom. "You know I didn't mean to hurt him, father!"

But Noyock said nothing to him, only told Stipock to go ahead.

Hoom felt the blanket come off him. The cold air was biting. Gentle hands touched his leg—fire ran up his spine.

"This is terrible, terrible," Stipock said softly.

"Can you heal him?" Noyock asked. "We've never had an injury this bad, at least not one that left the poor fellow alive."

"I'll need help."

Aven spoke up from the corner. "I'll help you."

"No!" Hoom hissed from his pain-clenched teeth. "Don't let him touch me."

Hoom couldn't see Aven turn away, or Esten put her arm around her husband to comfort his remorse. All he could see behind his closed eyes was the hatred on his father's face.

"You help me then, Noyock. Is that all right, Hoom?"

Hoom nodded, or tried to. Apparently Stipock understood his assent, for he began giving instructions. "You'll have to hold the boy by the armpits, from above. And don't try to spare him any pain. Gentleness won't help him now."

What's happening to me? What are you doing?

"Trust me now," Stipock said. "This is going to hurt like hell, Hoom, but it's the only way we can fix it so you'll ever walk again."

And then a hand gripped him at the ankle, which made Hoom moan, and another hand gripped him just below the break, high on his shin, which made him cry out in pain.

"Don't hurt him—" began his mother, and then silence, as Stipock said, "Now pull with all your strength, Noyock," and Hoom felt as if he were being pulled apart. The pain rose and rose and rose, until, suddenly, Hoom could feel no more pain, except that he knew he was virtually dead with it. Above the pain he floated, and felt the dispassionate movement of his body as Stipock pushed the fragment of shin back into place, where it fit again with a terrible snap (I don't feel it; it isn't me); as Stipock slid the kneecap back into position, forced the joint to fit again; as the leg, already used to the torture of the bones out of place, now began to feel the worse torture of the bones back together.

"Is that it?" he heard Noyock ask, from a great distance.

"We need wood and cloth strips," Stipock said. "Straight firm wood, no twigs or branches or green wood."

"I'll get it," Aven said, and "I'll get the cloth," said Esten, Hoom's mother. And then, at last, Hoom fell back down into the sea of pain and drowned in it, drifted down to the bottom, and slept.

He woke again, and it was dark. A tallow lamp sputtered by the bed. His head ached, and his broken leg throbbed dully; but the pain was much better, much eased, much gone, and he could leave his eyes open.

The room focused, and he saw Stipock sitting by his bed. "Hi," he said, and Stipock smiled. "How do you feel?" Stipock asked softly.

"The pain's not as bad."

"Good. We've done all we can do. Now it's up to your leg to heal."

Hoom smiled wanly.

Stipock turned toward somewhere else—a door, Hoom assumed—and said, "He's awake now. You can call the others." Then he turned back to Hoom and said, "I know you don't feel well, but some decisions have to be made, that only you can make."

Footsteps coming into the room, and one by one they came into Hoom's range of vision. First Noyock, looking grave. Then Esten, her eyes red from crying. And then Aven.

Seeing his father, Hoom turned his head upward, to the ceiling.

"Hoom," said Noyock.

"Yes," Hoom answered, his voice soft and husky.

"Stipock wants to take care of you," Noyock said. "He wants to take you out of your father's home, if you want to, and take care of you until you can walk again."

Hoom tried to control them, but the tears dripped out of the corners of his eyes anyway.

"But, Hoom, your father also wants to take care of you."

"No," Hoom said.

"Your father wants to say something to you."

"No."

"Please," said Aven. "Please listen to me, son."

"I'm not your son," Hoom said softly. "You told me so."

"I'm sorry for that. You know how it was. I went crazy for a minute."

"I want to go with Stipock," Hoom said.

Silence for a few moments, and then Aven bitterly spat out his feelings about Stipock, who came to steal children away from their parents. "I won't let you take the boy!" Aven said, and might have said more except that Noyock's voice, harsh with anger, cut through.

"Yes, you will, Aven!"

"Father!" Aven cried out, anguished.

"The law says that after a father has injured his child, the child must be taken by another family, for its own protection."

"Stipock isn't a family," Aven said.

"I will be," Stipock said, "when your son is living with me."

"It only makes sense, Aven," Noyock said. "Stipock can help the boy now—you can't."

"I can help him," Aven insisted.

"By pushing him out of windows?" Stipock quietly asked.

"Shut up, Stipock," Noyock answered mildly. "I'll ask Hoom one more time, and then that's it, and there'll be no complaint, no more discussion, and no resistance, or I swear I'll have you bound up and kept in a locked room until Jason comes again. Now, Hoom, will you stay with Stipock, or with your father?"

Hoom half-smiled. He felt a glow of satisfaction: the broken leg would be worth it, for the chance to make this choice. "Stipock *is* my father," Hoom said. And Aven's low moan of pain was some measure of repayment, Hoom felt, for the pain he had gone through. With that thought he closed his eyes and dozed.

But he became vaguely alert again a few minutes later. It seemed that Noyock and Stipock were alone in the room, and they were arguing.

"You see the harm it caused," Stipock said. "The law didn't give you any power to take this boy out of his father's home until his father nearly killed him."

"The law is the law," Noyock said, "and only Jason can change it."

"That's the point!" Stipock insisted. "The law needs to be changed. If Jason were here, he'd change it, wouldn't he?"

"Maybe," Noyock said.

"Then why can't *we?* Not just you and me, but all the people. Vote. Let the majority change the law."

Noyock sighed. "It's what you've wanted all along, Stipock. To let the majority of people in Heaven City change any one of Jason's laws they want."

"Just this law," Stipock said. "Just the law that lets fathers beat their children."

"Just this law? I'm not a fool, Stipock, though you seem to feel that everyone in Heaven City is stupider than a newborn big. Once we've changed one law that way, there'll be other laws to change, and people will begin to think all the laws are changeable."

"Aren't they?" Stipock asked. "Why don't you just ask them? On Jason's Day, when they gather at Firstfield, call a council, ask them to vote on whether voting should be allowed. See what they decide."

"I said, Stipock, that I'm not a fool. If I let them vote on anything, that becomes a lawful way for decisions to be made."

"So you aren't going to change the law?"

"Just let me think, Stipock."

"Let you? I'm begging you to. Do you really think the majority of people in this colony will decide stupidly? Don't you trust them?"

"I trust them, Stipock. It's you I don't trust." And Noyock left the room, his footfalls ringing in Hoom's ears.

"Stipock," Hoom whispered.

"Hmmm? Are you awake? Did we wake you?"

"That's all right." Hoom found it hard to use his voice. It was hoarse. Had he cried out that much from the pain? He didn't remember shouting at all—but his voice was as hoarse as if he had been yelling all day in the fields. "Stipock, what's a colony?"

"What? Oh, yes, I did use the word—it's still hard, even after all these months—"

"What is a colony?"

"It's a place where—it's when some people leave their homes behind, and go to a new place, and start to live there, far away from the others. Heaven City's a colony, because the—uh, the Ice People—they left the Empire and came across the space between the stars and lived here."

Hoom nodded. He had heard that story before—Stipock's miracle stories, they all called them behind his back. Wix didn't believe them, and Hoom wasn't sure.

"When we live across the river, we'll be a colony, then, won't we?"

"Yes, I guess so."

"Stipock."

"Yes."

"Move me across the river."

Stipock chuckled. "When you can walk again."

"No. Move me now."

"Your leg is bound up. You can't walk for months, Hoom."

"Then get my friends to carry me. Take me out of Heaven City. I want to get out of Heaven City. Even if I have to live in the open, in a tent. Get me out. Get me out." And Hoom's voice drifted away as he slept again.

Stipock sat studying the boy's quiet, gentle, but pain-scarred face. The lips were turned permanently downward; the forehead, even in sleep, was furrowed; the eyes were bagged with exhaustion, not crinkled with laughter as they should have been.

"All right," Stipock whispered. "Yes, now. That's a good idea, Hoom. Very good idea."

Two days later, two horses drew the cart that carried Hoom joltingly down Noyock's Road to Linkeree's Bay. Then, with a crowd of several hundred people gathered around, they carried Hoom on a plank out to the boat, which was waiting a few meters from shore. And the boat, this time in broad daylight, spread its white wings and danced skimmingly out of the bay into the current. Hoom laughed with pleasure—at his freedom, at the movement of the boat on the water, at his friends' proof of their true friendship. Dilna was at the tiller, and she smiled at him. Wix poked him now and then with his toe as he passed, working the sails, just to let him know he was noticed. And then they reached the other shore, and they set him down by a tree to watch as they cleared a patch of ground and laid the walls of a rough cabin. The floor was of planks, which had been cut the day before, and the door and windows were gaping holes. The roof couldn't be put on before dark, but they all promised they'd be back in the morning, and then carried Hoom inside. He looked around at the walls of his house.

228

"Well," asked Wix, "how is it?"

"Ugly as hell," Hoom said. "I love every inch of it." And then, before he could thank them and cry, they whooped and hollered their way out of the house and back to the boat.

It was getting dark, but there were plenty of blankets over him, and the stars were shining. Breakfast was in a bag on the floor beside him, and Hoom listened to the distant sounds of the boat being launched again.

As the sound grew softer, he listened to the breeze in the branches above him. Leaves were drifting lazily down; soon all the leaves would have turned colors and dropped, and the snow would come. Hoom felt a stab of loneliness—but he quickly forgot it in the satisfaction of being out of Heaven City. A leaf landed on his face, and he waited a moment before he brushed it away. Was this what it was like for Linkeree, in the old story, when he left Heaven City and built his own home in the forest? This feeling of not being one of a city, but of being an intruder among the trees?

He heard footsteps in the grass and leaves outside his door. He froze, afraid of who it might be. The ship was gone—had someone stayed behind? And why?

Dilna stood in the doorway.

"Dilna," Hoom said, sighing in relief.

"Hi," she said.

"I thought you went back with the others."

"I decided not to," she said. "Comfortable?"

Hoom nodded. "It's a good house."

"You promised me I could move in when the house was done," Dilna said.

Hoom laughed. "As soon as you want to," he said.

"Noyock promised me that he'd cross the river and marry us tomorrow. If you want to."

"I want to."

"Can I come in?"

"Of course, come in. I didn't know you were waiting for an invitation."

Dilna came in, her face lit only by starlight, and knelt beside him. "Do you always sleep with your clothes on?" she asked.

"No," he said, laughing at the idea. "But with a lumberyard tied around my leg, I've found it a little hard to get around."

"I'll help you," she said, and Hoom was surprised that he felt no embarrassment as she gently, carefully undressed him, moving his leg without hurting him, touching him so casually he felt no shame. Then she turned her back and undressed, also. "I didn't bring any more blankets. Any room to spare under yours?" she asked.

"I can't—I can't do anything," he said. "My leg—I can't—"

"Nobody expects you to," she said, touching his forehead softly. "There's plenty of time for that." She lay down beside him and pulled the blankets up to cover them both. Then she snuggled close to him. Her body was cold with the chilliness outside the blankets. She put her arm across his chest, stroked his cheek. "Do you mind?" she asked.

"No," he said.

"Better get used to it," she said. "Because I plan to sleep here for a good long time."

12

BILLIN'S voice sounded muffled in the heavy, smoky room, though he was shouting. Dilna sighed as she heard the same words again. "That damned History is our enemy! Every time something comes for a vote, Noyock pulls out the History and says, 'That isn't the way Jason did it! That isn't the way Kapock did it!' Well, I say, who the hell cares *how* they did it?"

Dilna carved savagely at the block of wood in her lap, as if it were Billins' head. It was stupid, this meeting every night in the tavern. Everyone in Stipock's Bay already agreed—they had to separate themselves from Heaven City. The laws had no relation to reality anymore—things were different here. But Billin didn't help anything with his fury, that so infected the others.

Even Stipock, she noticed, was watching Billin intently. But she more than half-suspected that Stipock was analyzing more than he was listening. Surely Stipock wasn't moved or impressed by Billin's talk! But Dilna wondered just the same. Could Billin possibly be doing just what Stipock wanted?

"The History is just paper! Only paper, and that's all! It can burn! And if that's the barrier that keeps us from making our own laws here, then I say, Burn it!"

Oh, clever, Dilna thought. The whole point is to win our independence, as Stipock had so often said, without losing our interdependence. If those on the other side of the river come to hate us, she silently asked, where would we get our copper, our tin, our brass? Paper? Ink? Flour? None of the tiny streams on *this* side of the river had enough force to turn a mill. But if Billin had his way, we'd rush over right now, burn the History, and then somehow persuade them to amicably let us be independent, while trade continued.

The chair next to hers scraped along the floor, and she looked up to see Stipock sitting down next to her.

"The aging philosopher comes to chat?" she asked.

"Aging," Stipock said. "It's worry, not years."

Billin's voice reached a climax. "Does it matter how the vote goes? As long as we own the boats, we decide what laws get enforced on this side of the river!" Some beery cheers arose from the audience.

"The man's an ass," Dilna said. "Even if you *were* the one who first pointed out that whoever owns the boats makes the laws on this side of the river."

"Billin gets a little too angry," Stipock said.

"As the great Stipock has always said," Billin shouted, "a man who rejects a government is no longer truly governed by it!"

"Is that what the great Stipock has always said?" Dilna asked, smiling.

"I wish to hell no one would ever quote me." He looked at the wood she was working on. "What are you carving?"

"A canehead for a rich old codger from Wienway. One of Wien's sons, in fact, who thinks a bit of bronze will buy anything."

"Won't it?" Stipock asked. She laughed. "Almost anything."

Stipock sat in silence, surveying the room. "Hoom isn't back yet?"

"You know how it is—once you start visiting with relatives—"

"Hoom and his father, under the same roof tonight. Will the house burn down, do you think?"

232

"Good chance," Dilna said, but she didn't laugh.

"And Wix is with him?"

"I assume so," she said. Suddenly she felt her knife hand gripped by Stipock's powerful fingers.

"Dilna. Hoom knows."

She gasped, before she could control herself. Damn, she thought, trying to cover the reaction. Damn, now whatever he suspects is confirmed. "Hoom knows what?" she said, doing a bad job of acting innocent.

"I said Hoom knows. And no one else matters. I'm just warning you, Dilna. Hoom loves you too much to do anything about it. Unless you leave him. If you leave him, you'll have to kill him."

"What are you talking about? I have no intention of leaving Hoom. What an idea."

"Good thing," Stipock said, releasing her wrist.

"Damn you," Dilna said.

"You're an idiot," Stipock said. "No one on this side of the river is half of Hoom's quality as a man."

"And what do *you* know," she said bitterly, "about quality in a man?"

"Enough," he said, and he got up and left, as Dilna tried to force her trembling hands to carve true. She couldn't, and she, too, walked out of the public house.

She went down the dusty road toward the house that she and Hoom had shared since their marriage. It was much more elaborate now—prosperity had helped it grow—but the original cabin was still there, a back room now.

She went inside, suddenly bone weary, wishing she could go to sleep and wake on another planet, as Stipock kept saying people did. A crazy man. For all these years, we've followed a crazy man. No wonder we do crazy things.

The house was clean inside, and the cupboards were full. Hoom, for all his mildness and lack of initiative, was a good provider. She sold her carvings because it made people prize her work, not because they needed the money. And it was like

233

Hoom—to dig up young trees, plant them, and sell the fruit. He only needed to plant once, and he reaped forever, only pruning now and then. His orchards spread from the Heaven River far inland. Tame trees. Hoom thought he could tame anything or anybody. Except me, she thought bitterly. Only I cannot be tamed, no matter how I long to be.

Why Wix? she wondered. And why now? Why a week ago? Why not ten years from now, or never, or always, so that Hoom would never have loved me, would never have been hurt. And how the hell did Hoom know? Too many questions. Does everyone know?

And if Stipock had only been guessing, she had certainly confirmed his guess. What a fool I am, Dilna reminded herself.

When Hoom got home Dilna was asleep, but she roused herself with a groan when she heard the door open, wrapped a blanket around her, and went into the common room, where Hoom and Wix were saying good night. Wix waved a greeting at her, and then disappeared silently as Hoom swung the door shut.

"Well?" Dilna asked. "How did the meeting go?"

"I'm tired," Hoom said, collapsing on a chair in an exaggeration of weariness.

"Tell me," Dilna insisted.

"And what will you give me if I do?" Hoom asked with a lazy smile. Dilna sighed and walked over to him. She sat on his lap, wrapping the blanket around them both. He rubbed his hand across her bare stomach and laughed. "Ah, the wages I get in this house!"

"Tell me," Dilna said, "or I'll put roaches in your bed."

"You would," he said. "So I'll tell you: Noyock's willing."

"Good," she said. "That'll defuse that bastard Billin."

"Don't call names. What's much more important, my dear, is that father's willing, too."

"You spoke to your father?"

Hoom smiled, but he didn't look amused. "It would have

234

interfered with the negotiations if I hadn't. After all, he is the leader of the Uniters."

"That's one nice thing about the opposition—they're very orderly, always appointing leaders."

"We don't have to appoint one: we have one already."

"But Stipock refuses to say what he wants," Dilna said, getting up and walking to the cooking fire, which still had enough heat to stir it back to flame. "Want some broth?"

"As a second choice," Hoom said.

She put the kettle over the flames, its brass long since blackened by smoke. "What did Aven say?"

"That if we were willing to accept the general leadership of the Warden, they'd consent to a separate vote and a separate tax."

"No, silly," she said. "What did he say afterward?"

"He tried to get all emotional and pretend that there was a reconciliation. But I left as soon as I could."

Dilna felt strangely irritated. "It was awfully petty of you, not to let things smooth over."

Hoom didn't answer, and she knew he was angry. Oh well, what the hell. He'd forget as soon as she climbed into his bed. Instant forgiveness, she called it. Privately, of course—it would never do to let Hoom know how transparent he was.

Change the subject: "Any doubt about the vote?"

"No. Even if half the Uniters don't go along with the compromise—which is likely enough, too many old people believe the History says that Jason has commanded us always to be united no matter how widely we spread out—we'll have enough votes to turn the difference."

The broth had already been warm, and now it was steaming hot. She ladled some into a bowl and carried it to Hoom. "Thank you," her husband said as she went back for a bowl for herself. They drank the broth in silence. When it was gone, Hoom went outside to relieve himself and Dilna went to the bedroom and turned down the blankets on his bed. Even though Hoom never

235

treated her like a possession (as a lot of the older men treated their wives, and too many younger ones, too), she still liked to do small services that made his life more comfortable.

As she turned back the blankets she wondered: Does he know?

She thought of how Wix had looked afterward, half-covered with damp leaves and his face twisted in—what, grief? Regret? Disappointment? He should have married, the bastard, and then he never would have been tempted by her, nor she by him. There was no way Hoom could know.

He came into the room, stripping off his shirt as he walked. "Getting chilly now. Jason's due back in a month. From today. Noyock wanted us to wait until he came."

Dilna turned in surprise. "Actually, why not? That isn't a bad idea. After all, the whole idea of voting was put in after Jason's last visit—why not let Jason see it in action?"

"Because," Hoom said wryly, "he might take offense at it and abolish the practice, and every old bastard in Heaven City would give it up just like that. We haven't mentioned it much, but that's one of the reasons Stipock's been pushing us to get the decision *now*, before the old god returns from the Star Tower."

"So Stipock *does* have opinions."

"One or two," Hoom said. "So do I. I'm of the opinion that I married the most desirable woman in Heaven City."

As he caressed her she laughed and said, "What about the most beautiful?"

"Goes without saying," he answered. But she wondered anyway whether he knew: why had he chosen to call her desirable? Did he know *who* had desired her? And been satisfied?

She didn't go back to her own bed until nearly morning, wondering as she did why she had insisted on that arrangement a year after they married. A sign of independence, she supposed. Everybody had to have their little signs of independence.

Because Hoom's orchard needed little tending at this time of year, he spent most of the day in the house, and there was a constant stream of visitors. Dilna usually would have been in the

236

common room joining into the conversations, but today she didn't feel like it, and instead she climbed up onto the shingled roof (Wix's innovation, and it had made him rich before he turned eighteen) and lay there, occasionally carving, but usually looking up at the clouds that promised rain (but not a drop fell, of course, for the winds were from the west and not until they shifted to the north would the fall rains begin).

Once she climbed to the crest of the roof and looked out across the river, where now four boats made regular trips back and forth. Eternally back and forth—boring. Wix and Hoom talked of following the current, going down the river to see where it led. As soon as the vote was taken and things were settled. Well, that's tomorrow, Dilna thought, and I'll be packed five minutes after they vote.

She wondered vaguely why she was so anxious to get away, but when her mind made a connection to that day a week ago in the woods to the west, she slid halfway down the roof (damn the splinters, I'll slide if I want) and carved furiously for a while.

She had fallen asleep on the roof when Hoom found the ladder and climbed up. She was surprised to see it was nearly evening.

"Trying to kill yourself?" Hoom asked, concerned.

"Yes," she answered, and then realized that Hoom really had been concerned. "No, Hoom, I couldn't possibly fall off."

"Yes you could," Hoom said, and then he helped her carry her things back down the ladder.

"The visitors all gone?"

Hoom nodded and led the way into the house. "But they aren't all happy about the compromise."

"Why not?"

"Billin says he can't tolerate having the Warden over him. Though why he should hate Noyock so badly I don't know."

"He's a fool sometimes," Dilna said. "Noyock's bound to be replaced next month when Jason comes. Who knows? Maybe Stipock will be Warden—now there's a thought that makes me want to throw the vote away!"

237

Hoom laughed. "Stipock Warden? The way he feels about Jason? I should tell you—there's even talk of separating from Jason himself. That's what Billin wants, anyway."

Dilna was silent for a while. Separate from Jason? Well, of course, no one thought Jason was God anymore, at least not in Stipock's village on this side of the river. But *separate?*

That made her uneasy. She was eager to cut ties—but all the ties? That felt like Hoom's feud with his father: wrong somehow, a wound that should be healed, not widened. And would Jason stand for it? He had tools—like the little box he had held in his hand when he killed the ox that went wild. Would he turn that against a man? The thought made her shudder. Of course not. But they'd never separate from Jason—that was just Billin's talk.

Hoom and Dilna spent the evening weaving and sewing together, and then went to bed.

In the morning she felt a familiar nausea, and vomited before breakfast.

"Well?" Hoom asked her as she came back from the privy.

"Damn," she said. "Why now?"

"It's hard to pick the time," he said, laughing. "This one we'll have," he said. He held her tightly around the waist. She smiled at him, but there was nothing behind the smile. She knew when her last fertile time had been—damn Stipock for even telling them about the cycle within the cycle—and it was possible, just possible, that Wix was the father. And he and Hoom looked so different.

Don't borrow trouble, she told herself. I've got months yet, and heaven knows the chances are better that it'll look like Hoom.

As always, Hoom misunderstood what she was worried about. "Two miscarriages aren't that bad," he said, consoling her. "Plenty of women have had two and then on the third pregnancy, the baby was born. Which do you want, a boy or a girl?"

"Yes," she answered, reviving the old joke from their last

238

pregnancy, and then she told him she felt good enough to go to Firstfield.

"Are you sure?"

"Once I throw up I'm always fine," she said. "And I'm sure as hell not missing the vote."

So they walked to the shore and got in Hoom's small boat. This time Dilna was at the tiller, the less strenuous job, while Hoom tended sail. The wind from the west and the current from the east made crossing tricky—every gust of wind meant quick adjustments so the boat wouldn't veer in the current. But they sailed into Linkeree's Bay, where dozens of other boats were already landed, and still more were just coming across the river.

The group from Stipock's Bay walked to Firstfield together, as their friends and sympathizers—mostly young—from Heaven City joined them along the way. The talk was cheerful and neutral—about anything but the upcoming vote—and they arrived in Firstfield in good humor.

Once there, however, they quickly got down to business. "What's the count?" Hoom asked, and Wix smiled as he said, "I don't think anybody stayed home today. On either side."

"How will the vote turn out?" Dilna asked.

"Well, Aven's sure that at least half his people will vote for the compromise. And with ours, there's no chance of it failing." Wix looked around. "Even Billin's smiling and looking happy. And he swore he'd do anything before he'd let the Warden keep power over us."

Hoom put his arm around Dilna. "When it comes down to it, Billin's a pretty sensible man. Just loves to hear himself talk."

But Dilna was watching Billin as he chattered happily not far away, surrounded by his supporters. Billin had been talking for weeks of how nothing short of complete freedom from the Warden—and from Jason—would be acceptable to him. He seems too happy right now, she thought.

I'm just depressed because of the pregnancy, she thought.

But she was not the only one depressed when the *no* vote was

239

considerably louder than the *yes* vote. Concerned, Wix leaped to his feet at the same time as Aven, and both of them shouted for a count. "Closer than we thought it would be," Wix said as he sat down. "Trust the diehards to yell louder."

But the count made it even more obvious. In favor of the partial independence were a clear majority of the Uniters. But among the people of Stipock's Bay, fully two-thirds were *opposed*.

Noyock finished the count, and shook his head. "People of Heaven City, I don't understand you!" he shouted.

Aven leaped to his feet. "*I* understand! Those crossriver bastards make all kinds of promises, but nothing comes of it!"

Many of the older people grumbled their agreement, and Billin shouldered his way through the crowd to the front. "May I speak?" he asked. Noyock shook his head. "Anybody who wants to listen to you, Billin, is free to. But I'm closing the council. Heaven City stands as a unit. The vote was against separation, and that's all I can do."

Noyock walked away from the front, and many of the older people gathered around him followed him away from Firstfield. Billin, undisturbed, began to shout.

"Why did we vote against the so-called compromise?" he asked.

"Who the hell cares!" Wix shouted back, and those who had voted for it laughed.

"We voted against that so-called compromise because it was a trap set by these Jason-loving old men, to keep us under the thumb of their precious Warden! Well, we don't need you here in Heaven City, and we don't have to settle for your outmoded, rigid, stupid laws and decisions! We'll cross that river, and take all the boats with us, and you can keep your Heaven City and we'll be a new city! Stipock City! A place where people are free!"

A thin cheer arose from those who had voted with Billin— and a few others.

240

"Let's get out of here," Dilna said.

"I agree," Hoom said.

"What I want to know," Wix shouted, even as he was walking through the crowd to leave with them, "is what you plan to do for metal if we don't cross the river!"

"That's Wix for you!" Billin shouted. "If he didn't think of a plan himself, he doesn't like it!" Laughter. "Well, Wix, three days ago Coren, Rewen, and Hanlatta came back from a little exploring party to the north of the river. And sure enough, they found what they were looking for! Copper! Tin! A supply as good as anything here on this side of the river! We're independent in *every* way now! So let the old men and the old women sit over here for the rest of their lives. *We'll* build a city that's a decent place to live in! We'll have no Warden! We'll have no God who tells us what we can and cannot do! We'll have no . . . ."

Dilna, Hoom, and Wix were far enough up Noyock's Road that they didn't have to listen anymore. Several of their friends were with them, and the silence was depressing as they walked up the hill.

Soon, however, they began joking, clowning, mocking each other and the events of the day. And by the time they reached the crest of the hill, they were laughing.

Stipock was standing, alone, on the hill.

"Didn't you go to the council?" Hoom asked him.

Stipock shook his head. "I knew how it would end."

"I didn't," Hoom said. "I wish you'd told *me*. Before we set ourselves up as idiots." Hoom laughed, but the mood was suddenly somber again.

"I might have been wrong," Stipock said. Wix laughed, spoke loudly so all could hear: "Do you hear that? Write it down— it's the first time we've heard him say it. Stipock might have been wrong!"

Stipock smiled thinly. "The feelings run too deep. Too many people love to hate. People aren't willing to work together."

"As the man who taught us that division was a wonderful

241

thing, it's odd you should suddenly love peace and cooperation so much."

Stipock looked very tired. "You don't know. I was born and raised in the Empire. Too many laws, so much oppression, everything far too rigid. And overnight I was put here, and I had to fight those laws, relieve that oppression, loosen things up."

"Damn right," Wix said.

"Well," Stipock said, "it can get a little out of hand." And then he looked down from the hill toward Linkeree's Bay. And all the eyes followed his, and saw the flames and the smoke rising. The boats were burning.

They shouted, and most of them ran down the hill, screaming threats that they couldn't possibly carry out, shouting for them to stop, not to burn the boats.

Only Dilna stayed with Stipock, and they walked slowly down the road toward the bay. "Your plans didn't work, did they, Stipock."

"Or worked too well. The one thing I didn't count on, you see, was the fanaticism of the people I converted too well, and this kind of reaction from the people I antagonized too much."

"There it is, you know," Dilna said. "You're just like Jason in your own way, Stipock. Twisting people around to do what you want them to do. Playing God with their lives. And what do you think will be left when the smoke dies down?"

And Dilna sped up, leaving Stipock walking slowly behind her.

At the burning ships, Wix and Hoom were having a shouting match with Aven and Noyock. Dilna ignored them. Just watched the flames and the red coals of burnt wood.

". . . Have no right! . . ." she heard her husband shout, and she only sighed, marveling at how people who hated laws pleaded for rights when their opponents, too, turned lawless.

". . . Won't have this city split apart by children. . . ." came Noyock's voice, angry and yet still, in his own way, trying to reason.

242

"Our homes are on the other side!" Wix cried out. And Noyock answered, "We'll let anyone who swears to loyally support and obey the laws Jason gave us build a new boat and cross the Heaven River."

"You don't have the right to stop us!" Hoom shouted again, and this time Aven answered his son.

"I heard what you people were saying—separation whether we voted for it or not. 'We own the boats,' you say! Well, you and your damned Stipock made us start changing the laws by majority vote. And so you damn well better be ready to abide by majority vote! And we're going to see to it you do, whether you like it or not!"

And Dilna couldn't see the flames anymore, for the tears running down her cheeks. I'm pregnant, she told herself. That's why things like this could make me cry. But she knew that it wasn't pregnancy. It was grief and fear. Grief for what was happening to people; fear of what would happen next.

What could the people from Stipock's Bay do, anyway? They had all come—there was no one left on the other side to bring a boat and take them across in the night. No one could swim the river—the current was too swift, and it was three kilometers wide at the narrowest point. They had none of their carpentry tools, and the older people were brandishing their axes and torches as if they'd gladly break a head or two, if one were offered.

She left the fire and walked slowly to where Hoom and Wix were still arguing furiously with Aven and Noyock.

"We don't want any trouble," said Noyock, "but I won't let you break up the City!"

"Break it up! You call this holding it together?" Hoom shouted back.

Behind each group of leaders was a gathering crowd of supporters. Both crowds looked equally angry; but the crucial difference was the sharp tools the older men held in their hands. Dilna walked into the space between the two groups.

She said nothing, and after a few moments they realized that she wasn't joining into the argument on either side. "What is it?" Noyock asked.

"All this talk," Dilna said, "won't build the ships for us. And all the shouting doesn't find us a place to stay warm tonight. I want my husband to build me a shelter. We'll need tools to do it."

And Dilna turned around to find herself looking directly into Wix's eyes. She averted her gaze, found Hoom's concerned face. Behind her, she could hear Aven saying, "We can't give them tools—they'd build boats in a week. Not to mention busting our heads in."

Dilna whirled on him. "You should have thought of that before you stole our homes from us. I'm pregnant, Aven. Do you want me to spend the night in the open air?"

Noyock turned to Aven and said, mildly, "They're right. Maybe a few tools—enough to rig some kind of shelter before nightfall."

"Why?" Aven asked. "Not one of them but has parents that'd be only too glad to invite 'em back into their homes."

Wix's father, the usually gentle Ross, raised his hand and said, "That's right, there's no hard feelings. We'd be glad to give them food and shelter!"

Wix's face was twisted with fury. *"Give* us food and shelter! There's not one of us but has plenty of food and shelter across the river! You stole it from us! You don't give us one damn thing! It's ours by right!"

"Rights, rights!" shouted Aven. "You little lying bastards don't have any rights!"

Dilna turned back to Wix and Hoom. "Enough, enough," she said quietly. "In a brawl we'd lose. Whatever we do, we can't do it here."

"She's right," Hoom said. "Let's go."

"Where?" Wix asked.

Hoom looked up the hill toward Noyock's Town. "The forest just north of the Pasture. We can take fence rails and rig a shelter."

Dilna turned back to Noyock. "Do you hear that, Noyock? We're going to take fence rails from you and build shelter. That way we won't have to touch your tools."

Noyock, eager to end the quarrel without violence, agreed, and Hoom, Wix, and the rest of the crowd straggled away from the beach, heading back up the hill. It was already afternoon, and there was much to do before night.

Noyock caught Dilna's arm before she could leave the beach. "Dilna—please listen. I want you to know, this wasn't my idea. When I got here, the boats were already burning."

"There's a law," Dilna said, "about destroying another man's property. You're the man who loves the law—imprison these men until Jason comes."

"I can't," Noyock said miserably. "There are too many of them."

"There are more than a few of us, too," Dilna retorted. "This is Linkeree and the ax all over again. Only you're not Kapock."

As she walked away, Noyock called after her: "It wasn't me that worked so bloody hard to strip all the power away from the Warden, it was you! If I still had that power, I could protect you!" But she didn't turn to answer. When she got to the brow of the hill, she stopped and looked back at the beach. Noyock was still there alone, watching the last flames die. On impulse she ran back down the hill, all the way to where he stood. "Warden," she said, "we'll need a fire tonight. Will Jason approve, do you think, of our taking some of the wood from our ships to start it?"

He set his face like stone and turned away. She picked up a piece of wood that was still burning on one end, and whose other end had been in the water until then. And once again she climbed the hill.

The people of Stipock's Bay were gathered in a small clearing in the forest, trying to turn fence rails, branches, and dead leaves into lean-tos for the night. Few of them looked sturdy, and Dilna looked at the sky, grateful that the clouds had gone, and the sky was clear. When Wix saw the torch, he smiled. "Wise woman," he said, and called to several men to rig a fire. Again, they had to use fence rails, so the fire was built in a large square, hollow in the middle. "I only wish we could burn down the whole damn fence," Wix said, as he lit the fire.

"Burning's a good idea," said a voice from the edge of the clearing. Many of the people working turned to see who it was. Billin.

"Ah, Billin," said Wix. "I thought you were still down in Firstfield, giving a speech."

"The time for speeches is over."

"How clever," Wix said. *"Now* he realizes that."

"I just saw the ashes of our boats," said Billin, raising his voice to be heard by all. "I just saw the ruins of our last hope for peace! And I say to you—"

What he was going to say to them no one knew, because at that moment Wix strode forward and struck him so hard in the stomach that Billin's feet left the ground, and he collapsed, gasping, in the dirt.

"The ruins of our last hope for peace aren't on the beach, Billin!" Wix shouted. "The ruins are back in Firstfield, when you and the pebble-brained oxen who followed you wrecked the only compromise we could have had! It was you that caused the burning of our boats, Billin! So you can shut up for a few days, or I'll put you deep enough in the river that you'll be singing to the fishes for eternity!"

The silence rang out after Wix finished his impassioned speech. Then Billin groaned, and slowly dragged himself to his feet. Everyone got back to work. But when conversations resumed, they were more bitter than ever before.

When night fell, they gathered around the fire, staring at the flames. Some women from Noyock's Town and Linkeree's Bay brought food before dark. It wasn't enough, but it was something, and they swallowed their pride and ate it. Now they sat and watched the fence rails shrink in the fire.

"I've been thinking all day about what Billin said," Hoom

said in one of the dismal lulls in the conversation. "And I think he's right. Burning's a good idea."

"And what do we burn, the whole city?" asked Wix, scornfully.

"No, no," Hoom said. "But the old people, they've hated the boats from the beginning, the boats have meant our freedom from them. They burned them." Hoom stood up and walked around the fire. He was no orator, but the very quietness of his speech made them listen all the more. "Well, there's a few things they've been using as weapons against us. The Warden, for instance." Someone laughed and said, "Does that mean we burn Noyock?"

Hoom smiled and shook his head. "Noyock's done us no harm. Just his office. There's something else, though. The History."

Several people snorted. The History, constantly held over their heads as "proof" that things must be done the old way.

"They burned our boats," Hoom said. "So let's burn their History. It's far less harm than they've done to us. You know what our fields will be like if we let them sit for a month, unharvested. My fruit trees will be bare, with the fruit rotting on the ground. They've destroyed our homes and our livelihoods—nobody could say we've been excessive if we destroy their stupid History."

A few chuckled, and the idea began to look more appealing.

Wix spoke up. "Easily said. But they're armed against us, and they'll fight to protect it. It's—it's a God-thing to them, they keep it for Jason. They'll fight."

"So," Hoom said, "we won't announce what we're after. Not a large number of us, either. We'll just wait until everybody's asleep at Noyock's house, and we'll break in, rush up the stairs, and burn the damn thing before they even know what we're about."

"Break in? Is it that easy?"

"It will be for me. *I* can get in," Hoom said. And so the plan was made. The crescent moon was high in the sky as they

247

emerged from the forest, far to the west of their camp. Only one of them held a torch; the rest carried unlit torches and kindling wood. They walked in silence, and approached the tall house from the west, where it was less likely that anyone would be watching.

There were no lights in the house, and so they set immediately to work. Wix pointed to a spot beside the house, and the kindling was laid down. Then Hoom, who carried the lit torch, ignited the kindling. As it flamed, they all put their torches in. After a few minutes, they were all ablaze. Then Hoom raised his torch, and they all followed him to the kitchen door.

Hoom knocked on the door, and they waited, all of them standing close to the wall, so that someone glancing out a window wouldn't see them so readily. But the household wasn't expecting danger that night—a soft voice asked, "Who is it?"

"Grandmother?" Hoom asked.

"Hoom," said the voice behind the door, in relief and delight. "You've come home," she said as she opened the door. But the door was barely ajar when Wix and Billin muscled through, forcing their way past Riavain. It only took her a moment to see what was happening, and she cried out, "Fire! Help, fire! Quickly! They've come!"

No one stopped to silence her. Instead, Hoom led the way up the stairs to the second floor. As they reached it, several of his uncles and cousins emerged from their rooms, looking worried. "Where's the fire?" one of them asked, and Hoom said, "Downstairs, in the kitchen." For a moment the obvious ruse seemed to be working—the men headed for the stairs even as the torch-bearers charged upward toward the third floor. But then they realized who was carrying torches, and ran back up the stairs, trying to overtake them.

On the third floor, no one was fooled. Aven and Noyock stood in front of the door of the library. "You're not coming in here," Noyock said. "This won't help you a bit."

"But burning boats will?" Hoom snarled, and Wix shouted, "Get out of the way." Dilna realized, though, that at this moment

248

their attack would either succeed or fail—the men from the downstairs were right behind them, waiting, it seemed, for them to surrender. And talking would never get the door open.

"Talk is nothing!" Dilna shouted, and she swung her torch at the man behind her on the stairs. He recoiled instinctively—if he hadn't, the torch would have hit him in the head. But in recoiling, he lost his balance, and fell backward into the men behind him. Billin seized the opportunity, and while Dilna and a few others used their torches to keep the men on the stairs at bay, Billin rushed forward, swinging his torch at Aven and Noyock.

But they held their ground, and Billin faltered in his advance. This time it was Wix who recovered the momentum. "You've had fair warning," he snarled, and shoved his torch into Noyock's belly.

The pain of the blow drove the breath out of Noyock—and when Wix pulled the torch away, Noyock's shirt was on fire. He tried vainly to brush it off, but it spread quickly, and he screamed and fell to the floor, trying to smother the fire. Aven still blocked the door, and he was using his feet to try to keep Billin and Wix at bay.

"An ax!" someone shouted, and sure enough one of the uncles was brandishing a bronze-headed ax. He was swinging it in a circle over his head, causing as much danger for his own side as for Dilna and the others defending the stair, and Dilna ducked under the blade and jammed the tip of her torch upward against the man's chin. He dropped the ax—it clattered on the floor next to Hoom. Hoom picked it up and swung it savagely at the door, right at Aven's head.

This time Aven ducked, just in time, and the axhead was buried in the door, splintering it. Aven tried to strike at Hoom while he pulled it free, but Billin was too quick, forcing him back.

With a roar the men on the stairs tried to rush past, just as the door gave way on the ax's second blow. Dilna and the others couldn't stop them—but the work was nearly done. Wix and Billin threw their torches into the room—Wix's sputtered on the floor, but Billin's landed on a shelf, instantly igniting the papers

249

there. Then the stair landing was a melee, as Wix, Billin, and Hoom struggled to keep the older men from entering the room and putting out the fire.

Aven bellowed and charged his son, throwing him aside as he entered the smoky library. As he passed, Hoom brought down the axhandle on his father's head, sending him sprawling. At that moment, Wix shouted, "Let's get the hell out of here!" and began slugging his way to the stair.

The others tried to follow. One of them was unconscious on the floor. Dilna, who had been swept to a far corner by the rush on the stairs, tried to rouse him, but he didn't budge, and she got up to run for the stairs. As she did, the library erupted in a sudden roar, and for a horrible moment flames lashed out the door and threatened to start the whole landing on fire. Then they subsided a little, but flames danced now on the banisters, and as Dilna forced her way toward the stairs, she saw an inert body in the library, covered with flames, the feet already charring. She screamed, caught hold of Hoom, who was fighting his way down the stairs, and shouted in his ear, "Your father! Your father!"

The look on her face told him the story, and he, too, screamed, rushing back up the stairs. "Father!" he shouted, a throat-ripping cry. "Father!" But the flames forced him back. Several of the men on the stairs saw what was happening—there were three men unconscious on the landing. They struggled back up against the heat, pulled them out and down the stairs. But Hoom still stood there, tears streaming down his face, seemingly oblivious to the heat, screaming, "Father! Father!" When they finally dragged him down his face was black with smoke, and the front of his clothing was charred. Dilna, who was being held at the bottom of the stairs, saw his smoking clothing and blackened face, and fainted.

They gathered in Firstfield on Jason's Day, but this time there was no chatter or pleased expectation. Those who had borne torches that night were each surrounded by men, and their hands were bound, except Hoom, who was still so badly injured that a makeshift bed was provided for him. The other refugees from Stipock's Bay kept to themselves. They were unguarded, but they had nowhere else to go, nothing else to do. Jason was coming; and suddenly even those who had scoffed at him were afraid of his coming.

The sun was hidden from them by the shaft of the starship; the space opened in the side and the line descended. Dilna remembered four years ago, when she was only barely thirteen, coming with her mother to see Jason come. He had brought the hundred eleventh Ice Person with him. Stipock. And bitterly Dilna wished he had never come.

Jason's feet touched the ground, and he stood and walked to Noyock, who waited for him. Jason held out his arms to embrace the Warden, but Noyock only covered his face with his hands and wept.

Jason stopped directly in front of Noyock, his blue eyes staring at him. They stood like that, it seemed, for hours, though when Jason broke the pose and enfolded Noyock in his arms, the sun was still not out from behind the tower. The people watched, and the realization spread as a murmur among them. "Jason is crying too," they whispered.

"He knows," came the answer. "He already knows, without even a word spoken."

Jason whispered something in Noyock's ear, and then stepped away. Noyock turned to look after him, no longer sobbing, though his cheeks were smeared with tears. Jason strode toward the waiting crowd. "Where is Aven?" he called out.

There was no answer, only a rustle of whispers in the crowd. "Who has hidden Aven from me?"

And then some answers came. "Hoom killed him!" someone said. "He died in a fire," said another. But the answer that caught on, that many called out, was the one that fixed the blame on Hoom.

Jason walked to where Hoom lay, swathed in bandages on the makeshift bed.

251

"Did you kill Aven, Hoom?" Jason asked, loudly.

Hoom closed his eyes and answered, clearly. "Yes."

Jason knelt beside him, and many, unable to see, stood or crowded toward the front, to see what Jason would do. But Jason only touched the bandages on Hoom's forehead, and looked deeply into him, as if he could see into his mind. Dilna got up from her guards, and came to Jason. "It isn't true," she said. "Hoom didn't mean to kill his father. He was only trying to burn the History."

Jason stood, and looked around at the crowd. "Burn the History. And why did Hoom want to burn the History?"

Again silence. But now Wix leaped to his feet, and cried out in fury, "They burned our ships, that's why! They're all quick enough to tell you Hoom killed his father, but they're not so fast to tell you they burned our boats! Kept us from our City on the other side of the river! All our fields are rotten, our harvest is wasted, all because they burned our boats!"

Jason nodded, and Wix fell silent, sat down. "Burned the boats," Jason said. "And why did they burn the boats?"

The answers came quickly then. "They wanted to split the City! They wouldn't obey the Warden! They said they'd make their own laws! They didn't obey the majority!"

Jason raised his hands, and silence fell again. He raised his voice and said, "They wouldn't follow the majority. They wouldn't obey the Warden. And for this you kept them from tending their fields and their flocks. For this you kept Hoom from getting a crop from his trees."

A gasp came from many in the crowd, for no one could have told Jason about Hoom's trees. He knew. He already knew everything.

"And why wouldn't they let the Warden rule them?"

The answers were shouted back at him, but again and again the shouts included one name. Stipock.

"Stipock!" Jason shouted. "Stipock!"

And Stipock walked out of the crowd, made his way to the

front, and stood to face Jason squarely. "Stipock," Jason said. "It all seems to come back to you."

"I never meant," Stipock said. "I never set out to have it end as it did."

"What did you mean, then?"

"I just wanted to give them democracy."

Jason smiled grimly. "Well, you didn't. You gave them anarchy."

Stipock's face was sculptured deeply with regret. "Do you think I don't know?"

Jason stepped away from him, faced the crowd, and cried out, "Who should be punished for this!"

There was no answer.

"That's what I think, too." Jason looked at them angrily. "We couldn't fairly punish anyone, without punishing everyone, could we. Because you're all guilty of Aven's murder! Every one of you!"

"I'm not," a woman shouted, leaping to her feet. "I didn't have a part in any of the fighting!"

"You didn't?" Jason asked sharply. "Did you try to *stop* them?"

And the woman sat down again, her face dark.

"Go to your homes, all of you. Be about your business. And give tools to the people whose homes are across the river. Let them build boats and go home! I'll speak to you all in due time. Go home!"

And the crowd dispersed miserably, in dismal groups that silently walked home, cloaked in shame. Jason knew. Jason had seen. And Jason was *not* pleased.

Jason had even wept.

The snow was light on the fields and on the trees when word spread through Heaven City: "Jason is finished." And in fact he had talked to everyone, visited in every home. And now he went to the edge of the river, and splashed out to the large boat that waited for him. Wix reached out his hand, and helped him into the boat, where ten of the people from Stipock's Bay sat, holding oars.

"I wish," Wix said as the oarsmen pulled them away from shore, "I wish you could have seen the boats with sail on them. But the wind is from the north now."

"I've seen them with sail," Jason said. Wix wondered when, and how. And Jason answered his unsaid words: "I've seen them in your eyes, Wix."

They touched the other shore, and Jason walked unerringly to the public house. Gradually the people came in, filling the large room to overflowing. Jason stood at the long bar, sipping hot beer. When it seemed that all had come who were coming, Jason set down the cup and lifted himself onto the bar, where he sat as he spoke to them.

"I've talked to every one of you," Jason said, "and there are many of you—most of you—who have learned enough from the bitter experiences of this autumn. You're content now to live under the law and under the Warden. But you still want to stay on this side of the river, where you're still independent, where you're still a little lonelier, and therefore a little happier." And then he said the names, all the men and women who felt that way, and told them they could go home. "If I'm wrong, then stay," he warned—but he wasn't wrong. Only about forty people remained in the public house, and Jason waited until the others were all gone before he spoke.

"You are the ones who hate too much. You're the ones who don't want to follow the laws, no matter how it hurts other people; you're the ones who don't want any part of Heaven City. If there's anyone here who doesn't feel that way, you can leave."

They all stayed.

"Well then," Jason said. "You're no more responsible for the disaster this city suffered than are those who aren't content unless they force everyone to fit their image of what is right and good. You won't be punished. I think your memories are punishment enough."

No one looked at anyone else, except Stipock, who sat at the back of the room and looked at everyone in turn.

"Stipock," Jason said. "You wanted to lead your own city, didn't you? You wanted to wean some of the people away from believing and trusting in me."

"Damn right," Stipock said.

"Well, then, look around you. These are the people you've won over. You've had four years. I'm sure our bargain is satisfied in four years, isn't it?"

And Dilna looked at Hoom, who sat beside her, holding her hand. Bargain? she asked with her eyes, and he shrugged.

"It may well be," Stipock said.

"You haven't fulfilled your part, you know," Jason said. "I expected a bit more than a tallow lamp and boats on the river."

"I was busy," Stipock said.

"You'll be busier. Because you're all getting what you want —freedom. Separation from Heaven City. And I'll even let Stipock choose where you're going. What's the most valuable piece of land on this little planet, Stipock?"

Stipock only half-smiled, and shook his head. But Jason acted as if he had answered. "Do you love steel that much?" Jason asked. "Then that's where I'll send you—to the place where iron ore is close to the surface."

The words were meaningless to them—iron and steel they had never heard of. Jason looked around at them, and smiled. "Oh, the iron is desirable enough," he said. "Have you seen the metal of the Star Tower?" They had, of course. "That's steel," Jason told them. "And you make it from iron—if you can."

"When do we leave?" Stipock asked.

"Tomorrow. I'd advise you all to forget your warm clothing. And bring hats. The place you're going is pretty sunny." Then Jason stepped away from the bar, and left the public house.

The next morning those who were leaving gathered in a large cleared field where the wheat had rotted on the stem. They didn't wait long—a roaring sound came from the Star Tower, and soon a huge metal object hovered over them. Stipock told

255

the people to stand clear, and when they had shifted back, the metal craft settled to the ground. Many of them were filled right then with doubts—Jason really did fly, and the ship he flew in was bigger than a house.

But the door was open, and Jason was herding them inside, and they had little time to worry about whether Jason was, after all, everything he had been thought to be. Two rows of seats filled the middle section of the craft, and they nearly filled them all. Stipock was the last to enter, and the door closed behind him, though no one touched it. And as soon as Stipock sat down, the craft lifted gently from the ground, and as the earth receded below them, many were filled with a terrible vertigo, and some vomited.

"Where are we going?" someone asked Stipock, and Stipock turned around and spoke to the group generally. "We're going," he said, "to a very hard place. There aren't many places where fields will grow well. But there are things more precious than fertile soil."

Dilna leaned over closer to Hoom, and said softly, "You'd almost think Stipock wanted us to go to this place from the beginning." Hoom's only answer was a faint smile. He didn't talk much, even though he was virtually healed from his burning in the fire at Noyock's house.

They crossed an endless forest, and then the forest ended, and below them was nothing but blue, striped with white. "The sea," Stipock explained. "Water for kilometers in every direction, so it seems you can never find the end."

But they found the end, and under them was rock and sand, carved into canyons and hostile mountains, plateaus and occasional patches of green. From the air it was impossible to see the details, but it was plain enough to everyone, though they had never seen a desert, that the land below them was dead.

It was frightening to Dilna, to see so much space with nothing growing in it. It looked endlessly dry. She swallowed convulsively. Hoom's hand closed over hers, and drew her close, and his arm reached around her, and held her.

"Hoom," she whispered, "I've never loved anyone but you."

"And I trust you with my life," he answered; and it occurred to Dilna to wonder whether Hoom had told as great a lie as she had told.

Jason left them near trees, and a shallow stream ran nearby, but the earth underfoot was sand, and the air was hot and dry. They milled around aimlessly, until Jason said a few words wishing them luck, urging them to obey Stipock; then the star-pilot climbed back into the flying ship and the door closed behind him.

"Well, everybody," Stipock said. "Let's get moving—up into the trees. We'll follow the stream. Feels warm enough that we probably won't need to build houses tonight—give us all a chance to be lazy!" Stipock laughed, but no one joined him. The sandy soil didn't look like it would be easy to farm. The water trickled over rocks, but a thin film of dust covered its surface even as it moved.

They shouldered their burdens and followed Stipock into the tall, gaunt-looking trees. Dilna and Hoom were among the last, and Dilna turned around to see dust rise under the flying ship.

She stopped and watched as it rose into the air and moved away north over the sandy plain. Wait, she wanted to cry out to him. Wait for me!

Instead, she shifted her pack and smiled at Hoom, who was waiting for her. "Well," she said. "This is more fun than a broken leg." He laughed, and they hurried to catch up with the others.

13

IN his haste to get back with the good news, Billin slipped on a shale slope and cut his hand severely. Of course he swore; of course he shouted; and then he ripped up his good sleeve (the left) and bound the bleeding cut and walked on.

He still carried his pack, though the food was gone since yesterday—good cloth was far too scarce these days. In the hot gray days of autumn when they first arrived, they had thrown away all the clothing that modesty allowed. Now they knew better. The summer sun burnt, and clothing was the only defense.

The trees were already getting more open, and shorter. The rich loam of the mountains had given way to more sandy soil, loose and sliding and hard to walk on. He was almost there, following the trickling stream that kept Stipock's City alive.

It was late afternoon when Billin finally reached the irrigation ditch and the diversion dam. Wix's idea, of course, and brilliant, of course, but only a stopgap in their constant losing battle with the sun and the sand. Although they might have had a chance if Stipock weren't so dead set on getting the iron—no. We'd be losing anyway. But now, Billin thought exultantly as he lurched along down the path of the ditch, now we can live better than we did at Heaven City. Just reach out a hand and pick food from the trees. Water everywhere. We have to leave immediately.

A house (new since he had left, but hardly a surprise, and he noticed that they had built it higher, out of the reach of the sand) and Billin went to the door and knocked.

No one. Getting on toward dark—wait here or go on down?

Billin was too hungry to wait, and too eager to tell his news, though his legs were weak enough that he had to think of every step before they would move.

And then he saw Wix and Dilna coming in from the trees. He stopped and waited until they came up to him.

"Billin," they said as soon as they were close enough to see who it was, and they rushed up and embraced him and welcomed him home. Yet Billin was not too tired to wonder what Wix and the bitch had been doing in the woods (as if he and everybody didn't know—a miracle Hoom hadn't murdered them both by now, except that the sweet simple-minded ox didn't notice), and he smiled at them as he said, "How's Hoom doing?"

"Well," Wix said. Was Dilna blushing? Billin doubted it—she wasn't the blushing type. At least Cirith, ugly and foul-tempered as she was, stayed faithful to Billin and loved him desperately.

"You must be tired," Dilna said, and Billin didn't even have to agree. He just stumbled and Wix caught him before he fell, and then the two of them helped him to the nearest house that might be large enough for him to rest awhile before going on to his own home.

It was a struggle between hunger (stay awake until the fish is fried) and sleep. Sleep won.

He woke in his own bed with Cirith leaning over him, smiling.

"Good morning," Billin said.

"Stay in bed," Cirith ordered, losing the smile the moment she knew he was looking. "You're too tired and weak to get up."

"Then bring me something to eat, dammit," Billin said, lying back down.

"It was so good while you were gone," Cirith grumbled as

260

she brought a bowl from the fire. "No one to complain at me."

"How did you make it through the weeks?" Billin said. And then as Cirith set the bowl on his bed and made as if to walk away in a huff, he lunged over (spilling stew) and pinched her.

She whirled on him. "If you're *that* wide awake, Billin my boy, you'll have no more sympathy from *me!*" And then she was off to the children's bedroom. Billin lay back on his bed and sighed. It was so good to be home.

He vomited the stew, but was able to eat broth later on in the morning.

And after noon, Stipock, Wix, and Hoom came to see him.

"Three out of four," Billin said as they gathered around his bed. "I feel honored."

"Dilna's pregnant again," Hoom said proudly.

"How many does that make—three?" Billin asked.

"No, four, of course—unless it's twins."

Four of hers, Billin kept himself from saying, but only three of yours. Not my place to tell the fool what everybody else knows.

"You were gone three and a half months," Stipock said.

"The days just flew by," Billin said, smiling.

They waited, and Billin loved watching them as they tried not to seem eager. But he was even more eager than they, and he ended the game and told them.

"A swift-flowing river, plenty of water even during the heat of the summer. A bay, and there are trees every inch, except where there are thick berry bushes. While I was there I wasn't hungry for a minute—I would have brought you back some of the fruit, but it started spoiling in the heat this side of the mountains, and so I ate it."

But as Billin described the paradise he had found a hundred miles to the south (or more—who can tell when the distance is covered on foot, scaling cliffs and wasting days hunting for a path through an impassable barrier), he became more and more uneasy. Hoom and Wix kept glancing at Stipock—and Stipock just watched Billin, his face impassive.

"I tell you," Billin said, determined to fire them with the enthusiasm he felt for the place, "that we could leave the plow behind and live forever there by just gathering. It goes on like that for miles. And the ground is as rich as anything in Heaven City, I swear it, except there's plenty of rain—the mountains must catch all the clouds, keep them from coming to us—and it's warmer than Heaven City, and besides—from the mountains I could see another land across the water, not far—we could build a boat and cross to it, and that other land looks even richer than the one I was in."

At last Stipock answered, "Very interesting."

Billin sat up in bed—too abruptly, and his headache immediately punished him for the impetuosity. "The hell it's *interesting*, Stipock. It's bloody damn *perfect*, it makes this place look like a desert, which it is, if you had guts enough to admit it. You chose this place—well, fine, you made a mistake, but by damn I've found a place we could get to in two weeks! Two weeks, and our children wouldn't spend half the year crying for food and the other half blistering in the sun and crying out for water!"

"Relax, Billin," Hoom said. "Stipock didn't mean anything bad. It's just hard to believe a place could be *that* good—"

"If you aren't going to believe me," Billin said, "why the hell did you send me?"

"We believe you," Hoom said. Hoom the peacemaker. Hoom the cuckold. Billin turned away in disgust. What kind of people did he have to deal with? Stipock, who only cared about that damn iron ore which wasn't worth a quart of ox-urine, and who always pretended that he was thinking carefully about things when the truth was his mind had been made up about everything a million years ago and he'd never change it come flood or fire. Hoom, so kind that you could almost forget how stupid he was. Wix, always full of bright ideas—the kind of man that could only be trusted by a fellow with an ugly wife (like me, Billin reminded himself). And Dilna? Why the hell was Dilna always involved in decisions? At least she wasn't here now.

262

"If you believed me," Billin finally said, "you wouldn't be here, you'd be home packing food and getting ready to go."

"Sleep awhile," Wix said. "You're still tired. We'll talk tomorrow."

"What did I do *wrong!*" Billin shouted, his voice cracking from the weariness still in him. "I'm not a hornet, don't brush me away!"

"You haven't done anything wrong," Stipock said as he went to the door. But it was Hoom who turned around and said, "I'm glad you're back, Billin. I've missed you."

After they left Billin was too angry even to quarrel with Cirith, and she went to bed in a huff, worried about Billin's strange behavior. And Billin kept waking in the night—angry, though it took him a few moments after waking to remember what he was angry *about*. Why were they so reluctant? Did they actually *like* the desert?

"No," Cirith said. Billin realized that he had been talking aloud. There was a faint light in the room—early morning.

"Sorry I woke you," he said.

"That's fine. They don't like the desert, Billin," she said. "But about a week after you left, I guess they realized you might find something like what you found, and ever since then Stipock has been telling people how good it is to suffer, how it makes us strong."

"Don't tell me people believe that crap!" Billin's mouth tasted foul. He got out of bed and staggered on aching legs to get a drink.

"I don't know what people believe," Cirith said.

Billin looked at her from the table, where he was dipping water from the jar. "What do *you* believe?"

"Don't tell me you suddenly, after two years of marriage, want my opinion?"

"I don't want to *have* your opinion, I only want to *hear* it."

Cirith shrugged. "Stipock's right. It makes us strong."

"Crap."

263

She held up her arm, flexed a large muscle. "Behold," she said. "Strong."

"So I married an ox," Billin said. "It's still a desert and I found a place where our kids can smile without getting a mouthful of sand."

He came back to Cirith and sat on the floor beside her stool. She put her arms around him. "Billin, I believe you and I want to go to that place. But I don't think Stipock will ever give up on his iron. He wants to make carts that move without pulling or pushing them. He wants to make a mill that doesn't need a stream. He thinks he can do it with iron."

"And I think he's crazy," Billin said.

"I thought you loved Stipock."

"Like a brother," Billin said. "Like a stupid, bull-headed, lovable, cold-as-a-fish brother. It's morning and I'm already sick of today."

"Let me make it better," she said, and he let her; and even though he was still a wreck from the exertions of the last month, it was wonderful.

"I take it all back," he said afterward. "That place wasn't perfect. It needed you."

"You hurt my thumb," she said, and then it was time to fix breakfast for little Dern, while Blessin pumped away on Cirith's breast. Billin tried getting out of bed, but he couldn't manage it. "Maybe this afternoon," he said.

But that afternoon he slept again, and as the sun set he woke to find Hoom beside his bed.

"Hello, Hoom. How long have you been waiting there?"

"Not long."

"Good."

Long pause. Billin decided that whatever Hoom had come to say must not be very pleasant, or he would have said it by now.

"Say it," Billin urged.

"We've talked about it—"

"We meaning the four Wardens of Stipock City—"

Hoom sat up rigidly. "How can you call us that?"

264

"You came to tell me," Billin said. "So tell me. You four have talked about it and you decided—or rather, Stipock decided and the three of you chirped back what he wanted to hear—and now you want to warn me not to tell people about what I found in the south."

"You don't have to see it that ugly unless you really want to."

"I should cover my eyes? I see what *is*."

Hoom smiled. "Does anybody see what is?"

"Least of all you, even when it's in front of your face."

"Sometimes," Hoom answered mildly (he doesn't understand, Billin thought contemptuously), "only the blind pretend to see. If you insist on telling people about what you *say* you found— what you *believe* you found—you'll only hurt yourself. No, that's not true—you'll hurt them, too, because they'll want so badly to believe in a place like that."

"Of course they'll want to believe it."

"For your own sake, then," Hoom said. And he left.

Billin felt better than he had since coming back—but even so, he would have stayed in bed if anger hadn't pulled him up and into his clothes and out the door of the house.

"Where are you going?" Cirith snapped as she saw him leaving.

"Visiting."

"At this time of night nobody wants to see you," she said.

"Mind your kitchen, woman," Billin answered. She kept grumbling after he left.

He went first to Serret's and Rebo's house. They were busy with putting children to bed (they had been twinned twice since coming to Stipock City), but they greeted Billin kindly.

"Glad to see you up and about already," Serret said, and Rebo smiled and took off her apron (in tatters, Billin noticed, like all the cloth), bringing him a stool to sit on.

He immediately began telling them what he had found on his journey. They listened politely, smiled, nodded, answered his questions, asked a few (though not many). After a half hour of this Billin realized to his fury that they weren't excited about it.

265

And why not? Their children were worse off than most, with bloated bellies that even Stipock said were a sign of a lack of food.

"You don't believe me, do you?" Billin abruptly asked, even while Rebo cooed softly about how wonderful his description of the rainfall sounded.

"Well, of *course* we believe you," Serret answered. Billin wasn't fooled. He took his leave quickly, went to another house.

It was late, and the lights were blown out in most of the houses when Billin finally gave up and came home. Cirith was waiting for him. She looked worried when he finally came to the door.

"Are you all right?" she asked.

Billin nodded, then shook his head. "Not one of them," he said, and she understood, and for once there was no banter, no complaint, she just came to him and held him and in his weariness and frustration he cried. The tears turned to anger quickly enough.

"How did they do it?" Billin demanded, pulling away from her and tossing a chair across the room. One of the children woke at the noise, cried out.

"Shhh," Cirith said, heading for the children's room.

"Not on your life!" Billin retorted. "I want to know how they did it! How did those damn self-appointed gods get everybody to answer the same way—'Yes, Billin, so glad you had a good time there, Billin, we're so *pleased* that your journey was successful, Billin, now get the hell out and let us get some sleep, Billin'—"

Cirith came to him and took his arms and dug her fingers into them. "You must promise me," she said, "that you won't do anything to them."

"What do you mean? What could I do to them?"

"Promise you won't. Promise you won't quarrel with them, please, Billin."

"What do you think I could do? Hoom's the murderer around

266

here, Wix is the adulterer, all I do is talk and now nobody's listening."

"Promise me, and then I'll tell you."

"Tell me what?" Billin asked, suspiciously.

"What they did."

Billin looked at her carefully. "I promise. What did they do?"

"I didn't want to tell you before you went out because you wouldn't have believed me and if you'd known you would have gotten so angry—"

"Get to it, Cirith, dammit, tell me what you know!" Billin paced to the window.

"They told everybody for the last two days, while you mostly slept, they told them that you had been badly hurt in a fall and it damaged your mind—"

"I cut my *hand,* the bastards, where do they think my mind *is?*"

"*I* know that, but they told the others that you invented a dream place, a place where everything is perfect, but that it doesn't exist—"

Billin roared with rage. The child in the bedroom cried louder, and another cry joined in. "Do they say I'm a liar! They dare to call me a liar!"

"No, no, no," Cirith said. "They only say that you were hurt. They say that you really believe what you say, that your mind isn't working right—Stipock had a name for it, he called it 'hallucinations', I think—"

"Stipock has a name for everything—"

"Billin, you can't fight it, the more you say you *know* what you saw, the crazier they'll think you are—"

"Cirith!" Billin said, striding to her, looking her in the eye, "do *you* believe them? Or do you believe me?"

She looked at him for a long time, but then she looked away. "I don't know," she finally said.

This time Billin did not roar, because this time his anger dissipated in despair. "If you don't believe me, Cirith—"

267

"I *do* believe you, I do, Billin, I want to believe you so much, but that's it—what you tell about is so perfect, how can I trust it? It makes everything here so terrible, and Stipock says that this is the best place—"

"He says that because of the iron—"

"I know, I know, please go to bed now, Billin, you're tired—"

"I can't sleep."

But he did, and woke in the morning still filled with despair. Because sometime in the night he had wakened after dreaming of the place he had been to. The dream had seemed so real. He had tasted the fruits again, and swum again in the bay, and drunk from the cold river and lain in the grass growing thickly on the riverbanks. He had felt the rain cover him again, beating warm and fresh on his skin, making him clean.

And he wondered if it had been a dream before.

And, once he wondered, he knew that it had. How could it be real? He closed his eyes and tried to picture the place, tried to imagine the taste of the berries. But all he could taste was the dust that always hung in the air; all he could see when he closed his eyes was red.

So he didn't speak of it anymore, not for weeks.

It was time for the rains to come.

The rains didn't come.

"Don't worry," Stipock said. "These things vary by as much as two or three weeks."

After six weeks the rains still hadn't come; but the winds came on schedule. Last year the winds had been cooling, drying out the soaking earth (for that short time of rain and then wind, the colony had been bearable); this year the winds were hot and dry, the breath of dying, and after four days of dust and sand whipping into ears and eyes and noses and mouths, burning the skin of those caught outside, drying out or silting up every barrel of water, every cistern, filling every ditch, tearing leaves off the trees, after four days of that one of Serret's and Rebo's younger twins died.

268

They buried him in the sand during one of the brief lulls in the wind.

The next morning the dessicated body was in the open, the skin flayed away. The wind, by one of those cruel freaks of nature, had blown the baby so that it jammed its parents' front door closed. Serret swore as he shoved the door open that morning—screamed and wept when he found what had closed it so tightly.

They burned the body at noon. The wind kept putting the fire out.

And the next day two more babies died, and Wevin, Weerit's wife, died when her baby tried to come four months early.

They couldn't bury the bodies, and they couldn't burn them, so they carried them out into the sand and left them, knowing the desert would surely dry them out.

That evening Billin huddled into his last cloak and crept against the wind to Serret's and Rebo's house. While there he told them what the water had tasted like in the land he had found. But he knew they hated him for saying it, since they believed he was insane, and it made it hurt even worse.

And from time to time during the terrible three weeks that the wind lasted, Billin dropped a word here and there. "Fruit," he would say, "growing off the trees. Wet and sweet." The person he was talking to would frown and move away.

"Sweet water in a wide, cool river." And the person would lick his lips and then say, "Dammit, keep your madness to yourself."

"Rain," he would say, and a child nearby would say, "What's rain, Mama?" and the mother would weep and curse Billin for his cruelty.

And Billin cursed himself, for he, too, wondered if he were mad. For now that he himself doubted what he had seen, he didn't know why he kept talking about it, why every morning and every night and the hours in between he would keep seeing that fruit before his eyes again, bushes more red than green, and water.

"*Am* I crazy?" he asked Cirith.

"Hopelessly," she answered, and kissed him. But he didn't know if she was teasing; finally was sure that she was not.

And then the wind stopped. One morning everyone awoke to the sudden silence, to the sudden heat (even before sunrise) when the wind didn't penetrate the cracks in the woodwork.

They put on their ragged clothing and went outside to see. The sky was clear. The dust had settled (mostly) to the ground. And now, for the first time, they could see the damage. They saw their suffering by moonlight, and realized before daybreak that they were through.

The sand had built up against the trees, in some places ten or eleven meters above the old level. Houses that had been on level ground now seemed to have been built leaning against sand dunes that were higher than they.

The irrigation ditches were all gone, with no trace left of where they had even been.

Two hundred meters to the west lay the new course of the stream, a wide shallow trickling stream, full of mud and barely drinkable.

The few sheep were all dead, except a couple of lambs that had been kept indoors.

There was no scrap of food anywhere that was not impregnated with sand. That was no surprise, since sand was the main seasoning and the main flavor that they had known for months. But the people, as they talked, realized that all the children were complaining of the pain of defecating, for their stools were filled with sand. And now all the bellies were distended, because food was short.

And water less yet.

And then, as the sun broke over the horizon, promising the terrible, unending heat they had known before, Billin scrambled up a sand dune that leaned against a house and cried out at the top of his voice, "It's enough! We're finished here!"

They turned and looked at him.

270

"There's no hope here anymore! We have no water, we have no food, we have no clothing, our children are dying!"

In alarm, Wix and Hoom came running to him.

"Don't talk like that," Wix said.

"I take no orders from you," Billin said. Then he shouted to everyone, "It's listening to Stipock and Wix and Hoom and the Bitch that's got us where we are! I say I'm through taking their orders! Who made them Wardens! Who put them in charge?"

Hoom climbed up the dune and took Billin by the arm. "What did you call my wife, you bastard!" Hoom shouted at him.

"How did you know I meant your wife?" Billin said triumphantly. At that Hoom swung back his arm to hit him, but Billin dodged and cried out, "See! The murderer wants to kill again! Murderer!"

And at the word Hoom backed away, confused. By now all the people had gathered, even Stipock, who watched dispassionately from a few meters behind the rest.

Billin pointed his finger at Stipock and shouted (and his mouth was dry and it was hard to make the words come, but still he shouted), "There he is! The man who taught us that Jason wasn't God! Well, that's true enough. But neither are you, Stipock! You and your damned iron. Machines that fly through the sky! Where are they? What about a machine that keeps our children alive, what about that? Where's that, Stipock?"

People began to murmur to each other. Cirith came to the foot of the dune and spoke to her husband. "Billin, don't make people lose their hope," she said.

"Damn right," he answered. To the crowd he said, "I'm making you lose your hope, my wife says. Damn right, I say. Look around you! They say I'm crazy, but only a crazy man would look at this and still *hope!*"

"He's crazy!" Dilna shouted. "Don't listen to him!"

Billin ignored her. "Think for a minute! Think of this! You

271

all saw how much food I took with me. Enough for three weeks! How long was I gone? How long?"

Three months, they realized.

"Why didn't I starve to death? I came back so weary I was sick, came back hungry because I had run out of food two days before. But not *ten weeks* before! That's because I found *food!* Whether you believe all that I said or not, you have to believe this: I found *food* out there! And that's more than you'll find here!"

Billin looked at Stipock and still the man didn't show any emotion at all. Billin looked at the impassive face and realized he had no hope of persuading anyone. When Billin had stirred crowds before, he had done it with the words Stipock had taught him. And now Stipock was silent and stood there uncaring, because he *knew* that Billin couldn't persuade the crowd on his own.

So Billin slumped his shoulders, then looked up at the crowd again and said, "Never mind. I don't care what you do. Stay here and keep digging for the damned iron and wait for the sand to come again. But I'm going. Because even if I'm crazy and there's nothing out there, it's better to die *looking* for something than to die here in the sand, with the wind to dry us out because we've lost our power even to bury or burn the dead."

And then Billin let himself fall backward and slide down the dune to where Cirith caught him and cradled his head. The crowd stayed for a while, then went back to their homes to begin sweeping out the dust.

That night the wind came up again, as hard as ever, and the dust came back in and hung in the houses.

And the next morning at dawn Billin, Cirith and their two children loaded pitifully scrawny packs on their backs and left their house. They walked west to the stream and then set their faces south, uphill into the shadeless trees that had been stripped by the storms.

They had not gone more than a hundred meters when they heard a hoarse cry behind them. Billin turned and saw Serret and Rebo and their two surviving children (one from each set of twins) also loaded with meager packs.

"Wait for us!" Serret called again.

They waited.

"Billin, may we go with you?" Serret asked.

"I thought you didn't believe me," Billin said.

Rebo shrugged. "Does it matter whether we believe you?"

Billin smiled, a dry, ghastly grin, he knew, but the first time he had smiled in weeks. "Come along then."

They went up the stream all day. Gradually, as the miles went by, the sand grew less, and the stream was deeper, better to drink. They filled their waterbags and went on (after drinking deeply and pouring the clean water on their heads). And finally they came to a place where the stream bent to the west and their path went to the east a little.

Billin went to a tree that bore a small cut, and with his knife made the cut deeper and more plain. He turned the mark into an arrow, pointing the way they went. Then he looked ahead until he saw a tree with another small mark, and led them to it, where again he made the mark plainer. "In case others follow."

They were nearly out of food when they came to the mountains, but already the land was far greener, the trees and undergrowth lusher, water more plentiful. Billin killed a tree squirrel and they ate the meat. And while they camped there, with a fire and water enough to wash all over, two more families joined them.

"We saw your fire," they said, "and realized you weren't so far ahead as we had thought."

So they waited a few more days, killing more squirrels and catching some small freshwater fish in a mountain lake one of them found while exploring the area. And when they finally left, heading downhill this time, there were thirty of them, counting women and children—half of the colony. Billin knew now that he hadn't dreamed—everything was as he had remembered it, and he couldn't stop talking about what they would find at the bottom of the mountains.

And after another week they reached the end of the craggy paths and found themselves by a placid bay, with a coldwater river rushing down, and fruit trees and berries so thick around that there was hardly need to plant. Of course they *did* plant, because one never knew what other seasons might be like in a place like this—but who needed to bother with watering and tending the fields, when they knew the seeds would grow and the harvest would come without worry?

And Billin's children stopped wearing clothing as they played in the sun, day after day.

Over the weeks more and more people came down the mountains and into the village, where the only houses were roofs—no walls were needed, and the roofs were just to keep a few things dry when the rains fell, and to keep the sun off during the heat of the day.

At last Billin counted who was there and realized that between those who had died and those who were there, only seven people remained unaccounted for: Stipock, Wix, and Hoom and Dilna with their three children.

He told Cirith.

"Will they come, too, do you think?" she asked.

"I don't think so," Billin said. "What would they do here? The only way they know how to live is by telling other people what to do."

"You tell people what to do."

Billin laughed. "Only when they want to work. We built a boat—so what! Those who wanted to work on it did. The rest just did as they pleased. Next week maybe we'll go over to that other place across the water. Who knows? Who cares?"

"I see, now. You're just lazy." She laughed.

"Of course," Billin said. "And you're just fat."

Cirith looked ruefully at her bulging stomach. "I was hoping I was going to have a baby, but my time of month began yesterday, so it isn't that."

"It's berries. Always when I kiss you you taste like berries," Billin said.

Then they made love, without particularly caring that their house had no walls and that it was daytime. No one particularly looked. And when they were through, Cirith went naked to the stream to get water.

"Cirith, you forgot your clothes," Billin said reproachfully when she came back.

"I know," she said. "But who needs them in this heat? We all know what human bodies look like, don't we?"

And they laughed, joking about what life was like for all the poor people back in Heaven City who had to wear clothes to stay warm and who had to work in order to eat, who always tried to keep learning things.

"Who cares if you can read and write?" Billin asked. "I never knew anyone who said anything worth writing down."

And Cirith only belched and then left him, trotting down to swim naked in the bay. Billin joined her and swam for hours, mostly lying on his back in the water looking at the white sky, wondering what Jason would think if he could see them now. Probably tell them that people were only human when they were working to achieve something. Like Stipock—have a goal, have a purpose. Well, to hell with them, Billin thought, and then he laughed so loud that he swallowed seawater and had to paddle in to shore, coughing and sputtering all the way. To hell with them, he thought again as he lay in the warm sand of the shore. And tomorrow I'll explore that other land. Or the next day, maybe.

14

STIPOCK woke early one morning, and because there was no wind he dressed and left his house and walked among the dying houses of the village. He went from door to door, and almost every one was hanging on its hinges, or blown off, and no one was there to make repairs. At last he came to Hoom's and Dilna's house, and knocked, and they let him come in and sit on one of the beds as they served the small breakfast they had to Cammar and Bessa and Dallat. The children looked gaunt and old, and no one seemed to have the energy to speak or make a sound.

Wix came a little later, and sat beside Stipock on the bed, and said. "We're the last."

Breakfast done, there was little to do worth doing. No one had worked the mine for a month or more, and it was doubtless completely blocked by sand. The pitiful amount of iron they had taken from the hill this year was not enough to encourage them to dig for more. And Hoom voiced all their thoughts when he said, "If only we could eat iron."

Wix patted his trouser leg and dust rose into the air. Outside there was only a small breeze. The sand lay undisturbed, but the dust rose into the air, seeped through the many cracks in the house. Cammar kept sneezing.

Finally Stipock leaned back on the bed and addressed the ceiling. "We might have done it, you know."

Yes, yes, of course, if only.

"But you can't organize rebels to do a damn thing," Stipock said. And again they agreed.

"Doesn't matter now," said Wix. "They're all gone to where fruits hang on the trees and fish leap up into your hands and the squirrels come over and lie down in the pan for you." And they managed to laugh.

Without a word they all began to move, taking all the food and putting it in bags. Hoom and Wix took empty waterbags and went to the brook to fill them. Stipock went back to his house and gathered up the record he had kept of the village and the small supply of food he had left.

At noon they were ready to go.

"Where?" asked Dilna as they hid from the sun in her house.

"Home," said Hoom, and Stipock wondered at the fact that for some reason—or many—none of them suggested going south, to Billin's group. Pride, because they had refused to take the easy escape route that would lead to savagery, and wouldn't give in now? Or a longing for Heaven City? It didn't matter. Stipock was too tired to analyze. Jason had won every round of their duel, and had done it without breaking the bargain. Stipock couldn't deny it, and now he wanted to go back to Heaven City and surrender.

Satisfied? he could hear Jason saying.

Satisfied, he answered. Whatever the hell you're doing with this world, you do it better than I can. You know the people better than I do. And so, because it's the only game, I'll pay whatever price I have to in order to play. Your rules. But you can bet I'll play pretty damn well, whatever the rules might be.

"Stipock?" asked Dilna, and Stipock shook his head. "Sorry. Yes. Home. Heaven City."

They slept in the afternoon, and began their journey just before dark. The sky was cloudless, as always, and the moon was high and full, and the trees looked cool and welcoming as they left the dying village and walked out into the sparse forest. Stipock, Hoom, and Wix carried heavy packs and water bags. Dilna carried Bessa in a sack on her back, and held Dallat in her arms. Cammar walked, his small legs forced to work hard to keep up with the slow pace the adults took.

They drank copiously from the stream before they left, and began rationing immediately. And as the night grew cool, and then cold, they hurried their pace in order to keep warm.

Stipock brought up the rear, following several paces behind Hoom, who now was carrying a weary Cammar, at least for a kilometer or so. The bodies of the three adults ahead of him were not adult bodies, Stipock remembered. Only Wix was twenty, the others still in their teens. In the Empire they'd be children still, none of them at their majority. Here the weight of the world was on them. And they seemed strong enough to bear it.

Hoom, burdened with Cammar's weight, slowed down enough that Stipock overtook him. "Let me carry the boy," Stipock said. And Hoom willingly handed the child to Stipock, who held him to his shoulder. Cammar barely noticed—he was sleepy, and he rested his head. Hoom looked at the boy as they walked, and then said, "A beautiful boy."

"Yes," said Stipock. "Like his parents."

Hoom's face grew a little sadder, and he said, "I wonder if Wix will ever marry, and have more children." Not children of his own, Stipock noticed. More children.

"You're a kinder man than I am," Stipock said, softly.

Hoom shook his head. "Love and faithfulness can only be given, not demanded. All the same, I would have liked to have them."

Stipock was surprised at the pain behind the whispered words. After all these years of silence, of pretending not to know, why was Hoom saying it now?

"Dilna loves you," Stipock said. "And so does Wix."

279

"And I forgive them because of that. Or in spite of that. Stipock?"

"Yes?"

"If I die before we return to Heaven City, would you tell them? That I know? And that I forgive them?"

"You won't die. You're the strongest of us all, don't let the darkness and the sand get to you already, or you'll never stay sane through the desert."

Hoom only laughed. "Just taking precautions, old man."

And then they walked in silence for another hour, before Wix called out that they should stop and drink. They drank, a swallow each from one waterbag, and sat and rested for a few minutes. And then they were on their way again, until dawn.

They followed the pattern for days, walking among the trees at night, sleeping in the best shade they could find by day. They refilled the canteens at every stream, and in this area there were many.

But after a week, the trees began to thin, and the ground began to rise, and Stipock told them it was time to move due north. They reached a large river, and followed its course northward, but the water was brackish, and they only filled their bags at the sluggish streams that joined the river. Later, the streams became more rare, and they began to drink the river's water in order to keep their waterbags full.

They reached the crest of the mountains and left the river behind, descending to a dry plain of rock and sand. A few plants grew, and an occasional small animal moved at the edge of their vision. But no water at all.

And no rest from the heat. There was no shade, except behind rocks, and at noon even the rocks were no shelter, for the sun was directly overhead, and rocks had no shadows at noon. On the eighth day they ran out of water. On the ninth day they piled rocks over Bessa's corpse and went on, no one shedding tears because they were too tired, and their eyes were too dry.

They found an oasis of sorts on the tenth day in the desert, and drank the foul-tasting water, and filled their waterbags.

An hour later all were vomiting, and Dallat died of it. They buried him by the poisoned pool, and weakly walked on, emptying their waterbags before they left to forestall the possibility of their forgetting and drinking again.

They were lucky. The next day they found a clear spring in the side of a hill, and the water was good, and they drank and didn't get sick. They stayed at the spring for several days, building back their strength. But now their food was getting low, and with full waterbags they set out again.

Two days later they reached the top of a rocky rise, and stopped at the edge of a cliff that plunged nearly a kilometer, almost straight down. To the west they saw the sea, and to the east another sea, the water winking blue in the sunlight of early morning. And at the bottom of the cliff, the land funneled into a narrow isthmus between the seas. The isthmus was green with grass, and Stipock wasn't the only one, he knew, who breathed a great sigh of relief.

"Do you see the green down there, Cammar?" asked Dilna. The boy nodded gravely. "That's grass, and it means that we'll find water."

"Can I have a drink?" Cammar asked.

They found a way down the cliff before noon, and as they descended they realized that it wasn't nearly as sheer as it seemed. The slope was broken, but there were many possible paths. And that night, exhausted, they spread their blankets in the tall grass. When they woke in the morning, the grass was damp with dew, and their blankets were cold and wet.

At first they laughed, and plucked up grass and threw it at each other, getting soaked in the process. And then Dilna began weeping, and the others also grieved for the two children who had been granted no tears at their burial.

From then on the journey seemed easy enough, and they were hardened and ready to walk many kilometers every day. Even Cammar seemed to thrive on it, and often would run ahead of the others, calling back, "Too slow! Hurry up!"

The farther north they went, the thicker the grass and the

larger the bushes became. Soon they were passing many groves of trees, and tiny streams became brooks that they had to take their shoes off for. Eventually the shoes were put in the packs, and they hiked on bare feet, which were already toughened and hard as leather.

Six weeks after they had left the village to the sand and drought, they saw the snow-capped mountains rise ahead of them. "The headwaters of half the rivers in the world rise in these mountains," Stipock said, and they marched on. A week later they could no longer see the peaks because of the high, steep foothills they were traveling through. They followed the banks of a large river northward, and as it narrowed into a canyon they often had to walk in the river itself. They climbed cliffs to pass waterfalls, and often had to backtrack when seemingly easy paths ended in precipices and narrow defiles. And always the rivers flowed south and east, back in the direction they had come, and always the path ahead was uphill. They passed the last trees, and food became scarce, and they rationed again; but hunger was better then thirst, and it was summer, so that although they were cold, they were in little danger of freezing to death.

And then they noticed that the rivers seemed to flow in the other direction, northwest, and some of their routes were downhill. And one morning as they reached the top of a windswept, grassy hill, they saw what they had hoped to see: between two lower peaks in the distance, a green blanket of dense forest that went on and on, stretching forever into the distance.

"It's the largest forest in the world," said Stipock, "according to Jason's map. But nothing ahead should be as hard as what's gone on before." They sat down to rest and look at the hopeful view, and Cammar caught the mood of relief and happiness, and he ran back and forth around the crown of the hill.

"Jason never told us he had a map of the world," Wix said. "And yet you follow your memory of it as if you trusted it completely."

"I should," Stipock said. "I invented the machine that took

282

the geological survey. It's pretty accurate. The only inaccuracies are in detail—and in my memory."

Hoom was pulling up grass and letting the breezes catch it. "You know, Stipock, you kept telling us, again and again, that Jason wasn't God. And yet every time it comes to one of the miracles that Jason performs, you say, 'Of course he can do that.' And I think I understand it now. To you, what Jason does is commonplace. To you, God would have to be far more extraordinary. But to us, Jason's abilities are far out of reach. And that's enough to make him not at all ordinary, not a common man at all. To us, God. And why not?"

Stipock only leaned back. "I suppose that if a man sets out to manipulate the world in certain ways, and has the wit and the power to do it, then why not play God? I would have stopped Jason if I could. I couldn't. But does that—"

A piercing scream interrupted the conversation, and they all jumped to their feet. "Cammar!" Dilna shouted, and they quickly saw that he wasn't on the crown of the hill. They ran in different directions, and Stipock called, "Here! Come here!" He was at the northwest slope, the area they hadn't yet seen, and when they arrived in a group at the edge, they saw that the gentle hill they had climbed gave way to a jagged precipice on the other side. A torn patch in the grass at the edge showed where Cammar had fallen.

Dilna was frantic. "Cammar!" she cried out again and again. And then his answer came from surprisingly close. "Mama, I'm hurt!"

"Don't move, Cammar!" Hoom called, and Stipock shouted, "Where are you?"

"Here!" Cammar answered.

Hoom ran along the edge of the cliff a little way. "I can see him from here!" he called. "He's just over the crest of that little cliff, on a ledge!" Then Hoom waved and smiled, and the others knew then that Cammar must be all right—just out of sight over the edge. Hoom ran back to the others.

"Can we reach him?" Stipock asked.

"He's not very far," Hoom answered. "You'll lower me over the edge—I'm the lightest one who isn't pregnant," and he smiled at Dilna. She smiled back, reassured about Cammar's safety by Hoom's obvious confidence. "Just hold onto my legs."

In a few moments Stipock was gripping Hoom's left leg, and Wix his right, as the young man inched his way out over the edge, his arms reaching downward, out of the others' sight. "Lower!" Hoom called, and Stipock and Wix slid carefully down a little farther. "Lower!" Hoom called again, and Stipock answered, "We can't—"

But he was cut off by Hoom's urgent cry, "Don't jump for me, Cammar! Just stay there—don't jump!" and then a high-pitched child's scream, and Hoom lunged downward, desperately, tearing his foot out of Stipock's grasp. Hoom slid out of control, and only stopped with Wix gripping his right foot, with Wix himself in clear danger of being pulled over the edge. Hoom's left foot was over the edge and out of sight. Stipock didn't try for it, just clung to Wix to keep the two younger men from flying off into the chasm. Wix was panting, his fingers slipping on Hoom's leg. "I can't hold him," Wix said. "I can't hold him alone!"

"Let me help!" Dilna shouted, nearly hysterical with the terror of knowing that her son had fallen, that her husband was about to fall. She threw herself to the ground and slid forward, face down, toward the edge, out of control. "Dilna!" Stipock cried, and she was only stopped by grabbing at Wix, which jolted him enough that he lost his grip on Hoom's foot. Wix cried out in the agony of trying to force his fingers to grasp, but Hoom slid away, struck the ledge Cammar had been standing on, bounced limply out into midair, and for a moment it seemed that he'd fly into the abyss—and then he was out of sight.

Dilna was hysterical, screaming Hoom's name and beating at Wix. Both of them were in a precarious position, and Stipock was afraid that anything he did might break the equilibrium. But he decided, and acted quickly, pulling Dilna by force backward toward safer, more level ground. When she was well clear of the edge, still weeping uncontrollably, Stipock went carefully back and pulled Wix clear. It only took a meter's pulling to get the young man in a position where he could get himself back up to safe ground.

"I tried to hold him," Wix kept saying. "I really tried." And Stipock said yes, I know, yes, of course you did.

Then they heard Hoom's voice from below—not loud, but loud enough to be heard. Immediately they fell silent, and listened.

"Don't come down!" Hoom shouted. His voice echoed from the walls of the canyon.

"Where are you!" Stipock shouted.

"There's no way down here! Don't try!"

"Are you all right?"

"I think my back is broken! I can't move my legs at all!"

"How far down are you?"

"Don't come!" Hoom shouted, sounding more frantic. "It's too sheer! And the rocks are giving way under me—I won't be here long!" To Stipock's horror the boy began to laugh. "There's nothing under me from here! Five hundred meters, right down to the river!"

Dilna called out to him. "Hoom! Hang on! Please!"

"I already thought of that!" Hoom called back, and then they heard a distant scraping noise, and a cry from far below. Dilna gasped, but Hoom immediately called again, "I'm all right! I have hold of a rock! It seems stable!"

Stipock wracked his brain for an idea, a way of getting down to Hoom. But there was no rope any nearer than Heaven City, and to try to scale the cliff and bring up a man with a broken back without rope was inviting more deaths.

"I'm going down," Wix said softly.

"No you're not," Stipock answered.

"I'm going down, Stipock," Wix said. "I've got to help him!"

"Stay there, dammit!" Hoom shouted. "I don't want you to die with me!"

Wix was frantic. "I can't let him die!"

"Don't kill yourself for guilt," Stipock said coldly, and Wix

285

turned to Dilna for support. "I tried to hold onto him," Wix insisted.

"I know it," she answered. "We all did."

And then they fell silent. They stood several meters from the edge. Waiting. For what? Stipock realized that the situation was impossible. They were waiting for Hoom to fall asleep, or lose his grip, or die of his injuries. At best they were waiting for him to die of thirst. If they had to stay there waiting, they'd all go crazy.

Hoom realized all that, too, and said so. "I'm going to let go!" he called out.

"No!" Dilna wailed, and the canyon shouted it back at her. "No! No!"

"I can't hold on forever! What should I wait for? Jason's flying ship?"

"Is Cammar anywhere near you?" Wix called, trying to keep Hoom from talking himself into dying.

"He's dead!" came the answer.

"Can you see him?" Wix called. There was a long wait before Hoom answered. "There's a lot of blood on this rock," Hoom said. "It isn't mine. There's nothing between here and the river." Hoom's voice quavered as he spoke.

Dilna began to vomit, retching loudly. The sound was terrible, and Stipock wanted to scream in his helplessness. Wix was crying, more in frustration than grief.

"Stipock!" Hoom called.

"Yes!"

"Tell them for me!"

"I will!" Stipock called back.

"Tell us what?" Wix asked, looking up in dread. "What?"

"That he knew. And that he forgives you both."

Wix and Dilna were silent now. Hoom called from below, "But you, Stipock! I'll never forgive *you!*"

Stipock felt a terrible pain, a wrenching of his bowels, and he breathed heavily. The boy couldn't mean it.

"I'll never forgive you for not teaching me more before I died!"

And, relieved, Stipock slowly sat down. But the feeling of guilt was still there. Because it was Stipock who had brought Hoom to this.

Hoom didn't say anymore. There was a sliding of rock. No scream, no cry. No sound of the body landing below. And in the deep silence after the sound of Hoom letting go, the gurgle of the river far below seemed remarkably loud.

Wix and Dilna just sat there, saying nothing, not touching. After a while Stipock went farther up the hill and looked for bushes he could use to make a fire. When he got it going, he came back to the two young people and led them up the hill to the fire. They came passively enough, but they didn't look him in the eye. Stipock could guess what they were thinking. Years of betrayal, and the fact that they hadn't stopped, had never stopped. Knowing that *he* knew that they had betrayed him. No wonder, Stipock thought, that they sit on opposite sides of the fire. Guilt couldn't keep them apart when Hoom was alive; but now that he's dead, it will, for a time at least, separate them more thoroughly than marriage had ever done.

Dilna and Wix both cried out in the night, at different times. Stipock also slept badly. The next day they backtracked, and found another way down the northwest slope of the mountains. They never found the river that had taken Dilna's husband and son, and were just as glad of that.

The forest swallowed them, and the going was slow, and at last Dilna was too pregnant to travel. They built a house, then, and hunted in the forest, trapping small animals and birds and laying in food for the winter, Wix and Stipock both leaving the house for days at a time, to make sure the winter would not catch them unprepared.

The snows in the forest here fell deep, deeper than they ever had in Heaven City. The trees were taller, too, and denser, and the darkness at noon in the middle of winter, even though

287

the leaves had fallen from the trees, was dismal and depressing. But that winter Dilna's child was born. A son.

"You'll name it Hoom?" Stipock asked.

She shook her head. "Hoom told me he wanted a son named Aven." And there was little talk that day, though the snow confined them all indoors; they were thinking of death as the infant sucked pap from Dilna's breasts.

As night came, and they laid the logs for the night's fire, Dilna spoke from the bed where she lay, recovering from the birth. "I've been pregnant," she said, "six times. Six times, and Aven is all that I have now." As if in answer, the baby stirred and cried weakly. No one could think of anything to say to her.

And in the spring they set out again, following streams and rivers northward, trying to find a pass through the northern mountains that Stipock warned them of. And they found it soon —there was still snow on the ground as they hiked through the vast gap in the mountains, the peaks rising to the right and the left as they walked northward on the gentle hills.

It was nearing summer when they came to the Heaven River, the kilometers-wide torrent rushing westward to Heaven City. They stopped to build a small, crude boat, and two days after they launched it, they saw the shining metal of the Star Tower rise above the trees. Soon they saw boats ahead, plying back and forth across the river.

"Left bank? Or right?" asked Stipock, who was at the tiller.

"Left," Wix answered quickly.

"Left," Dilna agreed. They wouldn't try to hide among the people of Stipock's Bay, who would probably accept them more readily. They'd go to the Main Town. They'd find the Warden and take whatever answer he gave them.

They were greeeted with amazement and open pleasure by the people in Linkeree's Bay, and a crowd followed them up Noyock's Road, over the hill where the ashes of Noyock's house had been cleared and a four-story house erected on the site, and down the other side to Main Town.

The new Warden was Jobbin, a great-grandson of Hux, a man younger than Wix. He embraced them, and showed them a paper left by Jason when he had come to take Noyock into the Star Tower.

"Stipock," said the letter, "are you ready now?"

Yes, thought Stipock.

"You and all who returned with you—welcome home. Be happy here in Heaven City. And at least make an effort to avoid causing trouble." And Jason had signed his name at the bottom.

Having read the letter, Wix and Dilna and Stipock smiled at each other, and then settled down to tell their story. Stipock gave the records of his colony to Jobbin, who read them carefully. Several people also took turns writing the account of their journey as they told it. The travelers, in turn, read the History of the last few years. It was an unbroken story of peace, plenty, growth, happiness. When it was done, Dilna looked at Wix and then at Stipock, and said, "It's good to be home again, isn't it?"

And then the three of them went to live in different parts of Heaven City, and had as little to do with each other as possible. Someone once asked Stipock why—after all they had been through together, shouldn't they be close friends?

"We all died in a chasm in the mountains," Stipock answered. "And these new people you see are strangers, with unpleasant memories of someone who looked very much like us. When those memories are gone, perhaps we'll be friends." That was the most he ever said on the subject. Wix and Dilna never said a thing.

But it was Wix who led the expedition that mapped the Heaven River clear to its delta. And it was Stipock who first minted money, and who taught them to make charcoal, and who built the first windmill, and who taught them to make glass.

And Dilna's son Aven became Warden—many said the best Warden of all—and when Jason brought Arran from the Star Tower and married her, it was Aven who performed the ceremony.

Jason eventually took both Wix and Stipock and their wives into the Star Tower. But when he asked Dilna to come and sleep so

289

she could live forever, she refused. "I don't see anything wrong with dying," she said, "and I'd rather do it among friends than strangers, years from now, who never knew me." At her instructions, after she died her body was burned, and the ashes were scattered across Heaven River.

People kept having babies, and the babies kept growing up, and three hundred years after the starship first landed beside the Star River, half a million people were spread along the Heaven River, and it was time for the next step in Jason's plan.

16

LITTLE Reuben followed the bird into the forest. He did not look where he was going. He did not notice when he stepped through the cleared area that stretched all the way around the farm. But if he had, chances are he wouldn't have stopped. Because he was only four years old, and his education was not complete.

The bird, of course, being small, flew easily through the invisible barrier and on into the dense undergrowth of the Forest of Waters. But Reuben could still see the splash of red, now hopping back and forth on a branch. He did not know that it was hopping because even though the barrier was passable, it still caused such a disturbance in the tiny brain that it was all the bird could do just to stay on the branch.

Reuben ran through the invisible barrier, too—but it cost him far more than it cost the bird. Between the moment when his head first entered the field and the moment he hit the ground Reuben felt more pain than he had ever felt in his short life. It seemed like every nerve in his whole body was on fire, like huge thunders were erupting in his head, like lightning was dancing in his eyes. So great was the pain that he didn't notice that his shoulder struck a rock and bled profusely.

295

He didn't even notice the hideous scream he uttered.

And because his leg remained in the middle of the barrier after he fell, the pain went on and on and on.

He fainted, but not soon enough. When he woke in the dark house, with father and grandma bending over him, massaging his arms, he could still hear the terrible thunder in his ears, and white spots danced at the edges of the world, retreating just out of sight when he tried to look at them. And his leg was completely numb.

He heard nothing but the thunder, though grandma's lips moved, and she seemed to be angry. He wondered why his leg felt like it wasn't there. Grandma and father were arguing, it seemed, and he wondered why they were talking so soft that he couldn't hear them.

Grandma clapped her hands hard beside his ear. He thought she was trying to hit him, and he dodged. Father looked triumphant, but grandma shook her head. She reached down and rolled Reuben over on his stomach, so he was looking at the wall. Reuben didn't see anything, then, though he did feel a wind rushing past his ear—at least, his hair was stirred by something.

Then, as if from far away, he heard through the thunder a soft voice, calling his name. He rolled over quickly, to see who might be calling. But it was grandma, and she was only a few inches away. She seemed to be shouting. He answered, "I can't hear you, grandma, you sound so far away."

But she seemed pleased with that response, and father also looked relieved. Reuben didn't understand.

But he soon understood his useless leg.

Over the months his hearing gradually came back, but the feeling in his leg did not. He could swing the leg from the hip, but he had no control over what happened to the knee or foot. And so he was always falling down, always dropping things, and father and mother were impatient with him. But after a while he learned to walk by throwing his leg forward and bringing the heel down hard on the ground, which made his knee lock. Then he treated his leg just as if it were a crutch, as straight and hard as wood. He swung over it, then threw the leg forward again.

He could not see himself, but his older brothers and his older sister teased him unmercifully because of the way he walked. "You walk like a mantis," they said. "You walk like a crippled rabbit."

But one day grandpa came back. Reuben was old enough by now to notice that grandpa looked younger than father, and much, much younger than grandma. It was a mystery, but the kind of mystery that he knew not to ask questions about. Another mystery was why no one would answer him when he asked if there were other people outside the farm, and where they came from, and who was grandpa's father.

When grandpa came back he took Reuben into the shed behind the house and touched him with little cold boxes and spheres that frightened him and made him cry. But when grandpa left, grandma began massaging Reuben's leg for an hour every day.

Father complained about that, because it took so much time away from important work. But grandma answered, "That's what Jason said, my boy, and so that's what we'll bloody well do. The boy's leg is more important than the weeds."

Father looked angry, but went out of the room. Grandma kept on massaging.

It did no good.

When Reuben turned five, grandma began to take him out to the barrier now and then. He would go with her easily enough until he realized that they were near that partially cleared strip of ground. Then he began to cling to her skirt and try to hold back, try to pull her away.

"No, grandma, please!" But she took him right to the barrier, and then, every time, she said the same words.

"This is the wall of Worthing Farm. On this side of the wall is life and food and clear water and everything good. On that side of the wall is death and pain and terrible loneliness. What happens if you cross that barrier?" She said all this in such a dark and terrible voice that Reuben only cried and answered, "I don't know!"

So she told him. And when she finished, he was sobbing so hard he could barely breathe, and then grandma would take him away from the barrier. At night for weeks after one of those visits to the wall, he would have nightmares, and wake screaming "Jason!" he would call. "Help me!" But grandpa didn't come—only grandma, or mother, or father.

When Reuben turned six, he stepped on a sharp rock and cut his bad foot. But he rejoined—for he had felt the pain, like a little spark from miles away, but he had felt it.

When he told grandma, she didn't believe him, told him that he must get used to not having the use of his leg. But then father came and looked at Reuben with his vivid blue eyes (just like grandpa's) and said, "He's telling the truth, mother." And then grandma cried for joy and hugged him in her long, strong arms.

And because he was getting better, father began to give him more work to do. Reuben learned ropemaking and bucket making, and was taught all the seeds and which to plant at what day of the year and month. He learned the calendar and the names of all the weeds, but grandma never taught him how she did her trick of scratching a quill on thin strips of paper, and then say the same words from it every time. She taught no one how to do it, not even father.

When Reuben turned eight, father said he was old enough to come on the Walk.

Reuben didn't want to go, but when father decided, the children did it.

The Walk came every seventh day. Winter or summer, blizzard or wind or the hottest day of the year, they would leave at noon and walk to the northeast corner of Worthing Farm. There at the corner father would repeat the very words grandma had used. Except that when he said them, he not only made the children afraid, but he also seemed to be afraid himself. When the words were said, they walked in single file all the way around the barrier. Reuben could hardly stand to be so close to the edge. In the dark forest beyond he could imagine *them,* waiting. He knew them well: he had seen them in a hundred terrible dreams. Now, walking along the barrier, he felt the same sweating, freezing sensation that woke him up screaming in the night. He kept turning around to look, but they retreated out of sight before he could get a clear glimpse. He stayed as close to father as possible. Why doesn't he hurry? Reuben wondered. Doesn't he know they're watching us?

Then, after they had walked the whole border of the farm, three kilometers on a side, they came, wearily, to the Worthingstone. It was a smooth silver-colored cube, harder than any other rock, and it always gleamed in the sunlight. Etched into the stone by a power greater than any of them, because they knew *they* could never cut its surface, were strange marks. The same kind of marks grandma made on the paper.

JASON WORTHING
From the stars
Blue-eyed one
From this land
Jason's son

And at the Worthingstone father would say, his voice trembling with emotion, "This stone was marked by your grandpa. He set it here to protect us. As long as this stone is here, the enemies from outside Worthing Farm cannot harm us. But if any harm comes to the stone, or if any of the people of Worthing Farm leave, then our protection will end, and terrible death will come upon us all."

Then the Walk was over, and they gratefully left the barrier, walking slowly at first, then running, then bounding across the farm until they were at the dark house.

The light house, of course, they could not enter—it was grandma's, and it had the trick of flying off. Everyone had to hide in the dark house, and then there would be a terrible roaring, and then grandma *and* the light house were gone. Matthew told Reuben once, in whispers, behind the shed, "Father said once that she goes to grandpa."

Whenever grandma came back, she was quiet for days; but she seemed serene and happy all that time, going about her work with a smile. Father would ask her, "What's so grand that you're grinning all the time?"

But grandma only answered, "Why don't you look behind my eyes, and see?"

Whenever she said that, father turned away looking angry and ashamed. Matthew told Reuben it was because grandpa had once done terrible things to father for looking into grandma's thoughts. No one was allowed to look into grandma's thoughts.

"Will *I* be able to know what people think?" Reuben asked Matthew one day.

Matthew laughed. "You're too little!"

But it was about the time that Reuben turned twelve that three things happened to him. His leg was almost completely better. His chest and groin began growing hair. And he began to have flashes of what people thought.

It was then that the stranger came to Worthing Farm.

He was short, and dressed in clothing that seemed like another skin, only dark brown. Reuben, Matthew, father, and Jacob were hoeing the potatoes when he stepped from the forest. How he had got through the barrier no one knew. But he was strange, he was from outside, and he must be terribly powerful.

Reuben could not control his gift yet—but he did manage to catch glimpses. They were frightening. He saw images of great halls and huge towers, the world like a little ball in the distance, men and women in strange clothing doing strange things. He heard words and sentences that had no meaning, but that sounded vaguely wondrous, and also menacing. And he understood something else: this stranger was a man of power, a man of might, a man who was used to ruling other men.

300

He was everything that Reuben had learned to hate and fear from outside. And almost at the same time that Reuben realized that, father and Matthew and Jacob silently picked up their bronze-headed hoes and raised them high and advanced on the stranger.

Later, Reuben could not remember if the man had spoken or not. He only knew that the man looked coldly at them, and turned and walked back toward the barrier. Don't let him get away! Reuben silently shouted, and the others thought the same thing, because they ran to catch the man, kill him before he could get away and come back with more men with such frightening minds and such calm, confident power. But the man reached the edge, fiddled with something in his hands, and stepped easily through the barrier.

At the cleared space the men stopped, wordlessly watching as the stranger calmly walked back into the forest. When he was out of sight, they came away from the barrier, shaking with fear as they always did when the barrier was too close, too long.

They said little about the incident. Reuben assumed they didn't want to tell the women and worry them. But grandma looked at them all carefully at dinner, and asked, "What is it you're not telling me?"

And father smiled and answered, "Why don't you look behind my eyes and see?"

Grandma reached over and slapped his face, lightly. "I said tell me."

And so they told her about the stranger. When they were done, she leaped to her feet. "And you waited to mention this until now! I've raised fools for sons, but I had no idea how foolish!" And she ran out of the house. Soon came the roaring of the light house, and she was gone.

They assumed she'd be back soon, but she never came.

Reuben grew up and married his Uncle Henry's youngest daughter, Mary, and all their sons had bright blue eyes, and all of them, at puberty, could look behind each other's eyes and see each other's heart. Nothing else of importance happened to Reuben; he lived out his life within the confines of the farm, and grew old, and saw his great-grandchildren born.

One day, however, when he was very, very old, he went to the barrier alone, and stood there for a very long time. He wasn't sure why he had come. But finally, in order to ease the longing, he reached out his hand into the space where the barrier had always been.

And felt nothing.

He took a step forward, and still felt nothing. And another step, and another, and he was completely through the barrier to the other side, and had felt no pain, nothing at all.

He touched a tree on the other side. It felt like any other tree. The sky looked normal enough. And the leaves crunched underfoot just the same.

And then he walked back through the barrier, and fled back to his tiny room at the back of the old house, and stayed there, trembling, for an hour. He told no one of what he had found. But from that day on, he made his son Simon lead the Walk, and Reuben stayed away from the barrier for the rest of his life.

He was buried with his head pointing toward the Worthingstone.

17

JASON Worthing awoke from somec for the hundredth time within the pilot's cabin of the starship. But now he no longer exercised—it was all he could do to get out and walk around, force the blood to flow. He had long since ceased wondering how old he really was—he looked not older than forty, and felt ninety-nine. For three centuries the responsibility for a world had been on his shoulders; for forty years since then, he had been wakened every year or so to talk to Arran when she flew the scoutship from the farm to the starship. He assumed, when he got up, that it was she whose coming had roused him.

But the voice that spoke to him as he stood, flexing his arms beside the coffin, was a man's voice, and Jason looked up in shock.

The man was fairly old, but dressed in Empire fashions, though the color combinations were strange to Jason. And the old man laughed as he saw Jason's puzzlement. Jason looked into the stranger's mind, and then laughed.

"Abner Doon!" he said, shaking his head in disbelief. "I'd long since given up any hope! Abner Doon!"

And the old man embraced him. "Sweaty, aren't you," Doon commented.

"And still making a virtue out of discourtesy, I see," Jason said.

And they sat and looked at each other for a while. Finally Jason laughed again. "You know, I kept expecting any time, after the first hundred years here, that you'd turn up someday. I think I was still hanging on to some hope of that. What kept you?"

"Oh, things, you know. The revolution took a bit longer than I had expected to foment, that kind of thing. People are so damned unpredictable."

"I know," Jason said. They sat in silence for a moment.

"Oh, by the way," Doon said. "I took some liberties. I read all the Histories you've got stashed in here—fascinating reading. And the wreckage in the back of the ship here is self-explanatory. So instead of waking you and wasting your time on a guided tour, I made a few visits around your little planet."

"And is everything up to snuff?"

"Going nicely. You'll be interested to know that Wien's group —Wien's dead, by the way—made it to the lake without much trouble, and there's a magnificent little bronze-age town growing up along the shores, with farms spreading all over. And Noyock's quite ambitious—he's already sent colonists to five of the major islands. You've accomplished a great deal. A planet with no metals, and you've created a stable, religious society, progressive, well-governed, peaceful, knowledgeable—my congratulations."

Jason nodded, smiling.

Doon moved in for the kill: "So what the hell are you doing with that miserable little farm in the middle of the Forest of Waters?"

"Oh," Jason said. "You went there."

"Yes, I went there, and they damn near killed me before I got away. That's when I decided to come back here and wake you up. That farm is the opposite of everything else you've done —everywhere else, poets, music, a chance for a totally nontechnological culture of real beauty and refinement. And on that farm, everyone suspicious, murderous, ignorant, and hemmed in

304

by the strongest damn mindshield I've ever had the misfortune to bypass."

"Well," Jason said, "that's my showcase."

Doon snorted. "Papa's pride and joy."

"Exactly."

Doon looked up, startled. "You don't mean it!"

"Didn't you see their eyes?"

"I didn't come close enough. You mean that's your *family?*"

"That's where my genes are being stored. Inbred. There's a very small chance that a few idiots will start turning up after a while. But in the meantime, they're going to be getting my genes from every parent for a few generations."

Doon looked disturbed. Angry. He got up and walked to the control board. "Dammit, Jason! That's terrible. I mean, it's fine to want to improve the strain—but inbreeding like that can cause real harm. You just don't have the right to play with people's lives like that!"

Doon might have said more, but Jason started laughing uproariously, and it didn't take Doon long to join in.

"Oh, well," Doon finally said. "From one man who's spent his life playing God to another, I must say you've done a thorough job."

And Jason reached over and shook his hand.

The door from the storage area opened, and Arran came in. She rushed to the coffin, saw it was empty, and whirled to see Doon and Jason shaking hands, looking at her in surprise. "Arran," Jason said.

"That must be the stranger," Arran said.

"Arran?" asked Doon. "Not Arran Handully—"

"Correct," Jason said. "Not Arran Handully. Just Arran. My wife."

Arran stepped foward, eyeing Doon suspiciously. "He came to the farm, Jason, just as you said. Thomas and the boys drove him off, though—I came as soon as they told me."

"It's all right, Arran," Jason said. "He's a friend of mine."

Doon got up and offered her his hand. She took it carefully,

305

and Doon smiled. "Still beautiful," he said, "as beautiful as ever, though the years have deepened you, it seems."

"Have we met each other?" Arran asked, surprised.

"A long time ago," Doon said.

"Never mind, Arran." Jason took her arm, and she clung to him—clung as she had when they both looked young, and she was a bride, living for three glorious years in Heaven City as the wife of God, before the Dispersal, before she went to the farm in the Forest of Waters and raised a family in the strange fashion Jason had commanded.

"Is he—" she asked, then stopped.

Jason looked at her carefully, then smiled. "Yes, Arran. He's my father."

They spent three days together in the ship, telling Doon anecdotes that hadn't found their way into the History, he speaking of events in strange, far-off places that left Arran dazzled and filled her dreams. Doon and Jason pored over charts, talked about the past, the future. And then Doon said, "Well, Jason. I see you've thought of everything, and you don't need the advice of an old man anymore. Too bad I won't be around to see what happens when some superhuman descendent of yours comes out of the wood and demands his rights as Jason's Son!"

"Where are you going next?" Jason asked. Doon only smiled. "I think," he said, "that I'll go back home now."

"Aren't you going to visit any other colonies?"

"Oh, no. No, Jason. Actually, I probably shouldn't have visited here, either. But you see, I had to kill a couple of thousand years before I dared go home to Garden and find some subtle way of living out my last few years in peace and quiet. After all, even Hitler was forgotten after two thousand years, and I wasn't quite as bad as he." They both laughed, and then Jason put his arms around the old man and embraced him, and Doon hugged him back. "You're the prize in my collection, Jason. The best I ever found. That's the best part of being God, you know—when you create someone who surpasses you."

306

Doon went out to his own suborbital cruiser and, without looking back, closed the door and lifted off to rejoin his starship in orbit. Jason watched until the craft was out of sight.

Arran asked him when he turned around, "Well, Jason, do I go back to the farm now?"

He looked behind her eyes.

"You don't want to go back, do you?"

She shook her head, and her aging eyes filled with tears. "Let me stay here with you, now, Jason! They're all trained. They'll stay inside the farm for a thousand years!"

"More likely two hundred, with luck," Jason said. "That's all I could hope for. The barrier itself won't last more than another fifty or sixty years. Your work's done there, Arran. Far better than I could do it."

"Why," she asked, "didn't you want to stay with me there?"

"Oh, no, Arran, I *did* want to stay with you. But I can't always do what I want, you know. You see, there are things in my mind that the boys might have understood, if they'd had enough time. Things that would have destroyed everything."

"You mean they can see into *you,* too?"

"You can stay with me now, Arran, I want you to."

And she threw her arms around him and wept. "I'm old and ugly!" she cried. "And you're still young. You'll always be young! I've lost my life with you!" And he let her weep, saying softly, "We all lose parts of our life, Arran. It can't be helped." But for a fleeting moment he felt a bitter regret for all the life that he, too, had lost; he grieved for friends who had grown old and died while he slept in the coffin; friends whose minds had been stripped by somec, whose life and love had been lost; for the children that he hadn't really been able to enjoy, for the life he had never been able to taste. "Being God," he said, "is the worst damn job in the universe."

Then he led Arran to a coffin in the now-empty *B* tube, and put her to sleep. He sealed the tube carefully, inspecting everything to make sure that the components had lasted the time well. Then he went through the rest of the ship, preparing it as if for

307

deep space. The gap in the side he could do nothing about, but the interior locks in the ship were as able to withstand pressure as the exterior surface.

When he was satisfied with the condition of the starship, he sat in the control room and gently lifted the monstrous structure into the sky. He hovered it, so that the rotation of the planet moved the surface under him. Soon the land retreated to the east, and he was over the sea. He flew south, then, to a place far from any land, and gently settled the starship toward the surface of the ocean. The ship barely noticed contact with the water; it sank easily beneath the waves. And the structure was hardy enough to bear the pressure at the bottom; Jason knew that the ship had been built for far worse conditions than these; that perhaps thousands of years from now the metal would still be uncorroded, the ship's computers still capable of being revived, the ship's engines still able to bring her to the surface.

He wrote a message and laid it on the control board, spoke the same message into the ship's log, gave it to the computer so that any contact with the computer would print it out on the screen. Then he went to the coffin, lay down, put the sleep helmet on his head, and waited for his brain to be recorded. The job was done.

And then for no reason he could think of, Jason began to weep, softly, in his coffin. He was still weeping as the needle stabbed him and the somec scoured through his veins, and the agony of another thousand years of sleep began.

The ship lay waiting on the bottom. Sea creatures crawled along its surface, or made their homes in *A* tube, which lay open to the water. Every fifty years or so the ship would come to life, lights going on and off from one end of the ship to the other. The engines would fire, killing millions of infinitesimal plants and animals. Then the ship would go back to sleep again.

Each time it happened, a message flashed on the computer screen for a full minute:

"I am Jason Worthing. Think carefully before you waken me.

If my work has failed, I don't want to know it. And if it has succeeded, but wasn't good for the people after all, I would rather sleep on. My dream of the future is too good for me to be eager to wreck it with reality."

The bottomfish, with their self-made light to protect them from the darkness of the deep, scuttled in and out of the torn place in the starship's hull. To them it was just another rock that could shelter them, for a short time, from the death always waiting just around the corner in the night.

BARONET SF

The best in illustrated science fiction and fantasy in a dynamic new format, featuring the bestselling SF writers and the most popular graphic illustrators. Fully illustrated in color and black and white.

THE ILLUSTRATED ROGER ZELAZNY
Illustrated by Gray Morrow
014-6   ($8.95)   ☐

THE ILLUSTRATED HARLAN ELLISON
Illustrated by Steranko, Wayne McLoughlin, Ralph Reese, Tom Sutton, Alfredo Alcala, Overton Loyd, William Stout, and Mike Whelan.
038-3   ($8.95)   ☐

THE STARS MY DESTINATION, Vol. I
by Alfred Bester. Illustrated by Howard Chaykin.
052-9   ($8.95)   ☐

THE STARS MY DESTINATION, Vol. II
by Alfred Bester. Illustrated by Howard Chaykin.
061-8   ($8.95)   ☐

Baronet/Analog SF

If you enjoyed this book, you will enjoy these other fine books in our Baronet/Analog series of science fiction.

Baronet Book Catalog

Free catalog of our latest Baronet books,
yours for the asking.

Now it's easy to get the books you want. Choose from many popular-priced books in your favorite categories and order them conveniently by mail!

Just send us your name and address.

_____

Baronet Books
Mail Order Dept.
509 Madison Ave.
New York, NY 10022

Please send me your free catalog.

Mr./Mrs./Ms. _____

Address _____

City _____ State _____ Zip _____